Praise for *The Absolutist*

"A gripping, superbly plotted novel, filled with surprises that are by turns confounding, disturbing, and tremendously moving. For all its spellbinding narrative momentum, *The Absolutist* is, in the end, a sober meditation on the heartbreak that ensues when people and principles collide."

—Paul Russell, author of *The Unreal Life of Sergey Nabokov*

"Extraordinary...The narrative is by turns surprising and tragic in equal measure while its troubling conclusion will stay with readers long after they've closed the book."

—Carlo Gébler, author of *The Dead Eight*

"Powerful, poignant, and beautifully written. This will become a classic war novel." —*The Bookseller*

"A fable about forbidden love in the First World War...effortlessly readable." —*The Guardian*

"Political, personal, powerful...a fiercely interrogative novel that asks not just what it means to be a man but also what it means to be a human being in the extreme circumstances of war." —*Irish Times*

"A relentlessly tragic yet beautifully crafted novel." —*Publishers Weekly*

"A thought-provoking and surprising page-turner that for some readers may recall Ian McEwan's *Atonement*." —*Library Journal*

"Poetic, passionate, and poignant, *The Absolutist* is about self-discovery, friendship, and how far bravery can take us."

—*Interview Magazine*

"What is most memorable here is the timelessly doomed relationship between Tristan and Will, marked by tenderness and confusion and cruelty in the face of their own internalized repression...This is a wonderfully crafted tragedy that will stay with the reader."

—*Daily Beast* (Hot Read)

"What begins as a slow-building World War I period piece...grows deeper, more curious, and uneasy as it progresses—and midway through this sad and beautiful story, you realize you're in the hands of a quiet master...a taut and tragic tale of love and war, with a kick-in-the-gut ending."   —Amazon (Best Books of the Month)

"A powerful story about love, hate, courage, guilt, and war where nothing is simple and everything might not be as it seems."

—*Shelf Awareness*

"This is a different kind of journey into the darkness of war, told by a gifted, powerful novelist, and the result is a book with an often staggering emotional punch."   —*Book Page*

"An outstanding, thought-provoking look at the passionate choices we make, and how we react to life-changing situations. Much recommended for all readers, five full stars out of five."

—Yahoo (Editor's pick of the month)

"An unforgettable story that transcends genres."   —*Huntington News*

"A riveting look into what drives the relationships we have in spite of the world around us."   —*Seattle Gay News*

"This is great modern literature with fantastic artistic appeal and superb writing, a story of duty, honor, love, high passion, and integrity."   —*Book Reporter*

"Writing of this sensitivity and simply verbal beauty is rare. Boyne is rapidly becoming one of the great writers of the century."

Literary Aficionado

"An outstanding read, very highly recommended."

—*Historical Novel Society*

"[In] Boyne's fiction, there's a sense that people are fundamentally the sum of their traumas...Boyne's narrative grip is strong."

—*Literary Review*

"For me, the world totally ceased to exist while I was reading *The Absolutist*...If you plan on reading just one book this winter, this should be it."   —*Washington Blade*

THE ABSOLUTIST

THE
ABSOLUTIST

John Boyne

OTHER PRESS NEW YORK

Softcover reissue 2021
ISBN 978-1-63542-166-8

Originally published in Great Britain in 2011 by Doubleday,
an imprint of Transworld Publishers

Production Editor: Yvonne E. Cárdenas

Design revisions for this edition by Cassandra J. Pappas

This book was set in 11.5 pt Giovanni Book
by Falcon Oast Graphic Art Ltd.

1 3 5 7 9 10 8 6 4 2

Library of Congress Cataloging-in-Publication Data

Boyne, John, 1971–
    The absolutist / John Boyne.
        p. cm.
    "Originally published in Great Britain in 2011 by Doubleday."
    ISBN 978-1-59051-552-5 (trade pbk.) — ISBN 978-1-59051-553-2
(e-book)
    1. Soldiers—Fiction. 2. Gay men—Fiction. 3. World War,
1914-1918—Campaigns—Western Front—Fiction. 4. World War,
1914-1918—Conscientious objectors—Fiction. I. Title.
    PR6102.O96A27 2012
    823'.92—dc22

                                                     2012000433

For Con

TOMBLAND

Norwich, 15–16 September 1919

S EATED OPPOSITE ME in the railway carriage, the elderly lady in the fox-fur shawl was recalling some of the murders that she had committed over the years.

"There was the vicar in Leeds," she said, smiling a little as she tapped her lower lip with her index finger. "And the spinster from Hartlepool whose tragic secret was to prove her undoing. The actress from London, of course, who took up with her sister's husband just after his return from the Crimea. She was a flighty piece so no one could blame me for that. But the maid-of-all-work in Connaught Square, I rather regretted killing her. She was a hard-working girl of good Northern stock, who perhaps didn't deserve such a brutal ending."

"That was one of my favourites," I replied. "If you ask me, she got what was coming to her. She read letters that were not hers to read."

"I know you, don't I?" she asked, sitting forward now, narrowing her eyes as she examined my face for familiar signs. A sharp combination of lavender and face cream, her mouth viscous with blood-red lipstick. "I've seen you somewhere before."

"I work for Mr. Pynton at the Whisby Press," I told her. "My name's Tristan Sadler. We met at a literary lunch a few months ago." I extended my hand and she stared at it for a moment, as if unsure what was expected of her, before shaking it carefully, her fingers never quite closing on my own. "You gave a talk on untraceable poisons," I added.

"Yes, I remember it now," she said, nodding quickly. "You had five books that wanted signing. I was struck by your enthusiasm."

I smiled, flattered that she recalled me at all. "I'm a great admirer," I said, and she inclined her head graciously, a movement that must have been honed over thirty years of receiving praise from her readers. "As is Mr. Pynton. He's talked several times about trying to lure you over to our house."

"Yes, I know Pynton," she replied with a shudder. "Vile little man. Terrible halitosis. I wonder that you can bear to be near him. I can see why he employed you, though."

I raised an eyebrow, confused, and she offered me a half-smile.

"Pynton likes to be surrounded by beautiful things," she explained. "You must have seen it in his taste for artwork and those ornate couches that look as though they belong in the Paris atelier of some fashion designer. You remind me of his last assistant, the scandalous one. But no, there's no chance, I'm afraid. I've been with my publisher for over thirty years and I'm perfectly happy where I am."

She sat back, her expression turning to ice, and I knew that I had disgraced myself, turning what had been a pleasant exchange into a potential business transaction. I looked out of the window, embarrassed. Glancing at my watch, I saw that we were running about an hour later than planned and now the train had stopped again without explanation.

"This is exactly why I never go up to town any more," she declared abruptly as she struggled to open the window, for the carriage had begun to grow stuffy. "You simply cannot rely on the railways to bring you home again."

"Here, let me help you with that, missus," said the young man who had been sitting next to her, speaking in whispered,

4

flirtatious tones to the girl next to me since we departed Liverpool Street. He stood and leaned forward, a breeze of perspiration, and gave the window a hefty pull. It opened with a jolt, allowing a rush of warm air and engine-steam to spill inside.

"My Bill's a dab hand with machinery," said the young woman, giggling with pride.

"Leave it out, Margie," he said, smiling only a little as he sat down.

"He fixed engines during the war, didn't you, Bill?"

"I said leave it out, Margie," he repeated, colder now, and as he caught my eye we considered each other for a moment before looking away.

"It was just a window, dear," sniffed the lady-novelist with impeccable timing.

It struck me how it had taken over an hour for our three parties even to acknowledge each other's presence. It reminded me of the story of the two Englishmen, left alone on a deserted island together for five years after a shipwreck, who never exchanged a single word of conversation as they had never been properly introduced.

Twenty minutes later, our train shifted into motion and we were on our way, finally arriving in Norwich more than an hour and a half behind schedule. The young couple disembarked first, a flurry of hysterical impatience and rush-me-to-our-room giggles, and I helped the writer with her suitcase.

"You're very kind," she remarked in a distracted fashion as she scanned the platform. "My driver should be here somewhere to help me the rest of the way."

"It was a pleasure to meet you," I said, not trying for another handshake but offering an awkward nod of the head instead, as if she were the Queen and I a loyal subject. "I hope I didn't embarrass you earlier. I only meant that Mr. Pynton wishes we had writers of your calibre on our list."

She smiled at this—*I am relevant*, said her expression, *I matter*—and then she was gone, uniformed driver in tow. But I remained where I was, surrounded by people rushing to and from their platforms, lost within their number, quite alone in the busy railway station.

I emerged from the great stone walls of Thorpe Station into an unexpectedly bright afternoon, and found that the street where my lodgings were located, Recorder Road, was only a short walk away. Upon arriving, however, I was disappointed to find that my room was not quite ready.

"Oh dear," said the landlady, a thin woman with a pale, scratchy complexion. She was trembling, I noticed, although it was not cold, and wringing her hands nervously. She was tall, too. The type of woman who stands out in a crowd for her unexpected stature. "I'm afraid we owe you an apology, Mr. Sadler. We've been at sixes and sevens all day. I don't quite know how to explain what's happened."

"I did write, Mrs. Cantwell," I said, trying to soften the note of irritation that was creeping into my tone. "I said I would be here shortly after five. And it's gone six now." I nodded in the direction of the grandfather clock that stood in the corner behind her desk. "I don't mean to be awkward, but—"

"You're not being awkward at all, sir," she replied quickly. "The room should have been ready for you hours ago, only . . ." She trailed off and her forehead wrinkled into a series of deep grooves as she bit her lip and turned away; she seemed unable to look me in the eye. "We had a bit of unpleasantness this morning, Mr. Sadler, that's the truth of it. In your room. Or what was to be your room, that is. You probably won't want it now. I know I shouldn't. I don't know what I'll do with it, honestly I don't. It's not as if I can afford to leave it unlet."

Her agitation was obvious, and despite my mind being more or less focused on my plans for the following day, I was concerned for her and was about to ask whether there was anything I could do to help when a door opened behind her and she spun around. A boy of about seventeen appeared, whom I took to be her son: he had a look of her around the eyes and mouth, although his complexion was worse, scarred as he was by the acne of his age. He stopped short, taking me in for a moment, before turning to his mother in frustration.

"I told you to call me when the gentleman arrived, didn't I?" he said, glaring at her.

"But he's only just arrived this minute, David," she protested.

"It's true," I said, feeling a curious urge to jump to her defence. "I did."

"But you didn't call me," he insisted to his mother. "What have you told him, anyway?"

"I haven't told him anything yet," she said, turning back to me with an expression that suggested she might cry if she was bullied any longer. "I didn't know what to say."

"I do apologize, Mr. Sadler," he said, turning to me now with a complicit smile, as if to imply that he and I were of a type who understood that nothing would go right in the world if we did not take it out of the hands of women and look after it ourselves. "I had hoped to be here to greet you myself. I asked Ma to tell me the moment you arrived. We expected you earlier, I think."

"Yes," I said, explaining about the unreliable train. "But really, I am rather tired and hoped to go straight to my room."

"Of course, sir," he said, swallowing a little and staring down at the reception desk as if his entire future were mapped out in the wood; here in the grain was the girl he would marry, here

7

the children they would have, here the lifetime of bickering misery they would inflict upon each other. His mother touched him lightly on the arm and whispered something in his ear, and he shook his head quickly and hissed at her to stay quiet. "It's a mess, the whole thing," he said, raising his voice suddenly as he returned his attention to me. "You were to stay in number four, you see. But I'm afraid number four is indisposed right now."

"Well, couldn't I stay in one of the other rooms, then?" I asked.

"Oh no, sir," he replied, shaking his head. "No, they're all taken, I'm afraid. You were down for number four. But it's not ready, that's the problem. If you could just give us a little extra time to prepare it."

He stepped out from behind the desk now and I got a better look at him. Although he was only a few years younger than me, his appearance suggested a child play-acting as an adult. He wore a pair of man's trousers, a little too long for him, so rolled and pinned in the leg to compensate, and a shirt, tie and waistcoat combination that would not have seemed out of place on a much older man. The beginnings of a moustache were teased into a fearful line across his upper lip, and for a moment I couldn't decide whether in fact it was a moustache at all or simply a dirty smudge overlooked by the morning's facecloth. Despite his attempts to look older, his youth and inexperience were obvious. He could not have been out there with the rest of us, of that I felt certain.

"David Cantwell," he said after a moment, extending his hand towards me.

"It's not right, David," said Mrs. Cantwell, blushing furiously. "The gentleman will have to stay somewhere else tonight."

"And where is he to stay, then?" asked the boy, turning on her, his voice raised, a sense of injustice careering through his tone. "You know everywhere's full up. So where should I send him, because I certainly don't know. To Wilson's? Full! To Dempsey's? Full! To Rutherford's? Full! We have an obligation, Ma. We have an obligation to Mr. Sadler and we must meet our obligations or else we disgrace ourselves, and hasn't there been enough of that for one day?"

I was startled by the suddenness of his aggression and had an idea of what life might be like in the boarding house for this pair of mismatched souls. A boy and his mother, alone together since he was a child, for her husband, I decided, had been killed in an accident involving a threshing machine years before. The boy was too young to remember his father, of course, but worshipped him nevertheless and had never quite forgiven his mother for forcing the poor man out to work every hour that God sent. And then the war had come and he'd been too young to fight. He'd gone to enlist and they'd laughed at him. They'd called him a brave boy and told him to come back in a few years' time when he had some hair on his chest, if the godforsaken thing wasn't over already, and they'd see about him then. And he'd marched back to his mother and despised her for the relief on her face when he told her that he was going nowhere, not yet, anyway.

Even then, I would imagine scenarios like this all the time, searching in the undergrowth of my plots for tangled circumstances.

"Mr. Sadler, you'll have to forgive my son," said Mrs. Cantwell, leaning forward now, her hands pressed flat against the desk. "He is rather excitable, as you can see."

"It's got nothing to do with that, Ma," insisted David. "We have an obligation," he repeated.

"And we would like to fulfil our obligations, of course, but—"

I missed the end of her speech, for young David had taken me by the crook of the elbow, the intimacy of the gesture

9

surprising me, and I pulled away from him as he bit his lip, looking around nervously before speaking in a hushed voice.

"Mr. Sadler," he said, "might I speak to you in private? I assure you this is not how I like to run things here. You must think very badly of us. But perhaps if we went into the drawing room? It's empty at the moment and—"

"Very well," I said, placing my holdall on the floor in front of Mrs. Cantwell's desk. "You don't mind if I leave this here?" I asked, and she shook her head, swallowing, wringing those blessed hands of hers together once again and looking for all the world as if she would welcome a painful death at that very moment over any further discourse between us. I followed her son into the drawing room, partly curious as to the measure of concern that was on display, partly aggrieved by it. I was tired after my journey and filled with such conflicting emotions about my reasons for being in Norwich that I wanted nothing more than to go directly to my room, close the door behind me, and be left alone with my thoughts.

The truth was that I did not know whether I could even go through with my plans for the following day. I knew there were trains to London at ten past the hour, every second hour, starting at ten past six, so there were four I could take before the appointed hour of my meeting.

"What a mess," said David Cantwell, whistling a little between his teeth as he closed the door behind us. "And Ma doesn't make it any easier, does she, Mr. Sadler?"

"Look, perhaps if you just explained the problem to me," I said. "I did send a postal order with my letter in order to reserve the room."

"Of course you did, sir, of course you did," he replied. "I registered the booking myself. We were to put you in number four, you see. That was my decision. Number four is the quietest of our rooms and, while the mattress might be a little

10

lumpy, the bed has a good spring to it and many of our clients remark that it's very comfortable indeed. I read your letter, sir, and took you for an army man. Was I right, sir?"

I hesitated for a moment, then nodded curtly. "I was," I told him. "Not any more, of course. Not since it ended."

"Did you see much action?" he asked, his eyes lighting up, and I could feel my patience beginning to wane.

"My room. Am I to have it or not?"

"Well, sir," he said, disappointed by my reply. "That's rather up to you."

"How so?"

"Our girl, Mary, is up there at the moment, disinfecting everything. She kicked up a stink about it, I don't mind telling you, but I told her that it's my name above the door, not hers, and she'll do what she's told if she wants to keep her position."

"I thought it was your mother's name," I said, teasing him a little.

"Well, it's mine, too," he snapped indignantly, his eyes bulging in their sockets as he glared at me. "Anyway, it will be as good as new by the time she's done with it, I can promise you that. Ma didn't want to tell you anything, but since you're an army man—"

"An *ex*-army man," I said, correcting him.

"Yes, sir. Well, I believe it would be disrespectful of me not to tell you what's gone on there and let you make up your own mind on the matter."

I was intrigued now and a variety of possibilities came to mind. A murder, perhaps. A suicide. A straying husband caught by a private detective in the arms of another woman. Or something less dramatic: an unquenched cigarette catching flame in a waste-paper basket. A guest absconding in the night without settling his account due. More tangles. More wasteland.

"I'm happy to make up my mind," I said, "if only I—"

"He's stayed here before, of course," said the boy, interrupting me, his voice growing more animated as he prepared to let me have it, warts and all. "Mr. Charters, that's his name. Edward Charters. A very respectable chap, I always thought. Works in a bank in London but has a mother somewhere out Ipswich way and goes to see her on occasion and usually comes into Norwich for a night or two before heading back to town. When he does he always stays here. We never had any problems with him, sir. A quiet gentleman, kept himself to himself. Well dressed. Always asked for number four because he knew how good the room was, and I was happy to oblige him. It's me who organizes the rooms, Mr. Sadler, not Ma. She gets confused by the numbers and—"

"And this Mr. Charters," I said. "He refused to vacate the room earlier?"

"No, sir," said the boy, shaking his head.

"There was an accident of some sort, then? He was taken ill?"

"No, it was nothing like that, sir. We gave him a key, you see. In case he came back late. We give it to preferred clients. I allow it. It will be perfectly all right to give one to you, of course, what with you being ex-army. I wanted to join up myself, sir, only they wouldn't let me on account of—"

"Please," I said, interrupting him. "If we could just—"

"Yes, I'm sorry, sir. Only it's a little awkward, that's all. We're both men of the world, am I right, Mr. Sadler? I can speak freely?"

I shrugged. I expected I was. I didn't know. Wasn't even sure what the phrase meant, if I was honest.

"The thing is, there was something of a commotion early this morning," he said, lowering his voice and leaning forward in a conspiratorial fashion. "Woke the whole bloody house up, it did. Excuse me, sir," he said, shaking his head. "It turned out that Mr. Charters, who we thought was a quiet, decent gentleman, was anything but. He went out last night but didn't come home alone. And we have a rule about that sort of thing, of course."

I couldn't help but smile. Such niceties! Was this what the last four years had been about? "Is that all?" I asked, imagining a lonely man, kind to his mother in Ipswich, who had somehow found a little female companionship for the evening, perhaps unexpectedly, and had allowed himself to be taken over by his baser instincts. It was hardly anything to get excited about, surely.

"Not quite all, sir," said David. "For Mr. Charters's . . . companion, shall we say, was no better than a thief. Robbed him blind and when he protested held a knife to his throat and all hell broke loose. Ma woke up, I woke up, the other guests were out in the corridors in their night attire. We knocked on his door and when we opened it . . ." He looked as if he was unsure whether he should go on or not. "We called the police, of course," he added. "They were both taken away. But Ma feels wretched over the whole thing. Thinks the whole place is spoiled now. Talking about selling up, if you can believe that. Moving back to her people in the West Country."

"I'm sure that Mr. Charters feels wretched, too," I said, experiencing pangs of sympathy for him. "The poor man. I can understand the young lady being arrested, of course, if she had become violent, but why on earth was he? Surely this is not a question of morality?"

"It is, sir," said David, standing up to his full height now and looking positively affronted. "It most certainly is a question of morality."

"But he hasn't broken the law, as far as I understand it," I said. "I don't quite see why he should be held accountable for what is, after all, a personal indiscretion."

"Mr. Sadler," said David calmly. "I shall say this plain, as I think you might have misunderstood me. Mr. Charters's companion was not a young lady, I'm afraid. It was a boy." He nodded knowingly at me and I flushed a little and looked away.

"Ah," I said, nodding my head slowly. "I see. That."

"So you can understand why Ma is upset. If word gets about . . ." He looked up quickly, as if he had just realized something. "I trust you will be discreet about this, sir. We do have our livelihoods to consider."

"What?" I asked, staring at him and nodding quickly. "Oh yes, of course. It's . . . well, it's nobody's business but your own."

"But it does leave the matter of the room," he said delicately. "And whether you wish to stay in it or not. As I say, it is being thoroughly cleaned."

I thought about it for a moment but could see no objections. "It really doesn't bother me, Mr. Cantwell," I said. "I'm sorry for your difficulties and for your mother's distress, but if the room is still available for the night, I am still in need of a bed."

"Then it's all settled," he said cheerfully, opening the door and stepping back outside. I followed him, a little surprised by how quickly our interview had been terminated, and found the boy's mother still in place behind the desk, her eyes darting back and forth between us.

"Mr. Sadler understands everything perfectly," announced her son. "And he would like to avail himself of the room after all. I have told him that it will be ready in an hour. I was right to do so, I presume?" He spoke to her as if he were already master of the house and she his servant girl.

"Yes, of course, David," she said, a note of relief in her voice. "And it's very good of you, sir, if I may say so. Would you care to sign the register?"

I nodded and leaned over the book, writing my name and address carefully on the ledger, the ink splashing a little as I struggled to control my grip of the pen in my spasmodic right hand.

"You can wait in the drawing room, if you wish," said David, staring at my trembling index finger and, no doubt, wondering. "Or there's a very respectable public house a few doors down if you require a little refreshment after your journey."

"Yes, that I think," I said, replacing the pen carefully on the desk, aware of the mess that I had left behind me and embarrassed by it. "May I leave my holdall here in the meantime?"

"Of course, sir."

I leaned down and took my book from inside the bag, fastened it again and glanced at the clock as I stood up.

"If I'm back by half past seven?" I asked.

"The room will be ready, sir," said David, leading me towards the door and opening it for me. "And once again, please accept my apologies. The world's a funny place, sir, isn't it? You never know what kind of deviants you're dealing with."

"Indeed," I said, stepping out into the fresh air, relieved by the breeze that made me pull my overcoat tightly around my body and wish that I had remembered my gloves. But they were inside, in the bag, in front of Mrs. Cantwell, and I had no desire to engage in any further conversation with either mother or son.

To my surprise, I realized for the first time that day that it was the evening of my twenty-first birthday. I had forgotten it entirely until now.

I made my way down the street but before entering the Carpenter's Arms public house, my eyes drifted towards the brass plaque that was nailed prominently above the door, where the words PROPRIETOR: J. T. CLAYTON, LICENSED TO SELL BEERS AND SPIRITS were etched in a black matted script. I stopped short for a moment and stared at it, holding my breath, a sensation of dread soaring through my veins. I longed for a cigarette and patted my pockets, hoping to find the packet of Gold Flakes I had bought in Liverpool Street that morning, already knowing that they were lost, left behind on my train-carriage seat when I reached up to help the novelist with her suitcase before disembarking, and they probably lay there still, or had found their way into the pockets of another.

PROPRIETOR: J.T. CLAYTON.

It had to be a coincidence. Sergeant Clayton had been a Newcastle man, as far as I knew. His accent had certainly betrayed him as one. But had I heard that his father had been something high up at a brewery? Or was I confusing him with someone else? No, it was ridiculous, I decided, shaking my head. There must be thousands of Claytons spread across England, after all. Tens of thousands. This couldn't be the same one. Refusing to succumb to painful speculation, I pushed open the door and stepped inside.

The bar was half filled with working men, who turned to glance at me for only a moment before looking away and returning to their conversations. Despite being a stranger, I felt at ease there, a contentment born out of a sense of isolated companionship. As the years have passed, I have spent far too many hours in pubs, hunched over unsteady, ale-stained tables, reading and writing, tearing at beer mats as I've raised my characters from poverty to glory while dragging others down from mansion to gutter. Alone, always alone. Not drinking too much, but drinking all the same. A cigarette in my right hand, a scorch mark or two on my left cuff. That caricature of me, writing my books in the corner snugs of London saloons, the one that irritates me so and has caused me, in later life, to rise up, bristling and whinnying in interviews like an aggravated horse, is not, in fact, a mistaken one. After all, the clamour of the crowded public house is infinitely more welcoming than the stillness of the empty home.

16

"Yes, sir?" said a hearty-looking man standing behind the bar in his shirtsleeves, wiping a cloth along the countertop to remove the beaded lines of spilled beer. "What can I get for you?"

I passed an eye across the row of taps that stood before him, some of the names unfamiliar to me, local brews perhaps, and chose one at random.

"Pint, sir?"

"Yes please," I said, watching as he selected a glass from the rack behind him and then, in an instinctive gesture, held it by its base up to the light to examine it for fingerprints or dust marks before, satisfied, tilting it at a precise angle against the tap and beginning to pour. There were flakes of pastry in his heavy moustache and I stared at them, both repulsed and fascinated.

"Are you the proprietor?" I asked after a moment.

"That's right, sir," he said, smiling at me. "John Clayton. Have we met before?"

"No, no," I said, shaking my head as I rooted a few coins out of my pocket. I could relax now.

"Very good, sir," he said, placing the pint before me, apparently unconcerned by my question. I thanked him and made my way across to a half-empty corner of the pub, where I removed my coat and sat down with a deep sigh. Perhaps it had been for the best that my room had not been ready, I decided, staring at the dark brown ale settling in the glass before me, its frothy head winking as the tiny bubbles made their way north, anticipating as I did so the great satisfaction that first mouthful would offer me after my train journey. *I could sit here all night*, I thought. *I could become very drunk and cause a scene. The police might arrest me, lock me in a cell and send me back to London on the first train tomorrow morning. I wouldn't have to go through with it. The whole thing would be taken out of my hands.*

I sighed deeply, dismissing the notion, and took my book from my pocket, glancing for a moment at the jacket with the feeling of safety that a set of bound-together pages has always afforded me. On that mid-September Monday of 1919, I was reading *White Fang* by Jack London. My eyes focused on the dust-jacket image: a silhouetted cub testing the air beyond some trees, the shadows of their branches suggesting a road cut deep into the heart of the mountains ahead, the full moon guiding his way forward. I turned to where my page holder rested, but before reading, I glanced again at the title page and the words inscribed there: *To my old pal Richard*, it said in black ink, the characters elegant and well formed. *No less of a mangy ol' dog than White Fang himself, Jack.* I had found the book a couple of days earlier on a stall outside one of the bookshops on Charing Cross Road and it was only when I had taken it home and opened it that I noticed the inscription. The bookseller had charged me only a ha'penny for the second-hand volume so I presumed that he had overlooked the words written inside, but I considered it a great bonus, although I had no way of knowing whether the Jack who signed himself "Jack" was the Jack who had written the novel or a different Jack entirely, but I liked to believe that it was him. I traced my right index finger—the one whose inconsistent trembling always caused me such trouble—along the letters for a moment, imagining the great author's pen leaving its trail of ink along the page, but instead of being offered a curative through literature, which in my youthful fancy I hoped it would, my finger trembled even more than usual and, repulsed by the sight, I pulled it away.

"What are you reading, then?" asked a voice from a few tables away, and I turned to see a middle-aged man looking in my direction. I was surprised to have been addressed and turned the novel around to face him so that he could read the title, rather than simply answering his question. "Never heard of that one," he said, shrugging his shoulders. "Any good, is it?"

"Very good," I said. "Terrific, in fact."

"Terrific?" he repeated, smiling a little, the word sounding unfamiliar on his tongue. "Well, I'll have to look out for it if it's terrific. I've always been a reader, me. Mind if I join you? Or are you waiting for someone?"

I hesitated. I had thought that I wanted to be alone, but when the offer of company was made I found that I didn't mind so very much.

"Please," I said, indicating the seat next to mine, and he slid across and placed his half-finished pint on the table between us. He was drinking a darker beer than mine and there was an odour of stale sweat about him that suggested a long, hard-working day. Curiously, it wasn't unpleasant.

"The name's Miller," he said. "William Miller."

"Tristan Sadler," I replied, shaking his hand. "Pleased to meet you."

"And you," he said. He was about forty-five, I thought. My father's age. Although he did not remind me of my father in the slightest for he was of slender build, with a gentle, thoughtful air, and my father was the opposite. "You're from London, aren't you?" he asked, sizing me up.

"That's right," I said, smiling. "Is it that obvious?"

"I'm good with voices," he replied, winking at me. "I can place most people within about twenty miles of where they grew up. The wife, she says it's my party trick but I don't think of it that way. It's more than just a parlour game to my way of thinking."

"And where did I grow up, Mr. Miller?" I asked, eager to be entertained. "Can you tell?"

He narrowed his eyes and stared at me, remaining silent for almost a minute, save for the sound of his heavy, nasal breathing, before he opened his mouth again, speaking cautiously. "I should think Chiswick," he said. "Kew Bridge. Somewhere around there. Am I right?"

I laughed, surprised and delighted. "Chiswick High Street," I said. "My father has a butcher's shop. We grew up there."

"We?"

"My younger sister and I."

"But you live here? In Norwich?"

"No," I said, shaking my head. "No, I live in London now. Highgate."

"That's quite a distance from your family," he said.

"Yes," I replied. "I know."

From behind the bar, the sound of a glass crashing to the floor and smashing into a million fragments gave me a jolt. I looked up and my hands clenched instinctively against the side of the table, only relaxing again when I saw the shrugged shoulders of the proprietor as he bent down with pan and brush to clear up his mess, and heard the delighted, teasing jeers of the men sitting close to him.

"It was just a glass," said my companion, noticing how startled I had become.

"Yes," I said, trying to laugh it off and failing. "It gave me a shock, that's all."

"There till the end, were you?" he asked, and I turned to look at him, the smile fading from my face as he sighed. "Sorry, lad. I shouldn't have asked."

"It's all right," I said quietly.

"I had two boys out there, you see. Good boys, the pair of them. One with more than his share of mischief about him, the other one a bit like you and me. A reader. A few years older than you, I'd say. What are you, nineteen?"

"Twenty-one," I said, the novelty of my new age striking me for the first time.

"Well, our Billy would have been twenty-three now and our Sam would have been about to turn twenty-two." He smiled when he said their names, then swallowed and looked away. The use of the conditional tense had become a widespread disease when discussing the ages of children and little more needed to be said on the matter. We sat in silence for a few moments and then he turned back to me with a nervous smile. "You have the look of our Sam, actually," he said.

"Do I?" I asked, strangely pleased by the comparison. I entered the woods of my imagination again and made my way through gorse and nettle-tangled undergrowth to picture Sam, a boy who loved books and thought that one day he might like to write some of his own. I saw him on the evening he announced to his parents that he was signing up, before they came to get him, that he was going out to join Billy over there. I pictured the brothers finding solidarity on the training ground, bravery on the battlefield, heroism in death. This was Sam, I decided. This was William Miller's Sam. I knew him well.

"He were a good boy, our Sam," whispered my companion after a moment, then slapped the flat of his hand three times on the table before us as if to say, No more of that. "You'll have another drink, lad?" he asked, nodding at my half-finished beer, and I shook my head.

"Not yet," I said. "But thank you. You don't have a tab on you, by any chance?"

"Of course," he replied, fishing a tin box out of his pocket that looked as if it had been with him since childhood, opening it and handing me a perfectly rolled cigarette from a collection of about a dozen. His fingers were dirty, the lines on his thumb heavily defined and darkened by what I decided was manual labour. "You wouldn't see better in a baccie's, would you?" he asked, smiling, indicating the cylindrical precision of the smoke.

"No," I said, admiring it. "You're a dab hand."

"Not me," he said. "It's the wife who rolls them for me. First thing every morning, when I'm still about my breakfast, she's sat there in the corner of the kitchen with a roll of papers and a packet of gristle. Takes her only a few minutes. Fills the box for me, sends me on my way. How's that for luck? There's not many a woman would do that."

I laughed, satisfied by the cosy domesticity of it. "You're a lucky man," I said.

"And don't I know it!" he cried, feigning indignation. "And what about you, Tristan Sadler?" he asked, using my full name, perhaps because I was too old to be addressed with the familiarity of "Tristan" but too young to be called "Mr." "Married gentleman, are you?"

"No," I said, shaking my head.

"Got a sweetheart back in London, I suppose?"

"No one special," I replied, unwilling to admit that there was no one who was not special either.

"Sowing your wild oats, I expect," he said with a smile, but without that leering vulgarity with which some older men can make such remarks. "I don't blame you, any of you, of course, after all you've been through. There'll be time enough for weddings and young 'uns when you're a bit older. But, my Lord, the young girls were thrilled when you all came home, weren't they?"

I laughed. "Yes, I expect so," I said. "I don't know really." I was beginning to grow tired now, the combination of the journey and the drink on an empty stomach causing me to feel a little drowsy and light-headed. One more, I knew, would be the ruination of me.

"You have family in Norwich, do you?" asked Mr. Miller a moment later.

"No," I said.

"First time here?"

"Yes."

"A holiday, is it? A break from the big city?"

I thought about it before answering. I decided to lie. "Yes," I said. "A few days' break, that's all."

"Well, you couldn't have picked a nicer place, I can tell you that," he said. "Norwich born and bred, me. Lived here man and boy. Wouldn't want to live anywhere else and I can't understand anyone who would."

"And yet you know your accents," I pointed out. "You must have travelled a bit."

"When I was a pup, that's all," he said. "But I listen to people, that's the key to it. Most people never listen at all. And sometimes," he added, leaning forward, "I can even guess what they're thinking."

I stared at him and could feel my expression begin to freeze a little. Our eyes met and there was a moment of tension there, of daring, when neither of us blinked or looked away. "Is that so?" I said finally. "So you know what I'm thinking, Mr. Miller, do you?"

"Not what you're thinking, lad, no," he said, holding my gaze. "But what you're feeling? Yes, I believe I can tell that much. That don't take a mind reader, though. Why, I only had to take one look at you when you walked through the door to figure that out."

He didn't seem prepared to expand on this so I had no choice but to ask him, despite the fact that my every instinct told me to leave well alone. "And what is it, then, Mr. Miller?" I asked, trying to keep my expression neutral. "What am I feeling?"

"Two things, I'd say," he replied. "The first is guilt."

I remained still but kept watching him. "And the second?"

"Why," he replied, "you hate yourself."

I would have responded—I opened my mouth to respond—but what I might have said, I do not know. There was no opportunity anyway, for at that moment he slapped the table again, breaking the tension that had built between us as he glanced across at the wall clock. "No!" he cried. "It's never that time already. I'd best get home or the missus'll have my guts for garters. Enjoy your holiday, Tristan Sadler," he said, standing up and smiling at me. "Or whatever it is you're here for. And a safe trip back to London when it's over."

I nodded but didn't stand up. I simply watched him as he made his way to the door, turned for a moment and, with a raised hand, exchanged a quick goodbye with J. T. Clayton: Proprietor, Licensed to Sell Beers and Spirits, before leaving the bar without another word.

I glanced back at *White Fang*, lying face up on the table, but reached for my drink instead. By the time I finished it, I knew that my room would be available to me at last, but I wasn't ready to go back yet, so I raised a finger in the direction of the bar and a moment later a fresh pint was before me: my last, I promised myself, of the evening.

My room at Mrs. Cantwell's boarding house, the infamous number four, was a bleak setting for the apparently dramatic events of the previous night. The wallpaper, a lacklustre print of drooping hyacinths and blossoming crocuses, spoke of better, more cheerful times. The pattern had faded to white in the sun-bleached square facing the window, while the carpet beneath my feet was threadbare in places. A writing desk was pressed up against one wall; in the corner stood a washbasin with a fresh bar of soap positioned on its porcelain edge. I looked around, satisfied by the efficient English under-statement of the room, its brisk functionality. It was certainly superior to the bedroom of my childhood, an image I dismissed quickly, but less considered than the one I had furnished with a mixture of thrift and care in my small flat in Highgate.

I sat on the bed for a moment, trying to imagine the drama that had played out here in the small hours of the morning: the unfortunate Mr. Charters, wrestling for affection with his boy, then struggling to retain his dignity as he became the victim of a robbery, an attempted murder and an arrest all within the space of an hour. I felt sympathy for him and wondered whether he had even secured his desperate pleasures before the horror began. Was he part of an entrapment scheme or just an unfortunate victim of circumstance? Perhaps he was not as quiet as David Cantwell believed him to be and had sought a satisfaction that was not on offer.

Rising slowly, my feet tired after my day's travelling, I removed my shoes and socks and hung my shirt over the side of the chair, then remained standing in the centre of the room in trousers and vest. When Mrs. Cantwell knocked on the door and called my name, I considered putting them on again for the sake of decorum but lacked the energy and anyway, I decided, it was not as if I was indecent before the woman. I opened it and found her standing outside carrying a tray in her hands.

"I'm so sorry to disturb you, Mr. Sadler," she said, smiling that nervous smile of hers, honed no doubt by years of servility. "I thought you might be hungry. And that we owed you a little something after all the unpleasantness earlier."

I looked at the tray, which held a pot of tea, a roast-beef sandwich and a small slice of apple tart, and felt immediately grateful to her. I had not realized how hungry I was until the sight of that food reminded me in a moment. I had eaten breakfast that morning, of course, before leaving London, but I never ate much in the mornings, just tea and a little toast. On the train, when I grew hungry, I found the dining car pitifully understocked and ate only half a lukewarm chicken pie before setting it aside in distaste. This lack of food, coupled with the two pints of beer in the Carpenter's Arms, had left me ravenous, and I opened the door further to allow her to step inside.

"Thank you, sir," she said, hesitating for a moment before looking around as if to ensure that there was no further sign of the previous night's disgrace. "I'll just lay it on the desk here, if that's all right."

"That's very kind of you, Mrs. Cantwell," I said. "I wouldn't have thought to bother you for food at this time."

"It's no bother," she said, turning around now and smiling a little, looking me up and down carefully, her attention focused for so long on my bare feet that I began to feel embarrassed by them and wondered what she could possibly find of interest there. "Will you be lunching with us tomorrow, Mr. Sadler?" she asked, looking up again, and I got the sense that she had something that she wanted to discuss with me but was anxious to find the appropriate words. The food, while welcome, was clearly a ruse.

"No," I said. "I'm meeting an acquaintance at one o'clock so will be gone by the late morning. I may head out and see a little of the city if I wake early enough. Will it be all right if I leave my things here and collect them before catching the evening train?"

"Of course." She hovered and made no move to leave the room; I remained silent, waiting for her to speak. "About David," she said eventually. "I hope he didn't make a nuisance of himself earlier?"

"Not at all," I said. "He was very discreet in what he told me. Please, don't think for a moment that I—"

"No, no," she said, shaking her head quickly. "No, I don't mean that. That business is behind us all now, I hope, and will

26

never be mentioned again. No, it's just that he can sometimes ask too many questions of servicemen. Those who were over there, I mean. I know that most of you don't like to talk about what happened but he will insist. I've tried speaking to him about it but it's difficult." She shrugged her shoulders and looked away, as if defeated. "*He*'s difficult," she said, correcting herself. "It's not easy for a woman alone with a boy like him."

I looked away from her then, embarrassed by the familiarity of her tone, and glanced out of the window. A tall sycamore tree was blocking my view of the street beyond and I found myself staring at its thickset branches, another childhood memory surprising me by how ruthlessly it appeared. My younger sister, Laura, and I gathering horse chestnuts from the trees that lined the avenues near Kew Gardens, stripping their prickly shells away and taking them home to string into weapons; a memory I dismissed just as quickly as it had arrived.

"I don't mind so very much," I said, turning back to Mrs. Cantwell. "Boys his age are interested, I know. He's, what . . . seventeen?"

"Just turned, yes. He was that angry last year when the war ended."

"Angry?" I asked, frowning.

"It sounds ridiculous, I know. But he'd been planning on going for so long," she said. "He read about it in the newspaper every day, following all the boys from around here who went off to France. He even tried to sign up a couple of times, pretending to be older than he was, but they laughed him straight back to me, which, to my way of thinking, sir, was not right. Not right at all. He only wanted to do his bit, after all, they didn't need to make fun of him on account of it. And when it all came to an end, well, the truth is that he thought he'd missed out on something."

"On having his head blown off, most likely," I said, the words ricocheting around the walls, splattering shrapnel over both of us. Mrs. Cantwell flinched but didn't look away.

"He wouldn't see it like that, Mr. Sadler," she replied quietly. "His father was out there, you see. He was killed very early on."

"I'm sorry," I said. So the accident at the threshing machine was fiction, after all.

"Yes, well, David was only just thirteen at the time and there never was a boy who loved his father as much as he did. I don't think he's ever got over it, if I'm honest. It damaged him in some way. Well, you can see it in his attitude. He's so angry all the time. So difficult to talk to. Blames me for everything, of course."

"Boys his age usually do," I said with a smile, marvelling at how mature I sounded when in truth I was only her son's elder by four years.

"Of course I wanted the war to end," she continued. "I prayed for it. I didn't want him out there, suffering like the rest of you did. I can't even imagine what it must have been like for you. Your poor mother must have been beside herself."

I shrugged and turned the gesture quickly into a nod; I had nothing to say on that point.

"But there was a part of me, a small part," she said, "that hoped he would get to go. Just for a week or two. I didn't want him in any battles, of course. I wouldn't have wanted him to come to any harm. But a week with the other boys might have been good for him. And then, peace."

I didn't know whether she was referring to peace in Europe or peace in her own particular corner of England but I said nothing.

"Anyway, I just wanted to apologize for him," she said, smiling. "And now I'll leave you to your tea."

"Thank you, Mrs. Cantwell," I said, seeing her to the door and watching for a moment as she scurried down the corridor, looking left and right at the end as if she didn't know which direction she should go in, even though she had most likely lived there for nearly all her adult life.

Back inside my room, with the door closed again, I ate the sandwich slowly, conscious that to rush it might upset the fragile equilibrium of my stomach, and sipped the tea, which was hot and sweet and strong, and afterwards I began to feel a little more like myself. I could hear occasional movements in the corridor outside—the walls of my room were paper-thin— and resolved to be asleep before any of my neighbours in rooms three or five returned for the night. I could not risk lying awake: it was important to feel refreshed for the day that lay ahead of me.

Setting aside the tray, I stripped off my vest and washed my face and body in cold water at the sink. It quickly dripped down upon my trousers so I pulled the curtains, turned the light on and stripped naked, washing the rest of myself as well as I could. A fresh towel had been laid on the bed for me but it was made from the type of material that seemed to grow wet very quickly and I rubbed myself down with it aggressively, as we had been shown on our first day at Aldershot, before hanging it over the side of the basin to dry. Cleanliness, hygiene, attention to detail, the marks of a good soldier: such things came instinctively to me now.

A tall mirror was positioned in the corner of the room and I stood in front of it, examining my body with a critical eye. My chest, which had been well toned and muscular in late adolescence, had lost most of its definition in recent times; it was pale now. Scars stood out, red and livid across my legs; there was a dark bruise that refused to disappear stretched across my abdomen. I felt desperately unattractive.

Once, I knew, I had not been so ugly. When I was a boy, people thought me pleasant to look at. They had remarked as much to me and often.

Thinking of this brought Peter Wallis to my mind. Peter and I had been best friends when we were boys together, and with thoughts of Peter it was but a short stroll to Sylvia Carter, whose first appearance on our street when we were both fifteen was the catalyst for my last. Peter and I had been inseparable as children, he with his curly rings of jet-black hair, and me with that unhelpful yellow mop that fell into my eyes no matter how often my father forced me into the chair at the dinner table and cut it back quickly with a heavy pair of butcher's scissors, the same ones he used to cut the gristle from the chops in the shop below.

Sylvia's mother would watch Peter and me as we ran off down the street together with her daughter, the three of us locked in youthful collusion, and she would worry about what trouble Sylvia might be getting herself into, and it was not an unjustified concern, for Peter and I were at an age when we talked of nothing but sex: how much we wanted it, where we would look for it, and the terrible things we might do to the unfortunate creature who offered it.

During that summer we all became most aware of each other's changing bodies when we went swimming, and Peter and I, growing older and more confident in ourselves, attracted Sylvia's teasing stares and flirtatious remarks. When I was alone with her once, she told me that I was the best-looking boy she had ever seen and that whenever she saw me climbing from the pool, my body sleek with water, my swimming trunks black and dripping like the skin of an otter, I gave her the shivers. The remark had both excited and repelled me, and when we kissed, my lips dry, my tongue uncertain, hers anything but, the thought passed through my mind that if a girl like Sylvia, who was a catch, could find me attractive, then perhaps I wasn't too bad. The idea thrilled me, but as I lay in bed at night, bringing myself off with quick, dramatic fantasies that were just as quickly dispelled, I imagined scenarios of the most lurid kind, none of which involved Sylvia at all, and afterwards, spent and feeling vile, I would curl up in the sweat-soaked sheets and swallow back my tears as I wondered what was wrong with me, what the hell was wrong with me, anyway.

That kiss was the only one we ever shared, for a week later she and Peter declared that they were in love and had decided to devote their lives to each other. They would marry when they were of age, they announced. I was mad with envy, tortured by my humiliation, for, without realizing it, I had fallen desperately in love; it had crept up on me without my even noticing it, and seeing the pair of them together, imagining the things that they were doing when they were alone and I was elsewhere, left me in bitter twists of anguish, feeling nothing but hatred for them both.

But still, it had been Sylvia Carter who had told me when I was an inexperienced boy that my body had given her the shivers, and as I looked at it now, beaten and bruised from more than two years of fighting, my once-blond hair a muddy shade of light brown and lying limply across my forehead, my ribs visible through my skin, my left hand veined and dis-coloured in places, my right prone to the most inexcusable shakes and shudders, my legs thin, my sex mortified into mute-ness, I imagined that if I were still to give her the shivers they were more likely to be spasms of revulsion. That my com-panion in the railway carriage had thought me beautiful was a joke; I was hideous, a spent thing.

I pulled my shorts and vest back on, unwilling to sleep naked. I didn't want the sensation of Mrs. Cantwell's well-worn sheets against my body. I couldn't abide any touch that might suggest intimacy. I was twenty-one years old and had already decided that that part of my life was over. How stupid of me. Twice in love, I thought as I closed my eyes and placed my head on the thin pillow that raised me no more than an inch or two from the mattress. Twice in love and twice destroyed by it.

The thought of that, of that second love, made my stomach turn violently and my eyes spring open as I leaped from the bed, knowing that I had no more than a few seconds to reach the sink, where I threw up my beer, sandwich, tea and apple tart into the washbasin in two quick bursts, the undigested meat and spongy bread forming a deeply unpleasant picture in the porcelain base, a mess that I washed away quickly with a jug of water.

Perspiring, I collapsed on to the floor, my knees pressed up against my chin. I wrapped my arms around them, pulling my body close as I pushed myself hard between the wall and the base of the washbasin, scrunching my eyes up tightly as the terrible images returned.

Why did I come here? I wondered. What was I thinking? If it was redemption I sought, there was none to be found. If it was understanding, there was no one who could offer it. If it was forgiveness, I deserved none.

I woke early the following morning after a surprisingly undisturbed sleep and was the first to use the bath that served the needs of the six rooms in Mrs. Cantwell's establishment. The water was tepid at best, but it served its purpose and I scrubbed my body clean with the same bar of soap that had been left for me in my room. Afterwards, having shaved and combed my hair in the small mirror that hung over the washbasin, I felt a little more confident about what lay ahead, for the sleep and the bath had revived me and I did not feel as unhealthy as I had the night before. I held my right hand out flat before me and watched it, daring the spasmodic finger to tremble, but it held itself still now and I relaxed, trying not to think about how often it might betray me as the day developed.

Not wishing to engage in conversation, I decided against taking breakfast in the boarding house and instead crept downstairs and out of the front door shortly after nine o'clock without so much as a word to my host or hostess, who I could hear busying themselves in the dining room and bickering away like an old married couple. I had left the door of my room ajar with my holdall atop the bed covers.

The morning was brisk and bright; there were no clouds in the sky, no suggestion of rain later, and I was grateful for that. I had never been to Norwich before and purchased a small printed map from a street stall, thinking that I might spend an hour or two strolling around the city. My appointment was not until one o'clock, which left me ample time to see a few of the local sights and return to my lodgings to freshen up before making my way to our designated meeting place.

I crossed the bridge on Prince of Wales Road and stopped for a moment, staring down into the Yare as it flowed quickly along, and recalled for a moment a soldier I had trained with at Aldershot and fought alongside in France—Sparks was his name—who had told me the most extraordinary story one evening when the two of us were on top-duty together. It seemed that he had been crossing Tower Bridge in London one afternoon some four or five years earlier when, halfway across, he was stopped short by an overwhelming conviction that at that precise moment he was exactly halfway through his life.

"I looked left," he told me. "I looked right. I looked into the faces of the people walking past me. And I just knew it, Sadler. That this was it. And right then, a date popped into my mind: 11 June 1932."

"But that would make you, what, no more than forty?" I said.

"But that's not all," he told me. "When I got home again, I took a scrap of paper and worked out that if it really was the halfway point of my life on that very day, then what date should be my last. And you'll never believe what it came to?"

"Never!" I said, astonished.

"No, it wasn't the right date," he replied, laughing. "But it was close. It would have been August 1932. Either way, it's not much of an innings, is it?"

He made it to neither. He had both legs blown off just before Christmas 1917 and died of his injuries.

I put Sparks from my head and continued northwards, climbing the steep gradient of the street, and found myself walking along the stone walls of Norwich Castle. I considered climbing the hill towards it and examining the treasures that might be on display inside but decided against that, suddenly uninterested. Castles such as this, after all, were nothing more than the remains of military bases where soldiers might camp out and wait for the enemy to appear. I did not need to see any more of that. Instead I turned right, walking through a place that identified itself by the rather morbid name of Tombland, and in the direction of the great spire of Norwich Cathedral.

A small café attracted my notice and with it a reminder that I had eaten no breakfast. Rather than continuing on, I decided to stop for something to eat, waiting only a few moments in a corner window seat before a rosy-cheeked woman with a high hat of thick red hair came over to take my order.

"Just some tea and toast," I said, happy to be sitting down again for a few minutes.

"A couple of eggs with that, sir?" she suggested, and I nodded quickly.

"Yes, thanks. Scrambled, if that's possible."

"Of course," she replied, nodding pleasantly and disappearing back behind the counter as I switched my focus to the street. I regretted not having brought White Fang with me for it seemed like a decent opportunity to relax, enjoy my breakfast and read my book, but it was left behind in my holdall at Mrs. Cantwell's. Instead, I watched as the passers-by went about their business.

The street was filled mostly with women carrying string bags filled with their early-morning shopping. I thought about my mother, about how she had made the beds and cleaned the flat every morning at this time when I was growing up, while my father poured himself into his great white coat and took up his position behind the downstairs shop counter, carving up the fresh joints for the regular customers who would come his way over the next eight hours.

I had been terrified of everything associated with my father's job—the boning knives, the animal carcasses, the bone saws and rib pullers, the bloodstained overalls—and my squeamishness did not endear me much to him. Later, he taught me how to use the knives correctly, how to separate the joints of the pigs or sheep or cows that hung in the cold-room out back and were delivered every Tuesday morning with great ceremony. I never cut myself but, although I grew reasonably proficient at the art of butchery, I was never a natural at it, unlike my father, who had been born to it in this same shop, or his father, who had come over from Ireland during the potato famine and somehow managed to scrape together enough money to go into trade.

My father hoped that I would follow him into the family business, of course. The shop was already called Sadler & Son and he wanted our fascia to be an honest one. But it never came to pass. I was expelled from home just before I turned sixteen and returned only once, over a year and a half later, on the afternoon before I left for France.

"The truth is, Tristan," my father said that day as he steered me carefully out on to the street, his thick fingers pressing tightly on my shoulder blades, "it would be best for all of us if the Germans shoot you dead on sight."

The last thing he ever said to me.

I shook my head and blinked a few times, uncertain why I allowed these memories to destroy my morning. Soon my tea, eggs and toast were before me and I realized that the waitress was still hovering, her hands pressed together like those of a supplicant in prayer, a smile spreading across her face, and I glanced up, my loaded fork suspended in the air between plate and mouth, wondering what she might want of me.

"Everything all right, sir?" she asked cheerfully.

"Yes, thanks," I said, and the compliment was apparently enough to satisfy her, for she scurried back behind her counter before attending to her next task. I was still unaccustomed to being able to eat at my leisure, having spent almost three years in the army eating whatever was put in front of me, whenever I could, trapped between the poking elbows of other soldiers who stuffed their faces and masticated their food as if they were rutting pigs in a farmer's backyard and not a group of Englishmen who had been brought up with their mothers' manners. Even the quality of the food and the new abundance of it had the power to surprise me, although it was still nothing like as good as it had been before the war. But to walk into a café like this one, to sit down and look at a menu and say, "Do you know, I think I might have the mushroom omelette," or "I'll try the fish pie," or "One portion of the sausage and mash, please, and yes to the onion gravy"—this was an extraordinary sensation, the novelty of which is almost impossible to articulate. Simple pleasures, the result of inhuman deprivations.

I paid my few pence, thanked the woman and left the café, continuing along towards Queen Street in the direction of the cathedral spire, and looked up at the magnificent monastic building as it came into sight, and the precinct wall and gates that surrounded it. I take great pleasure in churches and cathedrals. Not so much for their religious aspect—agnosticism has been my declared denomination—but for the peace and tranquillity offered within. My twin contradictory places of idleness: the public bar and the chapel. One so social and teeming with life, the other quiet and warning of death. But there is something soothing to the spirit about resting awhile on the pews of a great church, breathing in the chilly air perfumed by centuries of incense and candle-burning, the extraordinary high ceilings that make one feel insignificant in the greater scheme of natural design, the artworks, the friezes, the carved altars, the statues whose arms reach out as if to embrace their observer, the unexpected moment when a choir above, rehearsing its matins, bursts into song and lifts the spirit from whatever despair brought one inside in the first place.

Once, outside Compiègne, our regiment had rested for an hour about a mile from a small *église* and, despite having been marching all morning, I decided to stretch my legs towards it, more as a means of escape from the other soldiers for a few minutes than out of a desire for spiritual awakening. It was nothing special, a fairly rudimentary building both outside and in, but I was heartsick by how abandoned it seemed, its congregation scattered to safety, the trenches or the graveyard, its atmosphere emptied of the once-attendant conviviality of the faithful. Walking outside again, thinking that I might lie on the grass until summoned back to the line, perhaps even close my eyes in the noonday sun and imagine myself in happier surroundings, I found another of my regiment, Potter, leaning on the opposite side of the church at a slight angle, one hand resting forward against the wall as he relieved himself noisily against the centuries-old stonework, and I ran towards him without a second thought, pushing him off his feet and to the ground, where he fell in surprise, exposed to all, his stream of urine coming to an unexpected halt but not before splattering over his trousers and shirt. He was on his feet a moment later, pulling himself together, cursing loudly, before knocking me off my own and seeking satisfaction for the humiliation. We had to be separated by a handful of other soldiers. I accused him of desecration and he accused me of something worse— religious mania—and although the charge was false, I did not deny it, and as our tempers started to fail us we stopped trading insults and were eventually released after facing each other, shaking hands, and calling ourselves friends once again before heading back down the hill. But the sacrilege had disturbed me nevertheless.

I made my way through the nave of the cathedral now, glancing surreptitiously at the dozen or so people who were scattered in silent prayer around the church, and wondered from what hardships they sought relief or for what sins they begged absolution. At the crossing, I turned and looked up towards the place where the choir would stand on a Sunday morning, offering worship. I walked south from there and an open door led me outside to a labyrinth where a few children were playing a game of catch in the bright morning, and continued along the wall towards the eastern end of the cathedral, where I found myself brought to a halt by a single grave. It stood out. Its stark nature surprised me, a simple stone cross resting atop a two-tiered base, and I leaned forward to discover that this was the grave of Edith Cavell, our great nurse-patriot, who had helped hundreds of British prisoners of war escape from Belgium through her underground route and had been shot in the autumn of 1915 for her trouble.

I stood up and offered not a prayer, for that was of no use to anyone, but a moment of contemplation. Nurse Cavell had been proclaimed a heroine, of course. A martyr. And she was a woman. The people of England seemed to celebrate this fact for once in their history and I felt a great sense of joy at discovering her grave in such an unexpected fashion.

Footsteps on the gravel alerted me to the approach of someone else, two people, in fact, whose steps had fallen in time with each other, like a night patrol circling a compound. I walked a little further past the grave and turned away, pretending to be engaged in a study of the stained-glass windows above.

"We should be making the final list by about three o'clock," the young man—who had the look of a sacristan—was saying to his older companion. "Assuming we can get through the earlier business quickly."

"It will take as long as it takes," the other man replied insistently. "But I'll have my say, I promise you that."

"Of course, Reverend Bancroft," came the reply. "It's a diffi-cult situation, we're all aware of that. But everyone there understands your pain and grief."

"Nonsense," snapped the man. "They understand nothing and they never will. I will have my say, you may have no doubt on that score. But I need to get home quickly afterwards. My daughter has arranged something. A . . . well, it's difficult to explain."

"Is it a young man?" asked the sacristan in a flippant voice, and the look that he received in response put a stop to any further enquiries of that sort.

"It won't matter too much if I'm late," said the reverend, his tone betraying deep uncertainty. "Our meeting is far more important. Anyway, I haven't quite decided on the wisdom of my daughter's plans yet. She gets notions, you see. And not always very sensible ones."

They turned to start walking again and at that moment, the reverend caught my eye and smiled. "Good morning, young man," he said, and I stared at him, my heart beating faster inside my chest. "Good morning," he repeated, stepping towards me, smiling in an avuncular fashion and then seeming to think better of it, as if he could sense the potential of a threat, and moved back again. "Are you quite all right? You look as if you've seen a ghost."

I opened my mouth, unsure how to reply, and I believe that I must have shocked the two of them entirely as I spun around, turned on my heels and ran back in the direction of the gate through which I had entered, almost tripping over a raised hedge to my left, a small child to my right and a series of paving stones in front of me, before finding myself inside the cathedral once again, which seemed monstrous now but also claustrophobic, ready to take me within its grasp and hold me there forever. I looked around the confusing space, desperate for a way out, and when I found it, I ran through the nave of the church, my boots sounding heavily on the tiles and sending their drumlike rhythms echoing into every corner of the building as I made for the doors, aware that the heads of the faithful were turning in my direction now with a mixture of alarm and disapproval.

Outside I breathed quickly, desperate to fill my lungs, and felt a horrible clamminess begin to seep through my skin, covering my body, my earlier relaxed state replaced by one of terror and remorse. The serenity imparted by the cathedral had left me and I was a man alone again; here in the unfamiliar surroundings of Norwich, with a task to complete.

But how could I have been so stupid? How could I not have remembered? It was all so unexpected though; the name— Reverend Bancroft—and then the expression on his face. The likeness was uncanny. I might have been back on the training grounds of Aldershot, or the trenches of Picardy. It might have been that dreadful morning when I ascended from the holding cells in a terrible, vengeful fury.

By now it was time to start making my way back towards the boarding house in order to freshen up before my appointment.

I walked away from the cathedral and took a different route, turning left and right on the criss-crossing streets.

It was I who had initiated the correspondence with Marian Bancroft. Although we had never met, Will had spoken of her often and I envied their extraordinary closeness. I had a sister myself, of course, but she had been only eleven when I left home, and even though I had written to her shortly after, my letters never received any reply; I suspected that they were intercepted by my father before they could reach her. But did he read them himself, I often wondered? Did he steal them away and tear open the envelopes, scanning my scrawling handwriting for news of where I was and how I was scraping a living together? Was there even a part of him that wondered whether one day my letters might stop, not because I had given up writing, but because I was no longer alive, the streets of London having swallowed me whole? It was impossible to know.

The war had been over for almost nine months by the time I finally plucked up the courage to write to Marian. It had been on my mind for a long time, a sense of responsibility that had kept me awake night after night as I tried to decide what to do for the best. A part of me wanted to dismiss her from my thoughts entirely, to pretend that she and her family did not exist. What help could I be to them, after all? What possible comfort could I offer? But the idea lingered and one day, tortured by guilt, I purchased what I considered to be an elegant packet of notepapers and a new fountain pen—for I wanted her to think well of me—and composed a letter.

Dear Miss Bancroft,
    You don't know me, or maybe you do, maybe you have
heard my name mentioned, but I was a friend of your brother,
Will. We trained together before we were sent over there. We

were in the same regiment so we knew each other well. We were friends.

I must apologize for writing to you out of the blue like this. I don't know what you've been going through over these last couple of years, I can't imagine it, but I know that your brother is never very far from my thoughts because, no matter what anyone says, he was the bravest and kindest man I ever knew and there were plenty of brave men out there, I can promise you that, but not so many kind ones.

Anyway, I write to you now because I have something belonging to Will that I thought I should return. The letters you wrote to him while he was over there. He kept them all, you see, and they fell to me. Afterwards, I mean. On account of our friendship. I assure you that I've never read any of them. Only I thought that you might like them back.

I should have written before now, of course, but the truth is I haven't been well since my return and have had to take a little time for myself. Perhaps you can understand that. That's all over now, I think. I don't know. I'm not sure about things when I look to the future. I don't know if you are; I know I'm not.

I didn't mean to write so much really, I just wanted to introduce myself and say that if perhaps you would permit me to call on you some day, then I should very much like to do so and I could return the letters to you, for I wonder if it might not give you some degree of comfort when you think of your brother.

Maybe you come to London sometimes. I don't know if you do or not, but if you don't I wouldn't mind coming to Norwich. I hope this letter reaches you safely; you might have moved for all I know. I heard that sometimes in these cases people move because of all the trouble that comes about.

If you would write to me, I would like to set this matter right. Or, if you prefer not to meet, I could put the letters in a box and send them along to you. Only I hope you do agree to meet me. There are so many things I would like to tell you.

Your brother was my best friend, I said that already, didn't I? Anyway, I know this much, that he was no coward, Miss Bancroft, he was no coward at all. He was a braver man than I will ever be.

I didn't mean to write so much. But there's a lot to say, I think.

With respectful wishes,

Tristan Sadler

Without realizing it, I had walked directly past my turning for Recorder Road and found myself standing on the Riverside, staring across from where the stone pillars of Thorpe rose up to greet me. I found that my feet were taking me across the river and inside the station and I stood quietly, watching the people as they purchased their tickets and made their way towards the platforms. It was five minutes past twelve and there in front of me was the London train, set to go in another five minutes' time. A conductor was walking up and down crying, "All aboard!" and I put my hand in my pocket for my wallet, looking at the ticket that I was carrying for my return journey later that evening. My heart raced when I saw that it was valid all day. I could simply climb on board and go home, put the whole wretched business behind me. I would have lost my holdall, of course, but there was not much in it, just yesterday's clothes and the Jack London book. I could forward Mrs. Cantwell what I owed her and apologize for leaving without a word.

As I hesitated, a man approached me, hand extended, and asked whether I had any spare change. I shook my head, stepping back a little as he reeked of stale sweat and cheap alcohol; he walked on crutches for his left leg was missing, while his right eye was sealed over as if he had recently been in a fight. He wasn't a day over twenty-five.

"A few pennies, that's all," he said, growling at me. "Fought for my country, didn't I, and look how they left me. You can spare some change, can't you? Come on, you fucking bastard!" he cried, raising his voice now and shocking me with the unexpected vulgarity. "You can spare a few pennies for them what gave you freedom."

A lady who was passing by with a small boy immediately covered his ears and I noticed him staring at the man in rapt fascination. Before I could say anything to the man he lunged at me and I stepped back again at the very moment that a constable appeared and took a hold of him—gently, as it turned out—and said, "Come along, that's not going to solve anything, now is it?" And with that platitude, the man seemed to crumple inside himself and moved away, hobbling back towards the wall and returning to a seated position on the ground, where he became almost catatonic, holding his hand out in the air, not even expecting anyone to help him.

"Sorry about that, sir," said the constable. "He's not usually much trouble so we let him stay there as he gets a few shillings most days. Ex-army, like myself. Had rather a rough time of it, though."

"It's quite all right," I muttered, leaving the station, any thought of heading back to London quite gone now. I had come to do a job, it was important that I completed it. And it had nothing to do with the return of a packet of letters.

It was almost two weeks before I received a reply from Marian Bancroft and in the intervening time I had thought of little else. Her silence made me question whether she had received my note, whether her family had been forced to move to another part of the country, whether she simply wanted nothing to do with me. It was impossible to know and I was torn between regret at having written to her at all and a sense that I was being punished by her refusal to reply.

And then one evening, returning home late from a day of reading dreary, unsolicited manuscripts at the Whisby Press, I discovered a letter waiting for me under the door of my flat. I lifted it in amazement—I never received any post—and stared at the elegant handwriting, knowing immediately who it must be from, and went inside to make a cup of tea, staring at the envelope nervously as I did so and imagining the possible traumas that it might contain. Finally settled, I opened it carefully, removed the single sheet of paper, and was struck immediately by the faint smell of lavender that accompanied it. I wondered whether this was her particular perfume or whether she was a girl who stuck to the old-fashioned ways and put a drop of scent in her envelopes, regardless of whether she was writing a love letter, paying a bill or answering an unexpected correspondence such as my own.

Dear Mr. Sadler,

First, I should like to thank you for writing to me and apologize for taking so long to reply. I realize that my silence might have appeared rude but I think you will understand when I say that your letter both upset and moved me in unexpected ways and I was uncertain how to answer it. I didn't want to reply until I was sure of what I wanted to say. I think people often rush responses, don't you? And I didn't want to do that.

You speak very kindly of my brother and I was tremendously affected by this. I am glad that he had a friend "over there," as you call it. (Why is that, Mr. Sadler? Are you afraid to name the place?) I'm afraid I have a very contradictory feeling towards our soldiers. I respect them, of course, and pity them for fighting for so long in such terrible conditions. I am sure that they were terribly brave. But when I think of what they did to my brother, what these same soldiers did to him, well, I'm sure you can understand that at such times my feelings are less than generous.

If I try to explain all this I am not sure that there will be enough ink in the world to hold my thoughts, nor enough paper on which to write them down, and I dare say I would have trouble finding a postman who would deliver a document as long as the one I would need to compose.

The letters—I can't believe you have them. I think it is very kind that you want to return them to me.

Mr. Sadler, I hope you don't mind but I don't think I can come to London at present for personal reasons. I would like to meet you, but does it make any sense for me to say that I should like to meet you here, in streets that I know, in the place where Will and I grew up? Your offer to come here is a generous one. Perhaps I could suggest Tuesday the 16th of this month as a possible day? Or do you work? I expect you do. Everyone must these days, it's quite extraordinary.

Look, maybe you'd write again and let me know?

Sincerely,

Marian Bancroft

I hoped that I would have a free run of it when I stepped inside the boarding house but David Cantwell was there, placing fresh flowers in two vases that stood on side tables. He flushed a little when he saw me and I could tell that he was embarrassed.

"My mother's gone out," he explained. "So I'm left with this job. Woman's work, isn't it? Flowers. Makes me look like a pansy."

He smiled at me and tried to make me complicit in the pun but I ignored his feeble attempt at humour and told him of my intentions.

"I'm just going up to my room," I said. "Would you rather I left my holdall in your office or can I leave it up there?"

"The office is probably best, sir," he replied, a little archly now, perhaps disappointed by my unwillingness to treat him as if he were a friend of long standing. "We do have another guest booked in for the room and they're due in around two o'clock. At what time do you think you'll be back for it?"

"Not till much later than that," I said, although why I thought that I did not know. It was possible that my appointment would not last for anything more than ten minutes. "I'll stop in for it before I catch my train."

"Very good, sir," he said, going back to his flowers. I noticed that he was not quite as forthcoming as he had been the night before and, despite the fact that I was not looking for conversation, I couldn't help but wonder about the reason for it. Perhaps his mother had spoken to him and explained that talking about what had happened out there to someone who had experienced it might not be the kindest thing. Some servicemen lived off their stories, of course, as if they had actually enjoyed the war, but others, myself included, didn't.

I went upstairs, cleaned my teeth and washed my face, and combing my hair once again in the mirror decided that, although pale, I did not look too terrible. I felt as ready for this appointment as I ever would.

And so, no more than twenty minutes later, I found myself sitting in a pleasant café just off Cattle Market Street, glancing at the clock on the wall as it ticked its way mercilessly towards one o'clock, and the other customers around me. It was a traditional café, I felt, one that had perhaps been passed through a number of generations of the same family. Behind the counter was a man of about fifty and a girl of my own age—his daughter, I presumed, for she had the look of him. There weren't too many other customers, no more than half a dozen, which satisfied me, for I felt that it would be very difficult for us to talk if the room was completely full and noisy, and equally difficult if it was empty and our conversation could be overheard.

Dear Miss Bancroft,
    Thank you for your reply and your kind words. You owe me no apology for the delayed response. I was happy to get it, that's all.
    The 16th is fine for me. Yes, I do work but I have some holiday days due to me and I shall take them then. I look forward to meeting you. Perhaps you could suggest by reply where and when might be convenient.
    Sincerely,
    Tristan Sadler

The door opened and I looked up, amazed by the fright the noise gave me. My stomach was rolling with anxiety and I suddenly dreaded this encounter. But it was a man who had come inside, and he looked around, his eyes darting left and right in an almost feral fashion, before taking a seat in the far corner, where he was hidden behind a pillar. I thought he looked at me suspiciously for a moment before moving away from my sight line, and I might have thought more of it had I not already been so preoccupied.

Dear Mr. Sadler,
    Shall we say one o'clock? There's a nice café along Cattle Market Street, Winchall's it's called. Anyone can direct you there.
    Marian B.

I picked up a container of napkins from the table for something to do. My right hand immediately broke into a fresh spasm and the box fell from my grasp, spilling the napkins across the tablecloth and on to the floor. I cursed beneath my breath and reached down to pick them up, which was why I failed to notice when the door opened one more time and a lady stepped inside and made her way towards my table.

"Mr. Sadler?" she said breathlessly, and I looked up, my face flushed from leaning over, then stood up instantly, staring at her, words failing me now, words failing me.

WE'RE DIFFERENT, I THINK

Aldershot, April–June 1916

I DON'T SPEAK TO Will Bancroft until our second day at Aldershot Military Barracks but I notice him on our first.

We arrive in the late afternoon of the last day of April, some forty of us, a group of untidy boys, loud-mouthed and vulgar, stinking of sweat and bogus heroism. Those who already know each other sit together on the train, talking incessantly, afraid of silence, each voice competing to drown out the next. Those who are strangers hide in window seats, their heads pressed against the glass, feigning sleep or staring out as the scenery rushes past. Some make nervous conversation about the things they have left behind, their families, the sweethearts they will miss, but no one discusses the war. We might be on a day trip for all the nerves we dare show.

We stand around in groups as the train empties and I find myself next to a boy of about nineteen who glances around irritably, taking me in and dismissing me again with a single look. He wears a carefully coordinated expression of resignation mixed with resentment; his cheeks are fleshy and raw, as if he has shaved with cold water and a blunt razor, but he stands erect, staring around as if he cannot quite believe the high spirits of the other boys.

"Just look at them," he says in a cold voice. "Bloody fools, every last one of them."

I turn to look at him more closely. He's taller than I am, with a neat haircut and a studious appearance. His eyes are a little narrow-set and he wears a simple pair of owl-rimmed spectacles, which he removes from time to time to massage the bridge of his nose, where a small red indentation is clear to the eye. He reminds me of one of my former schoolteachers, only he is younger, and probably less prone to outbursts of gratuitous violence.

"It's a lot of nonsense, isn't it?" he continues, sucking deeply on a cigarette as if he wants to draw all the nicotine into his body in one drag.

"What is?" I ask.

"This," he says, nodding in the direction of the other recruits, who are talking and laughing as if this is all a terrific lark. "All of it. These idiots. This place. We shouldn't be here, none of us should."

"I've wanted to be here since it started."

He glances at me, thinks he has the measure of me already, and snorts contemptuously as he shakes his head and looks away. Crushing the spent tab beneath his heel, he opens a silver cigarette case and sighs when it reveals itself to be empty.

"Tristan Sadler," I say, extending a hand now, not wanting to get my military career off on a sour note. He stares at it for five seconds or more and I wonder whether I will have to draw it back in humiliation, but finally he shakes it and nods abruptly.

"Arthur Wolf," he says.

"Are you from London?" I ask him.

"Essex," he replies. "Well, Chelmsford. You?"

"Chiswick."

"Nice there," he says. "I have an aunt who lives in Chiswick. Elsie Tyler. You don't know her, I suppose?"

"No," I reply, shaking my head.

"She runs a florist on Turnham Green."

"I'm from Sadler & Son, the butcher on the high street."

"Presumably you're the son."

"I used to be," I say.

"I bet you volunteered, didn't you?" he asks, more contempt seeping into his voice now. "Just turned eighteen?"

"Yes," I lie. In fact my eighteenth birthday is still five months away but I have no intention of admitting this here in case I find myself back with a hod in my hand before the week is out.

"I bet you couldn't wait, am I right? I bet it was your present to yourself, marching down to the sergeant major, yes, sir, no, sir, anything you say, sir, and offering yourself up on a crucifix."

"I would have joined earlier," I tell him. "Only they wouldn't let me in on account of my age."

He laughs but doesn't pursue it any further, simply shaking his head as if I'm not worth wasting his time on. He is a man apart, this Wolf.

A moment later and I sense a commotion in the ranks. I turn to watch as three men in heavy, starched uniforms emerge from a nearby barrack and stride towards us. Everything about them stinks of authority and I feel a rush of something unexpected. Apprehension, certainly. Desire, perhaps.

"Good afternoon, gentlemen," says the man in the centre, the eldest of the three, the shortest, the fattest, the one in charge. His tone is friendly, which surprises me. "Follow me, won't you? We're not quite where we ought to be."

We gather in a pack and shuffle along behind him and I take the opportunity to look around at the other men, most of whom are smoking cigarettes and continuing low conversations. I pull my own tin from my pocket and offer one to Wolf, who doesn't hesitate.

"Thanks," he says, before, to my annoyance, asking for a second for later on. I shrug, irritated, but say all right, and he slips another from under the holding cord and perches it above his ear. "Looks like he's the one in charge," he says, nodding in the direction of the sergeant. "I need a word with him. Not that he's likely to listen to me, of course. But I'll have my say, I promise you that."

"Your say about what?" I ask.

"Take a look around you, Sadler," he replies. "Only a handful of these people will still be alive six months from now. What do you think of that?"

I don't think anything of it. What am I supposed to think? I know that men die—their numbers are reported in the newspapers every day. But they're just names, strings of letters printed together as news type. I don't know any of them. They don't mean much to me yet.

"Take my advice," he says. "Follow my lead and get the hell out of here if you can."

We stop now in the centre of the parade ground and the sergeant and his two corporals turn to face us. We stand in no particular order but he stares and remains silent until, without a word to each other, we find ourselves separating into a rectangle, ten men long and four men deep, each distanced from the next man by no more than an arm's width.

"Good," says the sergeant, nodding. "That's a good start, gentlemen. Let me begin by welcoming you to Aldershot. Some of you want to be here, I know, some of you don't. Those of us who have been in the service for many years share your emotions and sympathize with them. But they don't matter any more. What you think, what you feel, doesn't matter. You are here to be trained as soldiers and that is what will happen."

He speaks calmly, betraying the conventional image of the barracks sergeant, perhaps to put us at our ease. Perhaps to surprise us by how quickly he might turn on us later.

"My name is Sergeant James Clayton," he announces. "And over the next couple of months, during your time here, it is my responsibility to train you into soldiers, a job that requires as much intellect on your part as it does strength and stamina."

He looks around and narrows his eyes, his tongue bulging out his cheek as he considers the men—boys—lined up before him.

"You, sir," he says, lifting his cane and pointing it at a young lad in the centre of the front row, who made himself popular on the train with his quick wit and effervescent sense of humour. "Your name, please?"

"Mickey Rich," says the boy confidently.

"Mickey Rich, *sir*!" shouts the soldier standing at the sergeant's left shoulder, but the older man turns to him and shakes his head.

"It's perfectly all right, Corporal Wells," he says cheerfully. "Rich here doesn't understand our ways yet. He is utterly ignorant, aren't you, Rich?"

"Yes, sir," Rich replies, his tone a little less certain now, the "sir" being uttered with deliberate force.

"And are you happy to be here, Rich?" asks Sergeant Clayton.

"Oh yes, sir," says Rich. "Happy as a pig in shit."

The entire troop bursts into laughter at this and I join in nervously.

The sergeant waits until the laughter has died down, wearing an expression that suggests a mixture of amusement and contempt, but he says nothing before looking back through the rows and nodding in the direction of a second man. "And you?" he asks. "Who are you?"

"William Tell," comes the reply, and now there's another snigger, difficult to contain.

"William Tell?" asks the sergeant, raising an eyebrow. "Now there's a name. Brought your bow and arrow, have you? Where are you from, Tell?"

"Hounslow," says Tell, and the sergeant nods, satisfied.

"And what about you?" he asks, looking at the next man along.

"Shields, sir. Eddie Shields."

"All right, then, Shields. And you?"

"John Robinson."

"Robinson," acknowledges the sergeant with a brief nod. "And you?"

"Philip Unsworth."

"You?"

"George Parks."

"You?"

"Will Bancroft."

And so on and so on. A litany of names, some of them registering in my mind but none giving me any cause to look at anyone directly.

"And you?" asks the sergeant, nodding in my direction now.

"Tristan Sadler, sir," I say.

"How old are you, Sadler?"

"Eighteen, sir," I reply, repeating my lie.

"Glad to be here, are you?"

I say nothing. I can't think of the correct answer. Fortunately he doesn't press me on it because he has already moved on.

"Arthur Wolf, sir," says my neighbour.

"Wolf?" asks the sergeant, looking at him more closely; it's obvious that he knows something about this man already.

"That's right, sir."

"Well." He looks him up and down. "I expected you to be shorter."

"Six foot one, sir."

"Indeed," says Sergeant Clayton, his mouth creasing slowly into a thin smile. "So you're the chap who doesn't want to be here, yes?"

"That's right, sir."

"Afraid to fight, are you?"

"No, sir."

"No, sir, indeed not, sir, what an outrageous charge, sir! I wonder, can you imagine how many brave men over there don't want to fight either?" He pauses as his smile starts to fade. "But there they are. Fighting day in, day out. Putting their lives on the line."

I can sense a low murmuring in the ranks and some of the recruits turn their heads to look at Wolf.

"I'm not sending you home, if that's what you're expecting," says the sergeant in a casual tone.

"No, sir," says Wolf. "No, I didn't expect you would. Not yet, anyway."

"And you won't be put in confinement either. Not till I get orders to that effect. We'll train you, that's what we'll do."

"Yes, sir."

Sergeant Clayton stares at Wolf, his jaw becoming a little more clenched. "All right, Wolf," he says quietly. "We'll just see how this all turns out, shall we?"

"I expect to hear quite soon, sir," announces Wolf, no tremor audible in his voice, although standing next to him I can sense a certain tension in his body, an anxiety that he's trying hard to keep well hidden. "From the tribunal, I mean. I expect they'll be in touch to let me know their decision, sir."

"Actually, it is *I* who shall hear, Wolf," snaps the sergeant, losing his cool a little at last. "They will direct any communication through me."

"Perhaps you'd be good enough to let me know as soon as you do, sir," replies Wolf, and Sergeant Clayton smiles again.

"Perhaps," he says after a moment. "I'm sure you're all proud to be here, men," he continues then, looking around and raising his voice, addressing the pack now. "But you're probably aware that there are some men of your generation who feel no obligation to defend their country. Objectors, they call themselves. Chaps who examine their conscience and find nothing

59

there to satisfy the call of duty. They look like other men, of course. They have two eyes and two ears, two arms and two legs. No balls, though, that's a given. But unless you whip their pants off and make the necessary enquiries it can be fairly difficult to distinguish them from real men. But they're out there. They surround us. And they would bring us down if they could. They give sustenance to the enemy."

He smiles then, a bitter, angry smile, and the men in the ranks grumble and mutter to themselves, turning to look at Wolf with scorn in their eyes, each one trying harder than the last to impress upon Sergeant Clayton that they subscribe to no such beliefs themselves. Wolf, to his credit, holds his ground and acknowledges none of the hisses and catcalls that are coming his way, taunts that neither the sergeant nor his two corporals do anything to quell.

"Disgrace," says one voice from somewhere behind me.

"Bloody coward," says another.

"Feather man."

I watch to see how he will react to the abuse and it is then that I lay eyes on Will Bancroft for the first time. He's standing four men down from me and staring at Wolf with an expression of interest upon his face. He doesn't look as if he entirely approves of what the man is doing but he isn't joining in the chorus of disapproval. It's as if he wants to get the mark of a fellow who calls himself a conscientious objector, as if he has heard of such mythical creatures and has always wondered what one might look like in the flesh. I find myself staring directly at him—at Bancroft, I mean, not Wolf—unable to shift my gaze, and he must sense my interest for he turns and catches my eye, looking at me for a moment, then cocking his head a little to the side and smiling. It's strange: I feel as if I already know him, as if we know each other. Confused, I bite my lip and look away, waiting for as long as I can force myself to before turning to look at him again, but he's standing straight in line now, focused ahead, and it's almost as if the moment of connection never happened.

"That's enough, men," says Sergeant Clayton, and the cacophony quickly dies down as forty heads turn back towards the front. "Come up here, Wolf," he adds, and my companion hesitates only briefly before stepping forward. I can sense the anxiety beneath the bravado. "And you, Mr. Rich," he adds, pointing at his first interviewee. "Our resident pig in shit. The two of you, come up here, if you please."

The two men advance until they're standing about six or seven feet away from the sergeant and about the same distance from the front line behind them. There is absolute silence from the rest of us.

"Gentlemen," says Sergeant Clayton, looking towards the assembled men. "In this army, you will all be trained, as I have been trained, to honour your uniform. To fight, to handle a rifle, to be strong and to go out there and to kill as many of the fucking enemy as you can find." His voice rises quickly and angrily on that last phrase and I think, *There he is, that's who this man is.* "But sometimes," he continues, "you will find that you have worked your way into a situation where you have no weapons left and neither has your opponent. You might be standing in the centre of no-man's-land, perhaps, with Fritz standing in front of you, and your rifle might have vanished and your bayonet might have disappeared and you will have nothing left to defend yourself with but your fists. A terrifying prospect, gentlemen, isn't it? And if such a thing were to happen, Shields," he says, addressing one of the recruits, "what do you think you would do?"

"Not much choice, sir," says Shields. "Fight it out."

"Exactly," says the sergeant. "Very good, Shields. Fight it out. Now, you two," and here he nods in the direction of Wolf and Rich. "Imagine that you are in that very situation."

"Sir?" asks Rich.

"Fight it out, boy," says the sergeant cheerfully. "We'll call you the Englishman, since you showed a bit of spark, if nothing else. Wolf, you're the enemy. Fight it out. Let's see what you've got."

Both Rich and Wolf turn to each other, the latter with an expression of disbelief on his face, but Rich can tell where the land lies and he doesn't hesitate, clenching his right hand into a fist and punching Wolf directly in the nose, a sharp jab forward and back, like a boxer, so quickly surprising Wolf that he stumbles backwards, tripping over his feet, holding his face in his hands. When he rights himself again he looks in shock at the blood pouring from his nostrils over his fingers. But then Rich is a big lad with strong arms and a neat right-hook.

"You've broken my nose," says Wolf, looking at all of us as if he can't quite believe what has just happened. "You've only gone and broken my fucking nose!"

"So break his in return," says Sergeant Clayton in a casual tone.

Wolf stares down at his hands; the blood has slowed a little but there is a lot of it already, gathered in thick swirls on his palms. His nose is not broken, not really; Rich has just burst a few blood vessels, that's all.

"No, sir," Wolf says.

"Hit him again, Rich," says Clayton, and Rich jabs once more, this time to the right cheek, and Wolf stumbles back once again but manages to stay erect. He works his jaw, uttering a low cry of pain, and puts a hand to it, holding it there for a moment, massaging the bruise.

"Fight him, Wolf," says Clayton, very quietly, very slowly, enunciating each syllable clearly, and there's something in Wolf's expression that suggests to me that he just might, but he waits for twenty, thirty seconds, breathing heavily, controlling his temper, before shaking his head.

"I won't fight, sir," he insists, and now he is punched again, in the stomach, then once more in the solar plexus, and he's on the ground, cowering a little, no doubt hoping that this beating will soon come to an end. The men watch, uncertain how they should feel about the whole thing. Even Rich takes a step back, aware that it's hardly a fair fight when the other fellow won't stand his ground.

"For pity's sake," says Sergeant Clayton, shaking his head contemptuously, realizing that he's not going to get the brawl that he's been hoping for, the one that could leave Wolf seriously damaged. "All right, Rich, get back in line. And you," he says, nodding towards the prostrate Wolf, "get up, for God's sake. Be a man. He barely touched you."

It takes a minute or two but Wolf eventually rises to his feet unassisted and shuffles his way back into line next to me. He catches my eye; perhaps he sees the expression of concern there, but he looks away. He wants no pity.

"It's a beautiful day for a new beginning," announces Sergeant Clayton, stretching his arms out in front of him and cracking his knuckles. "A beautiful day to learn about discipline and to understand that I will tolerate neither humour nor cowardice in this regiment. They are my twin bugbears, gentlemen. Understand that well. You are here to train. And you will be trained."

And with that he turns around and strolls off in the direction of the barracks, leaving us in the hands of his two apostles, whose names are Wells and Moody, and who step forward now to tick our names off on a list that they hold in their hands, working their way down the line, letting each man leave once he has been accounted for, and leaving Wolf, of course, until the end.

My first real contact with Will Bancroft comes the following morning at five o'clock, when we're woken by Wells and Moody.

We're divided into barracks of twenty men, ten beds along one wall pointing into the centre, ten facing on the opposite side, an arrangement that Unsworth remarks is exactly his idea of what a field hospital might look like.

"Let's hope you don't find out any time soon," says Yates.

Having no brothers, I'm unaccustomed to sharing a room with anyone, let alone nineteen other young men who breathe, snore and toss and turn throughout the night, and I'm convinced that it will be all but impossible to sleep. However, to my surprise, my head has barely hit the pillow before a series of confused dreams begins—I must be exhausted from both the train journey and the emotion of being here at last—and then it's morning again and our two corporals are screaming at us to shift our fucking arses or they'll shift them for us with the toes of their fucking boots.

I have the last-but-one bunk on the left-hand wall, the side where, should the sun shine in the morning through the small window close to the ceiling, the light will fall directly on my face. Will was among the first inside the barracks and he took the bunk next to mine, the best place to be for he has a wall to one side of him and only one neighbour, me. Across from him and three beds down to the right is Wolf, who has received a great deal of pushing and shoving from the men since the previous night. To my surprise, Rich chose the bed next to his, and I wonder whether this was an act of apology or a threat of some sort.

Will and I acknowledged each other only briefly before falling into our bunks but as we leap from them again, me to my left, him to his right, we collide and fall backwards, nursing bruised heads. We laugh and offer a quick apology before lining up at the end of our beds, where Moody tells us that we're to make our way quick-smart to the medical tent for an inspection—another inspection, for I had one at Brentford when I enlisted—which will decide whether or not we're suitable to fight for the King's empire.

"Which is unlikely," he adds, "as I've never seen such a bunch of fucking degenerate misfits in my entire life. If this war depends on you lot, well, then, we better all spruce up on our *Guten Morgens* and our *Gute Nachts* because we'll need them soon enough."

Drifting outside towards the back of the group, dressed in nothing but our shorts and vests, our feet bare against the scratchy gravel, Will and I fall into line with each other and he extends a hand to me.

"Will Bancroft," he says.

"Tristan Sadler."

"Looks like we're to be neighbours for the next couple of months. You don't snore, do you?"

"I don't know," I say, having never considered it. "No one's ever said so. What about you?"

"I'm told that when I lie on my back I could raise the roof, but I seem to have trained myself to turn over on to my side."

"I'll push you over if you begin," I say, smiling at him, and he laughs a little and already I feel a camaraderie between us.

"I shouldn't mind it," he says quietly, after a moment.

"How many brothers do you have, then?" I ask, assuming that there must be some if he has been told about his nocturnal habits.

"None," he says. "Just an older sister. You're an only child?"

I hesitate, feeling a lump in my throat, unsure whether to answer truthfully or not. "My sister, Laura," I say, and leave it at that.

"I was always glad of my sister," he says, smiling. "She's a few years older than me but we look out for each other, if you know what I mean. She's made me promise to write to her regularly while I'm over there. I shall keep that promise."

I nod, examining him closer now. He's a good-looking fellow with a mess of dark, untidy hair, a pair of bright blue eyes that look poised for adventure, and round cheeks that crease into dimples when he smiles. He's not muscular but his arms are well toned and fit his vest well. I imagine that he has never had any difficulty finding bed-companions to roll him over on to his side if he grows too noisy.

"What's the matter, Tristan?" he asks, staring at me. "You've grown quite flushed."

"It's the early start," I explain, looking away. "I got out of bed too quickly, that's all. The blood has rushed to my head."

He nods and we stride on, bringing up the rear of our troop, who don't seem quite as enthusiastic or spirited at this early hour as they did when we descended from the train yesterday afternoon. Most of the men are keeping themselves to themselves and marching along quietly, their eyes focused more on the ground beneath their feet than the medical hut up ahead. Wells keeps time for us, calling out a fierce "Hup-two-three-four!" at the top of his voice, and we do our best to keep some sort of order but it's pretty hopeless really.

"Here," says Will a few moments later, looking directly at me, his expression growing more perturbed. "What did you make of friend Wolf, then? Pretty brave of him, wouldn't you say?"

"Pretty stupid," I reply. "Annoying the sergeant on his first day here. Not a good way to make friends with the men, either, is it?"

"Probably not," says Will. "Still, you have to admire his balls. Standing up to the old man like that, knowing that he'll probably get a pasting on account of it. Have you ever known any of those fellows? Those . . . what do you call them . . . conscientious objectors?"

"No," I say, shaking my head. "Why, have you?"

"Only one," he replies. "The older brother of a chap I went to school with. Larson was his name. Can't remember his Christian name. Mark or Martin, something like that. Refused to take up arms. Said it was on religious grounds and old Derby and Kitchener needed to read their Bible a little more and their rules of engagement a little less, and it didn't matter what they did to him, he wouldn't point a rifle at another of God's creatures even if they locked him up on account of it."

I hiss and shake my head in disgust, assuming that he, like me, thinks the man a coward. I don't object to those who are opposed to the war on principle or wish for its speedy conclusion—that's natural enough—but I am of the belief that while it's still going on, it remains the responsibility of all of us to join in and do our bit. I'm young, of course. I'm stupid.

"Well, what happened to him?" I ask. "This Larson fellow. Did they pack him off to Strangeways?"

"No," he replies, shaking his head. "No, they sent him to the Front to act as a stretcher-bearer. They do that, you know. If you refuse to fight they say the least you can do is be of assistance to those who will. Some are sent to work on the farms—work of national importance, they call it—they're the lucky ones. Some go to prison, they're not so lucky. But most of them, well, they end up here anyway."

"That seems fair," I say.

"Only until you realize that a stretcher-bearer at the Front has a life expectancy of about ten minutes. They send them over the trenches and out into no-man's-land to pick up the bodies of the dead and the wounded and that's the end of them. Snipers pick them off quite easily. It's a sort of public execution really. Doesn't seem quite so fair now, does it?" I frown and consider it. I want to reply carefully, for I already know that it's important to me that Will Bancroft thinks well of me and adopts me as his friend. "Of course I could have tried that myself, the whole religious thing," he adds, thinking about it. "The pater's a vicar, you see. Up in Norwich. He wanted me to go into the Church, too. I suppose that would have spared me the draft."

"And you didn't fancy it?"

"No," he says, shaking his head. "Not for me all that malarkey. I don't mind soldiering. At least, I don't think I'll mind it. Ask me again in six months. My grandfather fought in the Transvaal, you know. Was something of a hero out there before he was killed. I like the idea of proving myself as brave as he was. My mother, she's always kept a— Watch out now, here we are."

We step inside the medical hut, where Moody splits us into groups. Half a dozen take their seats on a group of bunks behind a row of curtains while the others stand nearby and wait their turn.

Will and I are among the first to be examined; he has chosen the last bed again and I take the one next to his. I wonder why he seems to have such a disdain for being in the centre of the room. For my part, I rather like being in the middle: it makes me feel part of something and somehow less conspicuous. I have an idea in my head that factions will develop soon among our number and those on the outskirts will be among the first to be picked off.

The doctor, a thin, middle-aged man wearing a pair of thick-rimmed spectacles and a white coat that has seen better days, indicates that Will should strip out of his clothes and he does so without embarrassment, pulling his vest over his head and tossing it carelessly on to the bed beside him, then dropping his shorts on the ground as if they matter not a jot. I look away, embarrassed, but it doesn't do much good, for everywhere I look, the other members of my troop, those sitting on the beds at least, have also stripped down to the altogether, revealing a set of malformed, misshapen and startlingly unattractive bodies. These are young men of no less than eighteen and no more than twenty, and it surprises me that they are for the most part so undernourished and pale. Sparrow chests, thin bellies, loose buttocks are on display wherever I look, except for one or two chaps who are at the other end of the extreme, overweight and corpulent, thick flabs of fat hanging around their chests like breasts. As I undress, too, I quietly thank the construction firm where I worked for the past eighteen months as a labourer for how it fed my muscle, before wondering whether my relative strength and fitness might see me called up for active duty sooner than is healthy.

I turn my attention back to Will, who is standing straight as a rod, both arms extended before him as the doctor peers inside his mouth, then runs a measuring tape across the expanse of his chest. Without thinking how it might look, I take him all in with a glance and am struck once again by how good-looking he is. Out of nowhere I have a sudden flashback to that afternoon at my former school, the day of my expulsion, a memory still buried deep inside me.

I close my eyes for a moment and when I open them I find that I am looking straight into Will's eyes. He's turned his head to look at me; it's another curious moment. I wonder, *Why isn't he looking away?* And then, *Why aren't I?* And the look lasts for three, four, five seconds before the corners of his mouth turn up into a slight smile and he looks away at last, staring directly ahead once again, exhaling three times, long and deep, the response, I realize, to the doctor holding a stethoscope to his back and asking him to breathe in deeply and out again.

"Thank you," says the doctor in a disinterested tone as he comes around to the front and tells Will that he can put his clothes back on. "Now," he says, turning his attention towards me. "Next."

I endure a similar examination, the same measuring of heart rate and blood pressure, height, weight and pulmonary ability. He grabs my balls and tells me to cough; I do so quickly, willing him to let go, then he orders me to extend both hands in front of my body and hold them there, as still as I can. I do as he asks and he seems pleased by what he observes. "Steady as a rock," he says, nodding and ticking off a box on his paperwork.

Later, after a terrible breakfast of cold scrambled eggs and fatty bacon, I find myself back in our barracks once again and kill a few minutes by taking in the lie of the land. The screened-off area at the opposite end from Will and me is where Wells and Moody sleep, their bunks offering a small degree of privacy from their useless charges. The latrine is outside, a single hut that contains a few pisspots and something worse, far more foul-smelling, and which we are informed we will be taking it in turns to empty every evening, starting that night, of course, with Wolf.

"You don't think they might have let us digest our breakfast first?" asks Will as we make our way to the drill ground, walking alongside each other again but this time more to the centre of the pack. "What do you think, Tristan? I feel as if I'm going to throw that whole mess up at any moment. Still, we are at war, I suppose. It's not a holiday camp."

Sergeant Clayton is waiting for us, standing erect in a freshly pressed uniform, and he doesn't move or even appear to breathe as we fall into line before him and his two apostles take their positions on either side.

"Men," he says finally, "the idea of seeing you engaging in exercise while wearing the colours of the regiment is abhorrent to me. For that reason, until I deem otherwise, you shall train and drill in your civvies."

A low murmur of disappointment rings out across the ranks; it's clear that many of the boys want nothing more than to put on the longed-for khaki fatigues here and now, as if the clothes themselves might turn us into soldiers immediately. Those of us who have waited a long time to be accepted into the army have no desire to wear the cheap, dirty clothes we arrived in for a moment longer than is necessary.

"Load of tosh," whispers Will to me. "The bloody army can't afford any more uniforms, that's all it is. It'll be weeks before we're kitted out."

I don't reply, nervous of getting caught talking, but I believe him. For as long as the war has been going on I've been following it in the newspapers and there are constant complaints that the army doesn't have enough uniforms or rifles for every soldier. The downside is that we will be stuck in our civvies for the foreseeable future; the upside is that we can't be called to France until we have a suitable kit to fight in. There's already uproar in Parliament about men sacrificing themselves without even having the proper uniform.

We begin with fairly rudimentary drilling techniques: ten minutes of stretching, followed by running on the spot while we build up a good perspiration. Then, quite suddenly, Sergeant Clayton decides that our file of five by four men is quite disordered and charges between us, pulling one man a step forward, pushing another a fraction back, dragging some poor unsuspecting lad to his right while kicking another further to the left. By the time he has finished—and I've received my own share of pushes and shoves during his manoeuvres—the lines don't look any more ordered or disordered than they did ten minutes earlier, but he seems more satisfied with them and I'm willing to believe that what is not obvious to my untrained eye is a glaring offence to his more experienced one.

Through it all, Sergeant Clayton complains loudly about our inability to hold formation, and his voice becomes so strained and his face so angry that I genuinely believe he might do himself an injury if he does not take care. And yet, to my surprise, when we are finished and dismissed, sent back to the wash house to scrub ourselves clean, he seems as composed and unflappable as he did when we first encountered him.

There's only one order left for him to give. Wolf, he decrees, has let the side down badly by not lifting his knees high enough as he marched.

"Another hour for Wolf, I think," he says, turning his head to Moody, who responds with a firm "Yes, sir" before Wells leads us back to where we started, our colleague standing alone in the middle of the parade ground, marching in a perfect formation of one as the rest of us leave him to it, apparently unconcerned for his welfare.

"The old man rather has it in for Wolf, doesn't he?" Will says as we lie on our bunks later that day, having been granted a thirty-minute reprieve before we are to report back for an evening march over some wild terrain, even the thought of which makes me want to groan out loud.

"It's to be expected," I say.

"Yes, of course. All the same, it's not very sporting, is it?"

I turn to him and smile, surprised. There's a bit of the toff in the way he speaks and I imagine that his upbringing as the son of a Norfolk vicar was perhaps a little more salubrious than mine. His language is refined and he seems to care about others. His kindness impresses me. It gathers me in.

"Was your father upset when you were drafted?" I ask him.

"Terribly," he replies. "But he would have been worse if I'd refused to fight. King and country mean an awful lot to him. What about yours?"

I shrug. "He didn't care very much."

Will nods and breathes heavily through his nose, sitting up and folding his pillow in two behind his back as he lights a tab and smokes it thoughtfully.

"Here," he says after a few moments, his voice growing quieter now so that no one else can hear him. "What did you think of that doctor chap earlier, then?"

"Think of him?" I reply, confused by the question. "I didn't think anything of him. Why do you ask?"

"No reason," he says. "Only I thought you seemed very interested in what he was doing, that's all. Not planning on running off to join the Medical Corps, are you?"

I feel my face begin to blush again—he had caught me staring at him after all—and turn over on the bed so he won't notice it. "No, no, Bancroft," I say. "I'm sticking with the regiment."

"Glad to hear it, Tristan," he says, leaning near enough towards me for me to smell a faint scent of perspiration coming my way. It feels as if his entire spirit is about to press down upon me. "Only we're stuck with a right group of no-hopers here, I think. Corporal Moody might have a point about that. It's good to have made a friend." I smile but say nothing; I can feel a sort of sting running through my body at his words, like a knife placing itself in the centre of my chest and pressing forward, hinting at the pain that is sure to follow. I close my eyes and try not to think about it too deeply. "And for God's sake, Tristan, stop calling me Bancroft, would you?" he adds, collapsing back on his own bunk now, the weight of his body throwing itself down so enthusiastically that it causes the springs to cry out as if they're in pain. "My name's Will. I know every bugger here calls each other by their surname but we're different, I think. Let's not let them break us, all right?"

Over the weeks that follow we endure such torturous training that I can't believe this is something I had wanted to be a part of for so long. Our reveille comes most mornings at five o'clock when, with no more than three minutes' warning by Wells or Moody, we're expected to wake, jump from our beds, dress, pull our boots on and line up in formation outside the barracks. Most days we stand there in a sort of daze, and as we begin to march out of the camp for the four-hour hike ahead our bodies cry out in pain. On these mornings I imagine that nothing could be worse than basic training; soon I will learn that I was wrong about that, too.

The result of such activity, however, is that our young bodies begin to develop, the muscle forming in hard packs around our calves and chests, a tightness appearing at our abdominal muscles, and we begin to look like soldiers at last. Even those few members of our troop who arrived at Aldershot over-weight—Turner, Hobbs, Milton, the practically obese Denchley—begin to shed their excess pounds and take on a more healthy aspect.

We're not obliged to march in silence and usually keep up low, grumbling conversations. I form good relations with most of the men in our troop but it's to Will that I cleave most mornings and he appears content to spend his time with me, too. I haven't experienced much friendship in my life. The only one who ever mattered to me was Peter, but he abandoned me for Sylvia and then, after the incident at school, my subsequent disgrace ensured that I would never lay eyes on him again.

And then, one afternoon on a rare hour's break in the barracks, Will comes inside to find me alone, my back turned to him, and he leaps upon me in a fit of enthusiasm, screeching and squawking like a child at play. I wrestle him off me and we roll around on the floor, grabbing and jostling, laughing at nothing. When he has me in a clinch, pinned to the floor, his knees on either side of my torso, he looks down at me and smiles, his dark hair falling in his eyes, and I am sure that he looks at my lips for moment, turns his head a little and stares at them, his body arcing forward just a touch, and I raise my knee slightly and risk a smile. We look each other—"Ah, Tristan," he says mournfully, his voice soft—and then we hear someone at the door and he jumps up, turning away from me, and when he looks back as Robinson enters the barracks I notice that he cannot, just now, catch my eye.

Perhaps it's not unusual, then, that I find myself seething with jealousy on an early-morning march when, having stopped to retie my bootlaces as I leave camp, I find that I have lost Will in the pack of men and, brushing my way through them quickly, careful not to appear too obvious in my intentions, I discover him walking ahead of the others with none other than Wolf, our conscientious objector, as his boon companion. I stare at them in surprise, for no one ever walks or talks with Wolf, on whose bed small white feathers appear every night from our pillows to such an extent that Moody, who has no liking for Wolf any more than the rest of us do, tells us to pack it in or our pillows will be stripped bare and we'll develop neck ache from stretching flat out on our mattresses with nothing to cushion our heads. I glance around, wondering whether anyone else has noticed this unusual pairing, but most of my fellow recruits are too focused on putting one foot in front of the other as they march along, heads bowed, eyes half closed, thinking about nothing other than getting back to base as quickly as possible and the dubious pleasures of breakfast.

Determined not to be left out of whatever they're discussing, I pick up the pace a little until I am alongside them both, falling into line next to Will, looking anxiously across at him as Wolf leans forward and smiles at me. I get the impression that he has been in the middle of a speech about something— it's never a conversation with Wolf, it's always a speech—but he grows silent now and Will turns to look at me, offering an expression which suggests that although he's surprised to see me he's pleased nonetheless.

Of course, one of the things that I like most about Will is the notion—completely real, at least in my head—that he genuinely enjoys my company. He laughs at my jokes, which come more freely and wittily whenever I am around him than they do in anyone else's company. He makes me feel as if I am just as good as him, just as clever, just as relaxed with other people, and the truth is that I feel anything but. And there is the sense, the ongoing sense, that he feels something for me.

"Tristan," he says cheerfully, "I wondered what had happened to you. I thought perhaps you'd gone back to bed. Arthur and I got talking. He was telling me about his plans for the future."

"Oh yes?" I ask, looking across at Wolf. "And what are they? Planning on making a run for the papacy, are you?"

"Steady on, Tristan," says Will, a note of criticism in his tone. "You know the pater's a vicar. Nothing wrong with the Church, you know, if it's the right thing for you. Couldn't manage it myself, of course, but still."

"No, of course not," I say, having momentarily forgotten the sainted Reverend Bancroft, preaching his sermons back in Norwich. "I only meant that Wolf sees the good in everyone, that's all." It's a pitiful response, designed to imply that I hold Wolf in high esteem, which I don't, for no other reason than that I suspect that Will does.

"Not the priesthood, no," says Wolf, apparently enjoying my discomfort. "I thought politics."

"Politics," I reply, laughing. "But there's no chance of that, surely?"

"And why not?" he asks, turning to me and, as ever, giving nothing away in his expression.

"Look, Wolf," I say. "I don't know whether you're right or wrong in your convictions. I won't presume to judge you on that."

"Really? Why not? You do most days. I thought you agreed with all those other fellows that I was a feather man."

"It's just that even if you are right," I continue, ignoring this, "you'll have a difficult job convincing anyone of it after the war. I mean to say, if a fellow were to stand for Parliament in my constituency and told the voters that he objected to the war and refused to fight in it, well, he'd have a tricky job making it off the platform intact, let alone garnering enough votes to win a seat."

"But Arthur isn't refusing to fight," says Will. "He's here, isn't he?"

"I'm here training," insists Wolf. "I've told you, Will, that once we're shipped out, I'll refuse to fight. I've told them that. They know it. But they don't listen, that's the problem. The military tribunal was supposed to make a decision on my case weeks ago, and still nothing. It's extremely frustrating."

"Look, what exactly are you objecting to?" I ask, not entirely sure that I understand his motivations. "You don't like war, is that it?"

"Nobody should *like* war, Sadler," says Wolf. "And I can't imagine that anyone really does, except for Sergeant Clayton, perhaps. He seems to relish the experience. No, I simply don't believe that it is right to take another man's life in cold blood. I'm not a religious man, not much anyway, but I think it's up to God to take us or leave us as he pleases. And anyway, what do I have against some German boy who's been dragged away from Berlin or Frankfurt or Dusseldorf to fight for his country? What does he have against me? Yes, there are issues at stake, political issues, territorial issues, over which this war is being fought, and there are legitimate grounds for complaint, I dare say, but there is also such a thing as diplomacy, there is such a thing as the concept of right-thinking men gathering around a table and sorting their problems out. And I don't believe those avenues have been exhausted yet. Instead we're all simply killing each other day after day after day. And I object to *that*, Sadler, if you really want to know. And I refuse to be a part of it."

"But, my dear fellow," says Will, a note of exasperation in his tone, "then it'll be the stretcher-bearer's job for you. You can't want that, surely?"

"Of course not. But if it's the only alternative."

"Small use to politics you'll be if you're picked off by a sniper in ten minutes flat," I say, and Will turns on me then, frowning, and I feel ashamed of what I've said. We make a point, all of us, of never talking about the consequences of the war, the fact that few of us, if any, are likely to live to see the other side of it, and it's against our code of conduct for me to make such a vulgar remark. I look away, unable to bear my friend's disapprobation, my boots stamping loudly on the stone beneath my feet.

"Something the matter, Sadler?" asks Wolf a few minutes later when Will has advanced again, this time laughing with Henley about something.

"No," I grunt, not even turning to look at him, my eyes focused firmly ahead at yet another prospective friendship that might push my nose even further out of joint. "Any reason why it should be?"

"You seem a little . . . irritated, that's all," says Wolf. "A little preoccupied."

"You don't know me," I say.

"There's really nothing to worry about," he replies in such a casual tone that it infuriates me. "We were just talking, that's all. I'm not going to steal him away from you. You can have him back now if you want."

I turn and stare at him, unable to find any words to express my indignation, and he bursts out laughing, shaking his head as he marches away.

Later, as punishment for my insensitivity, Will pairs off with Wolf again when we begin to train with the Short Magazine Lee-Enfield rifles—the Smilers, as we call them—and I find myself stuck with Rich, who has an answer for everything and considers himself the great wit of our group, but is known as something of a dunderhead when it comes to learning anything. He holds a rather curious position among us, for although he drives Wells and Moody to distraction with his idiocy and incurs the wrath of Sergeant Clayton almost every day, there's something pathetic about him, something likeable, and no one can ever be angry with him for long.

We each receive a rifle, and complaints that we are still wearing our civilian clothes, which are washed every third day to rid them of the caked mud and the stench of sweat that they bear, fall on deaf ears.

"They just want us to kill as many of the enemy as possible," remarks Rich. "They don't care what we look like. We could go over in our birthday suits for all Lord Kitchener would care."

I agree with him but think the whole thing is a bit much and say so. Still, it's something of a sobering moment for all of us when at last we are handed our Smilers, and an uneasy silence falls among us, terror that we might be called upon to use them, and soon.

"Gentlemen," says Sergeant Clayton, standing before us and stroking his own rifle in a perfectly obscene fashion, "what you hold before you is the means by which we will win this war. The Short Magazine Lee-Enfield rifles have a ten-round magazine, a bolt mechanism which is the envy of armies around the world and, for a short-range attack, a seventeen-inch bayonet attached to the end for the moment when you leap forward and want to spear the enemy in the face to let them know who is who and what is what and why the price of cabbage is the price of cabbage. These are not toys, gentlemen, and the chap that I see acting as if they are is the chap who will be sent on a ten-mile march with a dozen of these fine instruments tied to his back. Do I make myself clear?"

We grunt that he does, and our basic training in the use of the rifle begins. It's not easy to load and unload the mechanism and some are quicker to master it than others. I would say that I am about halfway down the pack on ability here and I glance across at Will, who is conversing with Wolf once again as they fill their magazines, empty them again, attach the bayonet, release it. Catching Wolf's eye for a moment, I grow convinced that they are discussing me, that Wolf can read me like a book, can see through to my very soul, and is telling Will all my secrets. As if I am shouting this aloud, Will turns at that very moment and looks at me, breaking into an elated smile as he waves his rifle dramatically in the air, and I smile back, waving mine in return, and receive a box on the ears from Moody for my troubles. As I rub them in pain, I see Will laughing in delight, and that alone makes it all worth the trouble.

"I can see that we have a few men who are faster learners than others," announces Sergeant Clayton when enough time has passed. "Let's have a little test of skill, shall we? Williams, step up here, please." Roger Williams, a fairly mild-mannered member of our troop, stands up and makes his way to the front. "And . . . Yates, I think," he continues. "You, too. And Wolf."

All three men gather at the front for what has become Wolf's daily ritual of humiliation. I can sense the delight of the men as he stands there, and I glance across at Will, who is frowning heavily.

"Now, gentlemen," says Sergeant Clayton, "the last man to take his rifle apart successfully and put it back together will . . ." He thinks about it and shrugs. "Well, I'm not sure yet. But I dare say it won't be much fun." He smiles a little and some of the sycophants among our company giggle in appreciation of the pathetic joke. "Corporal Wells, count them down if you would."

Wells gives them a "Three-two-one-begin!" and to my astonishment, as Williams and Yates struggle with their rifles, Wolf takes his apart without any bother at all and reattaches the whole thing in about forty-five seconds flat. There's a silence among the men, a potent disappointment, and his two opponents stop for a moment and stare at him in disbelief before rushing quickly to finish second.

Sergeant Clayton stares at Wolf in frustration. There's no question that he has done what has been asked of him and has completed the task in good time; there's simply no way that he can be punished for it now: it wouldn't be sporting and every man would know it. Will can't keep the smile off his face, I notice, and seems only a little shy of breaking into a burst of applause, but thankfully he manages to restrain himself.

"It astonishes me," says Sergeant Clayton eventually, sounding as if he genuinely means this, "that a man who is afraid to fight should show such skill with a rifle."

"I'm not afraid to fight," insists Wolf with an exasperated sigh. "I just don't care for it very much, that's all."

"You're a coward, sir," remarks Clayton. "Let us at least call things what they are."

Wolf shrugs his shoulders, a deliberately provocative gesture, and the sergeant grabs the rifle out of Yates's hands, checks that it isn't loaded, and turns to Moody once again. "We'll have one more go at it, I think," he announces. "Wolf and I shall take each other on. What do you say, Wolf? Can you stand a challenge? Or does that offend your finely honed moral convictions, too?"

Wolf says nothing, simply nods his head, and a moment later Moody gives another "Three-two-one-begin!" and this time there's no question about who the victor will be. Sergeant Clayton disassembles and reassembles his rifle with such astonishing speed that it's really quite something to observe. Many of the men applaud him, although I add only a per-functory clap to the embarrassing din. He turns and looks at us, delighted by his victory, and grins at Wolf with such a proud expression that it makes me realize what an infant this man really is, for all he has done is best a recruit at something that he has been doing successfully for years. There is no real victory in that. If anything, the challenge itself was shameful.

"Now, Wolf," he says, "what do you think of that?"

"I think you handle a rifle better than I ever shall," he replies, finishing the reassembly of his Smiler and taking his place back in line next to Will, who reaches his hand behind him and pats his back in a well-done gesture. Sergeant Clayton, however, cannot seem to decide whether Wolf's comment was meant as a compliment or a slight, and remains alone on the ground after he dismisses us, scratching his head and no doubt wondering how soon it will be before he can punish Wolf again for some perceived infraction.

The day that our uniforms finally arrive is the same day that Will and I have been rostered for guard duty and we stand together by the gates of the barracks in the cold night air, excited by our brand-new standard issue. Every man in the troop has been given a new pair of boots, two thick grey shirts, collarless, and a pair of khaki trousers, which are pulled high on our waists and kept in place with a neat set of braces. The socks are thick and I believe that for once my feet will be kept warm throughout the night. We've each been given a heavy overcoat, too, and it is in this fine new set of clothing that Will and I stand side by side, patiently scouring the expanse in the unlikely event that a battalion of German soldiers might appear over a hill in the middle of Hampshire.

"My neck hurts," says Will, pulling the shirt away from his skin. "It's a bloody rough material, isn't it?"

"Yes. But we'll get used to it, I dare say."

"After it's left a permanent ring around our necks. We'll have to imagine that we're aristocrats in the French Revolution and are giving Madame la Guillotine a clue for where to slice our heads off."

I laugh a little, seeing my breath appear before me. "Still, they're warmer than what we had before," I say after a moment. "I was dreading another night on guard duty in my civvies."

"Me, too. What about poor Wolf, though? Did you ever see anything as disgusting as that in all your life?"

I think about it before replying. Earlier in the day, when Wells and Moody were distributing the uniforms, Wolf found himself with a shirt that was too large and a pair of trousers that were too tight. He looked rather like a clown and the entire troop, save Will, was reduced to tears of laughter when he put them on and displayed himself for our merriment. I only stopped myself from joining in the hysteria through my desire not to have Will think badly of me.

"He brings it on himself," I say, frustrated by my friend's constant need to stand up for Wolf. "I mean, really, Will, why do you always take his side?"

"I take his side because he's in the regiment with us," he explains, as if it's the most obvious thing in the world. "I mean, what was it that Sergeant Clayton spoke to us about the other day? *Espert* . . . what was it? *Espert* something?"

"*Esprit de corps*," I remind him.

"Yes, that. The notion that a regiment is a regiment, a singular object, a unit, not a collection of mismatched men all vying for different levels of attention. Wolf may be unpopular among the men but that's no reason to treat him as if he were a monster of some sort. I mean he's here, isn't he? He hasn't run off to some hideaway in, I don't know, the Scottish Highlands or some godforsaken place. He might have run off up there and laid low till the war was over."

"If he's unpopular it's because he makes himself so," I explain. "You're not trying to tell me that you agree with the things he says, are you? The things he stands for?"

"The man talks a lot of sense," replies Will quietly. "Oh, I'm not saying that I think we should all hold our hands up and call ourselves conscientious objectors and head off home to bed. I'm not stupid enough to think that that would be a good idea. The whole country would be in a terrible mess. But damn it all, he has a right to his opinion, doesn't he? He has a right to be heard. There are some chaps who would have just scarpered and he didn't and I admire him for that. He has the guts to be here, to train with the rest of us while he waits to hear what the result of his case will be. If they ever get round to telling him. And the result of that is that he's subject to the bullying and despicable behaviour of a bunch of clots who don't have the sense to think that actually killing another human being is not something we should simply do on a whim, but is a most serious offence against the natural order of things."

"I didn't realize you were such a Utopian, Will," I say, a tone of mockery in my voice.

"Don't patronize me, Tristan," he snaps back. "I just don't like the way he's treated, that's all. And I'll say it again if I have to. The man talks a lot of sense."

I say nothing now, simply stare ahead and narrow my eyes, peering forward as if I've noticed something moving on the horizon when, of course, we both know full well that I haven't. I don't want to pursue this conversation any further, that's all.

I don't want to argue. The truth is, I actually agree with what Will is saying; I only hate the fact that he sees in Wolf a chap whom he respects and even looks up to, when I am no more to him than a friend to pal around with, someone he can talk to while he's going to sleep and double up with when it comes to joint activities, for we are each other's match in terms of speed, strength and skill, the three factors, according to Sergeant Clayton, which separate British soldiers from their German equivalents.

"Look, I'm sorry," I say after a long silence. "I quite like Wolf, if I'm honest. I just wish he wouldn't make such a song and dance about things, that's all."

"Let's not talk about it any more," says Will, blowing into his hands noisily, but I'm pleased to note that he doesn't say this in an aggressive tone. "I don't want to argue with you."

"Well, I don't want to argue with you, either," I say. "You know how much your friendship means to me." He turns to look at me and I can hear him breathe heavily. He bites his lip, looks as if he's about to say something, then changes his mind and turns away.

"Here, Tristan," he says after a moment, conspicuously changing the subject, "you'll never guess what today is."

I think about it for a moment and know immediately. "Your birthday," I say.

"How did you know?"

"Lucky guess."

"What did you get me, then?" he asks, his face bursting into that cheeky smile that has the power to dissolve all other thoughts from my mind. I lean forward and punch him on the upper arm.

"That," I say as he cries out in mock pain and rubs the injured area, and I grin back at him for a moment before looking away.

"Well, happy fucking birthday," I say, imitating our beloved Corporal Moody.

"Thanks very fucking much," he replies, laughing.

"How old are you, then?"

"You know full well, Tristan," he replies. "I'm only a few months older than you, after all. Nineteen today."

"Nineteen years old and never been kissed," I say, without really thinking about the words and ignoring the fact that he is not in fact a few months older than me but nearly a year and a half. It was a phrase my mother always used whenever anyone declared themselves to be a particular age. I don't mean anything by it.

"Steady on, old man," he says quickly, looking at me with a mixture of a smile and a hint of offence in his tone. "I've been kissed all right. Why, haven't you?"

"Of course," I say. Sylvia Carter had kissed me, after all. And there had been one other. Both utter disasters.

"Now if I was at home," says Will then, stringing out the words for a long time, playing a game that we always indulge ourselves with when we're on guard duty together, "I expect my parents would be throwing some sort of dinner party for me tonight and inviting all the neighbours in to throw presents at me."

"Sounds very posh," I say. "Would I be invited?"

"Certainly not. We only allow the upper echelons of society into our house. As you know, my father is a vicar, he has a certain position to uphold. We can't just let any old so-and-so through the door."

"Well, then, I should wait outside the house," I announce. "And stand guard, like we're doing here. It would remind us of this rotten place. I'd keep everyone out."

He laughs but says nothing and I wonder whether my suggestion has seemed a little overwrought to him.

"There is one you'd have to let through," he says after a moment.

"Oh yes? Who's that?"

"Why, Eleanor, of course."

"I thought you said your sister's name was Marian."

"It is," he says. "But what's that got to do with anything?"

"No, I only meant . . ." I begin, confused. "Well, who's Eleanor, then, if she's not your sister? The family Labrador or something?" I ask with a laugh.

"No, Tristan," he says, sniggering. "Nothing of the sort. Eleanor's my fiancée. I've told you about her, haven't I?"

I turn and stare at him. I know full well that he has never once told me about her and can see from the expression on his face that he knows the same thing. He seems to be making a point of saying it.

"Your fiancée?" I ask. "You're to be married?"

"Well, in a manner of speaking," he says, and I think I can hear a note of embarrassment, even regret, in his voice, but I'm not sure whether it's really there or whether I'm just imagining it. "I mean, we've been sweethearts for ever so long. And we've talked about marriage. Her family are well in with mine, you see, and I suppose it's just always been on the cards. She's a terrific girl. And not at all conventional, if you know what I mean. I can't stand conventional girls, Tristan, can you?"

"No," I say, digging the toe of my boot into the dirt and twisting it around, imagining for a moment that the soil is Eleanor's head. "No, they make me want to throw up."

I'm not entirely sure I know what he means when he says that she is not conventional, it seems an unusual turn of phrase, but then I remember him telling me he has been told that he snores something terrible and the phrase attacks me like a viper as I realize exactly what it is that he is saying.

87

"When this is all over, I'll introduce you to her," he says a few moments later. "I'm sure you'd like her."

"I'm sure I would," I say, blowing into my own hands now. "I'm sure she's an absolute fucking delight."

He hesitates for a moment before turning to me. "And what's that supposed to mean?" he asks quickly.

"What?"

"What you just said: 'I'm sure she's an absolute fucking delight.'"

"Don't mind me," I say, shaking my head angrily. "I'm just bloody cold, that's all. Aren't you freezing, Bancroft? I don't think these new uniforms are all they're cracked up to be."

"I've told you not to call me that, haven't I?" he snaps. "I don't like it."

"Sorry. Will," I say, correcting myself.

An unpleasant tension settles over us then and we don't speak for five, perhaps ten more minutes. I rack my brain for words but can think of nothing to say. The idea that Will and this miserable Eleanor tramp are somehow involved, have been for who knows how long, tortures me and I want nothing more than to be back in my bunk with my head buried in my pillow, hoping for the quick arrival of sleep. I can't imagine what Will is thinking but he is so silent now that I imagine he feels awkward, too, and I simultaneously try to analyse the reason why and try not to.

"Don't you have a sweetheart at home, then?" he asks me finally, the words sounding as if they are meant in a kindly way but coming out anything but.

"You know I don't," I say coldly.

"Well, how would I know that? You've never said one way or the other."

"Because I would have told you if I had."

"I didn't tell you about Eleanor," he counters. "Or so you claim."

"You didn't."

"It's just that I don't like to think about her up there in Norwich all on her own, pining away for me." He means it as a joke, something to soften the nasty atmosphere of the moment, but it does no good. It just makes him appear smug and arrogant, which is the opposite of his intention. "You know one or two of the chaps are married," he says now and I turn to look at him, interested at least in this.

"Really? I hadn't heard. Which ones?"

"Shields for one. And Attling. Taylor, too."

"Taylor?" I cry. "Who the hell would marry Taylor? He looks like Unevolved Man."

"Someone did apparently. It all took place last summer, he told me."

I shrug and act as if none of this is of any interest to me whatsoever.

"It must be awfully nice to be married," he says then, his voice becoming dreamlike. "Can you imagine coming home every night to find your slippers toasting beside a warm fire and a hot dinner waiting for you?"

"It's every man's dream," I say acidly.

"And the rest of it," he adds. "Whenever you want it. You can't deny that that doesn't sound like it's worth all the trouble."

"The rest of it?" I ask, playing stupid.

"You know what I mean."

I nod. "Yes," I say. "Yes, I know what you mean. You mean sex."

He laughs and nods. "Of course sex," he replies. "But you say it like it's a terrible thing. Like you want to spit the word out in horror."

"Do I?"

"Yes."

"Well, I don't mean to," I say haughtily. "It's just that I think there are some matters that are not fit for conversation, that's all."

89

"In the middle of my father's sermons, perhaps," he says. "Or in front of my mother and her chums during their Tuesday-night whist drives. But here? Come on, Tristan. Don't be such a prude."

"Don't call me that," I say, turning on him. "I won't be called names."

"Well, I didn't mean anything by it," he says defensively. "What has you all twisted up in knots, anyway?"

"Do you really want to know?" I ask. "Because I'll tell you if you do."

"Of course I want to know," he says. "I wouldn't have asked if I didn't."

"All right, then," I say. "Only we've been here for almost six weeks, haven't we?"

"Yes."

"And I thought we were friends, you and I."

"But we are friends, Tristan," he says, laughing nervously, although there is no humour to be found here. "Why ever would you think we're not?"

"Perhaps because in the course of those six weeks you've never once mentioned to me that you had a fiancée waiting for you at home."

"Well, you've never mentioned whether . . . whether . . ." He struggles to finish his sentence. "I don't know. Whether you prefer trains to boats. It's just never come up, that's all."

"Don't talk nonsense," I say. "I'm just surprised, that's all. I thought you trusted me."

"I do trust you. Why, you're the finest fellow here."

"Do you think so?"

"Of course I do. A chap needs a friend in a place like this. Not to mention in the place we're going next. And you're my friend, Tristan. The best I have. You're not jealous, are you?" he adds, laughing at the absurdity of it. "You sound just like

90

Eleanor, you know. She's forever goading me about this other girl, Rebecca, who she swears is sweet on me."

"Of course I'm not jealous," I say, spitting a little on the ground in frustration. For Christ's sake, now there's a Rebecca to be thrown into the pot. "Why would I be jealous of her, Will? It makes no sense." I want to say more. I'm desperate to say more. But I know that I can't. I feel as if we are at a precipice here. And when he turns to look at me, and swallows as our eyes meet, I'm sure that he can feel it, too. I can walk out over the ledge and see whether he'll reach out to catch me or I can take a step back. "Oh, just forget I said anything," I say eventually, shaking my head quickly as if to dismiss every unworthy thought from it. "I was just hurt that you didn't tell me about her, that's all. I don't like secrets."

A slight pause.

"But it wasn't a secret," he says quietly.

"Well, whatever it was," I say. "Let's forget about it, yes? I'm just tired, that's all. I don't know what I'm saying."

He shrugs and looks away. "We're both tired," he says. "I don't even know why we're arguing."

"We're not arguing," I insist, staring at him, feeling tears springing up behind my eyes because I would be damned rather than argue with him. "We're not arguing, Will."

He steps closer and stares at me, then puts a hand out and touches me gently on the arm, his eyes following it as if it's acting independently of him and he's wondering where it might travel next.

"It's just I've always known her," he says. "I suppose I've just always thought we were meant for each other."

"And are you?" I ask, my heart pounding so heavily in my chest as his hand remains on my arm that I am convinced he will be able to hear it. He looks up at me, his face caught in a mixture of confusion and sadness. He opens his mouth to say something, thinks better of it and, as he does so, our eyes remain locked on each other for three, four, five seconds and I'm sure that one of us will say something or do something, but I'm relying on him for I cannot risk it and now, for the briefest moment, I think he might but he changes his mind just as quickly and turns away, shaking his arm as if he wants to rattle it loose, cursing in exasperation.

"For fuck's sake, Tristan," he hisses and walks away from me, disappearing into the darkness, and I can hear his new boots tramping in the soil as he makes his way around the circumference of the barracks, on the lookout for anyone who has no business being there and upon whom he might take out whatever aggression he is feeling.

My nine weeks at Aldershot are almost at an end and I wake in the middle of the night for the first time since my arrival. In another thirty-six hours we are due to pass out, but it's not anxiety about what lies ahead for our regiment once we are officially soldiers that breaks my sleep. It's the sound of a muffled commotion coming from across the room. I raise my head off the pillow and the noises quieten for a moment or two before returning even stronger: an unsettling reverberation of dragging and kicking, then a shushing sound, a door opening, then closing, and silence again.

I open my eyes a little wider and look across at Will, asleep in the bed next to mine, one bare arm draped over the side, his lips slightly parted, a great bunch of dark hair falling over his forehead and into his eyes. Muttering something in his sleep, he flicks it away with the fingers of his left hand and rolls over.

And I fall asleep again.

At drill the following morning, Sergeant Clayton orders us into our ranks and we are an immediate eyesore to him, for sticking out in the second row, third spot along, is the empty place of a missing person, a soldier AWOL. It is the first time this has happened since we disembarked from the train in April.

"I feel I need barely ask this question," Sergeant Clayton says, "because I trust that if any of you men had an answer to it you would have already come to me. But does anyone know where Wolf is?"

There is complete silence from the ranks. No one turns their head as we might have done nine weeks earlier. We simply stand there and stare directly ahead. We have been trained.

"I thought not," he continues. "Well, I might as well tell you that our self-proclaimed conscientious objector has disappeared. Taken himself off in the night like the coward that he is. We'll catch up with him sooner or later, I can promise you that. If anything, I take a certain pleasure in the fact that when you pass out on Friday, there will not be a coward among your ranks."

I'm a little surprised by what he has said but don't think too much of it; I don't for a moment think that Wolf has absconded and am sure that he'll turn up sooner or later with a perfectly ridiculous excuse for his absenteeism. Instead, my mind has turned to questions of what will happen on Saturday morning. Will we be dispatched on the train to Southampton immediately and then find ourselves on an overnight passage to France? Will we be in the middle of things over there by Monday morning? Will I live another week? These are far more pressing concerns to me than whether or not Wolf has made a bid for freedom.

I am in Will's company, walking back later that afternoon from the mess hut towards the barracks, when I sense a great commotion ahead and notice the men gathered in groups, engaged in excited conversation.

"Don't tell me," says Will. "The war's over and we all get to go home."

"Who do you think won?" I ask.

"Nobody," he replies. "We both lost. Look out, here comes Hobbs."

Hobbs, having noticed us walking along, comes bounding over like a slightly overweight golden retriever. "Where have you chaps been?" he asks breathlessly.

"To Berlin, to see the kaiser and tell him to give it all up as a bad lot," says Will. "Why, what's the matter?"

"Haven't you heard, then?" asks Hobbs. "They found Wolf."

"Oh," I reply, a little disappointed. "Is that all?"

"What do you mean, 'Is that all?' It's enough, isn't it?"

"Where did they find him?" asks Will. "Is he all right?"

"About four miles from here," replies Hobbs. "In the forest where we went on marches in the early weeks."

"Up there?" I ask in surprise, for it's an unpleasant, squalid place, filled with marshes and freezing cold streams, and Sergeant Clayton had abandoned it long ago for drier terrain. "What on earth was he doing up there? That's no place to hide out."

"You really are quite dim, aren't you, Sadler?" said Hobbs, breaking into a broad grin. "He wasn't hiding out there. He was *found* there. Wolf's dead."

I stare at him in surprise, quite unable to take this in. I swallow, considering the awfulness of the word, and repeat it quietly, but as a question now, not a statement.

"Dead?" I ask. "But how? What happened to him?"

"I haven't got the full story yet," he says. "But I'm working on it. Seems he was discovered face down in one of the streams up there, his head split open. Must have been trying to run away, tripped over a rock in the dark and fell face forwards. Either the wound killed him or he drowned. Not that it matters either way; he's gone now. And good riddance, I say, to our resident feather man."

My instincts kick in and I grab Will's arm just as he lashes out to punch Hobbs in the face.

"What's the matter with you?" asks Hobbs, jumping back in surprise and turning on Will. "Don't tell me you've signed up to his rot, too? Not going to turn yellow on us on the eve of our getting out of this place, I hope?"

Will struggles against my arm for a moment longer, but I'm his match in strength and only when I feel his muscles slacken and his arm begin to relax do I release him. I watch him, though, as he glares at Hobbs, pure anger on his face, before he turns around and marches away, back in the direction from which we have come, throwing his arms up in the air in disgust as he does so before disappearing out of sight.

I decide not to follow him and instead return to my bunk and lie on my back, ignoring the conversations of the men around me who are coming up with ever more fantastic theories on how exactly Wolf has gone to his maker, and think about it myself. Wolf, dead. It seems beyond possible. Why, the man was only a year or two older than I, a healthy specimen with his whole life before him. I spoke to him only yesterday; he said that he'd played a geography quiz with Will while they were on duty together and Will had let himself down badly.

"He's not the brightest card in the pack, is he?" Wolf asked me at the time, infuriating me into silence. "I don't know what you see in him, really I don't."

Of course I know that there's a war on and that we will each face death sooner than we should in the natural order of things, but we haven't even left England yet. We haven't seen the back of Aldershot, for that matter. Our barrack of twenty is already down to nineteen, the slow inevitable crumbling of our numbers beginning before we pass out. And all these other boys laughing about it, calling him a coward and a feather man, would they find as much to celebrate if I had died? If Rich had? Will? It's too much to bear.

And still I despise myself for what I'm thinking. For while I no longer have reason to be jealous of his friendship with Will, God forgive me but I feel a certain satisfaction that it cannot be revived.

When Will hasn't returned by nightfall, I go in search of him, as we are by now less than ninety minutes from curfew. It's our last night together as recruits, for the following day we will pass out and be told of the army's plans for us, and in celebration of this we have been given the evening off and are allowed to wander at will, with the condition that we are back in our bunks with lights out by midnight or Wells and Moody will know the reason why.

Some of the men, I know, have gone into the nearby village, where a local pub has been our gathering place on those rare occasions when we have been granted liberty. Some are with the sweethearts in the local villages they have got together with over the weeks here. Others have gone for long, private walks, perhaps to be alone with their thoughts. One poor fool, Yates, has said that he is taking a last march up the hills for old times' sake and has been ragged mercilessly by the men for his ardour. But Will has simply vanished.

I check the pub first but he isn't there; the landlord tells me that he was in earlier and sat alone in a corner. One of the locals, an elderly gentleman, offered him a pint of ale in honour of his uniform and Will refused, casting an aspersion on his warrant badge, and a fight nearly ensued. I ask whether he'd been half-cut when he left but am told no, he'd had two pints, no more than that, then stood up and left without another word.

"What does he want to go starting fights in here for?" the landlord asks me. "Save all that for over there, I say."

I don't respond, simply turn around and leave. The notion runs through my head that Will may have run off in anger at what has happened to Wolf and means to desert. *Bloody fool*, I think, for he'll be court-martialled if—*when*—he's caught. But there are three separate paths leading from where I stand and he could have taken any of them; I have no choice but to make my way back to the barracks and hope that he's been smart enough to return there while I've been gone.

As it happens, I don't need to go that far, for halfway between pub and camp, I discover him by chance in one of the clearings in the woods, a small, secluded area that overlooks a stream. He's sitting in the moonlight on a grassy bank, staring into the water and tossing a pebble casually from hand to hand.

"Will," I say, running towards him, relieved that he hasn't put himself in danger's way. "There you are at last. I've been looking for you everywhere."

"Have you?" he asks, looking up, and in the moonlight I can see that he has been crying; his cheeks are streaked with dirt where he's tried to dry the tears away and the skin below his eyes is fleshy and red. "Sorry about that," he says, turning away from me. "I just needed to be alone for a while, that's all. I didn't mean to worry you."

"It's all right," I say, sitting down beside him. "I thought you might have done something stupid, that's all."

"Like what?"

"Well, you know," I say with a shrug. "Run off."

He shakes his head. "I wouldn't do that, Tristan," he says. "Not yet, anyway."

"What do you mean, 'not yet'?"

"I don't know." He lets a deep sigh escape his lips and rubs his eyes once again before turning back to me with a sad smile on his face. "So here we are," he says. "The end of the road. Was it worth it, do you think?"

"We'll find out soon enough, I imagine," I reply, staring into the still water. "When we get to France, I mean."

"France, yes," he says thoughtfully. "It's all in front of us now. I believe Sergeant Clayton would be disappointed if we weren't all killed in the line of duty."

"Don't say that," I reply with a shudder.

"Why not? It's the truth, isn't it?"

"Sergeant Clayton may be many things," I say, "but he's not that much of a monster. I'm sure he doesn't want to see any of us dead."

"Don't be so naive," he snaps. "He wanted Wolf dead, that's for sure. And he got his way in the end."

"Wolf killed himself," I say. "Perhaps not on purpose but through his own foolishness. Only an idiot would go marching up through that forest in the middle of the night."

"Oh, Tristan," he says, shaking his head again and smiling at me, the low, quiet way he whispers my name reminding me of the time he had me pinned to the floor after our mock-wrestle in the barracks. His hand reaches out now and he pats me on the knee, once, twice, then lingers a third time before slowly moving it away. "You really are unbelievably innocent at times, aren't you? It's one of the reasons I like you so much."

"Don't patronize me," I say, annoyed by his tone. "You don't know as much as you think."

"Well, what else am I supposed to think?" he asks. "After all, you believe that Wolf was the author of his own misfortune, don't you? Only an innocent would think that. Or a bloody fool. Wolf didn't fall, Tristan. He didn't kill himself. He was murdered. Killed in cold blood."

"What?" I ask, almost laughing at the absurdity of his remark. "How can you even think such a thing? For God's sake, Will, he'd deserted the camp. He'd run—"

"He hadn't run anywhere," he says angrily. "He told me, only a few hours earlier, before going to sleep, that he'd been granted his status as a conscientious objector. The tribunal had finally come back with a resolution to his case. He wasn't even being sent out there as a stretcher-bearer on account of it. Turns out he was quite adept at mathematics and had agreed to help in the War Department and live under house arrest for the rest of the war. He was going home, Tristan. The very next morning. And then, just like that, he disappears. That's a pretty extraordinary coincidence, don't you think?"

"Who else knew about this?" I ask.

"Clayton, of course. Wells and Moody, those dark horsemen. And one or two of the other men, I suppose. It was starting to get around late last night. I heard some rumblings about it."

"I never heard a thing."

"That doesn't mean it wasn't the case."

"So what are you suggesting?" I ask. "That they took him out and murdered him on account of it?"

"Of course, Tristan. Do you mean to tell me that you think they're not capable of it? What have we been trained for, after all, if not for killing other soldiers? The colour of the uniform doesn't matter much. They all look the same in the dark, anyway."

I open my mouth to reply but am unable to find any words. It makes perfect sense. And then I remember waking in the middle of the night and the noises that I heard, the rustling of the bed sheets, the kicking of the blankets, the shushing and the dragging along the floor.

"Jesus," I say.

"Now you have it," he says in an exhausted tone, nodding his head. "But what can we do about it, anyway? Nothing. We've done what we came here to do. We've made ourselves fit and strong. We've trained our minds to believe that the man in front of us who doesn't speak our language is a piece of meat that needs stripping from the bone. We're perfect warriors now. Ready to kill. Sergeant Clayton's work is done. We're just getting a head start on the action, that's all."

99

He speaks with such anger, such a tangled mixture of dread and fear and hostility, that I want nothing more than to reach out and comfort him, and so I do. A moment later, his head is buried in his hands and I realize that he is weeping. I stare, unsure what to do, and he looks up, guarding one side of his face with the flat of his hand so I cannot see how upset he is.

"Don't," he says, between gulps. "Go back to the barracks, Tristan. Please."

"Will," I say, reaching forward. "It's all right. I don't mind. We all feel it. We're all lost."

"But, damn it," he says, turning his face to mine, swallowing as he takes me in. "Jesus Christ, Tristan, what's going to happen to us out there? I'm scared shitless, honest I am."

He reaches over, takes my face in his hands and pulls me to him. In my idle moments, imagining such a scene, I have always assumed that it would be the other way round, that I would reach for him and he would pull away, denouncing me as a degenerate and a false friend. But now I am neither shocked nor surprised by his initiative, nor do I feel any of the great urgency that I thought I would, should this moment ever come to pass. Instead, it feels perfectly natural, everything he does to me, everything that he allows to happen between us. And for the first time since that dreadful afternoon when my father beat me to within an inch of my life, I feel that I have come home.

BREATHING AND BEING ALIVE

Norwich, 16 September 1919

"Miss Bancroft," I said, returning the pile of fallen napkins to the table and standing up, a little flushed now and more than a little nervous. I extended a hand and she stared at it before removing her glove and shaking it in a brisk, businesslike fashion. Her skin was soft against my own rough hands.

"You found it all right, then?" she asked, and I nodded quickly.

"Yes," I said. "I arrived last night, actually. Shall we sit down?"

She took her coat off, hanging it on a stand near the door before leaning over the table for a moment and speaking quietly. "Can you excuse me for a moment, Mr. Sadler?" she asked. "I just want to freshen up."

I watched her as she walked towards a side door and I guessed that this café must be a particular favourite of hers as she had no difficulty locating the Ladies. I suspected that she had planned this manoeuvre: step inside, say hello, size me up, disappear for a few minutes to gather her thoughts, then come back ready to talk. As I waited, a young couple entered, chatting happily, and sat down, leaving a gap of only one empty table between me and them; I noticed a large burn-mark running along the side of his face and averted my gaze before he caught me staring. In the far corner I was dimly aware of the man who had come in earlier staring in my direction. He had moved out from behind the pillar and appeared to be watching me intently, but as I caught his eye he looked away immediately and I didn't think anything further of it.

"Can I get you some tea?" asked the waitress, coming over with pad and pen.

"Yes," I said. "Or rather, no. Do you mind if I wait until my companion comes back? She won't be long."

The girl nodded, not in the least put out, and I turned my attention once again to the street outside, where a group of schoolchildren was walking past now, about twenty of them in a crocodile, each small boy holding the hand of the boy next to him so they wouldn't get lost. Despite how nervous I was feeling, I couldn't help but smile. It recalled my own school-days and how, when I was eight or nine years old and our teacher would make us do the same thing, Peter and I always locked hands, squeezing tightly, determined not to be the first to cry out and demand release. Could it really be only twelve years ago, I wondered? It felt like a hundred.

"I'm so sorry to have kept you waiting," said Marian, returning to the table now and sitting down opposite me. As she did so, the couple glanced across and whispered something to each other. I thought that perhaps they were there on a liaison and didn't want their conversation to be overheard, for they stood up almost immediately and moved to a table by the furthest wall, throwing unpleasant looks at us as they went, as if it were we who had disturbed them. Marian watched them go, her tongue bulging slightly in her cheek, before turning back to me with a curious expression on her face, a mixture of pain, resignation and fury.

"It's perfectly all right," I replied. "I only got here about ten minutes before you."

"Did you say you arrived last night?"

"Yes," I said. "On the late-afternoon train."

"But you should have said. We could have met then if it was more convenient for you. You wouldn't have had to stay the night."

I shook my head. "Today is fine, Miss Bancroft. I just didn't want to leave it to chance in the morning, that's all. The trains from London can still be quite unreliable and I didn't want to miss our appointment if they were cancelled for whatever reason."

"It is dreadful, isn't it?" she said. "I had to be in London a couple of months ago for a wedding. I decided to take the ten-past-ten train, which should have got me to Liverpool Street by about midday, and do you know, I didn't arrive until just after two o'clock. When I got to the church, my friends had already exchanged their vows and were walking down the aisle towards me. I was so embarrassed I felt like running right back to the station and catching the first train home again. Do you think things will ever get back to normal?"

"Some day, yes," I said.

"When? I grow fearfully impatient, Mr. Sadler."

"Not this century, anyway," I replied. "Perhaps the next."

"Well, that's no good. We'll all be dead by then, won't we? Is it too much to ask for decent transportation during one's lifetime?"

She smiled and looked away for a moment, out towards the street where a second delegation of schoolchildren—girls this time—was marching past in similar military two-by-two formation.

"Was it awful?" she said eventually, and I looked up, surprised that she should ask such a loaded question so soon. "The train journey," she added quickly, noticing my disquiet. "Did you get a seat?"

Of course it was natural that we should make small talk at first; it was hardly as if we could just get straight into the reason for my visit. But it was a curious sensation to know that we were making small talk, and for her to know it, too, and for us each to be entirely aware that the other was engaged in a similar level of deceit.

"I didn't mind it," I replied, half amused by my misunderstanding. "I met someone I vaguely knew on board. We were sharing a carriage."

"Well, that's something, I suppose. Do you read, Mr. Sadler?"

"Do I read?"

"Yes. Do you read?"

I hesitated, wondering for a moment whether she meant could I read. "Well, yes," I said cautiously. "Yes, of course I read."

"I can't bear to be on a train without a book," she announced. "It's a form of self-defence in a way."

"How so?"

"Well, I'm not very good at talking to strangers, that's the truth of it. Oh, don't look so worried, I shall do my best with you. But it seems to me that every time I'm in a railway carriage there's some lonely old bachelor sitting next to me who wants to compliment me on my dress or my hair or my good taste in hats, and I find that type of thing rather frustrating and not a little patronizing. You're not going to pay me any compliments, are you, Mr. Sadler?"

"I hadn't planned on it," I said, smiling again. "I don't know much about ladies' dresses or their hair or their hats."

She stared at me and I could see that she liked the remark, for her lips parted and she offered what might have been a distant relation of a smile; it was obvious that she was still deciding what to make of me.

"And if it's not a bachelor, then it's some terrible old woman who interrogates me about my life and whether or not I'm married and do I have a position and what does my father do and are we anything to do with the Bancrofts of Shropshire and it goes on and on and on, Mr. Sadler, and the whole thing's a frightful bore."

"I can imagine it would be," I said. "No one ever talks to a chap much. Young ladies certainly don't. Young men don't. Old men . . . well, sometimes they do. They ask questions."

"Quite," she said, her tone letting me know immediately that she didn't want to pursue this line just yet. She reached for her bag and removed a cigarette case, plucked one out and offered a second to me. I was going to accept but changed my mind at the last minute and shook my head. "You don't smoke?" she asked, appalled.

"I do," I said. "But I won't just now, if you don't mind."

"I don't mind," she said, putting the case back in her bag and lighting up in a quick, fluid movement of thumb, wrist and flint. "Why should I mind? Oh, hello, Jane, good morning."

"Good morning, Marian," said the waitress who had approached me earlier.

"I'm back again, like a bad penny."

"We hold on to our bad pennies here. We'll grow rich off them some day. Ready to order, are you?"

"Are we lunching yet, Mr. Sadler?" she asked me, blowing smoke in my face and causing me to turn my head to avoid it; she immediately waved it away with her right hand and turned her head to the side when she took her next drag. "Or shall we just have tea for now? I think tea," she said, not waiting for an answer. "Tea for two, Jane."

"Anything to eat?"

"Not just yet. You're not in a hurry, Mr. Sadler, are you? Or are you ravenous already? It seems to me that young men are always ravenous these days. All the ones I know, anyway."

"No, I'm fine," I replied, unsettled by her brusqueness; was it a front, I wondered, or her natural manner?

"Then just tea for now. We may have something else a little later on. How's Albert, by the way? Is he feeling any better?"

"A little better," said the waitress, smiling now. "The doctor says the cast can come off in a week or so. He can't wait, the poor dear. Nor can I, for that matter. He gets the most frightful itches and brings the house down with his complaining about it. I gave him a knitting needle to slide down there, to help scratch it away, you know, but I'm always terrified that he'll push it too hard and cut himself. So I took it away, but then he complains even more."

"Dreadful business," said Marian, shaking her head. "Still, you have only a week to go."

"Yes. And your father, he's all right, is he?"

Marian nodded and took another drag of her cigarette, smiling as she did so and then looking away, making it clear that Jane was dismissed and that was an end to that particular conversation.

"I'll bring the tea," said the waitress, understanding perfectly and walking away.

"Terribly sad story," said Marian, leaning towards me once the waitress was out of earshot. "It's her husband, you see. They've only been married a few months. He was repairing some tiles on their roof about six weeks ago and he fell off. Broke his leg. And he'd only just got over a broken arm about a month before that. Brittle bones, I expect. It wasn't as if he fell a great distance."

"Her husband?" I asked, surprised. "It sounded to me as if you were talking about a child."

"Well, he is rather a child," she said with a shrug. "I don't care for him much myself, he's always up to some mischief or other, but Jane is sweet. She used to play with me and—" She stopped herself and her face fell, as if she couldn't quite believe what she had been about to say. She took a final drag from her

108

tab, then pressed it out, only half smoked, in the ashtray. "That's enough of that," she said. "Do you know, I'm rather thinking of giving these things up."

"Really?" I asked. "Any particular reason?"

"Well, the truth is I don't enjoy them as much as I used to," she said. "Also, I can't imagine it can be all that good for you, can you? Taking all that smoke into your lungs every day. It doesn't sound very sensible when you think about it."

"I can't imagine it does that much harm," I said. "Everyone smokes."

"You don't."

"I do," I replied. "I just didn't feel like it right now."

She nodded and narrowed her eyes as if she were sizing me up. We didn't speak for a while and it gave me an opportunity to examine her more closely. She was older than Will and I, about twenty-five I imagined, but there was no wedding ring on her finger so I assumed that she was still unmarried. She didn't look very much like him; he had been so dark and cheeky-looking, his features always ready to crinkle into a wink and a smile, but she was fairer than him, almost as fair as I was, and she had a clean, blemish-free complexion. She wore her hair in a tidy, efficient way, cut short below the chin line, without an ounce of vanity to the style. She was pretty—handsome, I should say—and wore only a light smear of lipstick that may in fact have been her natural colouring. I imagined that there was many a young man who might lose his head over her. Or have it bitten off.

"So," she said after a moment. "Where did you stay last night, anyway?"

"Mrs. Cantwell's boarding house," I replied.

"Cantwell's?" she asked, wrinkling up her face now as she considered it, and I almost gasped. *There he was!* In that expression. "I don't know them, do I? Where are they?"

"Quite close to the railway station," I said. "Near the bridge."

"Oh yes," she said. "There's a run of them along there, isn't there?"

"Yes, I think so."

"One never really knows the boarding houses in one's own town, does one?"

"No," I said, shaking my head. "No, I suppose not."

"When I go to London I stay at a very nice place on Russell Square. An Irishwoman called Jackson runs it. She drinks, of course. Mother's ruin by the gallon. But she's polite, her rooms are clean, she stays out of my business and that's good enough for me. Can't cook breakfast to save her life but that's a small price to pay. Do you know Russell Square, Mr. Sadler?"

"Yes," I said. "I work in Bloomsbury, actually. I used to live in south London. Now I live north of the river."

"No plans to move to the centre, then?"

"Not at the moment, no. It's frightfully expensive, you see, and I work at a publishing house."

"No money in it?"

"No money in it for me," I said, smiling.

She smiled, too, and looked down at the ashtray, and I thought she might be rather regretting putting her cigarette out, for she seemed anxious to have something to do with her hands. She looked over towards the counter, where there was no sign of the tea or, for that matter, any sign of our waitress. The older man who had been present when I arrived had vanished, too.

"I'm thirsty," she said. "What's keeping her, anyway?"

"I'm sure she'll only be a moment," I said.

In truth, I was starting to feel rather unsettled and wondered why on earth I had decided to come here in the first place. It was clear that neither of us felt relaxed in the other's company. I was quiet and offering little to the conversation other than quick responses and shy remarks, while Miss Bancroft—Marian—seemed to be a bundle of nervous energy, shifting from topic to topic without thought or hesitation. I didn't for a moment believe that this was who she really was; it was simply part of our meeting. She did not feel free to be herself.

"It's usually very reliable in here," she said, shaking her head. "I suppose I owe you an apology."

"Not at all."

"It's a good job we didn't order any food, isn't it? My goodness, all we asked for were two cups of tea. But you must be starving, Mr. Sadler, are you? Have you eaten? Young men are always ravenous, I find."

I stared at her, unsure whether she would remember that she had already made that very remark, but she appeared curiously oblivious to it.

"I had some breakfast," I replied after a moment.

"At your Mrs. Cantwell's?"

"No, not there. Somewhere else."

"Oh, really?" she asked, leaning forward, terribly interested now. "Where did you go? Was it somewhere nice?"

"I don't remember," I said. "I think—"

"There are a number of good places to eat in Norwich," she said. "I suppose you think we're terribly provincial here and can't provide good food. You London chaps always think that, don't you?"

"Not at all, Miss Bancroft," I replied. "In fact—"

"Of course, what you should have done was ask me in advance. If you had let me know that you were coming the night before, why, we might have invited you to dinner."

"I wouldn't have liked to put you to any trouble," I said.

"But it wouldn't have been any trouble," she said, sounding almost offended. "For heaven's sake, it's just one more person at the table. How much trouble could that be? Didn't you want to come to dinner, Mr. Sadler? Was that it?"

"Well, I didn't think about it," I said, becoming incredibly flustered now. "By the time I reached Norwich, I was tired, that's all. I just went straight to my boarding house and went to sleep." I decided not to tell her about the wait for the room or the reasons for that wait; neither did I mention my visit to the public house.

"Of course you were," she said. "Train journeys can be so tiresome. I like to bring a book to read. Do you read, Mr. Cantwell?"

I stared at her and could feel my mouth opening but no words coming out. It was as if I had been thrown into a situation that I had known would be utterly unbearable but had had no realization of just how bad it would be until now. The irony was that I knew this meeting would be difficult for me but I had never quite considered how terrible it might be for her. But sitting there before me now, Marian Bancroft was a complete bag of nerves and she seemed to be getting worse by the moment.

"Oh my stars, I've already asked you that, haven't I?" she said, bursting into an extraordinary laugh. "You told me that you liked to read."

"Yes," I said. "And it's Sadler, not Cantwell."

"I know," she said, frowning. "Why would you tell me that?"

"You called me Mr. Cantwell."

"Did I?"

"Yes. Just a moment ago."

She shook her head and dismissed the idea. "I don't think I did, Mr. Sadler," she said. "But it doesn't matter. What were you reading?"

"On the train?"

"Yes, of course," she said, a note of frustration seeping into her tone as she looked around and stared at the waitress behind the counter, who was placing two scones on two plates for the couple who had moved to the isolated seats and showing no signs whatsoever of bringing our teas.

"*White Fang*," I told her. "By Jack London. Have you read it?"

"No," she replied. "Is he an American author?"

"Yes," I said. "You know of him, then?"

"I've never heard of him," she said. "I just thought he sounded like one, that's all."

"Even with a name like London?" I asked, smiling at her.

"Yes, even with that, Mr. Cantwell."

"Sadler," I replied.

"Stop it, can't you?" she snapped, her face turning cold and angry as she slammed both her hands flat on the table between us. "Don't go on correcting me. I won't stand for it."

I stared at her, unsure what I could say or do to improve this moment; for the life of me, I couldn't understand where it had gone so wrong. Perhaps on the day that I had put pen to paper and written *Dear Miss Bancroft, You don't know me . . . but I was a friend of your brother.* Or perhaps before that. In France. Or earlier still. That day in Aldershot when I leaned forward in the line and caught Will's eye. Or he caught mine.

"I'm sorry," I said, swallowing nervously. "I didn't mean to offend you."

"Well, you did. You did offend me. And I don't like it. Your name is Sadler. Tristan Sadler. You don't have to keep telling me over and over."

"I'm sorry," I repeated.

"And don't keep apologizing, it's terribly annoying."

"I'm—" I stopped myself in time.

"Yes, yes," she said. She drummed her fingers on the table and looked at the half-smoked cigarette again and I knew there was a part of her that was weighing the etiquette of picking it up, rubbing away the charred end and relighting it. My eyes turned to it, too; there was more than half of it left there, and it seemed such a frightful waste. In the trenches, a half-smoked cigarette meant almost as much to us as a night alone in a foxhole with a few hours' sleep promised. I had lost track of the times that I had used even the smallest amount of tobacco, an amount that any sane person would toss on to the street without a second thought, as a companion for as long as I could make it last.

"What do . . . what do you like to read, Miss Bancroft?" I said eventually, desperate to salvage the situation. "Novels, I suppose?"

"Why do you say that? Because I'm a woman?"

"Well, yes," I said. "I mean, I know that many ladies enjoy novels. I enjoy them myself."

"And yet you're a man."

"Indeed."

"No, I don't care for novels," she said, shaking her head. "I've never really understood them, if I'm honest."

"In what way?" I asked, confused by how the concept of the novel could be a difficult one to understand. There were some writers, of course, who told their stories in the most con-voluted way possible—many of whom seemed to send their unsolicited manuscripts to the Whisby Press, for instance—but there were others, such as Jack London, who offered their readers such a respite from the miserable horror of existence that their books were like gifts from the gods.

"Well, none of the stories ever happened, did they?" asked Miss Bancroft. "I can never quite see the point of someone reading about people who never existed, doing things they never did, in settings they never visited. So Jane Eyre marries her Mr. Rochester at the end. Well, Jane Eyre never existed, nor did Mr. Rochester or the wild woman he kept in the cellar."

"It was an attic," I said pedantically.

"Regardless. It's a lot of nonsense, isn't it?"

"I think it's more of an escape than anything else."

"I don't need an escape, Mr. Sadler," she said, stressing my name now to ensure that she got it right. "And if I did I should book myself a passage to somewhere warm and exotic where I might become involved in espionage or a romantic misunderstanding, like the heroines of those precious novels of yours. No, I prefer to read about things that are actually true, things that really happened. I read non-fiction mostly. History books. Politics. Biographies. Things like that."

"Politics?" I asked, surprised. "You're interested in politics?"

"Of course I am," she said. "You think I shouldn't be? On account of my sex?"

"I don't know, Miss Bancroft," I said, exhausted by her belligerence. "I'm just . . . I'm just talking, that's all. Be interested in politics if you want to be. It doesn't matter to me." I felt that I couldn't possibly continue with this. Keeping up with her was more than I felt capable of doing. We had been together less than fifteen minutes but I felt that this must be what it would be like to be married to someone, a constant back and forth of bickering, watching out for any stray comment in a conversation that might be corrected, anything to keep gaining the upper hand, the advantage, bringing one closer to taking the game, the set and the whole blasted match without ever ceding a point.

"Of course it matters, Mr. Sadler," she said after a moment, quieter now, as if she realized that she might have gone too far. "It matters because you and I wouldn't be here together if it wasn't for politics, would we?"

I looked at her and hesitated for a moment. "No," I said, shrugging my shoulders. "No, I suppose we wouldn't."

"Well, then," she said, pulling open her bag and reaching again for her cigarette case, which, when she retrieved it, slipped

115

out of her hands and fell to the floor with a tremendous crash, scattering cigarettes around our feet in much the same way as I had dropped the napkins just before her arrival. "Oh, bloody hell!" she cried, startling me. "Look at what I've done now."

In a moment, Jane, our waitress, was beside us, reaching down to help gather them, but it was the wrong move on her part for Miss Bancroft had had quite enough for one day and stared at her so furiously that I thought she might attack her.

"Never mind them, Jane!" she shouted. "I can pick them up. Can we have our tea? Please? Is it too much to ask for two cups of tea?"

The arrival of the tea offered some respite from the intensity of our conversation and allowed us to focus on something trivial for a few minutes, rather than being forced to talk. Marian was clearly in a state of great tension and anxiety. In my selfishness, I had considered little but my own preoccupations before we met, but Will, after all, was her brother. And he was dead.

"I'm sorry, Mr. Sadler," she said after a long silence, putting her cup down and smiling across at me with a contrite expression; again, I was stuck by how pretty she was. "I can be an awful old hag sometimes, can't I?"

"There's nothing to apologize for, Miss Bancroft," I said. "Of course we're both . . . Well, this is not the most comfortable situation."

"No," she agreed. "I wonder if it might be easier if we dispensed with some of the formalities? Can I ask you to call me Marian?"

"Of course," I said, nodding. "And I'm Tristan."

"A knight of the round table?"

"Not exactly." I smiled.

"Never mind. Still, I'm glad that's out of the way. I don't think I could bear to be called Miss Bancroft for much longer.

It makes me sound like a maiden aunt." She hesitated, bit her lip, then spoke again in a less flippant tone. "I suppose I should ask you why you wrote to me."

I cleared my throat; so here we were at last. "It's like I said in the letter," I told her. "I have something of Will's—"

"My letters?"

"Yes. And I thought you might want them back."

"It was kind of you to think of me."

"I know he would have wanted me to return them to you," I said. "It seemed only right."

"I don't mean this to sound critical, but you have held on to them for rather a long time."

"I assure you, I've never so much as opened an envelope."

"Of course not. I don't doubt that for a moment. I just wonder why you took so long to get in touch, that's all."

"I haven't been well," I told her.

"Yes, of course."

"And I didn't feel I was up to meeting you."

"It's perfectly understandable."

She looked out of the window for a moment and then turned back to me. "Your letter came as more of a surprise to me than you might imagine," she said. "But I had heard your name before."

"Oh yes?" I asked cautiously.

"Yes. Will wrote often, you know. Particularly when he was training at Aldershot. We had a letter from him every two or three days."

"I remember," I said. "I mean, I remember that he used to sit on his bed with a notepad, scribbling away in it. The men used to rag him about it, said he was writing poetry or something, the way so many did, but he told me he was writing to you."

"Poetry is even more frightful than novels," she remarked with a shudder. "You mustn't think me a terrible philistine, you know. Although I can see how you might with the things I'm saying."

"Not at all. Anyway, Will didn't care what anyone said. He wrote, as you say, all the time. They seemed like awfully long letters."

"They were. Some of them," she said. "I think he had aspirations towards literature, you know. He employed some very arch phrases, trying to heighten the experience a little, I thought."

"Was he any good?"

"Not really," she said, then laughed. "Oh, I don't mean to belittle him. Please don't misunderstand me, Mr. Sadler."

"Tristan," I said.

"Yes, Tristan. No, I only mean that he was obviously trying to tell me things in those letters, to explain how he was feeling, the sense of dread and anticipation that came with training at Aldershot. He seemed to spend an awful lot of time looking forward to the war. Sorry, I don't mean 'looking forward' as in 'being excited' about it—"

"Looking ahead?" I suggested.

"Yes, just that. And it was interesting, because he said so much but also so little. Does that make sense at all?"

"I think so," I replied.

"He told us all about his routines, of course. And about some of the men who were training with him. And the man in charge—Clayton, was it?"

I felt my body grow a little rigid at the name; I wondered how much she knew of Sergeant Clayton's responsibility in the whole business or the orders he had given at the end. And the men who had obeyed him. "Yes," I said. "He was there from start to finish."

"And who were the other two? Left and Right, Will called them."

"Left and Right?" I asked, frowning, unsure what she meant by this.

"He said they were Sergeant Clayton's assistants or something. One always stood on his left side, the other on his right."

"Oh," I said, understanding now. "He must have meant Wells and Moody. That's odd. I never heard him refer to them as Left and Right before. It's rather funny."

"Well, he did, all the time," she said. "I'd show you the letters, Tristan, but do you mind if I don't? They are rather private."

"Of course," I said, not realizing how much I wanted to read them until she told me that I couldn't. The truth was that I had never really given much consideration to the content of his letters home. At Aldershot, I had never written to anyone. But once, during the course of the French campaign, I wrote a long letter to my mother, asking her forgiveness for the pain I had caused. I attached a note to my father in the envelope, telling him that I was well and keeping healthy, lying that things over there were not quite as bad as I had expected them to be. I told myself that he would be pleased to hear from me, but I never received a reply. For all I knew he had been the first to pick the letter off the mat some morning and had thrown it away, unopened and unread, before I could cast further shame on his household.

"They sounded like terrible terrors, Left and Right," she remarked.

"They could be," I said, considering it. "They were rather terrorized themselves, to be honest. Sergeant Clayton was a difficult man. When we were training he was bad enough. But when we were over there . . ." I shook my head and exhaled loudly. "He'd been before, you see. A couple of times. He's not a man I have any respect for—in fact, even thinking about him makes me feel ill—but he'd had it hard, too. He told us once about his brother being killed in front of him, about his . . . well, about his brains being splattered over his own uniform."

"Good God," she said, putting her cup down.

"It was only later that I learned he'd already lost three other brothers in the fighting. He didn't have it easy, Marian, that's the truth. Although it doesn't excuse what he did."

"Why?" she asked, leaning forward. "What did he do?"

I opened my mouth, fully aware that I was not yet ready to answer this question. I didn't even know if I ever would be. For, after all, to reveal Clayton's crime would be to admit my own. And I tried to keep that as firmly bottled up inside myself as possible. I was here to return a packet of letters, I told myself. Nothing more.

"Did your brother . . . did Will mention me much in those letters?" I asked after a moment, my natural eagerness to know overpowering my dread of what he might have told her.

"He certainly did," she said, hesitantly, I thought. "Particularly in the early letters. Actually, he spoke of you quite a lot."

"Really?" I said in as calm a tone as I could muster. "I'm pleased to hear it."

"I remember his first letter arrived only a couple of days after he got there," she said, "and he told me that it seemed all right really, that there were two troops of twenty and he'd been put in with a bunch who didn't seem the most intellectually stimulating lot."

I laughed. "Well, that's true," I said. "I don't think we had much education to share around, any of us."

"Then, in his second letter, a few days later, he sounded a little more down, as if the excitement of arriving had worn off and he was facing up to what he was left with. I felt bad for him then, and when I wrote back I told him that he had to make friends, to put his best foot forward, the usual nonsense that people who know nothing about anything, like me, say when they don't want their own days to be ruined by worrying about others."

"I imagine you're being hard on yourself there," I said gently.

"No, I'm not. I didn't know what to say, you see. I was rather excited about him going off to war. Does that make me sound like a monster? But you have to understand, Tristan, I was younger then. Of course I was younger, that's obvious. But I mean that I was less informed. I was one of those girls that I despise so much."

"And what girls are those?" I asked.

"Oh, you've seen them, Tristan. You live in London, they're everywhere there. And, I mean, for pity's sake, you came back from the war in your fine uniform, you must have been on the receiving end of so many of their favours."

I shrugged and poured more tea, putting extra sugar in mine this time and stirring it slowly, watching as the spoon created a whirlwind in the murky brown soup.

"Those girls," she continued with an irritated sigh, "they think that war is an enormous lark. They see their brothers and their sweethearts getting dressed up in their finery. And then they come back and the uniforms are more dishevelled but, oh my, don't the men look handsome and experienced. Well, I was just like that. I read Will's letters and I thought, *Oh, but you're there at least!* And what I wouldn't give to be there! I didn't realize just how difficult it was. I still don't, I imagine."

"And the letters told you all this?" I asked, hoping to steer her back towards this subject.

"No, I only fully understood after everything that happened. I only appreciated the cruelty of the place then. So, in a way, I was rather frustrated by my brother's tone. But then, after a while, the letters grew more cheerful and I was pleased about that."

"Oh yes?"

"Yes. He told me in his third letter about the chap who had the bunk next to his. A Londoner, he said, but not a bad bloke all the same."

I smiled and nodded, looking down at my tea, hearing him say the words in my head.

Ah, Tristan . . .

"He told me how you and he would pal around together, how everyone needed someone to talk to when they were feeling down and how you were always there for him. I was glad of that. I'm glad of it now. And he said that it made things easier because you were the same age and you were both missing home."

"He said I was missing home?" I asked, looking up in surprise.

She thought about it for a moment and corrected herself. "He said that you didn't talk about your home very much," she replied. "But he could tell that you missed it. He said there was something in your silence that was very sad."

I swallowed and thought about it. I wondered why he had never challenged me on this.

"And then there was all that business with Mr. Wolf," she said.

"Oh, he told you about him, did he?" I asked.

"Not at first. But later. He said that he'd met a fascinating chap who had all sorts of controversial views. He told me about them. You know what they were better than I, I dare say, so I needn't explain."

"No."

"But I could tell he was interested in Mr. Wolf's beliefs. And then after he was murdered—"

"It was never proven that Wolf was murdered," I said irritably.

"Do you believe he wasn't?"

"All I know is that there was never any proof," I said, aware even as I said it that it was a bootless answer.

"Well, I know that my brother was convinced of it. He said it was put about that an accident had taken place but he had no doubt in his mind that the poor boy was killed. He said he didn't know who did it, whether it was Sergeant Clayton, Left or Right, some of the other recruits, or a combination of all the above. But he was quite certain about it. They came for him in the dead of night, he said. I believe that was when he began to change, Tristan. With Mr. Wolf's death."

"Yes," I said. "Well, a lot of things took place over those few days. We were under enormous strain."

"After that, the carefree boy I had known, the boy who was frightened of course about what lay ahead, vanished and in came this new chap, a chap who wanted to talk about right and wrong rather than Right and Left." She smiled at her joke, then grew immediately serious once again. "He asked me to give him details of what the newspapers were saying about the war, the debates that were taking place in Parliament, whether there was anyone who was standing up for the rights of man, as he called them, over the sound of the rifles. I didn't recognize him in those letters, Tristan. But I was intrigued by who he had become and tried to help. I told him as much as I knew and, by then, you were all in France and his tone changed even further. And then . . . well, you know what happened then."

I nodded and sighed and we sat very quietly for what felt like a long time, considering our different memories of her brother, my friend.

"And did he . . . did he say anything more about me?" I asked eventually, feeling that the moment to discuss those letters had passed but by God I might never get the chance again and I had to know. I had to know how he felt.

"I'm sorry, Tristan," she said, looking a little shamefaced. "I have a rather awful thing to tell you. Perhaps I shouldn't, I don't know."

"Please do," I said, urging her on.

"The truth is that you were such a big part of his letters all through that time at Aldershot. He told me all the things you did together; it made you sound like a pair of mischievous children, if I'm honest, with your jokes and japes. I was glad you had each other and I rather liked the sound of you. I thought he was quite besotted with you, to be honest, as preposterous as that sounds. I remember once reading a letter and thinking, *Dear Lord, must I hear nothing more than what Tristan Sadler did this day or said on that day?* He really thought you were the bee's knees and the cat's pyjamas."

I stared at her and tried to smile but could feel my face turning into a rictus of pain instead and hoped she wouldn't notice.

"And then he wrote to say that you had all shipped out," she continued. "And the thing is, from that first letter after you left Aldershot, he never mentioned you again. And for a while I didn't like to ask."

"Well, why would you?" I asked. "After all, you didn't even know me."

"Yes, but . . ." And here she stopped for a moment and sighed before looking back up at me as if she had a terrible secret, the weight of which was almost too much for her to bear. "Tristan, this is going to sound rather odd but I feel I ought to tell you. You can make of it what you will. The thing is . . . I said that when I received your letter a few weeks ago it came as rather a shock to me. I thought I must have misunderstood and I went back to read Will's letters afterwards but it seems to be quite clear there, so I can only imagine that he was either confused by what was going on or had simply written your name when he meant to write another. The whole thing is very odd."

"It wasn't easy out there," I said. "When men wrote letters in the trenches, why, we often had no time or hardly any paper or pencils to do it. And the question of whether or not those letters even got through was one that we didn't like to think about too much. All that time and energy, perhaps for nothing."

"Yes," she said. "Only I think most of Will's letters did get through. And certainly all the ones from those first months in France, because I received one almost every week and I really can't imagine that he would have had time to write more than that. So he was writing and telling me what was happening, trying to spare me some of the worst moments to stop me worrying too much, and because you'd become something of a character in my head, because you'd been such a big part of his earlier letters, I finally summoned up the nerve to ask him in one of my replies exactly what had happened to you, whether you had been posted to the same place together and were still part of the same regiment."

"But we were," I said, confused by this. "You know we were. We trained together, we took the boat to France together, we fought in the same trenches. I don't think we were ever apart really."

"Yes, but when he replied," said Marian, hesitating, looking almost embarrassed by her words, "he told me that he had some bad news for me."

"Bad news," I said, more of a statement than a question, and I had a sudden anxious idea of what this might be.

"He said . . . I'm so sorry, Mr. Sadler, I mean, Tristan, but it's really not me who has this wrong because, as I said, I went back and checked, it was just that he must have been so confused, what with all the shelling and the bombing and those awful, awful trenches—"

125

"Perhaps you'd better just tell me," I said quietly.

"He said you'd been killed," she said, sitting up straight now and looking me directly in the eyes. "There, I've said it. He said that two days after you left Aldershot, only a few hours after you'd arrived at your entrenchment, you were picked off by a sniper. He said it had been quick and you hadn't suffered."

I stared at her again and began to feel dizzy in my head. Had I been standing, I think that I might have fallen over. "He said I was dead?" I asked, the words sounding obscene on my tongue.

"It must have been someone else," she replied quickly. "He spoke of so many people in his letters. He must have just got it wrong. But what a frightful mistake. Anyway, as far as I was concerned, there were the two of you, thick as thieves on the training ground, and off you go to France together, and the next thing I know, that's it, you're gone. I don't mind telling you, Tristan, that even though I had never met you it had quite an effect on me."

"My death did?"

"Yes. If that doesn't sound too preposterous. I suppose part of it might have been that I was projecting your death on to the very real possibility that Will might die, too, which in my own stupidity I had never really thought about very much before. I cried for days, Tristan. For a man I had never met. I said prayers for you, even though I rarely pray. My father, he said a mass in your memory. Can you believe it? He's a vicar, you see, and—"

"Yes," I said. "Yes, I knew that."

"And he was terribly sorry, too. I don't think he could think too much about you, if I'm honest, because he was so worried about Will. He loved him so much. As did my mother. But there we are. I thought you had been killed in the war. And then, about three years later, out of the blue, your letter arrived."

I turned and looked out of the window. The street had grown quiet and I found myself staring at the cobblestones, noting the different shapes and sizes of the pieces. Over the previous twelve months I had felt such pain, such remorse over what had happened to Will and my part in it. And I had grieved so much, too, my feelings for him so intense that I feared I would never be able to see past them. And now to hear this, to hear that he had effectively killed me off after our last night together in Aldershot. I had believed that he could not have broken my heart any more than he had—but now there was this. There was this.

"Mr. Sadler? Tristan?"

I turned back to her and saw that Marian was looking towards my right hand with a concerned expression. I glanced down and saw that it was twitching uncontrollably, the fingers dancing nervously as if independent of my brain. I stared at it as though it were not part of my body at all, but something that a passing stranger had left on the table and was planning to return for later, a curio of some sort, and then I felt mortified by it and placed my left hand over it, quelling the trembling for now.

"You'll have to excuse me," I said, standing up quickly, my chair making a loud scraping noise against the floor as I pushed it back, a sound that set my teeth on edge.

"Tristan—" she began, but I shook my head.

"I'll be back," I said, rushing towards the door to the Gents, on the opposite side of the room to the one through which she had disappeared earlier. As I reached it, terrified that I might not make it through in time before the horror of what she had told me overwhelmed me, I saw the man who had entered the café earlier, the one who had appeared to be watching me, suddenly jump to his feet and march hurriedly towards it, blocking my way.

"Excuse me," I said. "Please."

"I want a word with you," he said, in an officious tone, an aggressive one. "It won't take long."

"Not now," I snapped, uncertain why he was bothering me. I had never seen the man before in my life. "Get out of my way."

"I won't get out of your way," he insisted. "Now, look here, I don't want to cause any trouble, but you and me, we need to talk."

"Get out of my way!" I repeated, shouting it now, and I saw the couple and the waitress turn to look at me in surprise. I wondered whether Marian had heard me, but our table was around the corner and not in my sight line, so if she had I would not have known. I pushed the man roughly aside. He didn't struggle with me, and a few moments later I locked myself in the lavatory and placed my head in my hands, devastated. I was not crying, but there was a word being repeated over and over, I thought in my head but actually aloud, and I had to make a concerted effort to stop myself saying *Will, Will, Will* as I rocked back and forth, as if this was the only word that had ever mattered, the only syllable that held any meaning for me.

When I returned from the Gents, I felt embarrassed by my behaviour but was unsure whether Marian had even noticed how upset I had become. I didn't turn to look in the direction of the man who had insisted on speaking with me but I could sense his presence, smouldering like a dormant volcano in the corner of the room, and wondered who exactly he thought I was. His accent betrayed his Norfolk roots but as I had never been to this part of the country before there was no possibility that we had ever met. At the table, Marian and our waitress, Jane, were deep in conversation, obviously reconciled, and I looked from one to the other a little nervously as I sat down again.

"I was just apologizing to Jane," explained Marian, smiling across at me. "I think I might have been rather rude to her earlier. Which she didn't deserve. Jane was very kind to my parents. Afterwards, I mean," she said, choosing her words carefully.

"I see," I replied, rather wishing that Jane would go back behind her counter and leave us alone. "You knew Will, then?"

"I knew him since he was a boy," she said. "He was a few years behind me in school but I had a right crush on him back then. He danced with me once at a parish social and I thought I'd died and gone to heaven." She looked away as she said this, perhaps regretting her choice of words. "Well, I'd best be getting on," she said. "Can I get you anything else, Marian?"

"Some more tea, I think. What do you say, Tristan?"

"Fine," I said.

"And afterwards, we can go for a stroll and get something to eat. You must be hungry."

"I am now," I admitted. "But more tea first is fine."

Jane disappeared to fetch the tea and Marian followed her with her eyes for a moment as she busied herself behind the counter. "She wasn't the only one, of course," she said, leaning forward and lowering her voice in a conspiratorial fashion.

"The only one of what?" I asked.

"Who was half crazed for love of my brother," she said, smiling. "You'd never believe the way the girls around here threw themselves at him. Even my own friends were sweet on him and they were years older than he was."

"Oh, come on," I said, smiling. "You're only a few years older than me. You're not ready to be put out to pasture yet."

"No, of course not," she said. "But it used to drive me crazy. I mean, don't misunderstand me, Tristan, I loved my brother to distraction, but to me he was always just a rather messy, rather unkempt, rather mischievous little boy. When he was a child, the difficulty my mother had getting him to take a bath was quite extraordinary—he would scream the house down the moment the tin appeared—but then I suppose all little boys are like that. And some of the older ones, too, if the chaps I know are anything to go by. So when I saw the effect he had on women as he grew older, it took me quite by surprise, I don't mind telling you."

I nodded. I wasn't entirely sure that this was a line I wanted to pursue but there was a part of me, a masochistic part, that could not help itself.

"And he reciprocated their affections?" I asked.

"Sometimes," she said. "There was a string of them at one point. You couldn't walk down to the shops without seeing him strolling along with some hare-brained thing in her Sunday-best dress who'd put a few flowers in her hair for effect, thinking she might be the one to catch him. I couldn't keep track of them, there were that many."

"He was a good-looking fellow," I remarked.

"Yes, I suppose he was. It's hard for me to recognize it, being his sister. Almost as hard as it is for you, I suppose."

"Me?"

"Well, being a man."

"Yes."

"I used to rag him about it, of course," she continued. "But he never seemed to pay any attention to me. Most boys, of course, would have flown into a fury and told me to keep my nose firmly out but he just laughed and shrugged it off. He said he enjoyed going for long walks, and if some girl wanted to join him for the company, then who was he to stand in their way? To be honest, he never seemed particularly interested in any of them. That's why it was pointless to tease. He really didn't care."

"But there was a fiancée, wasn't there?" I asked, frowning, wondering what to make of all of this.

"A fiancée?" she asked, looking up and smiling at Jane as she placed the fresh pot before us.

"Yes, he told me once that he had a sweetheart back home and they were engaged to be married."

She stopped pouring then but held the pot in mid-air as she stared at me. "Are you quite sure?" she asked me.

"Perhaps I have it wrong," I said nervously.

Marian looked out of the window and remained silent for a few moments, considering this. "Did he say who she was?" she asked, turning back to me.

"I'm not sure if I can recall," I said, although the name was firmly emblazoned in my memory. "I think it was Ann something."

"Ann?" she asked, shaking her head. "I can't think of any Ann. Do you have it right?"

"I think so," I replied. "No, wait. I have it now. Eleanor. He said her name was Eleanor."

Marian's eyes opened wide and she stared at me for a few seconds before bursting out laughing. "Eleanor?" she asked. "Not Eleanor Martin?"

"I'm not sure of the surname," I said.

"But it must be her. She's the only one. Well, yes, he and Eleanor did have a thing, I suppose, at one point. She was one of those girls who were always hanging off him. I imagine she would have liked nothing more than to marry my brother. In fact," and here she tapped the table several times as if she had just recalled something of importance, "Eleanor Martin was the one who wrote him all those soppy letters."

"When we were over there?" I asked, surprised by this.

"Well, possibly, but I don't know anything about that. No, I mean she used to send these extraordinary letters to the house.

Frightful, scented things with little flowers crushed inside that fell out over his lap whenever he opened them and caused a terrible mess on the carpets. I remember once he asked me what I thought they were supposed to signify and I told him nothing at all, other than the girl's utter stupidity, because—and you can trust me on this, Tristan—because I've known her since she was a child, that girl has no more sense than a postage stamp. I remember that she would write long essays on the theme of nature—spring, rebirth, little bunny rabbits, all that rubbish— and she sent these along, convinced that they would somehow captivate my brother. I don't know who she thought he was, Lord Byron or someone. What a fool!" She raised her cup to her lips and held it there for a while. "But you say that he claimed they were engaged?" she asked, frowning. "But it can't be. If *she* had said it I could put it down to the fact that the girl's a complete idiot, but him? It doesn't make sense."

"Perhaps I have it wrong," I repeated. "We had so many conversations. It's impossible to remember half of them."

"I'm sure you must have it wrong, Tristan," she said. "My brother was many things but he would never have given up his life to share it with a fool such as her. He had more depth than that. Despite his good looks and his ability to captivate any woman in sight, he never seemed to take advantage of any of them. I rather admired him for that. When his friends were chasing girls like crazy, he seemed to lose interest entirely. I wondered whether it was out of respect for our father, who would not have been happy, of course, to have a son who was the village cad. Being a vicar, I mean. I find that many handsome young men are cads, Tristan. Would you agree with me?"

I shrugged my shoulders. "I really couldn't say, Marian."

"Oh, I'm sure that's not true," she said, smiling gently, teasing me a little, I thought. "You're almost Will's equal, as far as I can see. That lovely blond hair of yours and those sad, puppy-dog eyes. I say this strictly from an aesthetic perspective, Tristan, so don't get any ideas, since I'm old enough to be your grandmother, but you're rather a dish, aren't you? Good Lord, you've gone quite red."

She was speaking with such good humour, such unexpected joy in her tone, that it was hard not to smile back. This was not a flirtation, I knew, not anything of the sort, but perhaps it was the beginning of a friendship. I realized that she liked me, and I knew that I liked her, too. Which was unexpected. That was not what I had come here for.

"You're not old," I insisted, mumbling into my cup. "What age are you, anyway? Twenty-five? Twenty-six?"

"Didn't your mother ever tell you that it was rude to ask a lady's age? And you're just a boy. What are you, nineteen? Twenty?"

"Twenty-one," I said, and she frowned, thinking about it.

"But hold on, that would mean—"

"I lied about my age," I told her, anticipating the question. "I was only seventeen when I was over there. I lied in order that they would accept me."

"And I thought Eleanor was a fool," she said, although not unkindly.

"Yes," I muttered, looking down at my tea.

"Just a boy," she repeated finally, shaking her head. "But tell me, Tristan," she continued, leaning forward. "Tell me the truth. Are you a cad?"

"I don't know what I am," I said quietly. "If you want the truth, I've spent most of the last few years trying to work that out for myself."

She sat back then and narrowed her eyes. "Have you ever been to the National Gallery?" she asked me.

"A few times," I said, a little surprised by this abrupt change of topic.

"I go whenever I'm in London," she said. "I'm interested in art, you see. Which proves that I'm not a philistine, after all. Oh, I'm no painter, don't get me wrong. But I love paintings. And what I do is I visit the gallery and find a canvas that intrigues me and I just sit down in front of it and stare at it for an hour or so, sometimes for a whole afternoon. I let the painting come together before my eyes. I start to recognize the brushstrokes and the intention of the artist. Most people just take a quick glance and walk on, ticking off this, this and this along the way and thinking that they've actually seen the work, but how can you appreciate anything that way? I say this, Mr. Sadler, because you remind me of a painting. That last remark of yours, I don't quite know what it means but I feel that you do."

"It didn't mean anything," I said. "I was just talking, that's all."

"No, that's a lie," she said equably. "But I feel if I keep looking at you for some time, then I might begin to understand you. I'm trying to see your brushstrokes. Does that make sense?"

"No," I said firmly.

"And that's another lie. But anyway . . ." She shrugged and looked away. "It's getting a little cold in here, isn't it?"

"I'm fine," I said.

"I believe I'm a little distracted," she said. "I keep thinking about that business with Eleanor Martin. Such an odd thing for Will to have said. She still lives around here, you know."

"Really?" I said, surprised.

"Oh yes. Well, she's a Norwich girl born and bred. Actually, she got married last year to a chap who really should have known better, but he was from Ipswich and I suppose you take what you can find there. She's always about the town. We might run into her later if we're terribly unlucky."

"I hope we don't," I said.

"Why do you say that?"

"No reason. I'm just . . . not that interested, that's all."

"But why wouldn't you be?" she asked, intrigued. "My brother, your best friend, tells you that he is engaged to be married. I tell you that there was never any such engagement that I knew of. Why wouldn't you be interested in seeing this Helen of Troy who had so captured his heart?"

"Miss Bancroft," I said with a sigh, leaning back now and rubbing my eyes. She had referred to Will as my best friend and I wondered whether the corollary held true. I also questioned why her previous good humour was now tinged with a certain amount of barbarity. "What is it that you want me to say?"

"Oh, I'm Miss Bancroft again now, am I?" she asked.

"You called me Mr. Sadler a moment ago. I thought perhaps we were returning to formalities."

"Well, we're not," she replied abruptly. "And let's not argue, all right? I couldn't stand it. You seem like such a pleasant young man, Tristan. You mustn't mind if I appear out of sorts. I'll attack you one minute and call you a dish the next. It's a strange day, that's all. I am glad you made the journey, though."

"Thank you," I said. I noticed her glancing at my hand, my left one, though, not the twitching right, and I caught her eye.

"I just wondered, that's all," she said. "So many men your age seem to have got married since coming back from the war. You haven't been tempted?"

"Not even a little bit," I said.

"You didn't have a sweetheart waiting for you, then, back home?"

I shook my head.

"Well, so much the better for you," she said quickly. "In my experience, sweethearts are a lot more trouble than they're worth. If you ask me, love is a fool's game."

135

"But it's all that matters," I said suddenly, surprised to hear myself say such a thing. "Where would we be without love?"

"You're a romantic, then?"

"I'm not sure that I even understand what that means," I told her. "A romantic? I know that I have emotions. I know that I feel things deeply—too deeply, in fact. Does that make me a romantic? I don't know. Perhaps."

"But you men all feel things so deeply now," she insisted. "Friends of mine, boys who fought over there. You have an intensity now, a potent sadness, even a sense of fear. It's not at all like before. Why is that, do you think?"

"Isn't it obvious?" I asked.

"Yes. To an extent. But I'd like to hear you explain it to me."

I glanced down at the table and thought about it. I wanted to be honest with her, or as honest as I dared to be. I wanted my words to have meaning.

"Before I went over there," I said, not looking at her now but staring at the used cutlery laid out before me, "I thought I knew something about myself. I felt things then, of course. I knew someone, I . . . forgive me, Marian, but I fell in love, I suppose. In a childish way. And I got very hurt by it. No one's fault but my own, of course. I hadn't thought things through. I thought I had. I thought I knew what I was doing and that the other party had similar feelings for me. I was wrong, of course, quite wrong. I allowed things to get completely out of hand. Then when I went over there and fell in with the regiment, fell in with your brother, too, of course, well, I realized how silly I had been back then. Because suddenly everything, life itself, became an intensely heightened experience. It was as if I was living on a different plane from the one before. At Aldershot, they weren't teaching us how to fight, they were training us how to extend our lives for as long as possible. As if we were already dead, but if we learned to shoot straight and to use a bayonet with care and precision then we might at least have a few more days or weeks in us. The barracks were filled with ghosts, Marian. Does that make sense? It was as if we died before we left England. And when I wasn't killed, when I was one of the lucky ones . . . well, there were twenty of us in my barracks, you see. Twenty boys. And only two came back. One who went mad, and myself. But that doesn't mean we survived it. I don't think I did survive it. I may not be buried in a French field but I linger there. My spirit does, anyway. I think I'm just breathing, that's all. And there's a difference between breathing and being alive. And so, to your question, am I a romantic? Do I think in terms of weddings and falling in love any more? No, I don't. It seems so pointless to me, so completely and utterly trivial. I don't know what that says about me. Whether it means that there is something wrong in my head. But the thing is, there's always been something wrong in my head, you see. From ever since I can remember. And I never knew what to do about it. I never understood it. And now, after everything that has happened, after what I did—"

"Tristan, stop," she said, reaching forward suddenly and taking my hand, which was shaking noticeably, embarrassing me once again. I realized that I was crying a little, too, not heavily, just a few tears working their way down my cheeks, and I felt ashamed about that as well, and wiped them away with the back of my left hand. "I shouldn't have asked you about this," she said. "I was being flippant, that's all. You don't have to tell me anything you don't want to. Good Lord, you came all this way to meet me, to give me this great gift of your stories about my brother, and this is how I repay you. Can you forgive me?"

I smiled and shrugged my shoulders. "There's nothing to forgive," I said. "It's just . . . Well, you don't want to get any of us started on these things. You say you have some friends, some former servicemen, who came back?"

"Yes."

"Well, do they like to talk about it?"

She considered this for a moment and looked uncertain. "It's a difficult question to answer," she said. "I feel at times that they do, because they talk about it almost incessantly. But it always leaves them distraught. Just as it did with you a moment ago. But at the same time, I feel that they cannot stop themselves reliving every moment over and over. How long will it take, do you think?"

"I don't know," I admitted. "A long time."

"But it is over," she insisted. "It's over! And you're a young man, Tristan. You're only twenty-one years old, after all. My God, you were just a child when you were over there. Seventeen! You can't let it drag you down. Look at Will."

"How do you mean?"

"Well, he's dead, isn't he?" she said, a look of genuine empathy on her face. "He doesn't even get to be distraught. He doesn't get to live with his bad memories."

"Yes," I said, that familiar stabbing pain resurfacing inside my body. I exhaled loudly and rubbed the heels of my hands against my eyes for a moment, and when I took them away I blinked several times and focused on her face carefully. "Can we get out of here?" I asked. "I feel I need some fresh air."

"Of course," she said, tapping the table in immediate recognition that we had stayed too long. "You don't have to go back to London yet, though, do you? I'm enjoying our talk."

"No, not yet," I said. "Not for a few hours, anyway."

"Good. It's such a beautiful day, I thought we might go for a walk. I could show you some of the places where Will and I grew up. You really have to see some of Norwich—it's a beautiful city. Then we can have a late lunch somewhere. And there's just one thing I'd like you to do for me, but I'll tell you that in a while, if you don't mind. If I ask you now, I think you'll refuse me. And I don't want you to refuse me."

I said nothing for second or two but then nodded. "All right," I agreed, getting up and taking my overcoat from the stand as she put her own coat on. "Let me just pay for the teas," I said. "I'll meet you outside in a moment."

I watched her as she made her way towards the door and out on to the street, buttoning her coat as she stood glancing around for anyone she might recognize. She didn't resemble Will physically, of course. They were very different types. But there was something in the way that she carried herself, a certain confidence mixed with a sense that although her beauty would be noticed by others, she rather wished it wouldn't be. I found myself smiling as I looked at her and then turned back to pay for the teas.

"I'm sorry about before," I said to our waitress as she took my money and counted out change from the till. "I hope we weren't becoming a bit of a trial for you."

"You don't have to apologize," she said. "You were a friend of Will's, then?"

"Yes," I said. "Yes, we served together."

"It was a disgrace," she hissed, leaning forward, fire in her eyes. "What happened to him, I mean. It was an absolute disgrace. Made me ashamed to be English. You won't get many around here that will agree with me on that, but I knew him and I knew the kind of man he was." I swallowed and nodded, taking the coins from her and putting them silently in my pocket. "There's not many people I respect as much as I do Marian Bancroft," she continued. "She's one in a million, she is. Despite everything that happened, she offers such help to the ex-servicemen around her. You'd think, all things considered, that she would hate them. But she doesn't. I never know quite what to make of her, actually. She's a mystery."

I frowned, realizing that I hadn't even asked Marian what she did in Norwich, how she spent her days, how she filled her time. It was typical of boys like me; we were so wrapped up in ourselves that we didn't think the world held a place for anyone else. I heard a quick ringing sound, the chiming of the bell over the door as someone left, thanked Jane and said goodbye.

Before leaving the café, I patted my pockets, checking for my wallet and the packet of letters, which was still in my overcoat, and satisfied that all was in place I opened the door and went outside. Marian was right: it was a beautiful day. Bright and warm with no breeze but no overbearing sunshine either. It was a perfect day to go for a stroll and I had a sudden vision of Will walking along these cobbled streets next to some unfortunate lovesick girl who would be doing all she could to keep up with him, sneaking sly glances at his handsome face, dreaming that perhaps at the next turning, where no one could see them, he would do the most unexpected but natural thing in the world and turn to her, take her in his arms and pull her to him.

I shook my head, dismissed the idea, and looked around for Marian. She was standing no more than ten or twelve feet away from me, but not alone. The man from the café had followed her out and was standing before her, gesticulating wildly. I didn't know what to make of it and simply stared at them before registering that there was something aggressive about his behaviour. I walked quickly towards them.

"Hello," I said. "Everything all right here?"

"And you," said the man, raising his voice and jabbing a finger in my face as he glared at me with thunder in his eyes, "you can just take a step back, friend, because none of this concerns you and I swear I won't be responsible for my actions if you come any closer. Do you understand me?"

"Leonard," said Marian, stepping forward and placing herself between him and me. "This has nothing to do with him. You'll leave it alone if you know what's good for you."

"You don't tell me what to do, Marian," he said, which at least made me understand that these two knew each other and he wasn't just some stranger assaulting her in the street. "You won't answer my letters, you won't speak to me when I call at the house, and then you take up with someone else and flaunt it in front of my eyes. Who do you think you are, anyway?" he asked, this last question addressed to me, and I looked at him in astonishment, not knowing what I could possibly say in response. He was in a pure rage, his cheeks scarlet with anger, and I could see that it was all he could do to stop himself from pushing Marian out of the way and knocking me to the ground; instinctively, I took a pace back. "That's right, you'd better back away," he added, so pleased by this move that he began to advance further towards me, probably thinking that he could intimidate me. The truth was that I wasn't in the least frightened of him; I simply had no desire to involve myself in some sort of street brawl.

"Leonard, I said stop it!" shouted Marian, pulling at his coat and dragging him back. A few people passing on the street stared at us with a mixture of interest and contempt but kept walking, shaking their heads as if they expected nothing better of our type. "It's not what you think. You've got everything wrong, as usual."

"Got it wrong, have I?" he asked, turning to her as I studied him a little more closely. He was taller than me, with brown hair and a ruddy complexion. He looked like someone who knew how to handle himself. The only thing detracting from his strong physical presence was a pair of owl-type spectacles perched on his face, which made him look more academic. And yet the argument against this was the commotion that he was causing here on the street. "Got it wrong? When I see the two of you sitting there for almost an hour, chatting away to each other like a pair of cooing mynah birds? And I saw you take his hand, Marian, so please don't tell me there's nothing going on when I know what my own eyes are telling me."

"And what if there is something going on?" she shouted in reply, the colour coming into her cheeks, too. "What if there is? What business is it of yours, anyway?"

"Don't give me that," he began, but she stepped closer to him, her face almost in his as she roared at him.

"I'll say whatever I like, Leonard Legg! You have no hold over me. Not any more. You mean nothing to me now."

"You belong to me," he insisted.

"I don't belong to anyone!" she cried. "Least of all you. Do you think I'd ever look at you again? Do you? After what you did?"

"After what *I* did?" he said, laughing in her face. "That's rich, that is. Why, even the fact that I'm willing to put the past in the past and still marry you should show you the kind of man I am. Getting mixed up with a family like yours won't do me any favours, will it, and still I'm willing to do it. For you."

"Well, don't bother," she said, lowering her voice; in an instant she had regained her dignity. "Because if you think I would ever marry you, if you think that I would debase myself so much—"

"*You* debase *yourself*? Why, if my parents even knew that I was talking to you, let alone forgiving you—"

"You have nothing to forgive me for," she cried, throwing her arms in the air in frustration. "It is I who should forgive you. But I don't," she insisted, stepping close to him again. "I don't. And I never, ever will."

He glared at her, breathing heavily through his nose like a bull getting ready to charge, and for a second I thought that he was going to assault her, so I moved forward, and as I did so, he turned to look at me and the fury that filled him was transferred from Marian's direction to my own. Without warning I found myself on the ground in a daze, one hand pressed to my nose from which—to my surprise—there was no blood pouring, but my cheek felt raw and tender and I realized that he had missed my nose entirely and punched me right of centre, knocking me off my feet and sending me sprawling to the ground.

"Tristan!" cried Marian, rushing over and leaning down to examine me. "Are you all right?"

"I think so," I said, sitting up and looking at my assailant. Every fibre of my being wanted to stand up and hit him back, to punch him all the way to Lowestoft, if need be, but I didn't do it. Like Wolf, I would not fight.

"Come on, then," he said, goading me into action and assuming a stance such as a professional boxer might take, pathetic clown that he was. "Get on your feet, then, and show me what you've got."

"Get out of here, Leonard," said Marian, turning on him. "Go, before I call the police."

He laughed but seemed a little disturbed by this suggestion and perhaps irritated by the fact that I was refusing to stand up and fight him. He shook his head and spat on the ground, the phlegm landing only a foot or two from my left shoe. "Coward," he said, looking down at me contemptuously. "No wonder she likes you. It's what the Bancrofts go in for, after all, isn't it?"

"Just leave, please," said Marian quietly. "For God's sake, Leonard, can't you just leave me alone? I don't want you."

"This isn't over," he said, turning away. "Don't think this is over, because it isn't."

He took one more look at the two of us, huddled together on the pavement, and shook his head in contempt before making his way down one of the side streets and disappearing out of sight. I turned to Marian in confusion only to find her close to tears now as she held her face in her hands.

"I'm so sorry," she said. "Tristan, I'm so, so sorry."

Later, when I was back on my feet, we began to walk side by side along the streets of Norwich town centre. A slight bruise was forming on my cheek but no serious damage had been done. Mr. Pynton would no doubt look at me with disapproval the following day, remove his pince-nez and give a deep sigh, putting it all down to the high spirits of youth.

"You must think terribly of me," she said, after a lengthy silence.

"Why would I?" I asked. "It wasn't you who hit me."

"No, but it was my fault. At least partly, anyway."

"You know that man, obviously."

"Oh yes," she said in a regretful voice. "Yes, I know him, all right."

"He seems to think that he has some sort of hold over you."

"He did. Once," she replied. "We were an item once, you see."

"Are you serious?" I asked, rather surprised, for although I had pieced this together from the row earlier, I found it hard to imagine either Marian being involved with such a creature or a scenario in which a chap who had secured her hand would ever let it go.

"Well, don't sound so shocked," she said with a hint of amusement in her tone. "I have had my share of suitors in my time."

"No, I didn't mean—"

"We were engaged to be married. That was the plan, anyway."

"And something went wrong?"

"Well, obviously, Tristan," she said, turning to me in frustration. "I'm sorry, I shouldn't take it out on you," she added a moment later. "It's just . . . well, I'm terribly embarrassed by how he attacked you like that and I feel ashamed of myself on account of it."

"I don't see why," I said. "It seems to me that you broke it off just in time. You could have been married to the brute. Who knows what kind of life he might have led you?"

"Only I wasn't the one who broke it off," she explained. "It was Leonard. Oh, don't look so surprised, please. The truth is I would have had no choice but to throw him over in the long run but he got in first, which is to my eternal regret. You must realize why, surely?"

"It was over Will, wasn't it?" I said, everything becoming clear now.

"Yes."

"He threw you over because of what people might say?"

She shrugged her shoulders, as if she were embarrassed by it, even after so much time had passed.

"And you think I'm a cad," I said, smiling at her, which caused her to laugh. She looked across towards the market, where a group of about forty stalls were positioned together in a tight rectangle, each one covered with a brightly coloured tarpaulin; they were selling fruit and vegetables, fish and meat. There were a lot of people gathered around them, mostly women, shopping bags at the ready, passing what little money they had to the stallholders and engaging in long, complaining conversations with each other as they did so.

"He wasn't that bad really," she said. "I did love him once. Before all this, all that, I should say—"

"The war, you mean?"

"Yes, the war. Before that he was a different person. It's hard to explain. We've known each other since we were fifteen or sixteen. We were always sweet on each other. Well, I was sweet on him, anyway—he was in love with a friend of mine, or as much in love as you can be at that age."

145

"Everything's a mess at that age."

"Yes, I think you're right. But anyway, he threw this other girl over in favour of me, which led to terrible arguments between our families. And that girl, who was a good friend of mine, never spoke to me again. It was a terrible scandal. I'm quite ashamed when I look back on it, but we were young so there's no point losing any sleep over it. The fact remains that I was crazy about him."

"But you seem so mismatched," I said.

"Yes, but you don't know him. We are different, now. Well, everyone is, I suppose. But we were happy for a time. So he asked me to marry him and I said yes. Now I can scarcely think of anything worse."

I thought about it but remained silent. I knew little about the relations between men and women, the intimacies that bound them together, the secrets that might drive them apart. Sylvia Carter was the sole experience I had had with girls and it was hard to imagine that one kiss, six years before, could be the end of the thing for me, but it was, of course.

"Was he over there?" I asked, considering it, for he was about the same age as Marian, I thought, only a few years older than me. "Leonard, I mean."

"No, he couldn't go," she said, shaking her head. "He's terribly short-sighted, you see. He had an accident when he was sixteen. Fell off his bike, the clot, and hit his head against a stone. He was found unconscious in the road and by the time they got him to the doctor he didn't know who or where he was. The upshot was that he'd damaged some of the ligaments in his eyes. The right eye is almost entirely blind while the left gives him terrible gyp, too. He hates it, of course, although you'd never know there was anything wrong just by looking at him."

"No wonder he missed my nose when he punched me, then," I said, trying to suppress a smile, and Marian turned to me, complicit for a moment in my laughter. "I saw him earlier," I added. "In the café, I mean. He was watching us. He tried to engage me when I went to the bathroom."

"If I'd known he was there I would have left," she said. "He follows me around now, trying to make things right between us. It's tiresome."

"And because of his eyes, he couldn't enlist?"

"That's right," she said. "And, to be fair to him, he was terribly cut up about it. I think he felt that it made him less of a man in some way. Of his brothers—he had four of them—two enlisted before 1916 and the other two, the younger ones, came in on the Derby Scheme. Only one came back alive and he's very ill. Had some sort of a breakdown, I believe. Stays at home most of the time. I hear his parents have a rotten time of it, which gives me no pleasure. Anyway, I know that Leonard feels awful about the fact that he couldn't fight. He's quite brave, you see, and terribly patriotic. It was awful for him when it was all going on and he was the only young man here in town."

"Awful for him?" I asked, irritated by this. "I would say it was wonderful for him."

"Yes, I can see why you would say that," she agreed. "But try to see it from his point of view. He wanted to be over there with the rest of you, not stuck here with a bunch of women. He doesn't fit in at all with the men who came back. I've seen him sitting in the corner of the public houses, not mixing with the fellows he used to go to school with. How can he, after all? He can't share their experiences, he doesn't know what they've been through. Some of them try to involve him, I think, but he gets aggressive about it and I think they've given up. Why should they humour him, I suppose, is their attitude. They have nothing to reproach themselves for."

I shrugged my shoulders. I could see what she was getting at and was willing to admit that he probably felt bad about things but, still, I couldn't bring myself to sympathize with a man who had been lucky enough to escape the trenches simply because he felt emasculated by this same good fortune.

"Well, if he didn't get to fight then he's certainly making up for it now," I said. "What does he mean, anyway, hitting me like that?"

"I suppose he thought there was something between us," she explained. "And he can be terribly jealous."

"But he was the one who threw you over!" I said, instantly regretting the unchivalrous nature of my remark, and she turned to look at me, scowling.

"Yes, I'm well aware of that, thank you, but clearly he regrets it now."

"And you don't?"

She hesitated only briefly before shaking her head. "I regret that a situation came about that led him to feel he had to break it off with me," she said. "But I don't regret that he did it. Does that make any sense?"

"A little," I said.

"But now he wants me back, which is a bore. He wrote to me and said as much. He follows me around town, and shows up at the house whenever he's had too much to drink, which is a couple of times a week at least. I've told him there's no chance at all and he might as well resign himself to it but he's as stubborn as a mule. Really, I don't know what I'm going to do about him. It's not as if I can speak to his parents—they won't have anything to do with me. And it's not as if I can ask my father to talk to him. He won't even acknowledge that Leonard exists any more." She took a deep breath before expressing in words what we were both thinking. "What I need, of course, is my brother."

"Perhaps I should have said something," I said.

"What would you have said? You don't know him, you don't know the circumstances."

"No, but if you're upset about it—"

"I don't mean to be rude, Tristan," she said, looking at me with an expression that suggested she was not to be patronized, "but you barely know me. And I don't need your protection, as grateful as I am that you are willing to offer it."

"Of course not. I just meant that as your brother's friend—"

"But don't you see?" she asked. "That's what makes it worse. It was his parents, you see. They put the most awful pressure on him. They run a greengrocer's, here in town, and rely on the goodwill of the community to keep their business going. Well, of course everyone knew that Leonard and I were to be married, so after Will died most of the town stopped shopping at Legg's. They were looking for someone to attack, you see. And it wasn't as if they could take it out on my father. He was their vicar, after all. There were certain conventions that had to be upheld. So the Leggs were the next best thing."

"Marian," I said, looking away, wishing there was a bench nearby where we could sit quietly. I felt a strong urge to remain silent for a long time.

"No, Tristan," she insisted. "Let me finish. You might as well know it. We tried to carry on for a while but it was obvious that it was no good. The Leggs were shunning me, the town was shunning the Leggs, it was horrible, all of it, and so Leonard decided that he'd had enough and threw me over for his family's sake. Of course his father put it about within a few hours and, by the next day, everyone was shopping there again. Business could go on as normal, hurrah. Never mind that I was going through the worst time of my life, grieving for the brother I'd lost; never mind that the person I relied on most to see me through those days decided that he couldn't stand the sight of me. But now that things have begun to blow over and no one wants to talk about it any more, he's decided that he wants me back. Everyone around here wants to act as though nothing ever happened and there never was a boy called Will Bancroft who grew up around them and played on their streets and went out and fought their blasted war for them—" She was raising her voice now and I could see a few people passing by looking at her with expressions that suggested they were thinking, *Ah yes, the Bancroft girl, we shouldn't expect much more from her than shouting in the streets.* "Now that that's all behind us, Tristan, my poor Leonard has decided that he made a terrible mistake and damn his father and damn his mother and damn their blessed cash register but he wants me back. Well, he shan't have me, Tristan, he shan't have me. Not today, not tomorrow. Never."

"All right," I said, trying to calm her. "I'm sorry. I can see it now."

"People behave as though we are disgraced. Can you understand that?" she said, quieter now. Tears sprung into her eyes as she spoke to me. "Look at that couple in the café. Their brazen rudeness. Their insensitivity. Oh, Tristan, don't look at me like that. Don't pretend you didn't notice."

I frowned, remembering only the couple who had sat a few tables away from us before moving to a more secluded area to continue their assignation.

"They moved because of me," she cried. "When I came back from the Ladies and they saw who was sitting near them, they upped sticks and got as far away from me as possible. This is what I have to put up with every day. It's not as bad as it once was, that's true, it used to be horrendous, but in a way it's even worse now that people are talking to me again. It says that they've entirely forgotten Will. Which I never shall. They treat my parents, they treat me, like they want to say that they forgive us, as if they think we have something to be forgiven for.

But it's we who should be forgiving them for how they treated us and how they treated Will. And yet I don't say anything. I'm full of fine ideas, Tristan; you'd learn that about me if you were fool enough to stick around here any longer. But that's all they are. Fine ideas. In my heart, I'm just as much a coward as they all think my brother was. I want to defend him, but can't."

"Your brother was *not* a coward," I insisted. "You must believe that, Marian."

"Of course I believe it," she snapped. "I don't think it for a moment. How could I? I who knew him best. He was the bravest one of all. But try telling that to the people here and see how far it gets you. They're ashamed of him, you see. The only boy from the entire county during the whole war ever to be lined up in front of a firing squad and executed for cowardice. They're ashamed of him. They don't understand who he is. Who he was. They never have. But you do, Tristan, don't you? You know who he was."

SQUINTING IN THE SUNLIGHT

France, July–September 1916

A CRY OF DESPAIR and weariness emanates from the pit of my stomach as the wall behind me begins to crumble and dissolve into a slow-moving river of thick, black, rat-infused mud that slides down my back and slips into the gaps at the top of my boots. I feel the sludge seeping its way into my already sodden socks and throw myself against the tide, desperate to push the barricade back into place before I am submerged beneath it. A tail passes quickly across my hands, whipping me sharply, then another; next, a sharp bite.

"Sadler!" cries Henley, his voice hoarse, his breathing laboured. He's standing only a few feet away from me with Unsworth, I think, by his side and Corporal Wells next along the line. The rain is falling in such heavy sheets that I'm spitting it from my lips along with mouthfuls of foul dirt and it's difficult to make any of them out. "The sandbags—look, they're over here—pile them as high as you can."

I make my way forward, trying to pull my boots out of three feet of mud. The terrible sucking sound they make as they emerge reminds me of the echo of a man's last breath, deep and frantic, gasping for air, failing.

Instinctively I open my arms as a sandbag filled with excavated earth comes at me, almost knocking me off my feet when it hits me in the chest, but although I am winded I am equally quick to turn back to the wall, slamming the sandbag where I think the base must be, turning for another, catching it,

155

padding the wall again, and another and another and another. Now there are five or six of us all doing the same thing, piling the sandbags high, crying out for more before the whole bloody place collapses about us, and it feels like a fool's errand, but somehow it works and it is over and we forget that we have very nearly died today as we wait to die again tomorrow.

The Germans use concrete; we use wood and sand.

It's been raining for days, an endless torrent that makes the trenches feel like troughs for the pigs rather than defences in which our regiment can take cover as we launch our sporadic attacks. When we arrived, I was told that the chalky ground of Picardy, through which we have been advancing for days now, is less liable to crumble than that of other parts of the line, particularly those miserable fields towards Belgium, where the high wetlands make entrenchment almost impossible. I can scarcely imagine any place worse than where we are. I have only these whispers and rumours to take for comparison.

All around me, what was this morning a clear pathway is now a river of mud. Pumps arrive and three of the men have a go at them. Wells shouts something at all of us, his voice gravelly, lost in the conquering environment, and I stare at him, feeling close to laughter, a sort of disbelieving hysteria.

"For fuck's sake, Sadler!" he screams, and I shake my head, trying to make it clear that I didn't hear the order. "Do it!" he roars at me. "Do it or I'll fucking bury you in the mud!"

Above my head, over the parapet, I can hear the shelling beginning again, a prologue of sorts, for it isn't heavy yet, nowhere near as heavy as it has been over the last few days, anyway. The German trenches are about three hundred yards north of ours. On quiet evenings we can hear an echo of their conversation, occasional singing, laughter, cries of anguish. We're not that different, them and us. If both armies drown in the mud, then who'll be left to fight the war?

"Over there, over there!" shouts Wells, grabbing me by the arm and dragging me over to where Parks, Hobbs and Denchley are attacking their pumps. "There's buckets, man!" he yells. "This whole area must be drained!"

I nod quickly and look around. To my right, I'm surprised to see two grey tin buckets, the type that normally stand behind the reverse line, close to the latrines. Yates makes it his business to keep them as sanitary as possible. His obsession with maintaining hygiene in this place borders on the psychotic. What the hell are they doing here, I wonder as I stare at them? Yates will lose his mind if he sees them lying around like this. They can't possibly have rolled over in the rain and landfall, for the supervision trench stands between the reverse and the front and each is about eight feet deep. Someone returning them to where they belong must have been picked off along the way. If the buckets are at my feet, then the carrying-soldier is a few feet above me, lying on his back, staring up at the dark sky over northern France, his eyes glazed over, his body growing cold and hard and free. And it's Yates, I realize then. Of course it is. Yates is dead and we'll have filthy latrines for the foreseeable.

"What's the matter with you, Sadler?" shouts Wells, and I turn to him, apologizing quickly as I reach down to pick up the buckets, my hands covered in shit the moment I take their handles, but what matter, I think, what matter at all? Placing one at my feet I hold the other by top and base and scoop up a quarter-gallon of water and, looking up and checking the air, toss the great sodden mess north-east, towards Berlin, in the direction that the wind blows, watching as the murky effluent flies through the air and falls to the ground atop. Is it falling on him, I wonder? Is it falling on Yates? Obsessively clean Yates? Am I throwing shit all over his corpse?

"Keep at it, man!" shouts a voice to my left and whoever it is—Hobbs?—pumps more water away as I drive my bucket deep and deeper again, lifting the water out, sending it on its way, reaching down for more. And then a heavy body, running too fast and slipping in the mud, curses, rights himself and pushes past me and I fall, knocked head over feet, my face in the sludge and the water and the shit, and I spit out the noxious earth as I place a hand down to lever myself up, but my hand seems to just sink deeper and deeper into the mud and I think, *How can this be, how can my life have descended into such filth and squalor?* I used to go swimming on warm afternoons at the public baths with my friends. I would play conkers with the fallen horse chestnuts in Kew Gardens, boiling them in vinegar for a better chance of victory.

A hand reaches down to help me up.

There's a lot of shouting now, none of it making any sense, then a great rush of water in my face, and where did that come from, I wonder? Is the wind rising and taking the rain with it? My bucket is thrust hard back into my hands and I turn to see who has helped me; his face is dark and filthy, almost unrecognizable, but I catch his eye for a moment, the man who lifted me, the man who helped me, and we stare at each other, Will Bancroft and I, and say not a word before he turns away and presses on, going I know not where, sent not to help us but to make his way further along the trench and into who knows what type of dreadfulness ten, twenty, a hundred feet away.

"It's getting heavier," cries Denchley, looking up for a moment at the heavens, and I do the same, closing my eyes and letting the rain fall on my face, washing the shit away, and I know that I have only a few seconds to enjoy it before Wells screams at me again to fill my bucket and drain the area, to drain the fucking area before every one of us is buried here in these filthy fucking French fields.

And I go back to work, as I always do. I focus. I fill my bucket. I throw it over the side. I fill my bucket again. And I believe that if I keep doing it, then time will pass and I will wake up at home, with my father throwing his arms around me and telling me that I am forgiven. I turn to my right and make for a deeper pool, glancing down the trench, the twenty or thirty feet of it that I can see—trying to see where Will has vanished to, wanting to make sure that he is all right, and I wonder, as I always wonder at these moments, whether I will ever see him alive again.

Another day.

I wake and step out of the foxhole where I have tried to sleep for three or four hours and gather my marching order about me, my rifle and bayonet, the ammunition that slips into my pockets front and rear, my trowel, a depleted bottle of liquid that goes by the name of water but tastes of chloride of lime and which provokes sporadic attacks of diarrhoea, but if it's a choice between dehydration and the shits, I'll take the shits any day. My greatcoat is wrapped around me, the curved plates beneath my shirt digging into my skin, for they're an unhappy fit meant for a smaller man, but damn it, Sadler, they tell me, we're not running a department store here, it'll have to do. I tell myself that it is a Tuesday, although I have nothing to base that on. Naming the day offers some dull pretence of normality.

Mercifully, the rain has stopped and the sides of the trenches are holding fast and solidifying once again, the sand-bags piled up against each other, black and muddy from the previous day's packing. I'm on top-duty in twenty minutes and, if I'm quick, I can make it to mess for tea and bully beef before returning to take up my position. Walking along, I fall into line with Shields, who looks the worse for wear. His right eye is blackened and half shut; there's a trail of hardened blood running along his temple. It's shaped like the Thames, twisting south towards Greenwich Pier at his eyebrow, then

159

north to London Bridge at his forehead and disappearing into the depths of Blackfriars amid the untidiness of his lice-infested hair. I make no remarks; we are none of us as we should be.

"You up, Sadler?" he asks me.

"Twenty minutes."

"Just finished. Food and sleep, that's what I need."

"I'm thinking of going to the pub later," I tell him. "A few pints of mild and a game of feathers, if you're interested?"

He says nothing, doesn't even acknowledge the joke. We all say things like this from time to time and sometimes there's fun to be had in it but Shields shows no interest in banter right now. He leaves me as we reach Glover's Alley, which leads to Pleasant Way, which in turn splits off at the top left and turns right into Pilgrim's Repose. We live here, beneath the ground like cadavers, and carve streets into the terrain, then we name them and erect signposts to give us the illusion that we remain part of a common humanity. It's a maze down here, the entrenchment splitting off in so many directions before it links with one path, snubs another, provides a safe passageway to a third. It's easy to get lost if you don't know where you're going, and God help the man who is not where he is supposed to be when he is supposed to be there.

I make my way out of the front trench and into the super-vision, where our support lies, those small amounts of medical help we can muster together and some cots for the officers. Beyond here I can smell the food cooking and I make my way towards it eagerly, looking around the ill-kept mess row along the south-west-facing alley of the third line and see mostly familiar faces, some who are new, some who don't speak, some who never stop, some who are brave, some who are foolhardy, some who are falling mad. Some from Aldershot, before us and after. Some with Scottish accents, some with English, some with Irish. As I make my way along there is a low murmur of conversation, the suggestion of a greeting perhaps, and I take my helmet off as I reach the mess and scratch my head, not bothering to look at what this leaves under my fingernails, for my scalp is covered in lice, and my armpits, too, and my crotch. Everywhere that they can nest and breed. It repulsed me once but now I think nothing of it. I am a charitable host and we live peacefully together, them feeding off my filthy skin, me occasionally plucking them away and ending them between the pincer-nails of thumb and forefinger.

I take what I can find and eat quickly. The tea is startlingly good; it must have been made fresh only minutes before and it summons up a memory, something from boyhood, and if I work at it I dare say I could bring it to life, but I have neither the energy nor the interest. The bully beef, on the other hand, is atrocious. God only knows what is forced into these tins; it might be badger or rat or some unknown vermin that has the audacity to continue to exist here, but we call it beef and let that be good enough for it.

I force myself not to look around, not to search for him, because in that direction only pain lies. If I see him, I will be too afraid of his rejection to approach, and there is every possibility that in my anger I will simply launch myself over the top later, directly into no-man's-land, and take whatever is due to me. And if I don't see him, I will convince myself that he has been picked off in the last few hours and I will throw myself over anyway, an easy potshot for the snipers, for what is the purpose of continuing if he does not?

In the end, food in my stomach, the taste of tea in my mouth, I stand up and make my way back to where I started, congratulating myself on how well I have done; how I never searched for him, not once. From such moments, half-happy hours can be strung together.

Climbing back into the front trench I hear a commotion ahead and, although I have little interest in arguments, I have to pass it to get where I am going, so I stop for a while and watch as Sergeant Clayton, who has grown bone thin in these few short weeks since we arrived, is screaming at Potter, an exceptionally tall soldier who was popular back at Aldershot for his abilities as a mimic. In good times he can do a fine imitation not only of our leader but also of his two apostles, Wells and Moody, and once, in a surprisingly buoyant mood, Clayton asked him to perform his sketches for the entire regiment, which he did and it went off well. There was no malice to it although there was, I thought, an edge. But Clayton lapped it up.

The argument appears to concern Potter's height. He stands above us all at six feet and six inches in his stockinged feet, but add a pair of boots and a helmet atop his high-domed forehead and then he's rearing closer to six feet eight. We're all accustomed to him, of course, but it doesn't make his life any easier, for the trenches are no more than about eight feet deep and less than four feet wide at their northernmost part. The poor man can't walk tall with his head above the parapet or he'll lose his brains to a German bullet. It's hard on him, although we haven't time to care, but Clayton is screaming in his face.

"You make yourself a standing target!" he cries. "And when you do that, you endanger everyone in your regiment. How many times have I told you, Potter, not to stand tall?"

"But I can't do it, sir," comes the desperate reply. "I try to bend over but my body won't let me for long. My back aches something rotten on account of it."

"And you don't think an injured back is a small price for a head?"

"I can't crouch all day, sir," complains Potter. "I try. I promise I do."

And then Clayton screams a few random obscenities at him and rushes towards him, pushing him back against the wall, and I think, *That's the spirit. Just unsettle all those sandbags, why don't you, and put us all in even more danger? Why not throw all our artillery away while you're at it?*

The argument is still ringing in my ears as I turn away from the matinee performance and make my way back to my post, where Tell looks around anxiously, waiting for me, hoping that I'll appear, for if I don't, then I've probably been stupid enough to let myself get killed in the night and he will have to stay where he is until Clayton, Wells or Moody comes along and agrees to find someone to relieve him. Which might be hours and he can't leave his post, for that would be desertion and the punishment is a line of soldiers standing before you, their rifles raised, each one aimed at the patch of fabric pinned above your heart.

"Christ, Sadler, I thought you'd never get here," he cries, breaking away now and tapping me on the arm for good luck. "Everything all right beyond?"

"Fine, Bill," I reply—Tell is another who prefers to be addressed by his Christian name; perhaps it makes him feel that he is his own man still—and then step forward to dig my feet into position and pull the box-periscope down to eye level. I'm about to ask him whether he has anything to report but he's already gone and I sigh, narrowing my eyes as I look through the muddy glass, trying to distinguish between the horizon, the fields of battle and the dark clouds up ahead, and do everything in my power to remember what the fuck it is that I'm supposed to be looking out for anyway.

I try to count the days since I left England and decide that it is twenty-four.

We took the train from Aldershot to Southampton the morning after passing out and marched along the roads towards the docks at Portsmouth, families coming out on to the pavements to cheer us on to war. Most of the men revelled in the attention, particularly when some of the girls in the crowd jumped forward to plant kisses on their cheeks, but I found it difficult to concentrate when my mind was still so focused on the events of the previous night.

Afterwards, Will had dressed quickly and stared at me with an expression unlike any I had ever seen before. A mixture of surprise at what we had done, tainted by an inability to deny that he had been not only a willing participant but the prime mover. He wanted to blame me, I could see that, but it was no good. We both knew how it had begun.

"Will," I began, but he shook his head and tried to climb the bank that surrounded us, tripping over in his eagerness to get away and sliding back down before he could get a stronger foothold. "Will," I repeated, reaching out for him, but he shrugged me off impatiently and spun around, glaring at me, teeth bared, a wolf ready to attack.

"No," he hissed, disappearing over the top and into the night.

When I returned to my bunk, he was already in his bed, his back turned towards me, but I knew that he was still awake. His body was rising and falling in a controlled way, his breathing heavier than normal; it was the movement and respiration of a man who wants to give the impression of sleep but does not have the acting skill to be entirely convincing.

And so I went to sleep myself, sure that we would talk in the morning, but when I awoke, he was already gone before Wells or Moody had even sounded the bell. Outside, after roll call, he took his place in the final march far ahead of me, in the centre of the pack, that claustrophobic spot he usually hated, surrounded by newly anointed soldiers to his left, right, fore and rear, each one providing a defence, if one were needed, against me.

There was no chance to talk to him on the train either, for he made sure to sequester himself by a window in the heart of a noisy rabble and I was some distance away, confused and agitated by this clear rejection. It was only later that night as we sailed towards Calais that I found him alone by the railings of the boat, his hands gripping the metal tightly, his head bowed as if deep in thought, and I watched from a distance, sensing his torment. I might not have approached him at all had I not been convinced that we might never get another chance to talk, for once we stepped off the boat, who knew what horrors lay ahead of us?

My footsteps on the deck alerted him to my presence and he lifted his head a little, his eyes open now, but he didn't turn around. I could tell that he knew it was me. I kept some distance between us, looked out in the direction of France, took a cigarette from my pocket and lit it before offering the half-filled case to him.

He shook his head at first, then changed his mind and took one. As he put it to his lips I handed mine across, thinking that he could take the light, but he shook his head once again, abruptly, and dug in his pockets for a match instead.

"Are you frightened?" I asked after a long silence.

"Of course I am," he said. "Aren't you?"

"Yes."

We smoked our cigarettes, grateful that we had them so we wouldn't be obliged to talk. Finally he turned to me, his expression sorrowful, apologetic, then looked down at his boots, swallowing nervously, his eyebrows and forehead knitted together in despair.

"Look, Sadler," he said. "It's no good. You know that, don't you?"

"Of course."

"It couldn't . . ." He hesitated and tried again. "We're none of us thinking straight, that's the problem. This bloody war. I wish it was all behind us. We haven't even got there yet and I'm wishing it was over."

"Do you regret it?" I asked quietly, and he turned, his expression more aggressive than before.

"Do I regret what?"

"You know what."

"I've said, haven't I? It's no good. Let's just act as if none of it ever happened. It didn't really, if you think about it. It doesn't count unless it's, you know . . . unless it's with a girl."

I laughed; a quick, involuntary snort. "Of course it counts, Will," I said, taking a step towards him. "And why are you calling me Sadler all of a sudden?"

"Well, it's your name, isn't it?"

"My name's Tristan. You're the one who always says how much you hate the way we're referred to by our surnames. You said it dehumanizes us."

"And so it does," he replied gruffly. "We're not men any more."

"Of course we are!"

"No," he said, shaking his head quickly. "I didn't mean that. I meant we can't think that we're regular men now; we're soldiers, that's all. We have a war to fight. You're Private Sadler and I'm Private Bancroft and there we are and that's an end to it."

"Back there," I said, lowering my voice and nodding in the direction from which we had come, the direction of England, "our friendship meant a lot to me. At Aldershot, I mean. I've never been good with friends and—"

"Oh, for pity's sake, Tristan," he hissed, flicking the end of his cigarette overboard now and turning on me furiously. "Don't speak to me like I'm your sweetheart, all right? It sickens me, that's all. I won't stand for it."

"Will," I said, reaching out to him again, meaning nothing by it, simply hoping to stop him marching away from me, but he slapped my arm aside in a rough fashion, rather more violently than he had intended perhaps, for as I stumbled he looked back at me with a mixture of regret and self-hatred. Then he pulled himself together and continued to walk back towards the deck, where most of our fellows were gathered.

"I'll see you over there," he said. "None of the rest of it matters."

He hesitated for a moment, though, turned around, and seeing the expression of pain and confusion on my face, relented a little. "I'm sorry, all right?" he said. "I just can't, Tristan."

Since then we have barely spoken. Neither on the march to Amiens, when he kept a clear distance between us, nor as we advanced towards Montauban-de-Picardie, which, Corporal Moody reliably informs us, is the desecrated region where I stand with my eyes to the mud-smeared glass of my box-periscope. And I have tried to forget him, I have tried to convince myself that it was just one of those things, but it's difficult to do that when my body is standing here, eight feet deep in the earth of northern France, while my heart remains by a stream in a clearing in England where I left it weeks ago.

Rich is dead. Parks and Denchley, too. I watch as their bodies are taken out of the trenches and as much as I want to turn away, I can't. They were sent on a wiring party last night, over the top, to lay thick reams of barbed wire in front of our defences before the next spate of shelling began, and were picked off one by one by German snipers.

Corporal Moody is signing the paperwork that will be needed to transport the bodies out of here and he turns around at the sound of my footsteps, surprised to see me there.

"Oh, Sadler," he says. "What do you need?"

"Nothing, sir," I reply, staring at the corpses.

"Then don't stand around all day like a bloody idiot. You're off duty?"

"Yes, sir."

"Good. The trucks will be here shortly."

"Trucks, sir?" I ask. "What trucks?"

"We ordered replacement timbers for the new trenches and to repair some of the old," he tells me. "We can take most of the sandbags away once they get here. Reinforce the streets. Go up top and help with that, Sadler."

"I was just about to get some sleep, sir," I say.

"You can sleep any time," he replies, and there isn't even a hint of sarcasm in his tone; I think he actually means it. "But the sooner we get this done the more secure we'll all be. Go on, Sadler, look lively, they'll be arriving soon."

I climb out, marching back towards the reverse line without fear of being shot; the distance is too far for the German guns to reach us here. Up ahead, I see Sergeant Clayton gesticulating wildly with three men and when I get closer I realize that one of them is Will, one Turner and the other a slightly older man, perhaps in his mid twenties, whom I've never laid eyes on before. He has a mop of red hair that's been shorn close to the scalp and his skin looks raw and aged. All four turn as they hear me approach and I try not to look at Will, not wanting to know whether his initial reaction will be one of pleasure or irritation.

"Sadler," snaps Sergeant Clayton, looking at me with contempt, "what in hell do you want?"

"Corporal Moody sent me over, sir," I tell him. "He said you might need a hand with the trucks."

"Of course we do," he says, as if it's the most obvious thing in the world. "What's keeping them, anyway?" He looks down the rough path that has been carved into the terrain and shakes his head, then glances at his watch. "I'll be at supervision," he mutters, turning away from us. "Bancroft, make sure you come and find me when they get here, all right?"

"Sir," says Will, a brief acknowledgement before he turns away and looks down the road himself. I want to talk to him but it's awkward here, with Turner and the unknown redhead standing between us.

"I'm Rigby," announces the stranger, nodding in my direction but not extending his hand.

"Sadler," I say. "Where have you sprung from, then?"

"Rigby's a feather man," says Turner but without any aggression in his tone. Indeed, he says it as if it's a perfectly natural thing.

"Really?" I say. "And yet here you are all the same."

"GHQ keep moving me around," he tells me. "I expect they're hoping I'll get picked off one of these days. A German bullet rather than a British one, to save them the cost of the gunpowder. I've done six nights of stretcher-duty in a row, if you can believe it, and I'm still alive, which I suspect is something of a record. Unless I'm dead and so are you and this is hell." He sounds remarkably cheerful about the whole thing and is, I assume, therefore, completely mad.

I look down at the ground as the three men continue talking, tipping the toe of my boot hard against the earth, separating dirt from stone, and watching as some of the dried mud flakes off into the ground. There's no aggression towards the objectors any more, at least not towards those who have agreed to serve but not to fight. There would probably be a lot less sympathy towards those on the farms or in prison except, of course, we never see any of them. The fact is that everyone who is over here is at risk. It was different back at Aldershot. There we could play politics and stir ourselves up into fits of outraged patriotism. We could make Wolf's life a bloody hell and never feel the worse for it. We could drag him from his bed in the middle of the night and cave his head in with a rock. None of us will survive here anyway, that's the general belief.

Will is walking around in circles, keeping a fine distance from me, and it's all that I can do not to run towards him, shake him by the shoulders and tell him to stop all this nonsense.

"Rigby's a Londoner, like you," says Turner, and I look up to see that he's addressing me; I get the impression that Rigby's already said this and Turner's been forced to repeat it as all three of them are staring at me now.

"Oh yes?" I reply. "Where from?"

"Brentford," he tells me. "Do you know it?"

"Yes, of course. My family lives not far from there."

"Really? Anyone I might know?"

"Sadler's Butchers," I say. "Chiswick High Street."

He looks at me in surprise. "Are you serious?" he asks, and I frown, wondering why on earth I wouldn't be. I notice Will turning around now at the unexpected question and drifting carefully back towards our company.

"Of course I am," I tell him.

"You're not Catherine Sadler's son, are you?" he asks me then, and I feel a little light-headed to hear her name. All the way over here. In a field in France. With the bodies of Rich and Parks and Denchley decomposing a few hundred feet from where I stand.

"That's right," I say carefully, trying hard to maintain my composure. "How do you know my mother?"

"Well, I don't know her, not really," he says. "No, it's my own mother who's friends with her. Alison Rigby. You must have heard your mother talk of her?"

I think about it and shrug my shoulders. It rings a bell somewhere but then my mother has a network of female friends around the town and I have never taken the slightest interest in any of them.

"Yes, I think so," I say. "I've heard the name, anyway."

"What a piece of luck! What about Margaret Hadley? You must know Margaret."

"No," I say, shaking my head. "Should I?"

"Works in Croft's Café?"

"I know Croft's. But it's been a few years. Why? Who is she?"

"She's my girl," he replies, smiling brightly. "Thought you might have run into her, that's all. You see, her mother, Mrs. Hadley, who I expect will be my mother-in-law one day, runs fund-raisers for the war effort with my mother and yours. They're thick as thieves these days, the three of them. I can't believe you don't know Margaret. Pretty girl, dark hair. Your mother thinks very highly of her, I know that for a fact."

"I haven't been back in a while," I tell him. "I don't . . . well, my family and I, we're not close."

"Oh," he says, sensing perhaps that he might have fallen into difficult territory. "I'm sorry to hear that. Gosh, Sadler, I was terribly sorry to hear about your—"

"It's quite all right," I say, unsure how best to pursue this conversation but I don't need to, because Will is beside us now, separated from me only by Turner, and I'm surprised to see him there, surprised to realize that he is taking such an interest.

"She's all right, is she, Mrs. Sadler?" asks Will, and Rigby turns and nods at him.

"Last I heard she was," he replies. "Why? Do you know her, too?"

"No," says Will, shaking his head. "Only I suppose Tristan would like to hear that his mother's doing well, that's all."

"Pink of health, as far as I know," he says, turning back to me. "Margaret, my girl, well, she writes to me fairly often. Tells me all the news from home."

"That must be nice," I say, glancing across at Will, grateful for his intervention.

"It's been bloody awful for them, of course," he continues. "Margaret's brothers were both lost early on, in the first few weeks, in fact. Their mother was a wreck over it, still is really, and she's a wonderful lady. Of course, none of them were happy when I lodged my objections to the MTB but I had to stick to my principles, that's the truth of it."

"Wasn't it hard, though?" asks Will, leaning forward, taking a keen interest now. "Making your mind up to go ahead with it after all that?"

"Damned hard," he says through gritted teeth. "Still don't know if I've done the right thing, if I'm honest. All I know is that it makes sense to me somehow. I know I'd feel as if I was letting the side down if I stayed at home or whiled the years away in prison. At least here, bearing stretchers and doing whatever is asked of me, I feel I'm of some use. Even if I'm not willing to pick up a gun."

All three of us nod but make no comment. In a larger gathering, this man might feel more awkward telling us these things, but here, in such an intimate group, it isn't so difficult. We have no intention of arguing with him about it.

"They've had a hard run of it all the same back home," he continues, turning to me. "I expect your mother has told you all about it."

"Not much," I reply.

"Yes, hundreds of boys from home have fallen. Did you know Edward Mullins?"

I nod. A boy from the year ahead of mine in school. "Yes," I say, recalling a rather plump chap with bad skin. "Yes, I remember him."

"Festubert," says Rigby. "Gassed to death. And Sebastian Carter?"

"Yes," I say.

"He was done for at Verdun," says Rigby. "And what about Alex Mortimer? Did you know him?"

I consider the name for a moment and then shake my head. "No," I say. "No, I don't think so. Are you sure he was from my neck of the woods?"

"He was a blow-in. Originally from Newcastle, I think. Moved to London about three years ago with his family. Knocked about with Peter Wallis all the time."

"Peter?" I say, looking up in surprise. "I know Peter."

"Battle of Jutland," he says, shrugging his shoulders as if this is just another casualty, nothing significant, nothing to write home about. "Went down with the *Nestor*. Mortimer, on the other hand, survived it out there but the last I heard he was holed up in an army hospital somewhere outside Sussex. Lost both his legs, the poor bastard. Got his balls blown off, too, so that's him singing soprano in the church choir ever after."

I stare at him. "Peter Wallis," I say, careful to control the tremor in my voice. "What exactly happened to him?"

"Well, I'm not sure I remember all the details," he says, scratching his chin. "Didn't the *Nestor* get hit by the German cruisers? Yes, that's it. They got the *Nomad* first, then the *Nestor*. Bang, bang, sunk, one after the other. Not everyone was killed, thankfully. Mortimer survived it, as I say. But Wallis was one of the unlucky ones. Sorry, Sadler. Was he a friend of yours, then?"

I look away and feel as if I might collapse with grief. So we are never to be reconciled. I am never to be forgiven. "Yes," I say quietly. "Yes, he was."

"At long bloody last," says Turner suddenly, pointing ahead. "Here's the trucks. Want me to go and get the old man for you, Bancroft?"

"Please," says Will, and I can feel his eyes on me now as I turn to him. "A good friend?" he asks me.

"Once," I say, unsure how to describe him, unwilling to dishonour him in death. "We grew up together. Knew each other from the crib. We were neighbours, you see. He was the only . . . well, the best friend I had, I suppose."

"Rigby," says Will, "why don't you run over and ask the driver how much timber there is? Then at least we can tell Sergeant Clayton when he gets here. We'll have a better idea of how long it will take to unload."

Rigby looks at both of us and then, sensing the awkwardness of the moment, nods and moves away. Only when he's out of sight does Will step closer to me, and by now I am trembling, wanting to run away, wanting to be anywhere but here.

"Keep it together, Tristan," he tells me quietly, placing a hand on my shoulder as his eyes search to make and hold a connection with my own, his fingers pressing tightly around my flesh, sending a current of electricity through me despite my grief; it's only the second time he's touched me since England—the first was when he helped to lift me off the floor of the deluged trench—and the only time he's spoken to me since the boat. "Keep it together, yes? For all our sakes."

I step closer to him and he pats my arm in consolation, leaving his hand there longer than is necessary.

"What did Rigby mean when he said he was sorry to hear about . . . well, he didn't finish his sentence."

"It doesn't matter," I say, moving forward in my grief to put my head on his shoulder, and he pulls me to him for a moment, his hand at the back of my head, and I am almost certain that his lips brush the top of my hair, but then Turner and Sergeant Clayton come into sight, the loud voice of the latter complaining about some new disaster, and we separate once again. I wipe the tears from my eyes and look at him but he's turned away and my thoughts return to my oldest friend, dead like so many others. I wonder why in God's name I ever went to look at Rich, Parks and Denchley's bodies when I could have been in my foxhole all this time, grabbing a few minutes' sleep, and knowing nothing about any of this, nothing about home or Chiswick High Street, my mother, my father, Peter or the whole bloody lot of them.

We advance further north, taking a long, narrow row of German trenches with minimal casualties—on our side at least—and news of our success prompts a visit from General Fielding.

Sergeant Clayton is beside himself with anxiety all morning and insists on personal inspections of all the men to ensure that we strike the right balance between the cleanliness that hygiene regulations demand and the filth that confirms we are doing our jobs. He tells Wells and Moody to follow him as he works his way down the line, one with a bucket of water, the other with a bucket of mud, and personally scrubs or soils the face of any man he thinks does not reach his exacting standards. It is the most extraordinary scene. Of course he shouts and screams as he goes, a litany of abuse or exaggerated praise, and I fear for his sanity. Williams has told me that Clayton is one of triplets and that both his brothers were killed in the opening weeks of the war by hand grenades that exploded too soon as the pins were pulled out. I don't know if this is true or not but it certainly adds to the mythology of the man.

Later, when the general arrives, more than two hours late, the sergeant cannot be found and it turns out that he's in the latrine. His timing is almost comical. Robinson is sent to look for him and it's another ten minutes before Clayton reappears, red-faced and furious, staring at every soldier he passes as if somehow it is our fault that he chose that moment to take a shit. It's difficult not to laugh but somehow we control ourselves; the punishment would be membership of an after-dark wiring party.

Unlike Clayton, General Fielding seems a pleasant enough fellow, even rational, and shows concern for the welfare of the troops under his command, an interest in our continued survival. He makes an inspection of the trenches and the foxholes, speaking to men along the way. We line up as if he's visiting royalty, which he is in a way, and he pauses at every third or fourth man with a "Treating you all right, are they?" or a "Giving it your best foot forward, I hear" but when he reaches me he merely smiles a little and nods. He talks to Henley, who's from the same neck of the woods as he is, and within a minute or two they're exchanging gossip about the glories of the First XI cricket team from some public house in Elephant & Castle. Sergeant Clayton, hovering by Fielding's right shoulder, listens on and appears rather jumpy, as if he would prefer to control everything that is said to the general.

Later that night, after General Fielding has left us for the safety of GHQ, there comes the brittle sound of sustained shelling from about thirty or forty miles to the south-west of us. I break with my orders for a moment and turn my box-periscope towards the sky, watching as the sudden bursts of electric sparks signify the dropping of bombs on the heads of German or English or French soldiers—it scarcely matters who. The sooner everyone's killed, the sooner it's all over.

There's a sense of fireworks about the planes' shelling and I think back five years ago to the only time I ever saw such a display in real life. It was June of 1911, the evening of George V's coronation. My sister, Laura, was ill at the time, laid low by a fever of some description, so my mother was forced to stay at home and tend her while my father and I walked through London towards Buckingham Palace, waiting in the heart of the crowds for the King and Queen Mary to drive past on their return from Westminster Abbey. I didn't like it there. I was still shy of my twelfth birthday and small for my age, and stuck as I was in the centre of the throng I couldn't see anything except the overcoats of men and women pushing me on either side. I found it hard to breathe and tried to explain this to my father, but he let go of my hand when he started a conversation with whoever was standing next to him. The carriages began to pass and I ran after them in my excitement at seeing the royal couple, and soon I was lost entirely and unable to find my way back.

I didn't lose heart but searched for my father and called his name, and when he finally found me an hour later, he slapped me so hard and so unexpectedly across the face that I didn't even have the wherewithal to cry. Instead, I simply stood blinking at him as a woman leaped forward, shouting at my father and punching him in the arm in retaliation, a blow he ignored as he dragged me through the gathering, all the while telling me that I was never to run off on him again or there'd be worse in store for me. Soon we were standing near the Victoria memorial and as the light grew dark and the fireworks began, and the tenderness on my cheek began to rise into a purple bruise, my father took me quite by surprise, lifting me on to his shoulders and holding me there so that I was above the crowd for once, staring down at the heads of the other revellers. The sparks, rockets and colours exploded in the sky, and I looked around at the sea of men and women that stretched as far as my eyes could see and at all the other children perched on the shoulders of their fathers, looking at each other, grinning in the ecstasy of the moment.

"Sadler!" shouts Potter, six-foot-eight-in-his-boots-and-helmet Potter, pulling at my shoulder and dragging me down deeper into the trench. "What the hell's the matter with you? Get your fucking head out of the clouds."

"Sorry," I say, returning my box-periscope to its proper position and scanning the terrain ahead. I have a panic that, having lost my concentration for a few minutes, I will be suddenly faced with a group of twenty Germans on their bellies advancing towards me like snakes and it will be too late for me to raise the alarm, but no, it's peaceful out there, even if it is hellish in the heavens, and the gulf of terrain that separates two groups of terrified young men from opposite sides of the North Sea remains empty.

"Don't let the old man catch you daydreaming," Potter says, lighting a tab and taking a deep drag before rubbing his arms against the cold. "And poke your head out there like that one more time and I promise you that Fritz will have no hesitation in blowing it off."

"They couldn't get me from this distance."

"Want to test that theory, do you?"

I let out an exasperated sigh. Potter and I are not close; his popularity expanded as his mimicry became more accomplished and now he never listens to any voice but his own. He doesn't outrank me but seems to think he does on account of having some displaced duke somewhere on his family tree while mine, as he mentions often, are in trade.

"All right, Potter," I say. "I'll keep my head down, but your infernal shouting isn't helping matters either, is it?"

I turn back to scan the horizon, sure that I can hear something out there, but all seems to be still. I have a sense of unease, though; it doesn't feel right even if it looks clean.

"I'll speak when I want to speak, Sadler," Potter snaps. "And won't be told not to by the likes of you."

"The likes of me?" I ask, turning on him, for I am in no humour for this nonsense tonight.

"Well, you're all the same, aren't you? Haven't got the sense you were born with, any of you."

"Your father's a carpenter, Potter," I say, for I heard some-where that he ran his own lumberyard in Hammersmith. "That doesn't make you Jesus Christ."

"Watch your blasphemy, Sadler," he says angrily, standing to his full height now so his own head is peeping out over the top, exactly as he told me not to. He holds his cigarette in the air as he does so, the red-flamed tip just visible above the parapet, and I gasp in horror.

"Potter, your tab—"

He turns, notices what he's doing, and I am immediately rendered blind by what feels like a bucket of hot mucus being chucked in my face. I spit and blink, retching against the side of the trench as I throw myself to the ground, wiping whatever filth this is away from my eyes, and look across to see Potter's body lying at my feet, a great hole in his head from where the bullet entered, one eye completely gone—somewhere on my person, I suspect—the other hanging uselessly from its socket.

The sound of the shelling thirty miles away appears to grow louder, and for a moment I close my eyes, imagining myself elsewhere, and then I hear the voice of the woman who remon-strated with my father for hitting me, five years ago on the night of the coronation. "The lad's done nothing wrong," she'd said. "You should learn to show a little kindness towards the boy."

The weeks pass, we advance, we stop, we entrench, we fire our Smilers and throw our grenades, and nothing ever seems to change. One day we are told that the line across Europe is pressing forward and it won't be long now, and the next we hear that things look grim and we should prepare for the worst. My body is not my own any more: the lice have offered joint tenancy to the rats and vermin, for whom I am a chew-toy. I console myself by thinking that this is their natural terrain, after all, and I am the intruder. When I wake now to find a parasite nibbling at my upper body, its nose and whiskers twitching as it considers an attack, I no longer jump about and shout but merely brush it away with the palm of my hand, the way I would a fly buzzing around my head in St James's Park. These are the new normalities and I give them little thought, but follow instead my routine of standing at my post, holding the line, going over the top when it is my turn to risk death, eating when I can, closing my eyes and trying to sleep, letting the days pass, believing that one day either it will all be over or I will.

It is weeks now since Potter's brains were spattered over my uniform and it has been washed since, of course, but the dark red and grey stains around the lapels bother me. I've asked others about them but they shake their heads and tell me there's nothing there. They're wrong, of course. The marks are most definitely there. I can smell them.

I finish a shift of more than ten hours and am dead on my feet when I make my way to the reverse. It's late and we expect to be shelled later tonight; on account of this the candles are mostly out, but I see someone sitting alone in the corner of the mess and advance towards him, eager for a little conversation before sleep. But I hesitate when, upon getting closer, I see that it's Will. He's hunched over some sheets of paper, a pen twisted in an unusual way in his fist, and for the first time I realize that he is left-handed. I stare at him, desperate to speak, but turn around, my boots sounding in the dirt as I walk away, and then he says my name quietly.

"Tristan."

"Sorry," I say, turning back but not stepping forward. "I didn't mean to disturb you."

"You're not," he says, smiling. "Off duty, then?"

"Just this minute. I'd better get some sleep, I suppose."

"Sleep is that way," he says, indicating the direction from which I have come. "What are you doing over here?"

I open my mouth to respond but can't think of an answer. I don't want to tell him that I needed company. He smiles at me again and nods at the seat next to his. "Why don't you sit down for a few minutes?" he asks me. "It's ages since we've talked."

I walk over, trying not to feel irritated by his implication that this has been a mutual decision. There's no point in being angry with him, though; he's offered me the gift of his company and there's not much more that I want from life. Perhaps there will be an end to hostilities after all.

"Writing home?" I ask, nodding at the papers set out before him.

"Trying to," he says, gathering them up and shuffling them on the table before stuffing them into his pocket. "My sister, Marian. I'm always uncertain about what to say, though, aren't you? If I tell her the truth about how things are going out here, she'll only worry. And if I lie, then there seems to be no point in writing at all. It's a bit of a puzzle, isn't it?"

"So what do you do?" I ask.

"I talk about other things. I ask questions about home. It's small talk but it fills the pages and she always replies to me. I'd go bloody mad if I didn't have her letters to look forward to."

I nod and look away. The mess tent is completely empty, which surprises me. There are almost always people here, eating, drinking tea, their heads bowed over their settings.

"You don't write home?" he asks me.

"How do you know I don't?"

"No, I only meant I've never seen you write. Your parents, surely they'd like to hear from you?"

I shake my head. "I don't think they would," I tell him. "I got thrown out, you see."

"Yes, I know. But you've never told me why."

181

"Haven't I?" I ask, and leave it at that.

He says nothing more for a few minutes, takes a sip of his tea, then looks up again as if he's just remembered something. "What about your sister?" he asks. "Laura, isn't it?"

I shake my head again and look down, closing my eyes for a moment, wanting to tell him about Laura but unable to; it would require longer than we probably have.

"You've heard about Rigby, I suppose?" he asks after a while, and I nod.

"Yes," I say. "I was sorry to hear it."

"He was a sound chap," says Will gravely. "But really, every time they send a feather man out into no-man's-land, they're just praying that he'll be picked off. They don't care about the poor bastard they've gone out to retrieve, either."

"Who was that, anyway?" I ask, turning to him. "I never heard."

"Not sure," he replies. "Tell, I think? Shields? One of those."

"Another one of ours," I say, picturing the boys in their beds in Aldershot barrack.

"Yes. Only eleven of us left now. Nine gone."

"Nine?" I ask, looking up and frowning. "I counted eight."

"You heard about Henley?"

"Yes, but I included him," I reply, my heart sinking at the idea that another one has gone; I keep a close track of the boys from the barracks, of who is still with us and who has been killed. "Yates and Potter. Tell, Shields and Parks."

"Denchley," says Will.

"Yes, Denchley, that makes six. Rich and Henley. That's eight."

"You're forgetting Wolf," says Will quietly.

"Oh yes," I say, feeling my face flush a little. "Of course. Wolf."

"Wolf makes nine."

"He does, yes," I agree. "Sorry."

"Anyway, Rigby is still out there, I think. They might send a team out later tonight to collect him, although they probably won't. What a waste of bloody time, eh? Sending a stretcher-bearer to collect a stretcher-bearer. Then he most likely gets killed and we have to send another out to retrieve him. It's an endless bloody cycle, isn't it?"

"Corporal Moody says there are eighty more men marching our way so we should have reinforcements in a day or two."

"For all the good they'll do," he says grimly. "Bloody Clayton. And I mean that literally, Tris. Bloody Sergeant James Bloody Clayton."

Tris. One single syllable of intimacy and the world is put to rights.

"It's hardly his fault," I say. "He's only following orders."

"Ha!" He snorts, shaking his head. "Don't you see how he sends the ones he doesn't like over the sandbags? Poor Rigby, I don't know how he survived as long as he did, the number of times he went out there. Clayton had it in for him from the start."

"The chaps don't like a feather man," I say half-heartedly.

"We're all feather men at heart," he replies. He extends his hand towards the candle that is burning before him. There's not much life left in it and he hovers his index finger in the air, passing it through the flame quickly, then slower, then slower again.

"Stop it, Will," I say.

"Why?" he asks, half smiling as he looks at me, his finger holding steady for longer and longer in the flame.

"You'll burn yourself," I say, but he shrugs it off.

"It doesn't matter."

"Stop it!" I insist, grabbing his hand now, pulling it away from the candle, which flickers for a moment, casting shadows on our faces as I hold his hand in mine, feeling the rough, calloused skin that we've all developed. He looks down at my hand and then looks up, his eyes meeting mine. I notice that his face, which is filthy, is caked in mud beneath both eyes. He smiles slowly and the dimples appear—neither war nor trenches can do for them—and he pulls his hand back slowly, very slowly, leaving me unsettled, confused and, above all else, aroused.

"How are yours?" he asks, nodding at my hands. I place them flat in the air and every finger is motionless, as if they have been paralysed. It's become something of a party piece for me now among the men; my record is eight minutes without a single movement. He laughs. "Still steady as a rock. I don't know how you do it."

"Nerves of steel," I say, smiling at him.

"Do you believe in heaven, Tristan?" he asks in a quiet voice, and I shake my head.

"No."

"Really?" he asks, surprised. "Why not?"

"Because it's a human invention," I tell him. "It astonishes me when people talk of heaven and hell and where they will end up when their lives are over. Nobody claims to understand why we are given life in the first place, that would be a heresy, and yet so many purport to be completely sure about what will happen after they die. It's absurd."

"Don't let my father hear you say that," he says, smiling.

"The vicar," I say, remembering now.

"He's a good man really," says Will. "I believe in heaven, you know. I'm not sure why. Perhaps I just want to. I'm not particularly religious, but you can't grow up with a father like mine and not have a little bit of it in your blood. Especially when your father is such a decent man."

"I wouldn't know about that," I say.

"Ah yes, the Butcher of Brentford."

"Chiswick."

"Brentford's close enough. And it sounds better."

I nod and rub my eyes. I'm feeling tired now; perhaps it's time to say goodnight and return to my foxhole for sleep.

"That night," says Will, and I don't turn my head or raise my eyes but sit still, as steady as my hands were a few moments before. "Before, I mean."

"At Aldershot?" I say.

"Yes." He hesitates before speaking again. "Funny thing, wasn't it?"

I breathe heavily through my nose and consider it. "We were frightened, I suppose," I tell him. "Of what was coming next, I mean. It wasn't planned."

"No," he says. "No, of course not. I mean I've always thought that I might like to get married some day. Have a few little ones, that type of thing. Don't you want that, Tristan?"

"Not really," I say.

"I do. And I know it's what my parents would want."

"And they matter all that much, do they?" I ask bitterly.

"They do to me," he says. "But that night—"

"Well, what of it?" I ask, frustrated.

"Had you ever thought of it before?" he asks, looking directly at me now, and in the candlelight I can see pools forming in his eyes and I want to reach out and hold him and tell him that if he will just be my friend again, then that is all I need; I can live without the rest if I have to.

"I had," I say quietly, nodding my head. "Yes, I think it's . . . well, it's there, I mean. In my head. I've tried to rid myself of it, of course." I hesitate and he stares at me, waiting for me to continue. "It's no good, though," I concede. "It was there before I even knew what it was."

"One hears of men," he says. "There are court cases, of course. One reads about them in the newspapers. But it all seems so . . . so vile, don't you think? The secrecy involved. The subterfuge. The whole filthy sordid nature of it."

"But that is not of their own volition," I say, choosing my pronoun carefully. "They have no choice but to live secret lives. Their liberty depends on it."

"Yes," he agrees. "Yes, I've thought of that. Still, I have always thought that it would be nice to be married, haven't you? To a decent girl from a good family. Someone who wants a happy home."

"Someone conventional," I say.

"Ah, Tristan," he sighs, moving closer to me—the third time he's used these words—and before I can reply, his mouth is already on mine, urgently, and I almost fall backwards in surprise but manage to steady myself and allow it to happen, wondering at what point I'm allowed to let myself go and simply enjoy the embrace.

"Wait," he says, pulling away and shaking his head, and I think that he is about to change his mind, but the combined look of desire and urgency in his face suggests otherwise. "Not here," he says. "Anyone could come in. Follow me."

I stand as he leaves the tent and walk after him, practically running in case I lose him in the darkness of the night, away from the trenches, moving so fast and to such a distance that a part of me worries whether this might be considered desertion; another part is curious about how easily he finds this patch of hidden ground. Has he been here before? With someone else? Milton or Sparks, perhaps? Or one of the newer boys? Finally, however, he appears to feel safe, and he turns to me and we lie down and as much as I want this, as much as I want him, I remember that night at Aldershot and the way he looked at me afterwards. The way he has barely spoken to me between then and now.

"It will be all right this time, won't it?" I ask, pulling free for a moment, and he looks down at me, a dazed expression on his face and nods quickly.

"Yes, yes," he says, then moves down my body, touching every part of me as he goes, and this time I tell myself to ignore the voice in my head that says that this is simply a few minutes of pleasure in exchange for who knows how long of antipathy on his part because it doesn't matter; at least for these few minutes I can believe that we are no longer at war.

I scramble forward and raise myself to a half-crouch, then trip and fall over a body, someone I half recognize, a new boy, and I land with a crash in the mud. Digging my heels into the soil, I raise myself up, spitting dirt and grit from my lips, ignoring him, pressing on. It's pointless to wipe the filth away; I haven't been clean in months.

Launching myself out into no-man's-land gets more terrifying every time. It's Russian roulette: with every pull of the trigger the chances of your surviving the next shot diminish.

I can hear Wells or Moody, one of them, issuing orders further down the line but it's difficult to make out exactly what he's saying; the combination of strong winds and sleeting rain render it impossible to act on anything other than pure instinct. It's madness to go over in conditions like this but the orders came through from GHQ and are not to be questioned. Unsworth, petulant as ever, queried the wisdom of the move and I thought that Clayton was going to strike him down for it but he quickly apologized and made for the ladders, apparently fearing the enemy's guns less than our sergeant's wrath. Clayton seems to have completely lost control of whatever senses were left to him since General Fielding's visit. He doesn't sleep much and looks like death. The sound of his roaring can be heard from wherever one is positioned. I wonder that Wells or Moody don't do something about him; he needs to be relieved of his command before he does something that endangers us all.

I crawl forward on my belly, holding my rifle before me, my left eye firmly closed as I look down the viewfinder for anyone advancing in my direction. I picture myself locking eyes with a boy of my own age, both of us terrified, in the instant before we shoot each other dead. Above us the sky is lousy with aircraft and the dark blue that forces its way through the grey clouds holds a certain beauty, but it's dangerous to look up so I keep moving, my heart pounding in my chest, my breath escaping my body in staccato gasps.

Will and Hobbs were sent forward last night on a recce that took so long I became convinced we would never see either of them alive again. When they finally reappeared they reported to Corporal Wells that the German trenches were located about three-quarters of a mile north of ours but they had been built in separate runs, not connected to each other as they had been elsewhere. We could take them one at a time if we were careful about it, Hobbs said. Will remained silent and when Sergeant Clayton screeched, "And what about you, Bancroft, you stupid son of a bitch? What do you say?" he simply nodded and said that he agreed with Private Hobbs.

I turned away at the sound of his voice. I feel as if I would be happy never to hear it again.

It has been three weeks since our second encounter and he has neither spoken to me nor answered when I have addressed him. When he sees me approaching—walking in his direction, I mean, not seeking him out—he turns and walks the opposite way. If he enters the mess tent when I am eating, he changes his mind and returns to his own private inferno. No, he spoke to me once, when we turned a corner, ran into each other and found ourselves alone. I opened my mouth to say something and he simply shook his head quickly, raised the palms of his hands to create a barrier between us, and said, "Just fuck off, yes?" and that was the end of that.

There's a sound of artillery fire up ahead. *Hold the line,* comes the word from man to man, nineteen or twenty of us in an uneven row as we get closer to the enemy trench. The firing stops; a dim light can be seen, probably a candle or two, then muffled voices. What's the matter with them? I wonder. Why don't they see us coming and pick us off one by one? Why don't they just fucking *end* us?

But it is in such ways that wars are won, I suppose. One side lets down its guard momentarily, another takes advantage of it. And on this particular night it is our turn to be lucky. Another minute, no more, and we are all on our feet, our rifles raised and primed, hand grenades at the ready, and now there is a constant sound of gunfire and the explosive light of our bullets shooting through the night and down into the trenches below. There's shouting from beneath us, heavy sounds of timber being thrown to one side—I picture a group of German boys forgetting their duty and playing cards to relieve the tension— and then they swarm like ants below us, raising their guns too late, for we have the advantage of the higher ground and the element of surprise, and we continue to shoot and reload, shoot and reload, shoot and reload, the line breaking a little as we work our way down to cover the length of the trench, which Will and Hobbs have promised us is five hundred yards long, no more than that.

A buzzing sound races past my ear and I feel a sting and think I have been hit, but when I press my hand to the side of my head it comes away without any blood and in my con-fusion my anger rises and I lift my Smiler and point it indiscriminately at the men beneath me, pulling the trigger again and again and again.

A sound like a balloon being burst and the man next to me falls with a cry of anguish and I can't stop to help him but it flashes through my mind that this is Turner who has just fallen, Turner who once bested me at chess three times in a row and was the most ungracious of champions.

Ten gone, ten left.

I rush forward, to the side, trip, fall over another body and I think, *Please God, let it not be Will,* but no, when I look down, unable to stop myself, I see Unsworth lying with his mouth wide open and an expression of anguish on his face, Unsworth who had the audacity to question the wisdom of the strategy. He's already dead. Two weeks ago I found myself on duty with him, alone for several hours, and although we were not particular friends he told me that his girl back home had found herself in the family way and I congratulated him and said that I hadn't even realized he was married.

"I'm not," he said, spitting on the ground.

"Ah," I replied. "Well, these things happen, I suppose."

"Are you stupid, Sadler?" he said. "I've not been home in six months. It's got nothing to do with me, has it? The dirty whore."

"Well, that's all right then, isn't it?" I said. "You don't have to worry."

"But I wanted to marry her," he cried, his face red with humiliation and pain. "I love the bones of her. And I'm not five minutes out of the country and this happens."

Eleven–nine.

Forward again and we jump down, my first time in a German trench, screaming as if our lives depend on it as we race through unfamiliar lanes, and I find myself shooting in- discriminately as I go, turning at one point and felling an older man with the butt of my rifle, hearing the sound of his nose or his jaw breaking as he collapses.

We're there for how long I don't know, and soon we have taken it. We've taken the German trench. They're all dead around us, every last one of them, and Sergeant Clayton rises like Lucifer from the bowels of hell, gathers us together and tells us that we're good men, we've done our duty as he trained us to do, that this is an important victory for Good over Evil but we have to continue tonight, we have to press on, that there's a lesser trench another mile north-west of our position and we have to make our way there immediately or lose our advantage.

"Four of you will stay here to defend this land," he says and we each silently pray that we will be selected. "Milton, Bancroft, Attling, Sadler, you four, all right? It should be all clear now but keep your wits about you. Milton, take my pistol, all right? And take the lead, too. The rest of you will have to rely on your rifles if there's any trouble. Another regiment might advance on you from the east."

"And if they do, sir," asks Milton, unwisely, "how are we to defend ourselves?"

"Use your wits, man," Clayton says. "That's what you've been trained to do. But if I come back later and find that Fritz has retaken this trench, I'll shoot every last one of you myself."

And in the madness of the moment I burst out laughing, for his threats are utterly pointless; in such an eventuality we will have long since passed from this world into the next.

"I'm going to take a look around," says Will, disappearing around a corner with his rifle hanging lazily over his shoulder.

"Couldn't believe it when the old man said we were to stay behind," says Milton, grinning at me. "What a stroke of luck, eh?"

"I don't think so," says Attling, a skinny lad with huge eyes and an amphibian aspect. "I'd have been happy to go on."

"Easy to say," replies Milton scornfully, "when you know you don't have to. What do you think, Sadler?"

"Easy to say," I agree, nodding and looking around. The wood that the Germans have used for their fire steps is better than ours. The walls are made of rough-laid concrete and I wonder whether they had an engineer among their number when they entrenched here. There are dead bodies all around us but I've lost any revulsion for corpses.

"Look at these foxholes," says Milton. "They've done all right for themselves, haven't they? It's like luxury compared to ours. Stupid bloody bastards, letting us take them like this."

"Cards," says Attling, reaching down and picking up an eight of spades and a four of diamonds; my earlier idea about what was going on down here has proved strangely correct.

"How long do you think it will take them to take the next trench?" asks Milton, turning to me, and I shrug my shoulders and pull a cigarette from my front pouch.

"I don't know," I say, lighting up. "A couple of hours, perhaps? Assuming they can take it at all."

"Don't say that, Sadler," he replies aggressively. "Of course they'll take it."

I nod and look away, wondering what's keeping Will, and just at that moment I hear the sound of boots marching through the mud and he reappears from around the corner. Only this time he is not alone.

"Bloody hell," says Milton, turning around, the delighted expression on his face suggesting that he can't quite believe what he sees. "What have you got there, then, Bancroft?"

"Found him hiding in one of the shelters around the rear," says Will, pushing forward a young boy, who looks at each one of us in turn with an expression of pure terror on his face. He's extremely skinny, this lad, with a mop of blond hair and a fringe that looks as though someone recently took a pair of scissors to it and simply cut in a horizontal line to keep it out of his eyes. He's trembling but attempting to look courageous. Under the mud and the dirt, he has a pleasant, childlike face.

"Who are you, then, Fritzy?" asks Milton, speaking as though the boy is a halfwit, his voice loud and terrifying as he walks forward, hulking over him now, making the boy lean back in fear.

"*Bitte tut mir nichts,*" he says, the words coming out fast, tripping over each other.

"What's he saying?" asks Milton, turning to look at Attling as if he might know the answer.

"I haven't got a fucking clue," says Attling irritably.

"Sod all use to me, then, aren't you?" says Milton.

"*Ich will nach Hause,*" says the boy now. "*Bitte, ich will nach Hause.*"

"Shut the fuck up," snarls Milton. "No one understands a word you're saying. He the only one, then?" he asks, addressing Will.

"I think so, yes," replies Will. "It tails off around there. There are a lot of bodies, of course. But he's the only one left alive."

"Better tie him up, I suppose," I say. "We can take him with us when we move on."

"Take him with us?" asks Milton. "Why the hell would we do that?"

"Because he's a prisoner of war," says Will. "What do you suggest we do. Let him go?"

"No, of course I don't bloody suggest we let him go," says Milton sarcastically. "But we don't need a weight like him around our necks. Let's just get rid of him now and be done with it."

"You know we can't do that," says Will sharply. "We're not murderers."

Milton laughs and looks around, indicating the number of dead Germans at our feet; there must be dozens of them. As he does so, I see the German boy looking, too, and I can tell from his eyes that he recognizes all of them, that some were his friends, that he feels lost without them. He is willing them back to life to protect him.

"*Was habt ihr getan?*" asks the boy, turning and looking at Will, who—perhaps he suspects it—will be his protector, since he was the one who discovered him.

"Be quiet," says Will, shaking his head. "Sadler, can you take a look around and find some rope?"

"We're not tying him up, Bancroft," insists Milton. "Stop playing the bloody saint, all right? It's tedious."

"It's not up to you," replies Will, raising his voice. "He's my prisoner, all right? I found him. So I'll decide what's to be done with him."

"*Mein Vater ist in London zur Schule gegangen,*" says the boy, and I look at him, willing him to stay quiet, since his appeals are only adding to the danger of the moment. "Piccadilly Circus!" he adds with fake cheer. "Trafalgar Square! Buckingham Palace!"

"Piccadilly Circus?" asks Milton, turning on him in bewilderment. "Trafalgar fucking Square? What's he talking about?" Without warning, he slaps him hard across the side of his face with the back of his hand, so hard that one of his rotten teeth—we all have rotten teeth—flies out and lands on one of the bodies.

"Jesus Christ, Milton," says Will, advancing on him. "What the hell do you think you're doing?"

"He's a German, isn't he?" asks Milton. "He's the bloody enemy. You know what our orders are. We kill the enemy."

"Not the ones we've captured, we don't," insists Will. "That's what separates us, or it's supposed to. We treat others with respect. We treat human life with—"

"Oh, of course," cries Attling, joining in now. "I forgot, your old man's a vicar, isn't he? You been drinking from the altar wine too long, then, Bancroft?"

"Shut your mouth, Attling," snaps Will, and Attling, a coward, does that very thing.

"Look, Bancroft," says Milton. "I'm not going to argue with you. But there's only one way out of this."

"Will is right," I say. "We tie him up now, we hand him over to Sergeant Clayton later and let him decide what's to be done with him after that."

"Who bloody asked you, Sadler?" asks Milton, sneering at me. "Of course you're going to say that. Bloody Bancroft says the moon is made of cheese and you say pass me the crackers, someone."

"Shut your fucking mouth, Milton," says Will, advancing on him.

"I'll not shut my fucking mouth," he replies angrily, looking at the two of us as if we are so inconsequential that he might swat us away with as little concern as when he hit the German boy.

"*Bitte, ich will nach Hause,*" repeats the boy now, his voice breaking with emotion, and all three of us turn to him as he very slowly, very carefully, moves one hand towards the top pocket of his jacket. We watch him, intrigued. The pocket is so small and thin that it's hard to imagine there could be anything in there, but a moment later he removes a small card and holds it out to us, his hand trembling as he does so. I take it first and look at it. A middle-aged couple smiling at a camera and a small blond boy, standing between them, squinting in the sunlight. It's difficult to make out the faces as the photograph is rather grainy; it's obviously been in his pocket for a long time.

"*Mutter!*" he says, pointing at the woman in the picture. "*Und Vater,*" he adds, pointing at the man. I look at them and then at him as he stares up at us beseechingly.

"Oh for fuck's sake," says Milton, grabbing him now by the shoulder and pulling him back towards him, taking a few steps back in the mud so that Will, Attling and I are standing on the opposite side of the trench to him. He pulls the pistol that Sergeant Clayton gave him from his belt and flicks it forward, checking that it's loaded.

"*Nein!*" cries the boy loudly, his voice breaking in terror. "*Nein, bitte!*"

I stare at him desperately. He can't be more than seventeen or eighteen years old. My age.

"Put that away, Milton," says Will, reaching for his rifle now, too. "I mean it. Put it away."

"Or what?" he asks. "What are you going to do, Vicar Bancroft? You going to shoot me?"

"Just put the gun down and let the boy go," he replies calmly. "For God's sake, man, just think about what you're doing. He's a child."

Milton hesitates and looks at the boy and I can see that for a moment there is a degree of compassion in his expression, as if he is remembering the person he used to be before all this started, before he became the person standing before us now. But the German boy picks this moment to lose control of his bladder and a heavy stream of piss darkens the leg of his trousers, the leg pressed closest to Milton, who looks down and shakes his head in disgust.

"Oh for fuck's sake!" he cries again, and before any of us can do or say another thing, he lifts his pistol to the boy's head, cocks the trigger—"*Mutter!*" cries the boy again—and blows his brains over the walls of the trench, splattering red across a sign that points eastwards and says FRANKFURT, 380 MEILEN.

It's the following night before Will approaches me again. I'm exhausted. I haven't slept in forty-eight hours. I must have eaten something rotten, too, because my stomach cramps are growing more severe by the hour. For once, when I see him, I don't feel any excitement or hope, just tension.

"Tristan," he says, ignoring the three other men sitting near me. "Can we talk?"

"I'm not well," I say. "I'm resting."

"It'll only take a minute."

"I said I'm resting."

He looks at me and his face grows a little kinder. "Please, Tristan," he says quietly. "It's important."

I sigh and pull myself to my feet. I wish to Christ I could resist him. "What is it?" I ask.

"Not here. Come with me, will you?"

He doesn't wait for an answer, simply turns around and walks away, which irritates me in the extreme but of course I follow him. He doesn't walk in the direction of the new reverse trench but further down the line to where a row of stretchers lie next to each other, the bodies atop them covered with the jackets of the fallen men.

Taylor is under one of those coats; twelve–eight.

"What?" I ask, when he stares back at me. "What's the matter with you?"

"I've spoken to the old man," he tells me.

"Sergeant Clayton?"

"Yes."

"About what?"

"You know bloody well about what."

197

I look at him, unsure for a moment what he means. He can't have told him what we have done together, surely; we would both be court-martialled. Unless he's trying to blame me for it, have me removed from the regiment? He sees the disbelief on my face, though, and flushes slightly, shaking his head quickly to disabuse me of the notion.

"About the German boy," he says. "About what Milton did to him."

"Oh," I say, nodding slowly. "That."

"Yes, that. It was cold-blooded murder, you know it was. You saw it."

I sigh again. I'm surprised he wants to bring this up. I thought it was all over with. "I don't know," I say finally. "Yes, I suppose it was."

"Oh come on, there's no suppose about it. That boy, that child, he was a prisoner of war. And Milton shot him dead. He wasn't a threat in any way."

"It wasn't right, Will, of course it wasn't. But these things happen. I've seen worse. You've seen worse." I offer him a brief, bitter laugh and look at the stretchers that surround us. "Look around, for pity's sake. What does one more matter?"

"You know why it matters," he insists. "I know you, Tristan. You know the difference between right and wrong, don't you?"

I set my face like stone and stare at him, feeling angry that he dares to presume to know me at all after how he has behaved towards me. "What do you want from me, Will?" I ask him eventually, running the back of my hand across my tired eyes, my voice filled with exhaustion. "Just tell me, all right?"

"I want you to back up my story," he says. "No, that's wrong. I want you to simply tell Sergeant Clayton what happened. I want you to tell him the truth."

"Why would I do that?" I ask, confused. "You just told me that you already have."

"He refuses to believe me. He says that no English soldier would behave in such a fashion. He brought Milton and Attling in and they both deny it. They agree that there was a German boy alive when they left us there but they claim that he tried to attack us and that Milton had no choice but to shoot him in self-defence."

"They say that?" I ask, both surprised and not surprised at the same time.

"I'm for going to General Fielding about it," continues Will. "But the old man says that's out of the question without anyone else to corroborate my story. I've said that you saw it all."

"Jesus Christ, Will," I hiss. "Why are you dragging me into this?"

"Because you *were* there," he cries. "My God, man, why am I even having to explain it to you? Now, will you back me up or won't you?"

I consider it for a moment and shake my head. "I don't want to get involved," I say.

"You already are involved."

"Well, just leave me out of it then, all right? You've got some bloody nerve, Will, I'll give you that. You've got some bloody nerve."

He frowns and looks at me, cocking his head a little to the side as he takes me in. "And what's that supposed to mean?" he asks.

"You know precisely what it means," I say.

"Jesus Christ, Tristan. Are you telling me that because your feelings are bent out of shape, you're going to lie to protect Milton? You're going to do this to get back at me, are you?"

"No," I say, shaking my head. "That's not what I'm saying at all. Why must you continually distort what I say? I'm saying that on the one hand I don't want to get involved in this business because there's too much going on and I can't see what one extra dead soldier matters in the great scheme of things. And on the other hand—"

"One extra—?" he begins, sounding amazed at the casual nature of my phrase, although no more appalled than I am to hear myself say it.

"And on the other hand, since you're finally deigning to speak to me, I want nothing to do with you, Will. Can you understand that? I want you to leave me alone, all right?"

Neither of us says anything for a few moments and I know that this can go one of two ways now. He can grow aggressive with me or he can repent. To my surprise, he chooses the latter.

"I'm sorry," he says. Then, louder: "I'm sorry, all right?"

"You're sorry," I repeat.

"Tristan, can't you see how difficult this is for me? Why do you always have to be so bloody dramatic about everything? Can't we just . . . you know . . . can't we just be friends when we're lonely and soldiers the rest of the time?"

" 'Friends'?" I ask, almost ready to laugh. "That's your word for it, is it?"

"For God's sake, man," he snaps, looking around nervously. "Keep your voice down. Anyone might hear."

I can tell that I have unsettled him. He looks as if he wants to say something to me in return and takes a step towards me, a hand lifting slightly towards my face, then changes his mind, and retreats as if we barely know each other.

"I want you to come with me," he says. "I want us to go to Sergeant Clayton right now where you will tell him exactly what happened with the German boy. We will report it and insist that the matter be referred to General Fielding."

"I won't do it, Will," I say unequivocally.

"You realize that if you don't, then the matter is at an end and Milton will have got away with it?"

"Yes," I say. "But I don't care."

He stares at me long and hard, swallows, and when he finally speaks again his voice is quiet and exhausted. "And that's your last word on the matter?" he asks.

"Yes," I tell him.

"Fine," he says, nodding his head in resignation. "Then you leave me with no choice."

And with that, he takes his rifle off his shoulder, opens the magazine, empties the bullets into the mud, and places the gun on the ground before him.

Then he turns around and walks away.

UNPOPULAR
OPINIONS

Norwich, 16 September 1919

MARIAN AND I had lunch in the window seat of the Murderers public house on Timber Hill. The incident with Leonard Legg had been put behind us, although the bruise on my cheek served as a reminder of what had taken place outside the café.

"Is it sore?" asked Marian, noticing me touch the bump gingerly with my finger to test for pain.

"Not really. It might be tender tomorrow."

"I am sorry," she said, trying not to smile at my discomfort.

"It wasn't your fault."

"Still, it's not on and I shall tell him so next time I see him. He's probably gone off somewhere to lick his wounds. We won't see him again today if we're lucky."

I hoped that would be the case and busied myself with my food. In the time it had taken us to walk there we had avoided controversial topics and settled for bland small talk instead. Now, as I finished my lunch, I remembered that I knew very little of what Will's sister actually did here in Norwich.

"You didn't mind meeting me on a weekday?" I asked, looking up. "You were able to take time away from your job, I mean?"

"It wasn't difficult," she replied with a shrug. "I work mostly in a part-time capacity. And it's all voluntary, anyway, so it doesn't really matter if I show up or not. Well, no, that's not right. I only mean that it doesn't affect my standard of living since I'm not being paid."

"Can I ask what you do?"

She pushed away the last of her pie with a grimace and reached for a glass of water. "I work mostly with ex-servicemen like yourself," she told me. "Men who've been through the war and are having difficulty coming to terms with their experiences."

"And that's a part-time position?" I asked, a flicker of a smile on my lips, and she laughed and looked down.

"Well, I suppose not," she admitted. "The truth is I could work with them twenty-four hours a day, seven days a week, and I still wouldn't even scrape the surface of what needs doing. I'm really only a dogsbody, of course, for the doctors, who actually know what they're doing. I suppose it's what you'd call emotionally draining. But I do what I can. It would be better if I was a professional."

"Perhaps you could train as a nurse?" I suggested.

"Perhaps I could train as a doctor," she replied, correcting me. "It's not such an outlandish idea, surely, Tristan?"

"No, of course not," I said, blushing slightly. "I only meant—"

"I'm teasing you. There's no need to feel so awkward. But if I could go back a few years I certainly would have trained for medicine. I'd have liked to become involved in a study of the mind."

"But you're still a young woman," I said. "It's not too late, surely? In London—"

"In London, of course," she said, interrupting me and throwing her hands in the air. "Why is it that everyone from London always believes it to be the centre of the universe? We do have hospitals here in Norwich, too, you know. And we have injured boys. Quite a few of them, in fact."

"Of course you do. I seem to keep putting my foot in it, don't I?"

"It's very difficult for women, Tristan," she explained, leaning forwards. "Perhaps you don't fully realize that. You're a man, after all. You have it easy."

"You believe that, do you?"

"That it's difficult for women?"

"That I have it easy."

She sighed and gave a noncommittal shrug. "Well, I don't know you, of course. I can't speak for your particular circumstances. But trust me, things are not as difficult for you as they are for us."

"The last five years might make a lie of that statement."

Now it was her turn to blush. "Yes, of course you're right," she said. "But leave the war aside for a moment and examine our situation. The way in which women are treated in this country is almost unbearable. And, by the way, don't you think that half of us would have gladly fought alongside the men in the trenches had we been allowed? I know I would have been out there like a shot."

"I sometimes think that it's wiser to leave action and discussion to men."

She stared at me; she could not have looked more surprised had I jumped on the tabletop and burst into a rendition of "Pack Up Your Troubles in Your Old Kit Bag." "I beg your pardon?" she said coldly.

"No," I said, laughing now. "Those aren't my words. They're from *Howards End*. Have you read Forster?"

"No," she replied, shaking her head. "And I shan't if that's the type of rot he comes out with. He sounds like a most objectionable sort."

"Only it's a woman who utters the line, Marian. Mrs. Wilcox says it at a lunch thrown in her honour. Rather appals the company, if I remember correctly."

"I told you I don't read modern novels, Tristan," she said. "Leave the action and discussion to men, indeed! I never heard such a thing. This Mrs. Wilton—"

"Wilcox."

"Wilton, Wilcox, whatever she calls herself. She betrays her sex with such a statement."

"Then you wouldn't like what she says next."

"Go on, then. Scandalize me."

"I won't be able to remember it exactly right. But it's something to the effect that there are strong arguments against the suffrage. She remarks that she is only too thankful not to have the vote herself."

"Extraordinary," said Marian, shaking her head. "I'm appalled, Tristan. I'm frankly appalled."

"Well, she dies shortly after this speech so her views go to the grave with her."

"What does she die of?"

"Unpopular opinions, I suppose."

"Like my brother."

I remained silent, refusing to acknowledge the remark, and she held my gaze for a long time before turning away and allowing her face to relax.

"I was involved in the suffrage movement myself, you know," she said after a while.

"I can't say I'm surprised," I replied, smiling at her. "What did you do?"

"Oh, nothing very substantial. Went on marches, posted leaflets through letter boxes, that sort of thing. I never tied myself to the railings of the Houses of Parliament or stood outside Asquith's house, crying for equality. My father would never have allowed it, for one thing. Although he believed in the movement, he believed in it very strongly. But he has a great conviction that one must retain one's dignity, too."

"Well, you got your way in the end," I said. "The vote has been granted."

"The vote has *not* been granted, Tristan," she replied tartly. "*I* don't have a vote. And I won't have until I'm thirty. And even then only if I'm a householder. Or am married to one. Or possess a university degree. But you do already and you're younger than I am. Now, does that strike you as fair?"

"Of course it doesn't," I said. "In fact, I wanted to publish a treatise on that very thing, written by a man, if you can believe it, pointing out the inequality of the suffrage. It was remarkably salient and would have a caused a stir, I'm sure of it."

"And did you publish it?"

"No," I admitted. "Mr. Pynton would have nothing to do with it. He's not modern, you see."

"Well, there we are, then. You have your rights, ours are still to be won. Astonishing how everyone is willing to go abroad to fight for the rights of foreigners while having such little concern for those of their own countrymen at home. But look, I'd better shut up about all this. If I get started on the inequalities that we simply accept without question in this country then we could be here all afternoon."

"I'm in no hurry," I said, and she appeared to appreciate the sentiment, for she smiled at me and reached across to pat my hand, leaving hers atop mine for longer than necessary.

"Is something wrong?" she asked me a moment later.

"No," I said, taking my hand away. "Why do you ask?"

"You looked suddenly upset, that's all."

I shook my head and turned to look out of the window. The truth was that the touch of her hand on mine put me so much in mind of Will that it was a little overwhelming. I could see a lot of him in her face, of course. Particularly in her expressions, the way she turned her head at times and smiled, the dimples that suddenly rose in her cheeks, but I had never realized that

209

touch could be a common thread in families, too. Or was I fooling myself? Was it simply something that I was ascribing to her out of my sheer desire to feel close to Will again and atone for my actions?

"It must be very rewarding," I said finally, facing her again.

"What must be?"

"Helping the soldiers. The ones who are suffering."

"You'd think so, wouldn't you?" she replied, considering it. "Look, this is an awful thing to say, but I feel such resentment towards so many of them. Does that make sense? When they talk of what they've been through or when they speak of loyalty in the ranks and their sense of comradeship, it makes me want to scream so loudly that sometimes I have to leave the room."

"But there *was* loyalty," I said, protesting. "Why would you think otherwise? And there was, at times, an almost over-whelming sense of comradeship. It could be quite suffocating."

"And where was comradeship when they did what they did to my brother?" she snapped, her eyes filling with the same rage that provoked her, I imagined, to march out of those nursing wards or consulting rooms, controlling her fury. "Where was comradeship when they lined him up against a wall and turned their rifles on him?"

"Don't," I begged, placing a hand across my eyes, hoping that to close them would banish the images from my mind. "Please, Marian." The sudden rush of words produced terrible memories that sliced through my body.

"I'm sorry," she said quietly, surprised perhaps by how violently I had reacted against this. "But you can't blame me for feeling that there are double standards in those supposed bands of brothers. Anyway, there's no point in pursuing this. You stood by him to the very end, I know. I can see how upset you become whenever I mention his death. Of course, you were close. Tell me, did you hit it off immediately, the two of you?"

"Yes," I said, smiling now at the memory. "Yes, we had the same sense of humour, I think. And we had the bunks next to each other, so naturally we formed an alliance."

"Poor you," she replied, smiling, too.

"Why so?"

"Because my brother was many things," she said, "but clean was not one of them. I remember before he went over there going into his room in the mornings to wake him and nearly fainting from the stench. What is it with you boys and your terrible smells?"

I laughed. "I don't know about that," I said. "There were twenty of us in the barracks so I can't imagine it was particularly sanitary. Although Left and Right, as you put it, as he put it, saw to it that we kept our beds and reports in good order. But yes, we became friends quickly."

"And how was he?" she asked. "In those early days, I mean. Did he seem glad to be there?"

"I'm not sure he thought about things in those terms," I told her, considering her question carefully. "It was more that this was simply the next part of life that had to be got through. Some of the older men, I think they found it more difficult than we did. For us, as stupid as it sounds in retrospect, it seemed like a great adventure, at least at the start."

"Yes, I've heard others use those exact words," said Marian. "Some of the men I've worked with, the younger ones, I mean, they've spoken of it as if they never really understood what lay in front of them until they got over there."

"But that's it, you see," I agreed. "We were training but it didn't feel any different from practising football or rugby at school. Perhaps we believed that if we learned everything on offer to us, then sooner or later we would be sent out on to the pitch for a jolly good skirmish and when it was all over we'd shake hands and retire to the changing rooms for slices of orange and a hot shower."

"You know better now, of course," she muttered.

"Yes."

One of the bar staff came over and took our plates away and Marian tapped the table for a moment before looking up at me. "Shall we get out of here, Tristan?" she asked. "It's terribly warm, don't you think? I feel as if I might pass out."

"Yes, of course," I said, and this time she settled our account, and when we stepped out into the street I followed as she led the way, assuming that she had an idea in her mind of where we were going next.

"How soon was it before his tendencies began to show themselves?" she asked me as we walked along.

I turned to her in surprise, uncertain what she might be getting at. "I beg your pardon?" I said.

"My brother," she replied. "I don't remember him being much of a pacifist before he went away. He used to get into the most frightful scrapes at school, if I remember correctly. But then, once he decided not to fight any more, I had the most terrifying letters from him, full of anger and disappointment at what was going on over there. He became so disillusioned with things."

"It's hard to know exactly when it began," I said, thinking about it. "The truth is that, contrary to what the newspapers and the politicians would have you believe, not every soldier out there wanted to fight at all. Each of us fell at a different point on a spectrum from pacifism to unremitting sadism. Bloodthirsty fellows, saturated in some overzealous sense of patriotism, who would still be over there even now, killing Germans, if they were given the chance. Introspective chaps who did their duty, anything that was asked of them, but didn't care for it at all. We spoke before about Wolf—"

"The murdered boy?"

"Well, yes, perhaps," I said, still, for whatever reason, unwilling to cede this point. "I mean, he certainly had an influence on Will's way of thinking."

"They were close friends, too, then?"

"No, not close," I said. "But he intrigued Will, that's for sure."

"And you, Tristan, did he intrigue you, too?"

"Wolf?"

"Yes."

"No, not in the slightest. I thought he was something of a poseur, if I'm honest. The very worst kind of feather man."

"It surprises me to hear you say that."

"Why?" I asked, looking at her with a frown.

"Well, from the way you talk, it sounds to me as if you would have agreed with everything this man Wolf said. Look, I know we've only just met but you don't strike me as a great antagonist. You didn't even go after Leonard when he hit you earlier. What kept you from being as interested in Wolf as my brother was?"

"Well, he was . . . I mean, if you'd known him . . ." I was struggling now. The truth was that I had no answer to her question. I rubbed my eyes and wondered whether I really believed what I had said about Wolf, that he was a poseur, or whether it was simply the fact that he and Will had got along so well that had made me despise him so much. Was I that unjust? Was it nothing more than jealousy on my part that made me condemn a decent and thoughtful man? "Look, we might have held similar opinions in our hearts," I said finally, "but we just rubbed each other up the wrong way, that's all. And of course he died, he was killed, whatever is the correct form of words. Which certainly affected your brother in a very deep way."

"And that's how it began?" she asked me.

"Yes. But you must remember that all that took place here in England. Things didn't really come to a head until France. There was an incident, you see, one that precipitated Will's decision to lay down his arms. Although, in retrospect, I don't think it's right to put it all down to that single event either. There were other things that happened, I'm sure of it. Some that I witnessed, many that I didn't. It was a confluence of events over a long period of time and sustained months of unremitting strain. Does that make sense?"

"A little," she replied. "Only I feel there must have been one particular thing. To make him so aggressively anti-war, I mean. You said there was an incident that precipitated things?"

"Yes, it took place just after we took one of the German trenches," I said. "It's not a pleasant story, Marian. I'm not sure you want to hear it."

"Tell me, please," she said, turning to look at me. "It might help to explain things."

"There were four of us, you see," I said, nervous about recounting it. "We captured a German boy who'd been left alive, the last of his regiment." I told her the story of Milton and Attling, and how Will had found the boy in hiding and brought him to our attention. I left nothing out, from Will's determination to bring him back to HQ as a prisoner of war to the boy pissing his pants and igniting Milton's anger.

"You'll have to excuse my language," I said as I finished the story. "Only you wanted to hear it as it happened."

She nodded and looked away, troubled by this. "Do you think he blamed himself?" she asked.

"For the boy's death?"

"For the boy's murder," she said, correcting me.

"No, I don't think it was as simple as that," I replied. "He wasn't responsible for it, after all. He didn't shoot the boy. In fact, he did everything he could to save his life. No, I think he just hated the idea of it, the sheer bloody cruelty of it, and would have liked to have blown Milton's brains out immediately afterwards, if you want the truth. He told me as much."

"But he found the boy," she insisted. "He captured him. If he hadn't done that, then it never would have happened."

"Yes, but he didn't expect that it would have the result that it did."

"I think he must have blamed himself," she said in a determined voice, irritating me a little, for she hadn't been there and didn't know what had taken place. She hadn't seen the expression on Will's face as the German boy's brains splattered across Attling's uniform. She had only my rough attempts to describe the horror of it to draw upon. "I think it must have been that," she added.

"But it wasn't, Marian," I insisted. "You can't put it down to one thing. It's too simplistic."

"Well, what about you, Tristan?" she asked, turning to me, her tone growing aggressive now. "Weren't you upset by what you'd witnessed?"

"Of course I was," I said. "I wanted to pick up a rock and hammer Milton's brains in. What right-thinking man wouldn't? That boy was terrified out of his wits. He lived his last minutes in a state of pure fear. You'd have to be a sadist to take any pleasure in that. But then we were all terrified, Marian. Every one of us. It was a war, for pity's sake."

"But you didn't feel moved to join Will?" she asked. "You didn't feel as strongly about it as he did. You kept a hold of your rifle. You continued to fight."

I hesitated and thought about it. "I suppose you're right," I admitted. "The truth is I simply didn't feel the same way about that incident as your brother did. I don't know what that says about me, whether it means that I'm a callous person, or an inhuman one, or a man incapable of compassion. Yes, I felt it was unjust and unwarranted, but also I believed it was just another one of those things that happened every day over there. The fact is that I was constantly witnessing men dying in the most horrific ways. I was on edge every day and night for fear that I was going to be picked off by a sniper. It's an awful thing to say but I allowed myself to become immune to the random acts of violence. My God, if I hadn't become immune to it I would never have been able to—" I pulled myself up short and stopped in the street, astonished by the sentence that I had been about to utter.

"You'd never have been able to what, Tristan?" she asked.

"To . . . to carry on, I suppose," I said, trying to salvage the situation, and she looked at me, narrowing her eyes, as if suspecting that that was not what I had been planning to say. But for whatever reason she decided not to press me on it. "Where are we, anyway?" I asked, looking around, for we were no longer in the town centre but making our way back towards Tombland and the cathedral, where I had begun my day. "Should we turn back now, do you think?"

"I mentioned earlier that there was something I wanted you to do for me," she said quietly. "Do you remember that?"

"Yes," I said, for she had said it as we left the café but I hadn't thought much of it at the time. "That's why I'm here, after all. If there's something I can do to make things any easier for you—"

"It's not my well-being I'm concerned with," she said. "It's my parents'."

"Your parents'?" I asked, and then, looking around, I realized what she was getting at. "You don't live near here, do you?" I asked nervously.

"The vicarage is just down there," she said, nodding towards the curve at the end of the road, where a small lane led to a cul-

216

de-sac. "It's the house where I grew up. Where Will grew up. And where my parents still live."

I stopped, feeling as if I had walked directly into a stone wall. "My daughter has arranged something," her father had said when I had inadvertently met him at Nurse Cavell's grave. "I'm sorry," I said, shaking my head. "No, I can't do that."

"But you don't know what I want you to do yet."

"You want me to visit your mother and father. To talk to them about the things that happened. I'm sorry, Marian, but no. It's out of the question."

She stared at me, her forehead wrinkling into a series of confused lines. "But why ever not?" she asked. "If you can talk to me about it, then why not them?"

"That's completely different," I said, not entirely sure why it would be. "You were Will's sister. Your mother gave birth to him. Your father . . . No, I'm sorry, Marian. I simply don't have the strength for it. Please, you'll have to take me away from here. Let me go home. Please."

Her expression softened now. She could see how difficult this was for me and she reached out and placed a hand on both my arms, just above the elbows. "Tristan," she said quietly. "You don't know what it means to me to be with someone who speaks as highly of my brother as you do. People around here"—she nodded her head up and down the street—"they don't talk of him at all, I told you that. They're ashamed of him. It would help my parents enormously if they were to meet you. If they could just hear how much you cared for Will."

"Please don't ask me to do this," I said, beseeching her, panic rising inside me as I realized that there was almost no way out of this other than to run away. "I wouldn't know what to say to them."

"Then don't say anything," she said. "You don't even have to talk about Will if you don't want to. But let them meet you and give you tea and know that there is a boy sitting in their front room who was friends with their son. They died over there, too, Tristan. Can you understand that? They were shot up against that wall just as my brother was. Think of your own family, your own father and mother. If, God forbid, something had happened to you over there, don't you think they would have wanted their minds to be set at ease? They must love you as much as my parents loved Will. Please, just for a little while. Half an hour, no longer. Say you'll come."

I looked down the street and knew that I had no choice. *Do it*, I thought. *Be strong. Get it over with. Then go home. And never tell her the truth about the end.*

But even as I thought this, my head was dizzy with what she had said about my mother and father. What if I *had* died over there, I wondered? Would they have cared? After the way things had ended between us, I rather thought not. Everything that had taken place between Peter and me, the fool I had made of myself, the mistake that cost me my home. What was it my father had said to me when I was leaving, after all?

"It would be best for all of us if the Germans shoot you dead on sight."

Peter and I were friends from the cradle. It was always just the two of us until the day when the Carters arrived, spilling their furniture and carpets on to the street as they took possession of the house next door to my father's shop and two doors along from Peter's home.

"Hello, boys," said Mr. Carter, an overweight car mechanic with hair growing in tufts from his ears and up over the collar of his too-small shirts. He was holding half a sandwich in his hand and stuffed it in his mouth as he watched us kicking a football to each other. "Pass it!" he shouted, ignoring his wife's sighs of exasperation. "Pass it over here, lads. Pass it over here!"

Peter, stopping for a moment, stared at him before using the toe of his boot to kick the ball neatly up in the air, where it landed with enviable precision in his arms.

"For pity's sake, Jack," said Mrs. Carter.

He shrugged and made his way over to his wife, who was as corpulent as he was, and it was at that moment that Sylvia appeared. That this pair could have produced such a creature was a surprise.

"Got to be adopted," muttered Peter in my ear. "There's no way she's theirs."

Before I could say anything, my own mother appeared from the upstairs flat in her Sunday best—she must have known that the new neighbours were arriving that day and been watching out for them—and began a conversation that was a mixture of welcome and curiosity. The battle for who was lucky to be living next door to whom was already beginning while Sylvia simply stared at Peter and me, as if we were a new class of beast altogether, entirely distinct from the boys she had known in her previous neighbourhood.

"I won't go short on meat, anyway," said Mrs. Carter, nodding in the direction of our front window, where a couple of rabbits were hanging from steel hooks through their necks. "Do you always keep them out like that?"

"Out like what?" asked my mother.

"Open to the world. Where anyone can see them."

My mother frowned, unsure where else a butcher's shop could display its wares, but said nothing.

"If I'm honest," continued Mrs. Carter, "I'm more of a fish person, anyway."

Bored by their talk, I tried to get Peter to return to our game, but he pulled away from me and shook his head, dropping the football again before bouncing it a dozen or more times on his knee as Sylvia watched him silently. Then, ignoring him, she turned her attention to me and her lips turned upwards slightly, the hint of a smile, before she looked away and disappeared inside her front door to explore her new home.

And that, as far as I was concerned, was the end of that.

But it wasn't long before she became a near-constant presence in our lives. Peter was smitten by her and it became obvious that to try to exclude her from our company was to ensure that I would be excluded from his, the idea of which was very painful to me.

But then the strangest thing happened. Perhaps it was because of Peter's evident devotion or my apparent indifference, but Sylvia began to direct all her attention towards me.

"Shouldn't we call for Peter?" I would ask when she knocked on my door, full of ideas for an afternoon's entertainment.

She'd shake her head quickly. "Not today, Tristan," she'd say. "He can be such a bore."

It made me furious when she insulted him like that. I would have argued his case, but I suppose I was flattered by her attentions. She had a somewhat exotic air, after all—she had not grown up in Chiswick, for one thing, and had an aunt who lived in Paris—and it was obvious that she was beautiful. Every boy wanted to be her friend; Peter was desperate to secure her favours. And yet she was choosing to bestow them on me. How could I not have been flattered?

Peter noticed this, of course, and was driven half mad with jealousy, which left me in a quandary over how to solve the problem. The fact was that the longer I encouraged her, the less possibility there was of her throwing me over for my friend.

As my sixteenth birthday approached I grew more tormented. My feelings towards Peter had clarified themselves in my head by now—I recognized them for what they were—and they were only amplified by my inability to verbalize or act upon them. I would lie in bed at night, curled into a tight ball, half encouraging the most lurid fantasies to energize the dark hours, half desperate to dismiss them out of pure fear of what they implied. As the summer approached and Peter and I took to the islands past Kew Bridge, I would encourage play-acting on the river banks in an attempt to force a physical bond between us but was always forced to pull away at the moments of the most intense thrill for fear of discovery.

And so I allowed Sylvia to kiss me under the chestnut tree and I tried to make myself believe that this was what I wanted.

"Did you like it?" she asked as she pulled away, half drunk on what she considered to be her own desirability.

"Very much," I lied.

"Do you want to do it again?"

"Perhaps later. Anyone might see us out here."

"And so what if they do? What does that matter?"

"Perhaps later," I repeated.

I could tell that this was not the answer she expected and my continued indifference, my utter refusal to be seduced by her, finally brought her campaign to a crashing end. She simply shook her head, as if dismissing me from her mind once and for all.

"I'll be getting home, then," she said, taking off across the fields without me, leaving me there alone to ponder my disgrace. I knew immediately that I had lost her favour and didn't care in the slightest. *Move away*, I thought. *Go back where you came from. Take up with your aunt in Paris if you want. Just leave us all in peace.*

And then, a day or two later, Peter came to see me in a state of great excitement.

"There's something I have to ask you, Tristan," he said, biting his lip and trying to keep his enthusiasm at bay. "You'll give me a straight answer, won't you?"

"Of course," I said.

"You and Sylvia," he said. "There's nothing between you, is there?"

I sighed and shook my head. "Of course not," I told him. "How many times do I have to tell you?"

"Well, I had to ask," he said, breaking into a smile, unable to keep his news to himself any longer. "Look, the thing is that she and I, well, we're an item now, Tristan. It's all decided."

I remember I was standing up at the time and to my left was a small table where, before going to bed at night, my mother would leave a bowl of water and a jug for me to wash with in the morning. My hand instinctively went out and rested atop that table for fear that my legs might give way beneath me.

"Is that so?" I asked, staring at him. "Well, lucky you."

I told myself that it was all something and nothing, that sooner or later he would make some idiotic comment that would annoy her and she would throw him over—but no, it was impossible, I realized, for who in their right mind would ever secure Peter's affections and then discard them? No, she would betray him with another and then he would put her aside and return to me and agree that girls were a bad lot and it would be for the best if we stuck to each other from now on.

Of course that didn't happen. Something more real, an actual romance, unfolded before my eyes and it was painful to observe. And so I made my great mistake, the one that within a few short hours would see me expelled from school, home and family and from the only life I had ever known.

It was a school day, a Thursday, and I found myself alone with Peter in our classroom, a rare occurrence now, for Sylvia was almost always by his side, or, rather, he was almost always by hers. He was telling me about the previous evening, how he and Sylvia had gone for a walk along the river together and there had been no one around to catch them so she had allowed him to place his hand on the soft cotton fabric of her blouse. To "feel her up," as he put it.

"She wouldn't let me go any further, of course," he said. "She's not that type of girl, not my Sylvia." *My Sylvia!* The words revolted me. "But she said we might go back again this weekend if it's sunny and if she can find an excuse to get away from her dragon of a mother."

He was prattling on, twenty to the dozen, unable to stop himself in the intensity of his feelings. It was obvious how much she meant to him, and without pausing to think about the consequences of my actions, overwhelmed by the power of his own longings, I reached forward, took his face in my hands and kissed him.

The embrace lasted a second or two, no more than that. He pulled away in shock, gasping, tripping over his own feet as I stood still before him. He stared at me in confusion, then repulsion, wiped his hand against his mouth and looked at it as if I might have left a stain upon his skin. Of course I knew immediately that I had made a terrible miscalculation.

"Peter," I said, shaking my head, ready to throw myself on his mercy, but it was too late: he was already running from the room, his boots pounding along the corridor outside as he sought to put as much distance between the two of us as he could.

It's an astonishing thing: we had been friends all our lives but I never laid eyes on him again after that. Not once.

I didn't return to class that afternoon. I went home, complaining to my mother of a sick stomach, and thought about packing a bag and running away before anyone could discover what I had done. I lay on my bed, the tears coming quickly, then found myself in the bathroom, vomiting hard, feeling the tension of perspiration and humiliation combining to condemn me. I was probably still there when our headmaster appeared in the shop downstairs, not to purchase a leg of lamb or a few pork chops for his tea, but to inform my father of the complaint that had been made against me, of the most hideous and vile complaint, and to instruct him that I was no longer welcome as a student in his school, that if he had his way I would be dragged before the magistrates on a charge of gross indecency.

I stayed in my room, a curious sense of calm overtaking me as if I was no longer of my own body. I inhabited a different plane for a short time, an ethereal presence watching this young, hopelessly confused lad sitting on the side of his bed, lost to the world but interested to find out what might happen next.

I was sent away from home later that day and within a few weeks most of the bruises and welts that my father had inflicted on me had begun to heal and the scars across my back and face had lost some of their sting. My left eye unsealed itself and I was able to see normally once again.

I made no protest as I was kicked out on to the street, where Mrs. Carter watched me as she watered her hydrangeas and shook her head, disappointed at where her life had brought her, for she knew in her heart that she had been born for more than this.

"Everything all right, Tristan?" she asked.

The vicarage reminded me of something from a picture postcard. It was located at the end of a small cul-de-sac with a short road leading up to it lined with trees that were just beginning to shed their leaves, and its windows were bordered by a lush spray of dark green ivy. I glanced towards the immaculate front lawn, taking in the row of ferns and bedding plants growing next to a corner rock garden. It was idyllic, a stark contrast to the small flat above the butcher's shop in which I had spent my first sixteen years.

In the hallway, an enthusiastic small dog ran towards me, an inquisitive expression on his face, and as I reached down to pat him, he balanced with his hind legs on the floor and his front legs on my knees, patiently accepting all the pats and caresses that I was willing to bestow, his tail wagging in ecstasy at the attention.

"Bobby, get down," said Marian, shooing him away. "You're not frightened of dogs, are you, Tristan? Leonard couldn't bear to have one near him."

I looked at her, laughing a little; Bobby was hardly an intimidating presence. "Not in the least," I said. "Although we never had one. What breed is he, anyway? A spaniel?"

"Yes, well, a King Charles. Getting on a bit now, of course. He's almost nine."

"Was he Will's?" I asked, surprised that I had never heard Bobby's name mentioned before. Some of the men over there had spoken about their dogs with more affection than they did their families.

"No, not really. He's Mother's, if he's anyone's. Just ignore him and he'll stop pestering you eventually. Let's go into the drawing room, I'll just let Mother know you're here."

She opened the door to a comfortable parlour and I stepped inside, Bobby in tow, and looked around. It was as comfortable as I had expected it to be, the firmness of the sofas suggesting that the room was probably kept for special visitors, of which I, apparently, was one. I glanced down to find the dog sniffing around my ankles. I caught his eye and he stopped immediately, sitting on the floor and staring up at me, seemingly uncertain whether or not he approved of me yet. He cocked his head to the left, as though deciding, then began the process of trying to climb me once again.

"Mr. Sadler," said Mrs. Bancroft, coming in a moment later, looking a little flustered. "It's so good of you to call. I'm sure you're very busy. Get down, Bobby."

"It's my pleasure," I said, smiling at her, lying, pleased that Marian followed her mother in almost immediately with a pot of tea. More tea.

"I'm afraid my husband isn't here yet," she said. "He did promise to join us but sometimes he gets distracted by parishioners on the way home. I know he's looking forward to meeting you."

"It's quite all right," I said, unsettled by the fine china cups being set out on the table with their painfully small handles. Since Will's mother had appeared, my right index finger had started to shake in that uncontrollable manner once again and I rather feared that if I attempted to drink from one of them I would end up with its contents poured down my shirt.

"I'm sure he'll be along soon, though," she muttered, throwing a quick look out of the window as if that might ensure his timely presence. She was very much her daughter's mother, an attractive woman in her early fifties, composed, well turned out, elegant. "Have you both had a nice day?" she asked eventually, as if this were nothing more than a social visit.

"Very nice, thank you," I said. "Marian showed me around the city."

"There's not much to see, I'm afraid," she replied. "I'm sure that a Londoner must find us terribly boring."

"Not at all," I said, even as Marian sighed audibly from the armchair next to mine.

"Now, why would you say that, Mother?" she asked. "Why must we continually believe that we are less than those who happen to live a hundred miles away?"

Mrs. Bancroft looked at her and then smiled at me. "You'll have to forgive my daughter," she said. "She does get in a flap sometimes over the smallest things."

"I'm not getting in a flap," she said. "It's just . . . Oh, it doesn't matter. It just irritates me, that's all. Continually putting ourselves down like this."

There was a touch of the irritated teenager about Marian now, quite different from the self-assured young woman with whom I had spent most of the day. I glanced towards the sideboard, where a series of portraits of Will, taken at various points during his life, captured my attention. In the first, he was presented as a young boy, smiling cheekily in a football outfit, then he was a little older, turning around and staring as if he had been taken by surprise. And in a third, he was walking away, his face invisible, his hands in his pockets, his head bowed low.

"Would you like to take a closer look?" asked Mrs. Bancroft, noticing my interest, and I nodded, going over to the sideboard, where I took each one down individually and examined it. It was all that I could do not to run my finger along the contours of his face.

"You don't have any pictures of him in uniform, I see."

"No," said Mrs. Bancroft. "I did have one. When he first enlisted, I mean. We were terribly proud, of course, so it seemed like the right thing to do. But I took it down. I don't want to be reminded of that part of his life, you see. It's in a drawer somewhere but . . ."

Her voice trailed off and I didn't pursue it. It had been the wrong question to ask. A moment later, however, I noticed another portrait, this one of a man who was wearing a uniform, although not the type that Will or I had ever worn. He had a placid expression on his face, as if he were resigned to whatever Fate had in store for him, and a rather extraordinary moustache.

"My father," said Mrs. Bancroft, lifting the picture off the sideboard and staring at it with a half-smile. Her other hand caressed my arm for a moment in an unconscious gesture and I felt comforted by it. "Neither Marian nor William ever knew him, of course. He fought in the first Transvaal conflict."

"Oh yes," I said, nodding. When I was growing up, the Boer War and its predecessor were the great conflict memories of my parents' generation and they were often talked about still. Everyone had a grandfather or an uncle who had fought at Ladysmith or Mafeking, laid down their lives on the sloping hills of Drakensberg or come to a horrible end in the polluted rivers of the Modder. People spoke of the Boers, a race who had simply chosen not to be overrun by invaders from a different hemisphere, as the last great enemy of the British people and their war as our last great conflict. A bitter irony, I suppose.

"I barely knew my father," said Mrs. Bancroft quietly. "He was only twenty-three when he was killed, you see, and I was only three. My mother and he married young. I don't have many memories of him, but those that I have are happy ones."

"These bloody wars have a habit of taking all the men in our family," remarked Marian from her armchair.

"Marian!" cried Mrs. Bancroft, looking quickly back at me as if I might have taken offence.

"Well, it's true, isn't it?" she said. "And not just the men, either. My grandmother—my mother's mother, that is—she was killed in the Transvaal, too."

I raised an eyebrow, sure that she could not possibly have this right.

"Don't be so ridiculous, Marian," said Mrs. Bancroft, putting the picture down again and looking at me with an unsettled expression. "My daughter is liberated, Mr. Sadler, and I'm not sure that's entirely a good thing. I myself have never had any interest in being liberated." I was reminded again of Mrs. Wilcox, disgracing herself over a Schlegel lunch.

"All right, she wasn't killed in the Transvaal exactly," admitted Marian, relenting a little. "But she didn't survive my grandfather's death."

"Marian, please!" snapped Mrs. Bancroft.

"Well, why shouldn't he know? We've nothing to hide. My grandmother, Tristan, found herself unable to live without my grandfather and took her own life."

I looked away, certain that I did not want to be included in this confidence.

"It's not something that we talk about," said Mrs. Bancroft, her voice losing its anger now and becoming more sorrowful. "She was very young, my mother, when he was killed. And she was only nineteen when I was born. I imagine she simply couldn't handle the responsibility and the grief. I've never blamed her for it, of course. I've tried to understand."

"But there's no reason why you should blame her, Mrs. Bancroft," I said. "When these things happen, they're tragedies. No one does something like that because they want to; they do it because they are ill."

"Yes, I expect you're right," she said, sitting down again. "Only it was a great source of shame for our family at the time, a terrible irony after my father brought us such pride with his actions in the war."

"Curious, isn't it, Tristan," asked Marian, "how we consider the death of a soldier to be a source of pride rather than a source of national shame? It's not as if we had any business being in the Transvaal in the first place."

"My father did his duty, that's all," said Mrs. Bancroft.

"Yes, and a fat lot of good it did him, too," remarked Marian, standing up and walking towards the window, staring out at the rows of dahlias and chrysanthemums that her mother, no doubt, had planted in neat rows along the edges.

I sat down again, wishing I had never been brought here. It was as if I had walked onstage into the middle of a dramatic play, where the other characters are already engaged in a battle that has been going on for some years but which only now, upon my arrival, is allowed to reach a climax.

I heard the front door open and close; the dog sat up immediately, alert to a familiar presence, and I had a sense that whoever was standing outside the drawing room was hesitating before opening the door.

"Mr. Sadler," said Reverend Bancroft, entering the room a moment later, taking my hand in both of his and holding it there before him while looking me directly in the eyes. "We're so glad you were able to visit us."

"I can't stay long, I'm afraid," I replied, aware how rude this sounded as my first response to him but not caring very much. I felt that I had spent enough time in Norwich by now and was anxious to return to the station and London and the solitude of home.

"Yes, I'm sorry I was delayed," he said, glancing at his watch. "I had intended to be here before four but I got caught up with a parish matter and time just escaped me. I trust my wife and daughter have been keeping you entertained in the meantime?"

"He wasn't here for entertainment, Father," said Marian, standing by the doorway with her arms folded before her. "And I very much doubt whether he has received any."

"I was just about to ask Mr. Sadler about the letters," said Mrs. Bancroft, and we all turned to look at her. "My daughter said that you were in possession of some letters," she added, and I nodded quickly, grateful for the diversion.

"Yes," I said, reaching into my pocket. "I should have given them to you earlier, Marian. It was the point of my visit, after all."

I placed the packet on the table before me. Marian stared at it, a collection of envelopes tied up in a red ribbon, her neat handwriting visible on the outside of the uppermost one, but did not step forward yet. Her mother didn't pick them up, either; she merely sat and stared at them as if they were bombs that might go off if she handled them too roughly.

"Will you excuse me a moment?" said Marian finally, rushing from the room like a whirlwind, keeping her back to me the entire time, Bobby charging after her in pursuit of adventure. Her parents watched her as she left and bore stoic, mournful expressions.

"Our daughter might come across as a little brittle at times, Mr. Sadler," said Mrs. Bancroft, turning back to look at me with a regretful expression. "Particularly when she's with me. But she loved her brother very much. They were always very close. His death has damaged her badly."

"She doesn't come across as brittle at all," I replied. "I've only known her a few hours, of course. But still, I think I can understand her pain and her grief."

"It's been very difficult for her," she continued. "Of course it's been difficult for all of us, but we each handle adversity in our own way, don't we? My daughter has a very forceful way of expressing her grief while I prefer not to allow my emotions to be on display. I don't know if that's a good thing or a bad thing, it's simply the way that I was brought up. My grandfather took me in, you see," she explained. "After my parents' deaths. He was a widower, the only relative I had left. But he was not emotional, no one could accuse him of that. And I suppose he brought me up in the same way. My husband, on the other hand, is much more likely to wear his heart on his sleeve. I rather admire him for that, Mr. Sadler. I've tried to learn from him over the years but it's no good. I think perhaps the adults we become are formed in childhood and there's no way around it. Would you agree?"

"Perhaps," I said. "Although we can fight against it, can't we? We can try to change."

"And what are you fighting against, Mr. Sadler?" asked her husband, removing his spectacles and wiping the lenses with his handkerchief.

I looked away with a sigh. "The truth, sir, is that I am tired of fighting and would prefer never to have to do so again."

"But you won't have to," said Mrs. Bancroft, frowning. "The war is over now at last."

"There'll be another one along in a moment, I expect," I said, smiling at her. "There usually is."

She made no reply to this, but reached forward and took my hand in hers. "Our son was very keen to enlist," she told me. "Perhaps it was wrong of me to keep his grandfather's portrait on display all these years."

"It wasn't, Julia," said Reverend Bancroft, shaking his head. "You've always been proud of your father's sacrifice."

"Yes, I know, but William was always fascinated by it, that's the thing. Asking questions, wanting to know more about him. I told him all I could, of course, but the truth is that I knew very little. I still know very little. But I worry sometimes that it was my fault, William signing up like that. He might have waited, you see. Until they called him."

"It would only have been a matter of time, anyway," I told her. "It wouldn't have made any difference."

"But he would have been in a different regiment," she said. "Been sent over there on a different day. The course of his life would have been altered. He might still be alive," she insisted. "Like you."

I took my hand back and looked away. There was an accusation in those last two words, one that struck me to my core.

"You knew our son well, then, Mr. Sadler?" asked Reverend Bancroft after a moment.

"That's right, sir," I said.

"You were friends with him?"

"Good friends," I replied. "We trained together at Aldershot and—"

"Yes, yes," he said quickly, waving this aside. "Do you have any children, Mr. Sadler?"

"No," I said, shaking my head, a little surprised by the question. "No, I'm not married."

"Would you like some?" he asked me. "One day, I mean."

"I don't know," I said, shrugging my shoulders, unable to meet his eye. "I haven't given it a lot of thought."

"A man should have children," he insisted. "We are put here to propagate the species."

"There are plenty of men who do their share of that," I said light-heartedly. "They make up for the rest of us shirkers."

Reverend Bancroft frowned at this; I could tell that he wasn't pleased by the flippancy of the remark. "Is that what you are, Mr. Sadler?" he asked me. "Are you a shirker?"

"No, I don't believe so. I did my bit."

"Of course you did," he said, nodding. "And here you are, safe at home again."

"Just because I wasn't killed does not mean that I didn't fight," I said, annoyed by his tone. "We all fought. We put ourselves in terrible places. Some of the things we saw were horrific. We'll never forget them. And as for the things we did, well, I need hardly tell you."

"But you must tell me," he said, leaning forward. "Do you know where I was this afternoon? Do you know why I was late?" I shook my head. "I thought you might have overheard us. This morning, I mean. At the cathedral."

I lowered my head and felt my cheeks redden a little. "You recognized me, then. I wondered if you had."

"Yes, immediately," he replied. "In fact, this morning, when you ran off, I had a very clear idea of exactly who you were. My daughter had already told me of your impending visit. So you were very much to the fore of my mind. And you're the same age as William. Not to mention that I was sure you had played a part in the war."

"It's that obvious, is it?"

"It's as if you aren't entirely convinced that the world you've returned to is the one you left behind. I see it on the faces of the boys in the parish, the ones who came home, the ones Marian works with. I act as a sort of counsellor to some of them, you see. Not just on spiritual matters, either. They come to me looking for some kind of peace that I fear I am ill equipped to provide. Sometimes I think that many of them half believe that they died over there and that this is all some kind of strange dream. Or purgatory. Or even hell. Does that make sense, Mr. Sadler?"

"A little," I said.

"I've never fought, of course," he continued. "I know nothing of that life. I've lived a very peaceful existence, in the Church and here with my family. We're accustomed to the older generation looking down on the younger and telling them that they know nothing of the world, but things are rather out of kilter now, aren't they? It is your generation who understands the inhumanity of man, not ours. It's boys like you who have to live with what you have seen and what you have done. You've become the generation of response. While your elders can only look in your direction and wonder."

"This afternoon," I said, sitting down again, "you wanted to tell me where you were."

"With a group of parishioners," he said, smiling bitterly. "There's a plan to erect a monument, you see. To all the boys from Norwich who died in the war. Some type of large stone sculpture with the names of every boy who laid down his life. It's happening in most of the cities around England, you must have heard of it."

"Of course," I said.

"And most of the time, it's organized through the Church. The parish council looks after the fund-raising drives. We commission a sculptor to come up with a design, one is chosen, the names of all the fallen are collected and soon, in a workshop somewhere, a man sits down on a three-legged stool beside a mass of rock and, with hammer and chisel in hand, cuts lines into the stone to commemorate the boys we lost. Today was the day when the final decisions on this were being made. And I, of course, as vicar, was required to be there."

"Ah," I said, nodding quietly, already able to see where he was going with this.

"Can you understand what that is like, Mr. Sadler?" he asked me, tears filling his eyes.

"Of course not," I said.

"To be told that your own son, who has given his life for his country, cannot be represented on the stone because of his cowardice, because of his lack of patriotism, because of his betrayal? To hear those words spoken of a boy whom you have brought up, whom you have carried on your shoulders at football matches, whom you have fed and washed and educated? It's monstrous, Mr. Sadler, that's what it is. Monstrous."

"I'm very sorry," I said, aware as the words left my mouth how impotent they were.

"And what does sorry do? Does it bring my boy back to me? A name on a stone, it means nothing really, but still it means *something*. Does that make any sense?"

"Yes, of course. It must be difficult to bear."

"We have our faith to sustain us," said Mrs. Bancroft, and her husband threw her a sharp look, which suggested to me that he wasn't entirely convinced that that was the case.

"I don't know much about that, I'm afraid," I said.

"You're not a religious man, Mr. Sadler?" asked the vicar.

"No. Not really."

"Since the war, I find that the young people are either moving closer to God or turning away from him entirely," he replied, shaking his head. "It's confusing to me. Knowing how to guide them, I mean. I fear I'm becoming rather out of touch with age."

"Is it difficult being a priest?" I asked.

"Probably no more difficult than it is holding any other job," he said. "There are days when one feels one is doing good. And others when one feels that one is of no use to anyone whatsoever."

"And do you believe in forgiveness?" I asked.

"I believe in seeking it, yes," he said. "And I believe in offering it. Why, Mr. Sadler, what do you need to be forgiven for?"

I shook my head and looked away. I thought that I could stay in this house for the rest of my life and never be able to look this man and his wife directly in the eye.

"I don't really know why Marian brought you here," he continued, after it became clear that I was not going to reply. "Do you?"

"I didn't even know that she was planning on it," I said. "Not until we were already on the street outside. I presume she thought that it would be a good idea."

"But for whom? Oh, please don't misunderstand me, Mr. Sadler, I don't mean to make you feel unwelcome, but there isn't anything you can do to bring our son back to us, is there? If anything, you're just a further reminder of what took place in France."

I nodded, acknowledging his truth.

"But there are those people, you see, and our daughter is one of them, who must root around and root around, trying to discover the reason why things have happened. I'm not one of them and I don't believe my wife is either. Knowing the whys and the wherefores doesn't change a blasted thing, after all.

Perhaps we're just looking for someone to blame. At least . . ." He hesitated for a moment now and smiled at me. "I'm pleased that you survived things, Mr. Sadler," he said. "Truly I am. You seem like a fine young man. Your parents must have been pleased to have you back safely."

"Well, I don't know about that," I told him with a shrug, a throwaway remark that shocked his wife more than anything I had said so far.

"What do you mean?" she asked, looking up.

"Only that we're not close," I said, sorry now that it had come up at all. "It doesn't matter. It's not really something that I—"

"But that's ridiculous, Mr. Sadler," she announced, standing up and looking at me furiously, her hands on her hips in an attitude of despair.

"Well, it isn't my choice," I explained.

"But they know that you're well? That you're alive?"

"I think so," I said. "I've written, of course. But I never receive any reply."

She stared at me with an expression of outright ferocity on her face. "I fail to understand the world sometimes, Mr. Sadler," she said, her voice catching a little. "Your parents have a son who is alive but whom they do not see. I have a son whom I wish to see but who is dead. What kind of people are they, anyway? Are they monsters?"

I spent my final week before Aldershot debating whether or not I should see my family before I left. It seemed perfectly plausible that I would lose my life over there, and although we had not spoken in more than eighteen months, I felt there might be the possibility of a reconciliation in the face of such an uncertain future. And so I decided to pay a visit the afternoon before leaving for the training camp, alighting at Kew

Bridge Station on a chilly Wednesday and making my way along the road towards Chiswick High Street.

The streets blended together with a mixture of familiarity and distance; it was as if I had dreamed this place up but was being allowed to visit once again in a state of consciousness. I felt strangely calm and put this down to the fact that I had, for the most part, been happy here as a child. It was true that my father had often been violent with me but there was nothing unusual in that; after all, he was no more violent than the fathers of most of my friends. And my mother had always been a kind, if distant, presence in my life. I felt that I would like to see her again. I put her refusal to see me or respond to my letters down to my father's insistence that she cut off all communication with me entirely.

As I got closer to home, though, I found my nerves beginning to overwhelm me. The run of shops, with my father's butcher's at the end, came into sight. Next to it were the houses where Sylvia's and Peter's families lived. The flat where I had grown up was easy to spot and I hesitated now, taking refuge on a bench for a few minutes, pulling a cigarette from my pocket for Dutch courage.

I glanced at my watch, wondering whether or not I should abandon the whole thing as a bad lot and take the next bus back to my quiet flat in Highgate for a final, solitary dinner and a good night's sleep before the next day's train took me to my new life as a soldier, and had all but determined to do so, had even stood up and turned around on the street to head back towards Kew, when I collided with a person walking towards me who dropped a basket of shopping on the ground in surprise.

"I'm so sorry," I said, reaching down and gathering the apples, bottle of milk and carton of eggs that had fallen but remained mercifully intact. "I wasn't looking where I was going." I glanced up then, aware that the person I was talking to had not responded, and was taken aback to see who was standing there. "Sylvia," I said.

"Tristan?" she replied, staring at me. "It's never you."

I shrugged my shoulders, indicating that yes, it was, and she looked away for a moment, placing the basket on the bench beside us, and biting her lip. Her cheeks flushed a little, perhaps in embarrassment, perhaps in confusion. I felt no embarrassment at all, despite what she knew about me. "It's good to see you," I said finally.

"And you," she said, extending an awkward hand now, which I shook. "You've hardly changed at all."

"I hope that's not true," I said. "It's been a year and a half."

"Has it really?" she asked.

"Yes," I said, examining her now, noticing differences. She was still a beauty, of course, even more beautiful now at seventeen than she had been at fifteen, but that was to be expected. Her hair, a bright shade of sunshine blonde, lay loose around her shoulders. She was slim and dressed to compliment her figure. A slash of red lipstick gave her an exotic air and I wondered where she had found it; the fellows I worked with at the construction firm were forever on the search for lipstick or stockings for their sweethearts; luxuries like this were hard to come by.

"Well, this is awkward, isn't it?" she said after a pause, and I rather admired her for her refusal to pretend otherwise.

"Yes," I said. "It is a bit."

"Don't you ever want the ground to open up and swallow you whole?"

"Sometimes," I admitted. "Not as often as I once did."

She considered this, perhaps wondering exactly what I meant by it; I wasn't sure myself. "How are you, anyway?" she asked. "You look well."

"I'm all right," I said. "And you?"

"I work in a factory, if you can believe it," she told me, pulling a face. "Did you ever expect me to end up as a factory girl?"

"You haven't ended up as anything yet. We're only seventeen."

"It's hateful but I feel I must do something."

"Yes," I said, nodding.

"And you?" she asked carefully. "You're not yet—?"

"Tomorrow morning," I told her. "First thing. Aldershot."

"Oh, I know a few chaps who went there. They said it was all right, really."

"I shall find out soon enough," I said, wondering how long this would go on for. It felt false and uneasy and I suspected that both of us would have quite liked to lower our guard and speak to each other without artifice.

"You're back to see your family, I presume?" she asked.

"Yes," I said. "I thought it would be good to see them before I went off. It might be the last time, after all."

"Don't say that, Tristan," she said, reaching a hand out and touching my arm. "It's bad luck. You don't want to jinx yourself."

"Sorry," I said. "I only meant that it felt right to come back. It's been . . . well, I've already said how long it's been."

She looked embarrassed. "Shall we sit for a moment?" she asked, glancing towards the bench, and I shrugged as we sat down together. "I wanted to write to you," she said. "Well, not at first, of course. But later. When I realized what we had done to you."

"It was hardly your fault," I said.

"No, but I had a hand in it. Do you remember that time we kissed? Under the chestnut tree?"

"As if it was yesterday," I replied, smiling a little, almost laughing. "We were just children."

"Maybe," she said, smiling back. "But I fancied you something rotten."

"Really?"

"Oh yes. You were all I could think about for the longest time."

I thought about it. It seemed so strange to hear her say this to me. "It always surprised me that it wasn't Peter you liked the best," I said.

"I don't know why," she said. "I mean, he was lovely, I was very fond of him, but I only went with him because you rejected me. It all seems so silly now, doesn't it? So trivial. The way we behaved. But it felt so important back then. That's what growing up is like, I suppose."

"Yes," I said, still astonished that she could possibly have liked me more than Peter, astonished that anyone could. "And Peter?" I asked tentatively. "Is he still—?"

"Oh no," she said. "He left about eight months ago, I think. He's training for the navy, didn't you hear? I see his mother sometimes, though, and she tells me he's doing well. No, there are only girls around here now, Tristan. It's frightful. You'd have your pick of us if you stuck around."

As soon as the words were out of her mouth I could see that she regretted them, for she went scarlet and looked away, uncertain how to recover the moment. I felt embarrassed, too, and couldn't look at her.

"I have to ask," she said eventually. "All that business. With you and Peter, I mean. It wasn't what they said, was it?"

"Well, that depends," I replied. "What did they say?"

"Peter . . . well, he told me something. Something that you did. I said he must have got it wrong, that it couldn't be, but he insisted that—"

"He was telling the truth," I said quietly.

"Oh," she said. "I see."

I was unsure how to explain it to her, not even sure that I wanted to or needed to, but I had not spoken of this for so long that I felt a sudden urge to and turned to her. "He had nothing to do with it, you see," I explained. "He never would have felt the same. But it had always been there. In my mind, that is. There's always been something wrong with me on that score."

"Something wrong with you?" she asked. "Is that how you see it?"

"Of course," I replied, as if it was the most obvious thing in the world. "Don't you?"

"I don't know," she said. "I'm not sure it matters so much. I fell in love myself recently with someone entirely unsuitable. He threw me over the minute he got what he wanted. Said I wasn't potential wife material, whatever that might be."

I laughed a little. "Sorry," I said. "So you and Peter . . . ?"

"Oh no," she said, shaking her head. "No, that barely outlasted you. He was a poor substitute, that's the truth of it. And once you were gone I couldn't see the point of keeping up with him. I was only doing it to drive you insane with jealousy, for all the good it did me."

"That's astonishing to me, Sylvia," I said in disbelief. "To hear you say that."

"Only because you can't understand someone not thinking that Peter was the bee's knees. He was rather selfish, really, when you think of it. And mean. You were such close friends and the moment he realized how you . . . how you really felt, he dropped you like a hot potato. And after all those years, too. Vile."

I shrugged. My feelings for Peter hadn't entirely evaporated, although I could at least now recognize them for what they really were, an adolescent crush. Nevertheless I hated thinking of him in this context. I liked to think that he was still my friend, somewhere in the world, and that if we met again, which I hoped we would some day, all past enmities would be forgotten. Of course we never did.

"Anyway," she said, "he took it badly. Chased me around for months until my father had to put a stop to it. Then he wouldn't speak to me again. I saw him just before he went, though, and we had a decent chat but it wasn't the same. The problem was that for the three of us, nothing ever settled right, did it? He loved me but I didn't feel the same. I loved you and you weren't interested. And you . . ."

"Yes, me," I said, turning my face away from her.

"Is there anyone now?" she asked, and I looked back, surprised by how daring she was. I couldn't imagine anyone else asking such a scandalous question.

"No," I said quickly. "No, of course not."

"Why 'of course not'?"

"Sylvia, please," I said irritably. "How could there be? I shall stay alone."

"But you don't know that, Tristan," she said. "And you must never say it. Someone could come along and—"

I jumped up and blew warm air into my clenched fists, which had grown cold as we sat there. I was weary of this conversation. I didn't want to be patronized by her.

"I should be getting along," I said.

"Yes, of course," she replied, standing up now, too. "I hope I haven't upset you."

"No. Only I have to get to the shop and then back home again later. I still have a lot to do before I leave tomorrow."

"All right," she said, leaning forward and kissing me lightly on the cheek. "Take care of yourself, Tristan," she added. "And survive, do you hear me?"

I smiled and nodded. I liked the way that she had phrased it. I turned my head and glanced down the street towards my father's shop, seeing an old, familiar customer emerging with a bag of meat under his arm.

"Right," I said. "Here goes nothing. I hope at least one of the three of them will be happy to see me." I noticed a cloud fall across her face as I said this, her expression growing confused again for a moment and then full of understanding, even horror, and I stared at her, the smile fading from my face. "What?" I asked. "What's the matter?"

"'The three of them'?" she said, echoing my phrase. "Oh, Tristan," she said as she pulled me most unexpectedly towards her once again, triggering a memory of that afternoon under the chestnut tree when she had kissed me and I had pretended to love her.

There were no customers in the shop and no one behind the counter. By rights, my stomach should have been turning somersaults by now but instead I felt nothing. A sense of release, perhaps, if that even. I recognized the smells immediately, the sour mix of meat and blood and disinfectant, which took me right back to my childhood. Closing my eyes for a moment, I could see myself as a boy running down the back stairs into the cold-room on Monday mornings, when Mr. Gardner would arrive with the carcasses that my father would butcher through the week and sell to his customers, never wasting a cut, never mean with the weights. It was from that same cold-room that he emerged while I was remembering this, carrying a tray of pork chops, closing the door behind him with his shoulder.

On a countertop, far away from the reach of customers, I could see his fine range of boning knives and slicers, but I turned away from them in case they should give me ideas.

"With you in a minute, sir," he said, barely glancing in my direction as he pulled the glass cover off the display case before him and settled the tray in an empty spot. He hesitated for the briefest of moments, the tray hovering in the air, and then he closed the cover once again, looked up and steadied himself, swallowing, and to his credit appeared to be at a loss for words.

We looked at each other. I examined his face for signs of remorse, for anything that might indicate shame, and for a second I thought I could see it there. But just as quickly it vanished, and was replaced by a cold stare, a look of disgust, and an attitude of repugnance that a creature like me could have been spawned from his body.

"I leave tomorrow," I told him. "I have nine weeks of training at Aldershot. And then I go. I thought you'd want to know."

"I assumed you were already over there," he replied, picking up a bloodstained cloth from the counter and rubbing his hands in it. "Or did you not want to go?"

"I wasn't eligible for a long time on account of my age," I said, recognizing the slight.

"How old are you now, then?"

"Seventeen," I said. "I lied. Told them I was eighteen and they let me in."

He considered this and nodded. "Well, I'm not sure why you thought I'd be interested but I suppose it's worth knowing," he said. "So unless you're after a bit of mince or—"

"Why didn't you tell me?" I asked him, trying hard to keep my voice steady.

"Tell you?" he said, frowning. "Tell you what?"

"She was my sister, for pity's sake."

He had the decency to look away, to stare down at the joints of meat that were spread out before him and not answer me immediately. I saw him swallow again, consider an answer, turn to look at me with just a hint of regret on his face and then, perhaps sensing it himself, run a bloodied hand across his eyes and cheeks and shake his head.

"It had nothing to do with you," he said. "It was family business."

245

"She was my sister," I repeated, feeling the tears start to form now.

"It was family business."

We said nothing for a few moments. A woman slowed down as she approached the front window, examined some of the meat on display, then looked up, appeared to change her mind and carried on walking.

"How did you hear, anyway?" he asked me finally.

"I met Sylvia," I said. "Just today. After I got off the bus. It was a coincidence that we should run into each other. She told me."

"Sylvia," he said, snorting in disgust. "That one's no better than she ought to be. She was fast back then and she's fast now."

"You could have written to me," I said, refusing to speak about anyone but Laura. "You could have found me and told me. How long was she ill?"

"A few months."

"Was she in pain?"

"Yes. A great deal."

"Jesus Christ," I said, bending over slightly, an aching pain at the pit of my stomach.

"For God's sake, Tristan," he said, coming around from behind the counter now and standing before me; it was all that I could do not to take a step back from him in disgust. "You couldn't have done anything to help her. It was just one of those things. It spread through her body like wildfire."

"I would have wanted to see her," I said. "I'm her brother."

"Not really," he said in a casual tone. "You were once, I suppose. I'll give you that. But that was all a long time ago. I think she'd pretty much forgotten you by the end."

To my surprise, he put an arm around my shoulder then and I thought he was going to embrace me, but instead he turned me around and walked with me slowly towards the door.

246

"The truth is, Tristan," he said as he guided me back out on to the street, "you weren't her brother any more than you are my son. This isn't your family. You have no business here, not any more. It would be best for all of us if the Germans shoot you dead on sight."

He closed the door in my face then and turned away. I watched him as he hesitated for a moment in front of the display case, examining the various cuts of meat, counting them off in his head, before disappearing back into the cold room and out of my life forever.

"Perhaps I was wrong," said Marian as we made our way back through the city, walking in the direction of the railway station. "I rather ambushed you, didn't I? Bringing you in to meet my parents like that."

"It's all right," I said, lighting a much-needed cigarette and letting the smoke fill my lungs and calm my nerves. The only thing that might have matched it for pure pleasure was a pint of cold ale. "They're decent people."

"Yes, I suppose they are. We drive each other mad on a daily basis but I suppose that's par for the course. Given the choice, I'd like a home of my own. Then they could visit and we could be friends and there wouldn't be any more of these daily confrontations."

"I'm sure you'll marry some day," I said.

"A home of my own," she insisted. "Not someone else's. Like you have."

"Mine is just a small flat," I told her. "It's comfortable but, believe me, it's nothing like you have here."

"Still, it's all yours, isn't it? You answer to no one."

"Look, you really don't have to walk with me all the way back," I told her. "I don't mean to sound ungrateful but I'm sure I can find my way."

"It's all right," she said, shaking her head. "I don't mind. We've come this far together, after all."

I nodded. The evening was starting to close in, the sky was growing darker and the air colder. I buttoned my overcoat and took another drag of my cigarette.

"What will you do now?" she asked me after a few minutes, and I turned to her, frowning.

"I'll go back to London, of course," I said.

"No, I don't mean that. I mean tomorrow and the day after that and the day after that. What are your plans for the future, now that the war is behind us?"

I thought about it. "Tomorrow morning I shall be back at my desk at the Whisby Press," I said. "There will be manuscripts to read, rejection letters to send out, books to edit. We're doing a presentation of future titles to some booksellers next week so I have to prepare a few notes on each one."

"You enjoy working there, do you?" she asked.

"Yes," I said enthusiastically. "I like being around books."

"So you think you'll stay where you are? Seek promotion? Become a publisher yourself?"

I hesitated. "I might like to try my hand at writing," I told her; it was the first time I had admitted this aloud to anyone. "It's something I've dabbled in a little over the last few years. I feel I might like to take it more seriously now."

"There aren't enough novels in the world already?" she asked, teasing me a little, and I laughed.

"A few more won't hurt anyone," I said. "I don't know, I might not be any good, anyway."

"But you're going to try?"

"I'm going to try," I agreed.

"Of course, Will was a great reader," she said.

"Yes, I saw him with a book from time to time," I said. "Sometimes one or two of the fellows might have brought something with them and it would get passed from hand to hand."

"He was reading from the time he was three years old," she told me. "And he tried his hand at writing, too. He wrote a completion for *The Mystery of Edwin Drood* in a most ingenious way when he was only fifteen."

"How did it end?"

"In exactly the way that it should," she replied. "Edwin came home to his family, safe and well. Eternal happiness ensues."

"Do you think that's the ending that Dickens intended?"

"I think it's the ending Will believed would be the most satisfying. Why are we stopping?"

"This is Mrs. Cantwell's boarding house," I said, looking up the steps towards the front door. "I just have to collect my holdall. We can part here, if you like."

"I'll wait for you," she said. "The station's only across the road. Might as well make sure you get there safely."

I nodded. "I'll only be a minute or two," I said, running up the steps.

Inside, Mrs. Cantwell was nowhere to be seen but her son, David, was behind the reception desk, consulting a chart, the tip of a pencil pressed to his tongue.

"Mr. Sadler," he said, looking up. "Good evening."

"Good evening," I said. "I've just come to collect my holdall."

"Of course." He reached down and picked it up from behind the desk, passing it across to me. "Did you have a good day, then?"

"Yes, thanks," I said. "We've settled everything regarding the bill already, haven't we?"

"Yes, sir," he said, following me as I walked towards the door. "Will we be likely to see you again in Norwich?"

"No, I don't think so," I said, turning to smile at him. "I rather think this will be my one and only visit."

"Oh dear. We didn't disappoint you that much, I hope?"

"No, not at all. It's just . . . Well, I don't imagine my work will bring me through here again, that's all. Goodbye, Mr. Cantwell," I said, extending my hand, and he looked at it for a moment before shaking it.

"I want you to know that I tried to fight, too," he said, and I nodded and shrugged. "They said I was too young. But I wanted it more than anything in the world."

"Then you're a fool," I said, opening the door and letting myself out.

Marian took my arm as we made our way across to the station and I was both flattered and upset by the gesture. I had waited so long to write to her, spent so much time planning this meeting, and here I was, ready to return home, and I still had not steeled myself to tell her about her brother's last hours. We walked in silence, though, and she must have been thinking the same thing, for it was only when we entered the station itself that she stopped, removed her arm and spoke again.

"I know he wasn't a coward, Mr. Sadler," she said. "I know that. I need to know the truth about what happened."

"Marian, please," I said, looking away.

"There's something you're not telling me," she said. "Something that you have been trying to say all day but haven't been able to. I can tell, I'm not stupid. You're desperate to say it. Well, we're here now, Tristan. Just the two of us. I want you to tell me exactly what it is."

"I have to get home," I said nervously. "My train—"

"Doesn't go for another forty minutes," she said, looking up towards the clock. "We have time. Please."

I took a deep breath, thinking, *Will I tell her? Can I tell her?*

"Your hand, Tristan," she said. "What's the matter with it?"

250

I held it out flat in front of me and watched as the index finger trembled erratically. I watched it, interested, then pulled it away.

"I can tell you what happened," I said finally in a quiet voice. "If you really want to know."

"But of course I want to know," she replied. "I don't believe I can go on if I don't know."

I stared at her and wondered.

"I can answer your questions," I said quietly. "I can tell you everything. Everything about that last day. Only I'm not sure that it will offer you any solace. And you certainly won't be able to forgive."

"It doesn't matter," she said, sitting down on a bench. "It's the not knowing that is most painful."

"All right, then," I said, sitting next to her.

THE SIXTH MAN

France, September–October 1916

HOBBS HAS GONE MAD. He stands outside my foxhole and stares down at me, eyes bulging, before putting a hand over his mouth and giggling like a schoolgirl.

"What's the matter with you?" I ask, looking up at him, in no mood for games. In reply he just laughs even more hysterically than before with uncontrollable mirth.

"Keep it down!" cries a voice from somewhere around the corner and Hobbs turns in that direction, his laughter stopping instantly, and he makes an obscene comment before running away. I think no more about it for now and close my eyes, but a few minutes later there's an almighty commotion from further down the trench and it seems unlikely that I will be able to sleep through it.

Perhaps the war has ended.

I wander in the direction of the noise, only to find Warren, who's been here about six or seven weeks, I think, and is a first cousin of the late Shields, being held back by a group of men while Hobbs cowers on the ground in the very definition of supplication. He's still laughing, though, and even as some of the men move to pick him up, there's an expression of fear on their faces, as if they're not entirely sure what might happen if they touch him.

"What the devil's going on?" I ask Williams, who's standing beside me, watching the proceedings with a bored expression on his face.

"It's Hobbs," he says, not even bothering to look at me. "Looks like he's lost the plot. Came over to Warren while he was asleep and took a piss on him."

"Jesus Christ," I say, shaking my head and reaching into my pocket for a cigarette. "Why on earth would he do such a thing?"

"God knows," shrugs Williams.

I watch the entertainment until two of the medics arrive and coax Hobbs to his feet. He starts babbling to them in some unfamiliar dialect and they take him away. As he turns the corner out of sight I hear him raise his voice again, shouting out the names of English kings and queens from Harold onwards in perfect order, a hangover from his schooldays perhaps, but his voice grows fainter around the House of Hanover and disappears altogether just after William IV. He's taken to the medical tent, I presume, and from there will be shipped back to a field hospital. He'll either be left there to rot or be cured of his ailment and sent back to the Front.

Thirteen of our number gone, seven left.

I return to my foxhole and manage to sleep for a little while longer, but when I wake, just as the sun is beginning to go down, I find that I am shaking uncontrollably. My whole body is in spasm and although I have been cold since the day I arrived in France, this is something entirely different. I feel as if I've been laid out in a snowdrift for a week and the frost has entered my bones. Robinson finds me and is taken aback by the sight.

"Jesus Christ," I hear him say, then, raising his voice, he calls out, "Sparks, come and take a look at this!"

A few moments of quiet, then a second voice.

"His number's up."

"I saw him not an hour ago. He seemed all right."

"Look at the colour of him. He won't see sunrise."

Soon, I'm transported to the medical tent and find myself lying on a bunk for the first time in I know not how long, covered with warm blankets, a compress placed about my forehead, a makeshift drip tied to my arm.

I float in and out of consciousness, waking to find my sister, Laura, standing over me, feeding me something warm and sweet-tasting.

"Hello, Tristan," she says.

"You," I reply, but before I can continue the conversation, her pretty features dissolve into the far rougher, unshaven visage of a medic, one whose eyes have sunk further and further into the back of his skull, giving him the appearance of the walking dead. I lose consciousness again, and when I finally come to, I find a doctor standing over me, and next to him, unable to control his irritation, is Sergeant Clayton.

"He's no good to you," the doctor is saying, checking the fluid in my drip and tapping the tube sharply with the index finger of his right hand. "Not at the moment, anyway. Best thing for him is to be shipped back home for convalescence. A month or so, no more than that. Then he can come back."

"For God's sake, man, if he can convalesce there he can convalesce here," insists Clayton. "I'll not send a man back to England for bed rest."

"He's been lying here for almost a week, sir. We need the bed. At least if he goes home—"

"Did you not hear me, Doctor? I said I will not send Sadler home. You told me yourself that he's showing signs of improvement."

"Improvement, yes. But not recovery. Not a full recovery, anyway. Look, I'm happy to sign the documentation for the transfer if that's what you're worried about."

"This man," insists Clayton, and I feel his fist slamming down hard against the blanket, bruising my ankle as it connects with it, "has nothing wrong with him, nothing compared to those who have already lost their lives. He can stay here for the time being. Feed him up, rehydrate him, get him back on his feet. Then send him back to me. Is that understood?"

A long silence, then what I take to be a frustrated nod of the head. "Understood, sir."

I turn my head on the pillow. The hope of a return home had been held out to me for a few moments, then snatched away. As I close my eyes and drift off again I begin to wonder whether the entire scenario has even happened; perhaps it was a dream and I am just waking up now. This sense of confusion continues throughout most of the day and night that follow, but the next morning, as I wake to the sound of rain pelting down on the canvas tent in which we injured many lie, I feel the fog lifting from my mind and know that whatever has been wrong with me has been alleviated, at least, if not cured.

"There you are, Sadler," says the doctor as he sticks a thermometer in my mouth. He reaches a hand beneath the sheets as he waits for the reading, putting a hand over my heart carefully to find my pulse, feeling for what I hope is a steady rhythm. "You look better. You have a bit of colour in your cheeks at least."

"How long have I been here?" I ask.

"A week today."

I exhale and shake my head in surprise; if I've been in bed for a week, then why do I still feel so tired?

"I think you might be over the worst of it. We thought we were going to lose you at first. You're a fighter, aren't you?"

"I never used to be," I say. "What have I missed, anyway?"

"Nothing," replies the doctor, laughing a little. "The war's still going on, if that's what you're worried about. Why, what did you expect to miss?"

"Has anyone been killed?" I ask. "Anyone from my regiment, I mean."

258

He takes the thermometer from my mouth and stares at it, then turns to look at me with a curious expression on his face. "Anyone from your regiment?" he asks. "No. Not since you've been in here. None that I'm aware of. It's been fairly quiet out there. Why do you ask?"

I shake my head and stare at the ceiling. I've been sleeping for most of the past two days but want more. I feel as if I could sleep for another month if I was offered the chance.

"Much better," says the doctor cheerfully. "Temperature's back to normal. Or as normal as it gets out here, at any rate."

"Did I have any visitors?"

"Why, who were you expecting—the Archbishop of Canterbury?"

I ignore his sarcasm and turn away. It's possible that Will looked in on me from time to time; it's not as if this doctor has been watching my bed twenty-four hours a day.

"So what's next for me, then?" I ask.

"Back to active duty, I expect. We'll give you another day or so. Look, why don't you get up for a little bit? Go to the mess tent and get some food into you. Plenty of hot sweet tea if there's any to be found. Then report back here and we'll see how you're getting along."

I sigh and drag my body from the bed, feeling the weight of a full bladder pressing on my abdomen, and dress quickly before taking myself off to the latrine. As I open the flap of the tent and step out into the miserable, murky half-light, a great pool of water that has been sitting on the canvas above falls on me, drenching my head, and I stand there for a moment or two, a sodden mess, willing the elements to make me ill again so that I might return to the warmth and comfort of the medical tent.

But, to my disappointment, I only improve and am soon back on active duty.

*

Although I develop a rash on my arm later that day, which makes it feel as though it's on fire, after spending another afternoon in the medical tent waiting to be seen I'm finally given a cursory examination and told that there's nothing the matter with me, it's all in my head, and I can go to the trenches.

In the evening, standing alone at my box-periscope, my rifle slung over my shoulder as I stare across no-man's-land, I become convinced that there is a German boy of my own age standing on the opposite side, watching me. He's tired and frightened; he's spent every evening praying that he will not see us climbing over the sandbags because the moment we emerge from our muddy graves is the moment he will be forced to give the signal to his own comrades and the whole horrible business of engagement will begin.

No one mentions Will, and I am nervous about asking after him. Most of our original regiment are dead, or in Hobbs's case sent to a field hospital, so there isn't any reason why they should be thinking of Will. I am racked with loneliness. I haven't laid eyes on him since before I became ill. After my refusal to report Milton to Sergeant Clayton, he studiously avoided me. Then I became sick and that was the end of that.

When a group of men are selected by Sergeant Clayton for a recce in the dead of night over the sandbags and towards the German defences, of the sixty who leave us, only eighteen return, a disaster by any standards. Among the dead is Corporal Moody, who has taken a bullet in the eye.

Later that same evening, I discover Corporal Wells sitting alone with a mug of tea, his head bowed over the table, and I feel unexpected sympathy for him. I'm unsure whether it's appropriate to join him or not—we have never been particularly friendly—but I feel alone, too, and in need of company so I take the bit between my teeth, pour myself some tea, and stand before him.

"Evening, sir," I say carefully.

It takes him a moment to look up and, when he does, I notice that there are dark bags forming under his eyes. I wonder how long it has been since he has slept. "Sadler," he says. "Off duty, are you?"

"Yes, sir," I say, nodding at the empty bench opposite him. "Would you rather be alone or can I join you?"

He stares at the emptiness as if unsure of the etiquette of the moment, but finally shrugs and indicates that I might sit down.

"I was sorry to hear about Corporal Moody," I tell him after a suitable pause. "He was a decent man. He always treated me fairly."

"I thought I'd better write to his wife," he tells me, indicating the paper and pen before him.

"I didn't even know he was married."

"No particular reason why you should. But yes, he had a wife and three daughters."

"Won't Sergeant Clayton be writing to his wife, sir?" I ask, for that is the usual way these things work.

"Yes, I expect so. Only I knew Martin better than anyone else. I thought it might be best if I wrote, too."

"Of course," I say, nodding again, and as I lift my mug, I feel an unexpected weakness in my arm and spill tea across the table.

"For pity's sake, Sadler," he says, putting the paper and pen aside before they can be spoiled. "Don't be so damn nervous all the time, it gets on my wick. How are you, anyway? All better?"

"Quite well, thank you," I say, wiping the tea away with my sleeve.

"Thought we'd lost you at one point. Last thing we need, another man going down. There's not a lot of your original Aldershot troop left, is there?"

"Seven," I say.

"Six by my count."

"Six?" I ask, feeling the blood drain from my face. "Who's been killed?"

"Since you fell ill? No one as far as I know."

"But then it's seven," I insist. "Robinson, Williams, Attling—"

"You're not going to say Hobbs, are you? Because he's been sent back to England. He's in the nuthouse. We don't count Hobbs."

"I wasn't counting him," I say, "but that still leaves seven: Robinson, Williams and Attling, as I said, and Sparks, Milton, Bancroft and me."

Corporal Wells laughs and shakes his head. "Well, if we're not including Hobbs, then we're not including Bancroft," he tells me.

"He's all right, isn't he?"

"Probably in better condition than any of us. For the moment, anyway. But look here," he adds, narrowing his eyes a little, as if he wants to get a better reading of me. "You and he were tight once, weren't you?"

"We had the bunks next to each other at Aldershot," I say. "Why, where is he? I've been keeping an eye out for him in the trenches ever since I came back to the line but there's no sign of him."

"You haven't heard, then?"

I shake my head but say nothing.

"Private Bancroft," begins Wells, stressing each syllable as if it carries a great weight, "made an appointment for a conversation with Sergeant Clayton. He brought up that whole business of the German boy again. You've heard about that, I imagine?"

"Yes, sir," I reply. "I was there when it happened."

"Oh, that's right. He did mention it. Anyway, he wanted Milton brought up on charges, insisted on it in no uncertain terms. The sergeant refused for what must be the third time of asking and this time the conversation grew rather heated between the two. The upshot of it all was that Bancroft surrendered his weapons to Sergeant Clayton and announced that he would take no further part in the campaign."

"What does that mean?" I ask. "What happens next?"

"Sergeant Clayton told him that he was an enlisted man and he could not refuse to fight. To do so would be a dereliction of duty for which he could be court-martialled."

"And what did Will say?"

"Who's Will?" Wells asks stupidly.

"Bancroft."

"Oh, he has a Christian name, does he? I knew you two were friends."

"I told you, we just bunked next to each other in training, that's all. Look, are you going to tell me what's happening with him or not?"

"Steady on, Sadler," says Wells cautiously. "Remember who you're addressing."

"I'm sorry, sir," I say, running a hand across my eyes. "I just want to know, that's all. We can't . . . we can't afford to be another man down. The regiment . . ." I say half-heartedly.

"No, of course not. Well, Sergeant Clayton told him that he had no choice, he had to fight, but Bancroft announced that he no longer believed in the moral absolute of this war, that he felt the army was engaged in tactics which are contrary to the public good and God's laws. Has he ever displayed a religious fervour, Sadler? I wonder whether that might explain this sudden rush of conscience."

"His father's a vicar," I tell him. "Although I've never heard Bancroft talk about it much."

"Well, either way it won't do him much good. Sergeant Clayton told him that he couldn't register as a conscientious objector out here, it was too late for that nonsense. No military tribunals to hear his case, for one thing. No, he knew what he was signing up for, and if he refuses to fight then we're left with no alternative. You know what that is, Sadler. I don't need to tell you what we do with feather men."

I swallow and feel my heart pounding wildly in my chest. "You're not sending him over the sandbags," I ask. "A stretcher-bearer?"

"That was the general intention," he replies, shrugging his shoulders, as if this is a perfectly normal thing. "But no, Bancroft wouldn't have that either. He's gone the whole hog, you see. Declared himself an absolutist."

"I beg your pardon?"

"An absolutist," he repeats. "You're not familiar with the term?"

"No, sir," I say.

"It's one step beyond conscientiously objecting," he explains. "Most of those men oppose the fighting part of things, the killing and so on, but they are willing to help in other ways, in what they might deem to be more humanitarian ways. They'll work in hospitals or in GHQ or whatever. I mean, it's terribly cowardly, of course, but they'll do something while the rest of us risk life and limb."

"And an absolutist?" I ask.

"Well, he's at the far end of the spectrum, Sadler," he tells me. "He won't do anything at all to further the war effort. Won't fight, won't help those who are fighting, won't work in a hospital or come to the aid of the wounded. Won't do anything at all, really, except sit on his hands and complain that the whole thing's a sham. It's the thin end of the wedge, Sadler, it really is. Cowardice on the most extreme level."

"Will is not a coward," I say quietly, feeling my hands curling into fists beneath the table.

"Oh, but he is," he says. "He's the most frightful coward. Anyway, he's registered his status so now the only thing left is to decide what to do with him."

"And where is he now?" I ask. "Has he been sent back to England?"

"For an easy life? I should think not."

"I should think that if he was he would be imprisoned," I point out. "And I can't imagine there would be anything easy about that."

"Really, Sadler?" he says doubtfully. "The next time you're crawling on your belly across no-man's-land with the bullets whizzing past your head, wondering when you're going to be picked off like Martin Moody, you just remember those words. I expect at such a moment you might rather relish a couple of years in Strangeways."

"So is that where he's gone?" I ask, already feeling heartsore at the idea that I might not see him again, that like Peter Wallis, Will and I parted as enemies and I might die without our ever being reconciled.

"Not yet, no," says Wells. "He's still here at camp. Locked up at Sergeant Clayton's discretion. Court-martialled."

"But there hasn't been a trial yet?"

"We don't need a trial out here, Sadler, you know that. Why, if he was to lay down his gun during the fighting itself he'd be shot by the battle police for cowardice. No, there's a big push coming over the next twenty-four hours and I'm sure he'll come to his senses before then. If he agrees to get back into the thick of it, all will be forgotten. For now, at least. He may have to answer for it at a later date, of course, but at least he'll live to tell his side of the story. He's lucky, when you think about it. Were it not for the fact that every last man has been helping with the advancement or working on entrenchment he would have been shot by now. No, we'll hold on to him where he is for the time being and send him out when the battle begins. He's full of fine talk about never fighting again, of course, but we'll knock that out of him in time. Mark my words."

I nod but say nothing. I'm not convinced that anyone could ever knock anything out of Will Bancroft once he has an idea in his head, and want to say so but keep my peace. After a moment, Wells drains his mug and stands up.

"Well, I'd better get back to it," he says. "Are you coming, Sadler?"

"Not quite yet," I say.

"All right, then." He starts to walk away, then turns back and stares at me, narrowing his eyes again. "Are you sure that you and Bancroft aren't friends?" he asks me. "I always thought you were thick as thieves, the pair of you."

"We just had bunks next to each other," I say, unable to look him in the eye. "That's all we are to each other. I barely know him really."

To my astonishment, I see Will the following afternoon, seated alone in an abandoned foxhole near HQ. He's unshaven and pale; there's a lost expression on his face as he unsettles the dirt on the ground with the tip of his boot. I watch him for a moment without making my presence known to see whether he looks any different now that he has taken his great stand. It might be minutes later when he jerks his head up abruptly, then relaxes when he sees that it's only me.

"You're free," I say as I approach him, not bothering with any greeting despite the fact that we haven't laid eyes on each other for some time. "I thought they'd locked you away somewhere."

"They have," he tells me. "And they'll take me back there in a bit, I dare say. There's a meeting of some sort taking place in there and I expect they don't want me to hear what they're talking about. Corporal Wells told me to wait here until someone came to fetch me."

"And they trust you not to run off?"

"Well, where do you think I might go, Tristan?" he asks, smiling at me and looking around. He has a point; it's not as if there's anywhere to run off to. "You don't have a cigarette on you, by any chance? They took all mine away."

I dig around in the pocket of my coat and hand one across. He lights it quickly, his eyes closing for a moment as he takes the first draw of nicotine into his lungs.

"Is it very awful?" I ask.

"What?" he asks, looking up at me again.

"Being held like this. Wells told me what you're doing. I expect they're treating you horribly."

He shrugs his shoulders and looks away. "It's fine," he says. "Most of the time they just ignore me. They bring me food, take me to the latrine. There's even a bunk in there, if you can believe it. It's a lot more comfortable than being left to rot in the trenches, I can promise you that."

"But that's not why you're doing it, is it?"

"No, of course not. What do you take me for, anyway?"

"Is it because of the German boy?"

"He's part of it," he says, looking down at his boots. "But there's Wolf, too. What happened to him. His murder, I mean. It just feels like we've all become immune to the violence. I'm of the opinion that Sergeant Clayton would fall to his knees and burst into tears if he heard that the war had come to an end. He loves it. You realize that, Tristan, don't you?"

"He doesn't love it," I say, shaking my head.

"The man's half mad. Anyone can see that. Babbling half the day. Great rages, then weeping fits. He needs to be carted off to the funny farm. But look, I haven't asked how you are."

"I'm fine," I say, not willing to turn the conversation to me.

"You were ill."

"Yes."

"I thought you were a goner at one point. The doctor didn't give you much chance, anyway. Bloody fool. I told him you'd pull through. Said you were made of stronger stuff than he realized."

I laugh abruptly, flattered by this, then look back at him in surprise. "You talked to the doctor?" I ask.

"Briefly, yes."

"When?"

"Well, when I came to visit you, of course."

"But they told me no one came to visit," I tell him. "I asked and they seemed to think I was mad even to imagine it."

He shrugs his shoulders. "Well, I came."

Three soldiers appear from around the corner, new recruits I haven't seen before, and they hesitate when they see Will sitting there. They stare at him for a moment before one of them spits in the mud and the others follow suit. They don't say anything, not to his face, anyway, but I can hear the mutters of "Fucking coward" under their breath as they pass by. Following them with my eyes I wait until they're out of sight before turning back to Will.

"It doesn't matter," he says quietly.

I tell him to shove up and take a seat beside him. I can't stop thinking about the fact that he visited me in the medical tent, about what that means.

"Don't you think you could just put it all aside for now?" I ask. "These concerns of yours, I mean. Just until it's all over?"

"But what good would that do?" he asks. "The point must be made while the fighting is still going on. Otherwise it's entirely worthless. You must see that."

"Yes, but if you're not shot here for cowardice then they'll ship you off back to England. I've heard what happens to feather men in jails back home. You'll be lucky if you survive it. And after that, how do you think the rest of your life will turn out? You won't be welcome in polite society, that's for sure."

"I couldn't give two figs for polite society," he replies with a bitter laugh. "Why would I, if this is what it represents? And I'm not a feather man, Tristan," he insists. "This is not an act of cowardice."

"No, you're an absolutist," I reply. "And I'm sure that you think it justifies everything if you can ascribe a clean word to it. But it doesn't."

Will turns and stares at me, taking the cigarette from his mouth and using his thumb and index finger to remove a flake of tobacco that's trapped between his front teeth. He glances at it for a moment before flicking it into the dirt at our feet. "Why do you care so much, anyway?" he asks. "What good do you think it does talking to me here?"

"I care for the same reason that you visited me in hospital," I say. "I don't want to see you making a terrible mistake that you will regret for the rest of your life."

"And you don't think that you'll regret it?" he asks. "When this is all over and you're safely back home in London, you don't think that you'll wake up with the pictures of all the men you've killed haunting your dreams? Do you actually mean to tell me that you'll be able to move past it all? I don't think you've given it any thought at all," he adds, his voice growing colder now. "You talk of cowardice, you talk of feather men, and yet you direct your contempt at everyone but yourself. You can't see that, can you? How it's you who is the coward and not I? I can't sleep at night, Tristan, for thinking of that boy pissing his pants just before Milton put the gun to his head. Every time I close my eyes I see his brains being splattered over the trench wall. If I could go back, I'd have put a bullet in Milton myself before he could kill the boy."

"You'd have been shot for it if you had."

"I'll be shot anyway. What do you think they're discussing back there? The lack of decent tea in the mess tent? They're figuring out when's the best time to be rid of me."

"They won't shoot you," I insist. "They can't. They have to hear your case."

"Not out here they don't," he says. "Not in the field of battle. And who'd have turned me in if I had shot Milton? You?"

Before I can answer this there's a cry of "Bancroft!" from my left and I turn to see Harding, the new corporal sent over from GHQ as a replacement for Moody. "What do you think you're doing? And who the hell are you?" he asks as I jump to my feet.

"Private Sadler," I say.

"And why the devil are you talking to the prisoner?"

"Well, he was just sitting here, sir," I say, uncertain of what crime I might have committed. "And I was passing by, that's all. I didn't know that he was in isolation."

Harding narrows his eyes and looks me up and down for a moment as if he's attempting to decide whether or not I am cheeking him. "Get back to the trench, Sadler," he says. "I'm sure someone there must be looking for you."

"Yes, sir," I say, turning around and nodding at Will before I leave. He doesn't acknowledge my farewell, just stares at me with a curious expression as I walk away.

Evening time.

A bomb falls somewhere to my left and knocks me off my feet. I hit the ground and lie there for a moment, gasping, wondering whether that's the end of me. Have my legs been blown away? My arms dismembered? Are my intestines slipping out of my body and melting into the mud? But the seconds pass and I feel no pain. I press my hands to the soil and lift myself up.

I am fine. I am uninjured. I am alive.

I throw myself forward in the trench, looking left and right quickly to apprise myself of the situation. Soldiers are rushing past, filling positions three men deep along the front defence line, and Corporal Wells is at the end, shouting instructions at us. His arm rises and falls in the air as if he is chopping something, and as the first group steps back, the second takes a movement forward as the third, myself among them, lines up behind the second.

It's impossible to hear what is being said over the noise of shelling and gunfire, but I watch, breathing in quick gasps, and I can see that Wells is giving quick instructions to the run of fifteen men in the front line who look at each other for a moment before ascending the ladder and, heads held firmly down, throwing themselves over the sandbags and into no-man's-land, which is dark and lit up sporadically like a carnival.

Wells pulls a box-periscope down and stares through it, and I study his face, noticing the moments when he sees someone's been hit, the quick expression of pain that spreads across his features, then he pushes it to one side as the next line steps forward.

Sergeant Clayton is among us now and he stands on the opposite side of the line to Wells and shouts instructions at the troops. I close my eyes for a moment. How long will it be, I wonder, two minutes, three, before I am over the sandbags, too? Is my life to end tonight? I've been over before and survived, but tonight . . . tonight feels different and I don't know why.

I look in front of me and see a boy trembling. He's young, untested, a new recruit. I think he arrived the day before yesterday. He turns around and stares at me as if I can help him and I can see that his expression is one of pure terror. He can't be much younger than me, maybe he's older, but he looks like a child, a little boy who doesn't even know what he's doing here.

"I can't do it," he says to me, his Yorkshire voice low and pleading, and I narrow my eyes and force him to focus on them.

"You can," I tell him.

"No," he says, shaking his head. "I can't."

More screams from either side of the line and now a body falls from above, almost from the heavens, and lands among us. It's another of the new recruits, a lad I noticed not five minutes ago with a mop of prematurely grey hair, a bullet hole through his throat seeping blood. The boy in front of me cries out and takes a step back, almost pushing into me, and I shove him forward. I can't be expected to deal with him, too, when my own life is about to end. It's not fair.

"Please," he says, appealing to me as if I have some control over what is happening.

"Shut up," I say, no longer willing to play mother to him. "Shut the fuck up and step forward, all right? Do your duty."

He cries and I shove him again and he's at the base of the ladders now, standing in a row alongside a dozen or so others.

"Next line-up!" screams Sergeant Clayton and the soldiers place their feet nervously on the lowest rung of the ladders, holding their heads low so they do not peep over the top any sooner than they have to. My boy, the one in front of me, does, too, but he makes no move to ascend, keeping his right foot rooted firmly in the mud.

"That man!" screams Clayton, pointing at him. "Up! Up! Up now!"

"I can't do it!" cries the boy, the tears streaming down his face now, and God help me I've had enough, I've had enough of all of this, if I am to die, then let it end soon but it can't happen until my turn is called, so I press my hand beneath his buttocks and push him up the ladder, feeling his weight trying to force itself back against me. "No!" he cries, pleading with me, his body failing him now. "No, please!"

"Up, that man!" shouts Clayton, rushing over to us now. "Sadler, push him up!"

I do it, I don't even think of the consequences of my actions, but between us Clayton and I push the boy to the top of the ladder and there's nowhere for him to go now but over and he falls on his belly, the possibility of a return to the trench out of the question. I watch as he slithers forward, his boots disappearing from my eye line, and I turn to Clayton, who is staring at me with insanity in his eyes. We look at each other and I think, *Look at what we have just done*, and then he returns to the side of the lines as Wells orders the rest of us upward and I don't hesitate now, I climb the ladder and throw myself over and I stand tall, do not lift my rifle but stare at the chaos around me, and think, *Here I am, take me now, why don't you? Shoot me.*

I'm still alive.

The silence is astonishing. Sergeant Clayton addresses forty of us, standing in pathetic lines that look nothing like the neat rows we learned to form in Aldershot. I know only a few of these men; they're filthy and exhausted, some badly wounded, some half mad. To my surprise Will is present, standing between Wells and Harding, who each grip one of his arms as if there's a possibility that he might run away. Will has a haunted look and he barely glances up from the ground; only once, and when he does he looks at me but doesn't seem to recognize me. There are dark circles under his eyes and a raised bruise along his left cheek.

Clayton is shouting at us, telling us how brave we've been over the last eight hours, then condemning us as a bunch of frightened mice the next. He was never completely sane, I think, but he's lost it entirely now. He's blabbering on about morale and how we're going to win the war but refers to the Greeks rather than the Germans on more than one occasion and loses his train of thought over and over again. It's clear that he shouldn't be here.

I glance over towards Wells, the next most senior man, to see if he's aware how damaged our sergeant has become, but he's not paying much attention. It's not as if he can do anything, anyway. Mutiny is impossible.

"And this man, this man here!" shouts Clayton then, marching over towards Will, who looks up in surprise as if he has barely registered that he is even present in the moment. "This man who refuses to fight this fucking coward what do you think of him men not like you is he taught better taught better than that I know I was the one who taught him makes all sorts of outrageous suggestions then pops his head down on a pillow in his cell while the rest of you brave lads are here to train because it's only a few weeks before we head off to France to fight and this man this man here he says he's not in the mood to kill but he was a poacher before or so I heard . . ."

And on and on and on interminably, none of it making any sense, no sentences, just a sequence of garbled words gathered together and thrown at us while he spits and spews out hatred.

He walks away, then a moment later walks back, pulls off a glove and slaps Will across the face with it. We're immune to violence, of course, but the action takes each of us a little by surprise. It's both tame and vicious at the same time.

"I can't stand a coward," says Clayton, slapping him again, hard, and Will's head turns away from the beating. "Can't stand to eat with one, can't stand to talk to one, can't stand to command one."

Harding looks at Wells as if to ask whether they should intervene but Clayton has stopped now and turns back to the men, pointing at Will.

"This man," he declares, "refused to fight during this evening's attack. In light of this, he has been duly court-martialled and found guilty of cowardice. He will be shot tomorrow morning at six o'clock. That is how we punish cowards."

Will looks up now but doesn't seem to care. I stare at him, willing him to turn his head in my direction, but he doesn't. Even now, even at this moment, he won't allow me.

It's night-time now, dark, surprisingly quiet. I make my way towards the reverse, where a group of medics are placing casualties on stretchers for transport home. I glance at them for only a few moments and see Attling and Williams, and Robinson with his head split open by a German bullet. On a stretcher next to him lies the body of Milton, the murderer of the German boy, dead now, too. There are only three of us left, Sparks, Will and I.

How have I survived this long?

I make my way towards the sergeant's quarters and Wells is outside, smoking a cigarette. He looks pale and nervous. He takes a deep drag on the tab, sucking the nicotine far into his lungs, as he narrows his eyes and watches me approach him.

"I need to see Sergeant Clayton," I tell him.

"I need to see Sergeant Clayton, *sir*," he corrects me.

"It's important."

"Not now, Sadler. The sergeant's asleep. He'll have all three of us shot if we wake him before we have to."

"Sir, something needs to be done about the sergeant," I say.

"Something? What do you mean by that?"

"Permission to speak frankly, sir?"

Wells sighs. "Just spit it out, for Christ's sake," he says.

"The old man's gone mad," I say. "You can see it, can't you? The way he beat up Bancroft earlier? And that kangaroo court martial? It shouldn't even happen here, you know that. He should be taken back to GHQ, tried before a jury of his peers—"

"He was, Sadler. You were sick, remember?"

"It was done here, though."

"Which is allowed. We're in battle conflict. It's extraordinary circumstances. The military handbook makes it clear that in these conditions—"

"I know what it says," I tell him. "But come on, sir. He's going to be shot in—" I look at my watch. "Less than six hours. It's not right, sir. You know it's not."

"Honestly, Sadler, I don't care," says Wells. "Ship him back, send him over the top, shoot him in the morning, it doesn't matter a damn to me. Can't you understand that? All that matters is the next hour and the one after that and the one after that and the rest of us staying alive. If Bancroft refuses to fight, then let him die."

"But, sir—"

"Enough, Sadler. Go back to your foxhole, all right?"

I can't sleep; of course I can't. The hours pass and I watch the horizon, willing the sun not to rise. At about three o'clock I walk through the trench, my mind elsewhere, barely looking at where I'm going, when I stumble over a pair of outstretched feet and trip over, steadying myself quickly to avoid falling head first in the mud.

Looking behind me in a fury, I see one of the new recruits, a tall red-haired boy named Marshall, sitting up straight and pulling his helmet back from where he had placed it over his eyes while he slept.

"For God's sake, Marshall," I say. "Keep yourself tidy, can't you?"

"And what's it to you?" he asks, remaining in his seat and folding his arms as a challenge to me. He's young, one of those boys who has yet to see any of his friends' heads blown off before his eyes, and probably believes that the only reason this blasted war is still going on is because the likes of him have not yet been involved in it.

"What's it to me is that I don't want to trip over your feet and break my bloody neck," I snap. "You're a danger to everyone, sprawled out like that."

He whistles through his teeth and shakes his head, laughing, and waves me away. He's unlikely to allow himself to be challenged like this without response, particularly when some of the other new recruits are watching, too, spoiling for a fight, hoping for anything that might provide a break in their tedious routine.

"How about you get your head out of the clouds, Sadler, and then you won't have any accidents?" he suggests, putting the helmet back over his eyes and pretending that he's about to fall asleep again when I know, of course, that he is happy to keep his face covered until he's sure how this particular interview is going to end. It isn't something I plan, and even as I see my arm reach out I'm almost surprised by what I'm doing, but it takes only a moment for me to flip the helmet off his head and send it flying in a perfect arc through the air before it lands in a pile of mud, burying itself rim down so that it will need to be cleaned before being put back on his head.

"For God's sake, man!" he cries, jumping up and looking at me with a mixture of anger and frustration in his eyes. "What do you want to go and do a thing like that for?"

"Because you're a fucking idiot," I reply.

"Fetch my helmet for me," he says, his voice growing lower now in barely concealed fury. I'm aware of a few of the men gathering and can hear the sound of matches being struck as cigarettes are lit, something to keep the hands busy as they settle down for the entertainment.

"You can fetch it yourself, Marshall," I reply. "And next time, look lively when a superior officer passes by you."

"A 'superior officer'?" he asks, bursting out laughing. "And there was me thinking that you were just a lowly private like me."

"I've been here longer," I insist, the words sounding wretched even to my ears. "I know a lot more about who's who and what's what than you do."

"And if you want to keep knowing what's what, I'd suggest you fetch my helmet for me," he adds, smiling, his yellow teeth disgusting to observe.

I feel my lips twist themselves into a sneer. I've known boys like him before, of course. Bullies. I've seen them at school and I've seen them ever since and I've had enough of them. The wound on my arm, the one the doctors say doesn't even exist, is giving me unholy pain and I am so consumed with frustration over what is happening to Will that I can hardly keep my thoughts straight.

"I notice you show no signs of fighting," he says after a moment, looking around at the gathered men for support. "Another one of them, are you?"

"Of who?" I ask.

"Like that pal of yours, what's his name, Bancroft?"

"That's right," comes a voice from a few feet away, another of the new recruits. "You have him there, Tom. Bancroft and Sadler have been thick from the start, so I've been told, anyway."

"And are you a feather man like him?" asks Marshall. "Afraid to fight?"

"Will is not afraid to fight," I say, stepping forward now until I can smell his stinking breath.

"Oh, it's 'Will,' is it?" he asks, laughing contemptuously at me. " 'Will' is a brave man, is he? Easy to be brave when you're locked up safely, given three meals a day and a bed to sleep in. Maybe you'd like to join him there, Sadler, is that what it is? Or do you prefer 'Tristan'? Think this would all be a lot more fun if you and he were cuddled up together, the pair of you, playing smash and grab under the blankets?"

He turns to grin with his friends at this and they in turn burst into laughter at his pathetic joke, but it's enough for me and in a second my fist has made contact with his jaw and I send him flying off his feet with as much precision as I did the helmet a few moments before. His head crashes against one of the timbers of the trench wall as he falls, but it doesn't take him long to recover his senses and he's up and on me as the men's cries turn into cheers and jeers; they shout loudly when one of us lands an effective punch, laugh in our faces when we stumble or mis-hit in the mud. It becomes something of a free-for-all, Marshall and I lashing out in the confined space with the grace of a pair of pugnacious chimpanzees. I'm barely aware of what's taking place but it feels as if months of internalized pain are suddenly pouring out and, without realizing that I am securing a victory, I find myself astride him, punching him time and time again in the face, pushing him further into the mud.

There he is, his face, pulling back in the schoolroom after I kissed him.

And there, coming from behind his butcher's counter, placing an arm around my shoulders, telling me that it would be better for all if I was killed over there.

And there, embracing me by the stream at Aldershot before pulling his clothes together and running away with a look of contempt and revulsion.

And there again, somewhere in the back of the lines, telling me that it was all a mistake, men just sought comfort where they could find it at times like this.

I punch at every one of them and Marshall takes the blows and the world seems very black even as I feel arms pulling me from behind, dragging me off the boy and lifting me to my feet as the men cry, "Enough, enough, for God's sake, man, enough! You'll kill him if you're not careful!"

"You're a bloody disgrace, Sadler, you realize that, don't you?" asks Sergeant Clayton, stepping around from behind his desk and coming a little too close to me for comfort. His breath stinks and I notice a twitch at his left eye and the fact that he appears to have shaved only the left-hand side of his face.

"Yes, sir," I say. "I'm aware of it."

"A bloody disgrace," he repeats. "And you an Aldershot man. A man that *I* trained. How many of you are left now, anyway?"

"Three, sir," I say.

"It's two, Sadler," he insists. "We don't count Bancroft. The yellow-bellied bastard. Two of you left, and this is how you conduct yourself? How are the new recruits expected to fight the enemy if they have the living shit beaten out of them by you?" His face is red and his tone grows more furious with every word.

"Obviously it wasn't wise, sir," I say.

"Not wise? *Not wise?*" he roars. "Are you trying to be funny with me, Sadler, because I promise you that if you even try any of that nonsense with me, I'll have you—"

"I'm not trying to be funny, sir," I say, interrupting him. "I don't know what happened to me. I went a little mad, that's all. Marshall just rubbed me up the wrong way."

"Mad?" he asks, leaning forward and staring at me. "Did you say 'mad,' Sadler?"

"Yes, sir."

"Now, don't tell me you're trying to get out of here on some spurious grounds of insanity because I won't stand for that, either."

"Out of where, sir?" I ask. "Out of your office?"

"Out of France, you bloody idiot!"

"Oh. No, sir," I say. "Not at all. No, it was more of a temporary thing. I can only apologize. I tripped over him, words were exchanged, it all got a little heated. A bad mistake."

"You've put him out of commission for the next twenty-four hours," he tells me, his temper appearing to lessen now.

"I know I hurt him, sir, yes."

"That's a bloody understatement," he replies, stepping away, putting one hand down the front of his trousers and scratching deeply at his crotch without any embarrassment, before taking a seat, sighing to himself as he does so and running this same hand across his face. "I'm bloody exhausted, too," he mutters. "Woken up for this? Still," he adds, softening his tone, "I didn't know you had it in you, Sadler, if I'm honest. And that fool needed to be taken down a peg or two, I know that much. I'd have done it myself, the amount of gyp he gives me. But I can't, can I? Have to set an example to the men. Ignorant little bastard's given me nothing but trouble since the day he got here."

I stand at attention, slightly surprised by this turn of events. I haven't imagined that I would be seen as a hero in Sergeant Clayton's eyes, although he is a man who is generally impossible to read. He'll probably turn on me again in a moment.

"But look here, Sadler," he says. "I can't let this type of thing go unpunished. You realize that, don't you? It's the thin end of the wedge."

"Of course, sir," I say.

"So, what am I to do with you?"

I stare at him, unsure if this is a rhetorical question or not. *Send me back to England?* I feel like saying, but resist, sure that it will only reignite his anger.

"You'll spend the next few hours in confinement," he says finally, nodding his head. "And you'll apologize to Marshall in front of the men when he's back on duty tomorrow. Shake his hand, say all's fair in love and war, that sort of thing. The men need to see that you can't just start punching each other like that without there being consequences."

He looks towards the door and shouts out for Corporal Harding, who enters a moment later. He must have been standing outside all along, listening to the conversation.

"Take Private Sadler into confinement until sunrise, will you?"

"Yes, sir," says Harding, and I can tell by the tone of his voice that he is uncertain what Clayton means by this. "Where should I put him, exactly?"

"In con-fine-ment," the sergeant repeats, stretching out the syllables as if he's speaking to an infant or a halfwit. "You understand English, man, don't you?"

"There's only the cell where we're holding Bancroft, sir," Harding replies. "But he's meant to be in solitary."

"Well, they can be in solitary together," he snaps, ignoring the obvious contradiction as he waves us away. "They can nurse their grievances and get them out of their systems. Now get out of here, the pair of you. I have work to do."

"You do realize that it's the Germans you're supposed to be fighting, not our own men, don't you?"

"Very funny," I say, sitting down on one of the bunks. It's cold in here. The walls are damp and crumbling with earth; only a little light gets through from an opening near the ceiling and the barred cavity on the door.

"I must say I'm a bit surprised," says Will, considering it, sounding amused despite the circumstances. "I wouldn't have taken you for a scrapper. Were you like that in school?"

282

"On occasion. Like anyone else. Why, were you?"

"Sometimes."

"And yet now you won't fight at all."

He smiles then, very slowly, his eyes focusing so tightly on mine that eventually I am forced to look away. "And is that what you're here for really?" he asks me. "Was this all planned so you'd be thrown in here, too, and you might persuade me to change my mind?"

"I've told you exactly why I'm here," I say, annoyed by the charge. "I'm here because that damn fool Marshall had it coming to him."

"I don't know him, do I?" he asks, frowning.

"No, he's new. But look, let's not worry about him. Clayton's gone mad, anyone can see it. I think we can fight this thing if we try. We just need to talk to Wells and Harding and—"

"Fight what thing, Tristan?" he asks me.

"Well, this, of course," I say in amazement, looking around me as if any further explanation were unnecessary. "What do you think I'm talking about? Your sentence."

He shakes his head and I notice that he is trembling slightly. So he is afraid, after all. He does want to live. He says nothing for a long time and neither do I; I don't want to rush him. I want to wait for him to decide on his own.

"I've had the old man in here a few times, of course," he says finally, extending his hands out before him, turning them over to examine his palms as if he might find answers there. "Trying to get me to change my mind. Trying to get me to lift my gun again. It's no good, I tell him, but he won't wear it. I think he sees it as a slight on his own character."

"He probably doesn't want to have to report to General Fielding that one of his own men refuses to fight."

"And an Aldershot man at that," he replies, his head cocked a little to the side as he smiles at me. "The disgrace of it!"

"Things have changed. Milton's dead, for one thing," I say, wondering whether this particular piece of intelligence has made its way here. "So it doesn't matter any more. You can't bring him to justice, no matter what you do. You can give all this up."

He thinks about this for a moment, considers and dismisses it. "I'm sorry to hear he's dead," he tells me. "But it doesn't change anything. It's the principle that matters."

"It's not, actually," I insist. "It's life and death that matters."

"Then perhaps I can take it up with Milton in a couple of hours' time."

"Don't, Will, please," I say, horrified by his words.

"I hope there aren't any wars in heaven."

"Will—"

"Can you imagine it, Tristan? Getting away from all this only to find that the war between God and Lucifer continues up above? I'd have a difficult time refusing Him, wouldn't I?"

"Look, stop being so bloody flippant. If you offer to get straight back into the thick of it then the old man will let you off. He needs every soldier he can get his hands on. Yes, you might be prosecuted when the war is over but at least you won't be dead."

"I can't do it, Tris," he says. "I'd like to, I really would. I don't want to die. I'm nineteen years old, I have my whole life in front of me."

"Then don't die," I say, approaching him. "Don't die, Will."

He frowns a little and looks up at me. "Don't you have any principles, Tristan?" he asks me. "Principles for which you would lay down your life, I mean."

"No," I say, shaking my head. "People, perhaps. But not principles. What good are they?"

"This is why things have always been complicated between us, you see," he tells me. "We're very different people, that's the truth of it. You really don't believe in anything at all, do you? While I—"

"Don't, Will," I say, looking away.

"I don't say it to hurt you, Tristan, really I don't. I just mean that you run away from things, that's all. From your family, for example. From friendships. From right and wrong. But I don't, you see. I can't. I'd like to be more like you, of course. If I was, there'd have been more chance that I would have got out of this bloody mess with my life."

I can feel the anger bubbling inside me. Even now, even at this moment, he chooses to patronize me. It makes me wonder why I ever felt a thing for him.

"Please," I say, trying not to let my growing resentment overwhelm me, "just tell me what you want me to do to put this madness to an end. I'll do whatever you say."

"I want you to go to Sergeant Clayton and tell him that Milton killed that boy in cold blood. Do that if you really mean what you say. And while you're at it, tell him what you know about Wolf's murder."

"But Milton is dead," I insist. "And so is Wolf. What's to be gained by such a thing?"

"I knew you wouldn't."

"But it wouldn't mean anything," I tell him. "Nothing would be gained."

"Do you see the irony at all, Tristan?"

I stare at him and shake my head. He seems determined not to speak again until I do. "What irony?" I ask eventually, the words tumbling out in a hurried heap.

"That I am to be shot as a coward while you get to live as one."

I stand up and walk away from him, remove myself to the furthest corner of the room. "You're just being cruel now," I say quietly.

"Am I? I thought I was being honest."

"Why must you always be so cruel?" I ask.

"It's something I've learned here," he tells me. "You've learned it, too. You just don't realize it."

"But they're trying to kill us, too," I protest, standing up again now. "You've been in the trenches. You've felt the bullets flying past your head. You've been out in no-man's-land, crawling around among the dead bodies."

"Yes, and we do the same to them, so doesn't that make us just as bad as them? I mean it, Tristan. I'm interested to know. Give me an answer. Help me to understand."

"You're impossible to talk to," I say.

"Why?" he asks, sounding genuinely bewildered.

"Because you will believe whatever it is you choose to believe and you won't hear any argument about it one way or the other. You have all these opinions which help define you as a better man than anyone else, but where are your high-minded principles when it comes to the rest of your life?"

"I don't think I'm better than you, Tristan," he says, shaking his head. He looks at his watch and swallows nervously. "It's getting closer."

"We can put a stop to it."

"What did you mean by 'the rest of my life'?" he asks, looking across, his brow furrowed with irritation.

"You don't need me to spell it out for you," I say.

"I do, actually," he says. "Tell me. If you have something to say, just say it. You may not get many more chances, so spit it out, for pity's sake."

"Right from the start," I say, not hesitating for a moment. "Right from the start, you've behaved badly towards me."

"Is that so?"

"Let's not pretend otherwise," I say. "We became friends back there in Aldershot, you and I. I thought we were friends, anyway."

"But we *are* friends, Tristan," he insists. "Why would you think otherwise?"

"I thought perhaps we were more than that."

"And whatever gave you that impression?"

"Do you really need me to tell you?" I ask him.

"Tristan," he says with a sigh, running his hand across his eyes. "Please don't bring up that business again. Not now."

"You speak of it as if it meant nothing."

"But it did mean nothing, Tristan," he insists. "My God. What's the matter with you, anyway? Are you so emotionally crippled that you can't understand what comfort is when it stands in front of you? That's all it was."

"'Comfort'?" I ask, astonished.

"You must keep coming back to this, mustn't you?" he says, growing angry now. "You're worse than a woman, do you know that?"

"Fuck off," I say, although my heart isn't fully in it.

"It's true. And if you continue to talk about this, I'm going to call Corporal Moody and ask him to lock you up somewhere else."

"Corporal Moody is dead, Will," I tell him. "And if you had been part of what was going on around here and not hiding away in this useful little cubbyhole of yours, you'd know that."

This makes him hesitate. He looks away and bites his top lip.

"When did this happen?"

"A few nights ago," I say, brushing it away as if it means nothing; this is how immune I have become to the fact of death. "Look, it doesn't matter. He's dead. Williams and Attling are dead. Milton's dead. Everyone's dead."

"Everyone's not dead, Tristan. Don't exaggerate. You're alive, I'm alive."

"But you're going to be shot," I say, almost laughing at the absurdity of it. "That's what happens to feather men."

"I'm not a feather man," he insists, standing up now and looking angry. "Feather men are cowards. I'm not a coward, I'm principled, that's all. There's a difference."

"Yes, so you seem to believe. Do you know, if it had been a one-off, perhaps then I could have understood it. Perhaps I could have thought, *Well, it was the end of our training. We were worried, we were terrified of what lay ahead. You sought comfort where you could find it.* But it was you, Will. It was you who led me the second time. And then you looked at me as if I was something that repulsed you."

"Sometimes you do repulse me," he says casually. "When I think of what you are. And I realize that that's what you think I am, too, and I know differently. You're right. At such moments you do repulse me. Perhaps that's your life. Perhaps that's the way your destiny is to be shaped, but not mine. It's not what I wanted. It never was."

"Only because you're a liar," I say.

"I think you had better take care what you say," he says, narrowing his eyes. "We are friends, Tristan; I like to think we are, anyway. And I shouldn't like us to fall out. Not now. Not at this late stage."

"I don't want that either," I insist. "You're the best friend I have, Will. You're . . . Well, look"—I have to say it; our time is running out—"does it matter at all that I love you?"

"For God's sake, man," he hisses, a thread of spittle falling from his mouth on to the ground. "Don't speak like that. What if we were to be overheard?"

"I don't care," I say, coming over and standing before him. "Listen to me, just this once. When this is all over—"

"Get away from me," he insists, shoving me aside, with more force than he might have intended, for I stumble hard on to the ground and fall on my shoulder, a stab of pain shooting through my body.

He looks at me and bites his lip as if he regrets that for a moment but then his expression reverts to one of coldness.

"Look, why can't you just stay away from me?" he asks. "Why must you always be around? Why must you be always in my ear? To hear you say what you've just said, well, it turns my stomach, that's all. I don't love you, Tristan. I don't even like you very much any more. You were there, that's all it was. You were there. I feel nothing for you, except contempt. Why are you even in here? Did you orchestrate this? Did you fall over Marshall so that you would be dragged in here with me?"

He steps forward and slaps me on the face; not a punch, as he might deliver to another man, but a slap. My head turns with the force of it but I'm stunned into silence and inaction.

"Are you expecting something from me, Tristan? Is that what it is?" he continues. "Because you're not going to get it. Understand that, can't you?"

And now he slaps me again and I let him.

"Do you think I would have anything to do with a man like you?"

Right in front of me now, he slaps me for a third time; my right cheek is inflamed with pain but still I cannot hit him back.

"My God! When I think of what we've done together it makes me sick. Do you realize that? It makes me want to retch."

A fourth slap and now I rush at him, seeing red, ready to pounce, ready to punch him in my anger, but he misinterprets my actions and pushes me away and I fall again on my bruised shoulder and this time it hurts like hell.

"Get off me!" he shouts. "Jesus Christ, Tristan, I'm about to die and you want one last go at me for old times' sake, is that it? What kind of man are you, anyway?"

"That's not what I—" I begin, stumbling back to my feet.

"Fucking hell!" he snaps, leaning over me. "I'm about to die! Can't you just leave me alone for five fucking minutes to get my thoughts together?"

"Please, Will," I say, tears of anger spilling down my cheeks as I reach for him. "I'm sorry, all right? We're friends—"

"We're not fucking friends!" he shouts. "We were never friends! Can't you understand that, you fool?" He marches to the door and bangs on it repeatedly, shouting through the bars. "Get him out of here!" he yells, pushing me against the door. "I want a few minutes' peace before I die."

"Will," I say, but he shakes his head; still, he pulls me to him one last time.

"Listen to me," he says, whispering in my ear. "And remember what I tell you: I am not like you. I wish to fuck I had never met you. Wolf told me all about you, told me what you were, and I stayed your friend out of pity. Because I knew that no one else would be your friend. I despise you, Tristan."

I feel dizzy. I never would have believed that he could be so cruel but he seems to mean every word that he is saying. I feel tears coming to my eyes. I open my mouth but find I have no words for him. I want to lie on my bunk, my face to the wall, pretending that he doesn't exist, but at that moment I hear footsteps running down towards our door, a key in the lock. It opens. And two men step inside and stare at us both.

I stand in the courtyard for what seems an age, feeling as if my head will explode. There's a fireball of fury within me. I hate him. All he made me do, all he said to me. The way he led me on. I feel a searing pain in my shoulder from where he knocked me off my feet twice, and my face is tender from his slaps. I look back towards where he remains locked up, with Corporal Harding and the chaplain. I want to go back down there, grab him by the neck and bang his head on the stone floor until his brains have spilled out. I want him to fucking die. I love him but I want him to fucking die. I can't live in a world where he exists.

"I need one more!" shouts Sergeant Clayton to Wells.

But Wells shakes his head. "Not me," he says.

I look in front of me at the firing squad already assembled—the sun has risen, it's six o'clock—five men in a row, a gap for the sixth.

"You know I can't, sir," says Wells. "It has to be an enlisted man."

"Then I'll do it myself!" roars Clayton.

"You can't, sir," insists Wells. "It's against regulations. Just wait. I'll go back to the trench and find someone. One of the new boys, someone who doesn't know him."

I don't recognize the five boys lined up to shoot Will. They look terrified. They look clean. Two of them are visibly shaking.

I march over to them and Clayton looks at me in surprise. "You need a sixth man?" I ask.

"No, Sadler," says Wells, staring at me in astonishment. "Not you. Go back to the trenches. Find Morton. Send him to me, all right?"

"You need a sixth man?" I repeat.

"I said not you, Sadler."

"And I said I'll do it," I say, picking up the sixth rifle as the hatred courses through my veins. I twist my jaw to relieve some of the pain in my cheek but it feels like he's slapping me again every time I do so.

"There we are, then," snaps Sergeant Clayton, giving the signal to the guardsman to open the door. "Bring him up. It's time."

"Sadler, think about this, for God's sake," hisses Wells, grabbing me by the arm, but I brush him off and take my place in line. I want his fucking head on a plate. I check the round, lock it in place. I stand between two boys, ignoring them both.

"Corporal Wells, get out of the way," snaps Sergeant Clayton, and then I see him, I see Will being led up the steps by the guardsman, a black mask placed over his eyes, a piece of red cloth pinned above his heart. He walks hesitantly until he is standing at the stoop. I stare at him, I remember everything, I hear his words in my ears and it is all I can do not to rush at him and tear him limb from limb.

Sergeant Clayton gives the order for us to stand to attention, and we do, six men side by side, rifles raised.

What are you doing? I think, a voice of reason in my head, a voice pleading with me to think about what I'm doing. A voice I choose to ignore.

"Take aim!" cries Clayton, and in that moment, Will, brave to the last, whips his blindfold away, wanting to face his killers as they gun him down. His expression is one of fear but strength, too, resilience. And then he notices me standing in line and his expression changes. He is shocked. He stares. His face collapses.

"Tristan," he says, his last word.

And the command comes, and the index finger of my right hand presses on the trigger and, in a heartbeat, six guns have discharged, mine as quickly as anyone's, and my friend lies on the ground, unmoving, his war over.

Mine about to begin.

THE SHAME OF
MY ACTIONS

London, October 1979

✧

I SAW HER ONCE AGAIN.
It was almost sixty years later, the autumn of 1979. Mrs. Thatcher had come to power a few months earlier and there was a sense that civilization as we knew it was about to come to an end. My eighty-first birthday had been reported in the newspapers and I received a letter from a literary society, informing me that I was to be presented with a misshapen piece of bronze cast inside a block of wood with a silver pen emerging from its crown but it was mine only if I was willing to don a tuxedo, attend a dinner, deliver a short speech and an even shorter reading, and generally make myself available for a day or two to the press.

"But *why* can't I say no?" I asked Leavitt, my publisher, thirty-two years old, all braces and Brylcreemed hair, who was insisting that I accept the invitation; he had inherited me two books earlier when Davies, my long-term editor and friend, passed away.

"Well, it would be very rude, for one thing," he said, speaking to me as if I were an infant who needed chastising for refusing to come downstairs and say hello to the guests, sing a song or two. "The prize is rarely awarded. In fact you would be only the fourth recipient."

"And the other three are all dead," I remarked, looking at the names of those writers—two poets and a novelist—who had received it before. "That's what happens when you start accepting awards like this. There's nothing left to play for any more. And so you die."

"You're not going to die, Tristan."

"I'm eighty-one," I pointed out. "I admire your positivity but even you, Leavitt, have to admit that there's a very real possibility."

But the pleas went on and I found myself too exhausted to say no—resistance itself might have killed me—so I showed up and sat at a top table, surrounded by bright young things who made charming conversation and told me how much they admired me but how they were trying for a very different effect with their work, although, of course, it was vital for young people to continue to read those who had gone before.

The society furnished me with seven extra tickets for the event, which I thought was a bit inconsiderate as they knew that I had spent my life as a single man and had no family at all, not even a nephew or niece to keep me company and collect my letters after I passed away. I considered sending them back, or distributing them at a nearby university where I offer occasional talks, but in the end I offered them to certain loyal people who had looked after my business interests over the years—agents, publicists and so on, most of whom had long since retired—and they seemed only too happy to give up an evening to spend time celebrating me, a throwback of sorts to when we were all on the cutting edge of things together.

"Who would you like to sit next to you at the dinner?" a secretary asked, calling me up in the middle of the morning; a great disturbance as I write between the hours of eight and two.

"Prince Charles," I said, without giving it much thought. I had met him once at a garden party and he'd rather impressed me with some off-the-cuff remarks about Orwell and poverty, but that was about as far as our acquaintance went.

"Oh," said the secretary, sounding a little put out. "I don't think he's on the guest list."

"Well, then, I shall leave that in your capable hands," I replied, hanging up the phone and then taking it off its cradle for the rest of the day.

In the end a young man was placed to my left—he had recently been named the greatest young writer in the world, or some such thing, on the basis of a short novel and a collection of stories. He had flowing blond locks and reminded me a little of Sylvia Carter in her prime. As he spoke, he waved a cigarette about and blew smoke in my face. I found him almost unbearable.

"I hope you don't mind," he said, reaching under the table for a bag from Foyles of Charing Cross Road. "I bought some of your books earlier. Would you mind signing them?"

"Not at all," I said. "To whom should I make them out?"

"Why, to me, of course," he said, grinning, delighted with himself. I was certain that a night devoted to me was simply a ruse designed to ensure his presence at the party.

"And who might you be?" I asked politely.

Books duly signed, bag returned to the safety of the under-table, he winked at me and placed a hand on my forearm.

"I read you at uni," he confided in such a careful tone that it was rather like he was admitting to an unhealthy interest in young girls of school-going age. "I must admit I hadn't heard of you until then. But I thought some of your books were bloody good."

"Thank you. And the others? Not so 'bloody good'?"

He winced and considered it. "Look, it's not for me to say," he said, scattering ash over his prawn cocktail before proceeding to tell me of the various flaws they contained, how it was all very well to place such and such in a certain context, but throw in a complication like this or that and the whole house of cards fell down. "But look, we wouldn't have the literature of today if the last few generations hadn't been there to lay down such solid foundations. You deserve high praise for that at least."

"But I'm still here," I pointed out, a ghost at my own table.

"But of *course* you are," he said, as if he were confirming the fact for me; as if I had asked the question in order to reassure myself because of some ongoing dementia, an uncertainty about my continued existence.

Anyway, the point is that I went along and speeches were made, photographs taken, books signed. There was a telegram from Harold Wilson, who claimed to be an admirer but misspelled my name. (He addressed me as "Mr. Sandler.") Another from John Lennon.

"You fought in the Great War?" a journalist from *The Guardian* asked me in a long interview to coincide with the presentation of the prize.

"I didn't think it was all that great," I pointed out. "In fact, if memory serves, it was bloody awful."

"Yes, of course," said the journalist, laughing uncomfortably. "Only you've never written about it, have you?"

"Haven't I?"

"Not explicitly, at least," he said, his face taking on an expression of panic, as if he had suddenly realized that he might have forgotten some major work along the way.

"I suppose it depends on one's definition of explicit," I replied. "I'm pretty sure I've written about it any number of times. On the surface, occasionally. A little buried, at other times. But it's been there, hasn't it? Wouldn't you agree? Or do I delude myself?"

"No, of course not. I only meant—"

"Unless I've failed utterly in my work, that is. Perhaps I haven't made my intentions clear at all. Perhaps my entire writing career has been a busted flush."

"No, Mr. Sadler, of course not. I think you misunderstood me. It's clear that the Great War plays a significant part in your—"

At eighty-one, one has to find one's fun where one can.

I stayed in a hotel in London on the night of the dinner, having left the city some fifteen years earlier and retired, as they say, to the country. Despite numerous requests from old friends to linger in the bars of London with them until the small hours and put my health and life expectancy at peril, I said my goodbyes at a respectable hour and made my way back to the West End, looking forward to a decent night's sleep and the early train home. And so it was with some surprise that I heard one of the porters calling out to me as I passed the reception desk.

"Sadler," I said, waving my key in the air, assuming he took me for some octogenarian interloper. "Eleven-o-seven."

"Of course, sir," he said, coming over and halting me before I could get into one of the lifts. "Only I'm supposed to tell you that there's a lady waiting to see you. She's been in the residents' bar for about an hour now."

"A lady?" I said, frowning. "At this time of night? There's not some mistake?"

"No, sir. She asked for you by name. Said that you knew her."

"Well, who is she?" I asked impatiently. The last thing I wanted was to be hounded by another journalist or a reader at this late hour. "Is she carrying a bundle of books under her arm?"

"I didn't see any, sir, no."

I looked around, considering it. "Look, do me a favour, will you?" I said. "Go in and tell her that I've gone to bed for the night. Apologies and all that. Ask her to contact my agent— he'll know what to do with her. Hold on, I have his card here somewhere."

I rooted in my pocket and took out a handful of business cards, staring at them with a sense of exhaustion. So many names, so many faces to remember. None of which I was ever any good at.

"Sir, I don't think she's a fan. Might she be a relative perhaps? She's rather elderly, if I may say so."

"You may if she is," I told him. "But no, there's no chance that she's a relative. Did she leave a note for me at all?"

"No, sir. She said to tell you that she'd come all the way from Norwich to see you. She said you'd know what that meant."

I stared at him. He was rather beautiful and, of course, the fires never go out.

"Mr. Sadler? Mr. Sadler, are you all right?"

I made my way into the darkened lounge nervously, loosening my tie a little, and searched the room. It was surprisingly busy for that time of night but there was no mistaking her. She was the only lady of advanced years in the room, for one thing. But I think I would have known her anywhere. Despite the passing of so many years, she had never been far from my thoughts. She was reading a book, not one I recognized, and looked up, though not in my direction, when (I suppose) she sensed me watching her, and I thought that a shadow of sorts crossed her face. She lifted her wine glass and brought it to her lips but seemed to think better of it and returned it to the table. I remained motionless in the centre of the floor for rather a long time; only when she turned and offered me a slight inclination of the head did I come forward and take the seat opposite her. She had chosen well; a slight alcove, away from others. Flattering lighting. Good for both of us.

"I read about your award in the newspaper," she told me without any preamble as I sat down. "And I happened to be in London for my grandson's wedding, which was yesterday. I don't know why exactly but I thought I would call on you. It was a last-minute decision. I hope you don't mind."

"I'm glad you did," I replied, which seemed to be the polite thing to say, although I was uncertain exactly how I felt to see her again.

"You remember me, then?" she asked with a half-smile.

"Yes, I remember you."

"I knew you would."

"The wedding," I said, struggling to find a safe topic while I composed my thoughts. "Was it enjoyable?"

"As much as these things ever are," she said with a shrug, nodding at the waiter when he offered to refill her glass; I ordered a small whisky, then changed my mind and increased the measure. "All we ever do is eat and drink together, Tristan," she said. "Curious, isn't it? Anyway, yes, it was fine, I suppose, although I don't care for the girl much. She's a floozy; there, I've said it. She'll run Henry a rare dance, I can see it now."

"Henry is your grandson?"

"Yes. My eldest girl's youngest boy. I have eight grand-children, if you can believe it. And six great-grandchildren."

"Congratulations."

"Thank you. I suppose you're wondering why I came?"

"I haven't really had time to wonder," I said, thanking the waiter as he left my drink. "You've taken me a bit by surprise, Marian. You'll have to forgive me if I'm not at the top of my game."

"Well, you're as old as the hills," she said lightly. "Although I'm even older, so there we are. The fact that we're both even compos mentis is a triumph of good food and healthy living, I expect."

I smiled and took a slow dram of my whisky. She hadn't changed really. There was still the quick absurdity of her speech, the urgent wit and literacy of her.

"I suppose I should congratulate you," she said after a moment.

"Congratulate me?"

"On your award. I'm told it's quite prestigious."

"Yes, I'm told the same thing," I replied. "Although it's rather ugly, if I'm honest. I wonder that they couldn't have commissioned something beautiful."

"Where is it, then? Up in your room?"

"No, I left it with my agent. It was rather heavy. They'll send it along, I dare say."

"Your photograph was on the front page of *The Times*," she said. "I was reading about you when I took the train up on Monday. And you were a clue in the crossword. You've done well for yourself."

"I've been fortunate," I agreed. "I've been permitted to live the life I wanted. To a certain degree, anyway."

"I remember that day, just before we parted, you told me that you'd been dabbling in writing for a little bit but that you planned to start taking it more seriously when you got back to London. Well, you certainly did that, didn't you? There's quite an impressive number of books to your name. I've never read any of them, I have to admit. Is that rude?"

"Not at all," I said. "I wouldn't expect you to have. You didn't like novels, as I recall."

"Actually, I came around to them in the end. Just not yours. I saw them in bookshops all the time, of course. And I use the library and they're great fans of yours there. But I never read one myself. Do you ever think of me, Tristan?"

"Most days," I admitted without hesitation.

"And my brother?" she asked, apparently unsurprised by my admission.

"Most days," I repeated.

"Yes."

302

She looked away now and had some more wine, closing her eyes for a moment as the grape entered her bloodstream.

"I don't know what I'm doing here," she said a moment later, looking across at me and smiling, a rather demented sort of smile. "I wanted to see you but now I don't know why. I must seem mad. I haven't come to attack you, if that's what you're worried about."

"Tell me about your life, Marian," I said, interested in what she might have to say. The last image I had of her was her sitting on the platform at Thorpe as a group of people stared at this distressed, weeping woman, and then her charging towards the glass of my window seat as the train pulled out of the station. I had gasped, thinking she meant to throw herself under the wheels, but no, she had simply wanted to attack me, that was all. If she had got her hands on me, she might have killed me. And I might have let her.

"My goodness," she said. "You don't want to know about my life, Tristan. It would seem terribly boring compared to yours."

"Mine is a lot more humdrum than people might imagine," I told her. "Please. I'd like to know."

"Well, the potted version, perhaps. Let's see. I'm a teacher. Or I was, anyway. I'm retired now, obviously. But I trained as a teacher shortly after my marriage broke up and remained in the same school for, goodness me, it must be over thirty years."

"Did you enjoy it?"

"Very much. Small children, Tristan. The only ones I could handle. Stand one on top of the other and if you're still taller than them, you're safe. That was always my rule. Four- and five-year-olds. I loved them. They were a great delight to me. Some of them were just wonderful." Her face broke into a radiant smile.

"Do you still miss it?" I asked her.

303

"Oh, every day. It must be so wonderful to have a career like yours where no one ever tells you that you have to give it up. Novelists only seem to get better as they grow older, don't they?"

"Some of them," I said.

"Have you?"

"I don't think so. I think I might have reached my peak around middle age and I've been stuck, paddling the same water, ever since. I'm sorry to hear that your marriage ended badly."

"Yes, well, it was inevitable that it would. I never should have married him, that's the truth of it. I must have been mad."

"And yet you had children together?"

"Three. Alice is a vet, she has three children of her own and is doing very well for herself. Helen is a psychologist and she has five, if you can believe it. I don't know how she manages it. They'll both be retiring soon, of course, which makes me feel as old as the hills. And then there's my son."

"The youngest?"

"Yes. Well, he's in his early fifties now, so he's not exactly young."

I continued to look at her, not saying a word, wondering what she might tell me about him.

"What?" she asked after a moment.

"Well, does he have a name?"

"Of course he has a name," she said, looking away, and I realized suddenly what it was and felt ashamed for asking. I reached for my drink, my safety ground.

"My son has struggled with life, if I'm honest," she said after a moment. "I don't know why exactly. He had the same up-bringing as his sisters, almost exactly, but where they've excelled he has found himself disappointed at every turn."

"I'm sorry to hear it."

"Yes, well. I do what I can for him, of course. But it's never enough. I'm not sure what will happen after I'm gone. His sisters find him terribly difficult."

"And his father?"

"Oh, Leonard is long gone. He died in the 1950s. Married someone else, emigrated to Australia and was killed in a house fire."

I stared at her, the name coming back to my mind without any problem. "Leonard?" I asked. "Not Leonard Legg?"

"Why, yes," she said, frowning as she looked at me. "How would you . . . ? Oh yes, of course. I'd completely forgotten. You met him that day, didn't you?"

"He punched me in the face."

"He thought that we were involved in a romantic liaison."

"You married him?" I asked, appalled.

"Yes, Tristan, I married him. But as I told you, the marriage ended within a decade. We made each other miserable. You look surprised."

"I am rather," I said. "Look, I didn't know him, of course. Only I remember all the things you said that day. How you were set against him. He'd let you down so badly, I mean."

"We were married quite soon after that," she said. "I don't want to say it was the worst decision of my life, because I have three children from the marriage, but it certainly showed very poor judgement on my part. I went back to him the next day, you see. After you left. I needed someone and he was there. I can't explain it. I know it must seem . . . stupid."

"It doesn't seem anything," I said. "It's not for me to judge you."

She glared at me, looking suddenly offended. "No, it's not," she said. "Look, he was there and I wanted someone to take care of me at that moment. I let him back into my life but in the end he left it again and that was the end of that. Let's stop talking about me. I'm sick of me. What about you, Tristan? You never married? The papers didn't say."

"No," I said, looking away. "But then you knew that I couldn't. I explained all that to you."

"I knew that you *shouldn't*," she replied. "But who knows how dishonest you might have been? I rather expected you would in the end. People did in those days. They still do, I imagine. But you didn't, anyway."

"No, Marian," I said, shaking my head, taking the blow on the chin as it was intended. "No, I didn't."

"And was there ever—I don't know what people call it, I'm not modern, Tristan—a companion? Is that the right word?"

"No," I said.

"There was never anyone?" she asked, surprised, and I laughed a little, surprised by her surprise.

"No," I said. "Not a single person. Not once. No liaisons of any description."

"Well, goodness me. Wasn't it lonely? Your life, I mean."

"Yes."

"You're alone?"

"Yes."

"You live alone?"

"I am entirely alone, Marian," I repeated quietly.

"Yes, well," she said, looking away for a moment, her expression hardening now.

We sat like that for some time and finally she turned back to me. "You look well, anyway," she said.

"Do I?"

"No, not really. You look old. And tired. I'm old and tired myself, I don't mean it unkindly."

"Well, I am old and tired," I admitted. "It's been a long run."

"Lucky you," she said bitterly. "But have you been happy?"

I thought about it. This was one of the more difficult questions of life, I felt. "I've not been unhappy," I said. "Although I'm not sure if that's the same thing. I've enjoyed my work very much. It's brought me a great deal of satisfaction. But of course, like your son, I have struggled at times."

"With what?"

"Can I say his name?"

"No," she hissed, leaning forward. "No, you can't."

I nodded and sat back. "It might mean something to you, or it might not," I said, "but I have lived with the shame of my actions for sixty-three years. There hasn't been a day that I haven't thought about it."

"I'm surprised you've never written about it if you feel that strongly."

"I have, actually." An expression of dismay crossed her face and I shook my head quickly. "I should clarify that," I said. "I've written about it, only I've never published it. I thought I'd leave it behind. For after I'm dead."

She leaned forward, intrigued now. "And what have you written, Tristan?"

"The whole story," I told her. "Our lives at Aldershot, the way I felt about him, the things that happened. Our time in France. A little about my life before that, some things that happened to me as a child. And then the trouble, the decisions your brother made. And what I did to him in the end."

"Murdering him, you mean?"

"Yes. That."

"Because you couldn't have him."

I swallowed and looked down at the floor, nodding my head. I was as unable to look her in the eye now as I had been her parents all those years ago.

"Anything else?" she asked. "Tell me. I have a right to know."

"I've written about our day together. How I tried to explain things to you. How I failed."

"You've written about me?"

"Yes."

"So why haven't you published it, then? Everyone praises you so much. Why not give them this book, too?"

I thought about it, pretending that I was trying to decipher the reason, only I knew it well enough. "I suppose the shame would be too much for me," I said. "For anyone to know what I had done. I couldn't live with the way that people would look at me. It won't matter after I'm gone. They can read it then."

"You're a coward, Tristan, aren't you?" she asked me. "Right to the end. A terrible coward."

I looked up at her; there wasn't a lot she could say to hurt me. But she had found something. Something true.

"Yes," I said. "Yes, I suppose I am."

She sighed and looked away, her expression suggesting that she might scream if she wasn't careful. "I don't know why I came here," she said. "But it's late now. I have to go. Goodbye, Tristan," she said, standing up. "We shan't meet again."

"No."

And with that she was gone.

She was right, of course. I have been a coward. I should have delivered this manuscript years ago. Perhaps I was waiting for the story to find a conclusion of sorts, sure that it would come sooner or later. And it has finally come tonight.

I returned to my room shortly after she left. Holding my right hand out before me I noticed that my spasmodic index finger was perfectly still now; the finger that had pulled the trigger that sent the bullet into my lover's heart, satisfied at last. I removed the manuscript from my briefcase; I take it with me whenever I travel, you see. I like it to be close at hand. And I write now of our conversation, that short, final encounter between Marian and me, and I hope that it has given her some satisfaction, even though I am sure that wherever she is right now she is unable to sleep, and if she does then she will be haunted by nightmares from the past.

And then I reach into my case for something else, something I also keep close to hand, for the moment when it feels right to use it.

Soon they will find me here, in this bedroom, in an unfamiliar hotel, and the police will be called, and the ambulance service, and I will be carried away to some cold morgue in the heart of London city. And tomorrow, the newspapers will run my obituary and say that I was the last of that generation to go and what a shame, another link with the past gone, but look what he left us, my Lord, look at the legacy he has left behind to honour his memory. And soon afterwards this manuscript will appear, my final book, published between hard covers, edited by Leavitt. There will be outrage and disgust and people will turn on me at the last, they will hate me, my reputation will forever be destroyed, my punishment earned, self-inflicted like this gunshot wound, and the world will finally know that I was the greatest feather man of them all.

John Boyne was born in Ireland in 1971 and is the author of twelve novels for adults, most recently the *New York Times* best seller *The Heart's Invisible Furies, A Ladder to the Sky*, and *A Traveler at the Gates of Wisdom*, as well as six novels for teens and young adults including the #1 *New York Times* bestselling *The Boy in the Striped Pajamas*, which was made into an award-winning feature film. It also won two Irish Book Awards, was short-listed for the British Book Award, reached the top of the *New York Times* best sellers list, and has sold more than five million copies. His novels are published in forty-five languages. Boyne lives in Dublin.

Please visit him at www.johnboyne.com